Messages

lets get jack n da box

Already had Jamba juice.

jamba juice! i bet when you were born da doctor said "its kind of a boy!"

u probally drive a Kia minivan wit adam lambert floor mats

you enjoy capshuring butterflys and keeping dem in a hot pink jar with snail and hard designz

u cry wen u watch football

u want 2 adopt a unicorn

e no
the girliest text mess
a female language i ble
inja star a :) is my sord
it wrks luv me they b
ersent fluant langauge
a i say kk and they bo
rushin spy wit. speak ju
z B gittin wit other bit
soft and sweet 2 eacJ
oennett. i know wat wa
d Dats fabulus And Kk a
they think im sinstive
r hear dat song dat g

texts from bennett

MAC LETHAL

Gallery Books

New York London Toronto Sydney New Delhi

G

GALLERY BOOKS
A Division of Simon & Schuster, Inc.
1230 Avenue of the Americas
New York, NY 10020

First Gallery Books trade paperback edition September 2013

GALLERY BOOKS and colophon are registered trademarks of
Simon & Schuster, Inc.
For information about special discounts for bulk purchases,
please contact Simon & Schuster Special Sales at 1-866-506-1949
or business@simonandschuster.com.

The Simon & Schuster Speakers Bureau can bring authors to your
live event. For more information or to book an event contact the
Simon & Schuster Speakers Bureau at 1-866-248-3049 or visit our
website at www.simonspeakers.com.

Designed by Jason Snyder

Manufactured in the United States of America

10 9 8 7 6 5 4 3 2

Library of Congress Cataloging-in-Publication Data is available.

ISBN 978-1-4767-0687-0
ISBN 978-1-4767-0688-7 (ebook)

For Rocky

ne no mo?

the girliest text messa

a female language i ble

inja star a :) is my sord

it wrks luv me they b

ersent fluant langauge

a i say kk and they bo

ushin spy wit. speak ju

z B gittin wit other bit

soft and sweet 2 eaco

bennett. i know wat wa

d Dats fabulus And Kk a

they think im sinstive

ear dat song dat g

Part 1

why was every1 given me dirty looks and wisparing behind my bacc? haters

> Our grandparents renew vows after 50 years of marriage and you come to the ceremony in soccer shorts and flip-flops?

what.. it warm outside it aint even a real wedding

> You ate a McDonald's fish filet in the front row of the ceremony.

So what. Mcdonald got the best fish sanwich

Induction
1

"I'm thirteen percent black, man!"

My cousin Bennett was always saying and texting stupid stuff, so this proclamation came as no surprise to *me*.

But for his part, Mr. Cole stood with his shiny head cocked to the side, his mouth a quarter open, wheezing against the moist August air. He was shrouded in a bathrobe with HOLIDAY INN embroidered above the right breast pocket. His Jheri-curled hair was glistening in the sunbeams. And he was armed with a bowling pin, and it was clear that someone was about to get their skull busted open by it.

His Yorkshire terrier, Franklins, aloof to the situation, was sitting on his butt, left leg propped up, licking his balls. Normally I wouldn't take the lowbrow route and point out when a dog is licking his balls, but I was so terrified by the idea of being concussed by Mr. Cole's bowling pin that I could either look at my cousin Bennett, in his sagging purple nylon pants, or I could admire Franklins's profound focus on cleansing his eggplant-colored ball sack.

And I knew if I looked at Bennett I would end up killing him myself. I had no idea why Mr. Cole was mad. All I knew was that my cousin was most likely guilty of something terrible.

I had just gotten home from the studio and was getting ready to water my jalapeño and tomato garden when I noticed Bennett and my neighbor Milton Cole, arguing across the low backyard fence.

Both were talking over each other and cursing a lot. I had swiftly walked up to see what was wrong.

On a physical combat level, Bennett was in way over his head. We both were. But I had no idea why they were arguing. I just knew that out of all the people in my new subdivision one could get into an altercation with, Mr. Cole, my fifty-one-year-old, stocky—ex–Black Panther—neighbor was the *worst* choice. The man had been imprisoned for twelve years on a federal kidnapping charge, stemming from road rage after a sixteen-year-old kid cut him off in rush-hour traffic. He was so angered by the kid's "lack of respect for elders," that he dragged the boy out of his car, threw him in the back of his Lincoln Town Car, drove to the kid's parents' house, and threatened to kill the father if he didn't teach his son how to drive better. He's a fucking lunatic. Plus he named his very effeminate dog Franklins—after plural $100 bills.

"I paid a family tree company to locate my roots—and my grandpa's mom is from Africa!" Bennett declared.

Really, Bennett? A family tree company? I thought. Bennett had a very bad lying problem. It didn't help that he was a *bad liar*, as well.

Turning to me with confusion emblazoned across his face, Mr. Cole studied me from top to bottom. Then he looked back at Bennett and did the same to him. I wasn't exactly sure why he was studying us so closely, but I'm guessing he was searching for any possible remnants of melanin on either one of our bodies. Bennett and I are as Caucasian as it gets, our epidermises are pasty with a light-pink hue. I have been told by professional physicians to spend fifteen minutes a day in the sun, so I can avoid suffering a vitamin D deficiency. The problem is, fifteen minutes in the sun will give me a *sunburn*. It's that bad.

Point being, we have *zero* African in our bloodlines.

Mr. Cole appeared homicidal. "Y-Y-You just a sissy-ass white mothafucka! I'd s-s-s-s-s-s-s-snap yo mothafuckin' neck if I wouldn't end up in . . . L-L-Lan-Lansing again," he peppered out.

Mr. Cole lifted the bowling pin above his head and was seconds away from delivering a shattering blow to Bennett's cranium. Bennett leaned back and weakly raised his arms to protect himself. I was in a heated trance, unsure of whether I should jump between them, hop the fence and tackle Mr. Cole, or just stand there watching, avoiding damage altogether. The thing I was *quite* certain of, however, was that when someone stutters through his death threat, it's kind of hilarious.

Don't laugh, I reminded myself.

He cocked back his arm, making us now mere milliseconds away from Bennett's demise. Fortunately for us, right then Mr. Cole seemed to sense the fear in both of us and perhaps got a little too cocky. In a moment of spontaneity, he decided to say something vengeful and horrifying to preface the blow—something those super badass motherfuckers do in shitty, low-budget action movies before they blow up a building and walk away all slowly, unaffected by it.

Unfortunately for him, his brain was so overwhelmed by anger and frustration, that when it was time to hit us with his deadly catchphrase—he malfunctioned worse than before. Ramping up his emotional radiator to such egregious levels, the stutter shut his entire body down.

He began rapidly making weird noises, and instead of proclaiming something undeniably macho, he just stood there gurgling horrifically.

"F-f-f-f-f-f-f-f-f-faaaahhhhh . . . !" He burped. I stared back down at Franklins's balls, clenching my teeth, holding my laughter in for dear life. Mr. Cole's lower jaw zigzagged away from his upper jaw. His eyes rolled into the back of his head. "Flaaahhhhhhh."

Every second was an eternity in which I might fall to the ground, laughing my ass off. He was just convulsing, making guttural noises, his entire body in stutter-induced paralysis, unable to be moved by his brain.

Bennett and I took the opportunity to step back out of harm's way, relying on the waist-high chain-link fence for protection in case he regained control of his body and lunged.

The stutter only got worse. The vague letter *F* sounds gave way to a strange whistle. Horrendous, cacophonic squeaks and hums filled our yards. His eyes crossed; he was foaming at the mouth;

his jaw stuck open. I could see an amalgam cavity filling in the back of his mouth.

"Vvvvvvhhhhhhhhhhnnnnnn," he . . . uh . . . said? Moaned? I don't know how to describe it.

Don't laugh. Don't laugh. Don't laugh. I tried to think of atrocious things to erase any frivolity. I started thinking of Hitler. I started thinking of Mao. I started thinking of Hitler and Mao, in bikinis, on the beach, frolicking and skipping, while holding hands.

Wait, shit, that's going to make me laugh.

Okay, back to Franklins's balls. Nothing funny about Franklins's balls.

Meanwhile, Bennett had little regard for the fact that we were minutes away from being bludgeoned to death by a bowling pin. Nonchalantly, with a smirk on his face, he looked at Mr. Cole and, with genuine curiosity, little respect, and zero fear, asked, "What the fuck is wrong with you, homie? You choking on something?"

Flabbergasted by Bennett's irreverence, a calm, killer instinct came over my neighbor. He stopped making noises. His eyes opened to the size of oysters, and he stared directly at both of us. One eye on Bennett, one eye on me.

"Fuck. You." He finally got out in two clean, decisive stabs.

Which was oddly satisfying for me, maybe satisfying for Bennett, and definitely satisfying for Mr. Cole.

"Fuck you, you racist kid." But his tone had changed. His voice cracked and became a little more nasally. There was disappointment and confusion in his larynx. His swagger was less predatory, and it seemed like his feelings were genuinely hurt by something.

What had Bennett done?

"Okay, hang on a second," I interjected, "Mr. Cole, wha—"

But before I could ask him what the problem was, he turned around and stomped back toward his house, Franklins in tow. I stood there silently, giving him time to walk back into his house, before turning to Bennett.

"What the fuck was that about?" I asked Bennett, half-whispering. "Seriously! Dude? What the fuck did you do?!"

"I don't know! Fuck! That dude is a dick, mane!" Bennett pleaded.

Now, my cousin had a way of saying things that most people are uninitiated to. He spoke with a pure, midwestern ghetto twang. Words like *man* came out "mane." Words like *dude* became "doo." And words like *reciprocity* weren't pronounced at all. People like Bennett don't know what reciprocity means.

"How he gonna get mad at people jus' like him?" he said.

I turned around and walked to my back patio, reservation and anger battling inside me. I was sealing my mouth and holding in any hostile accusations until I knew the whole story. I had been borderline verbally abusive to Bennett and his family for the past few weeks and wanted to exhibit patience and tolerance.

But, Jesus, my house was a fucking mess, I thought as I walked inside.

Excessive partying, psychotic damsels on designer drugs, and my white-trash family tree branch had performed a coup d'état on my once very clean and organized home. In order for me to even sit down in my favorite chair at my kitchen table, I had to scoop a basketball, a magazine covered with crumbs of marijuana and cigar guts, and an empty bottle of Actavis promethazine cough syrup with codeine (an oddly popular drink among the gangsta community).

I plugged my phone into the wall closest to the table to let it charge.

"Uh, why did Mr. Cole just try to kill us, Bennett?" I asked my cousin, only to realize he hadn't followed me into the kitchen. I could hear him rapping to himself in a distant room.

After a few minutes of quietly decompressing, my phone turned on. I had missed several texts but quickly skipped all of them as they popped up, to locate my conversation with Bennett from earlier.

DISCLAIMER: What you're about to read is 100 percent real. Yes, my cousin Bennett really texts/types/writes like this. I imagine you know this already, because you're reading a fucking book about the way Bennett texts, for Chrissakes. But on the off chance you're an overprotective mother rummaging through her son's bookshelf, trying to discover if he's on drugs or not (he is), or a prisoner doing a bid in some ruthlessly cold, concrete state prison, trying to pass the time by reading, hoping you'll get out early (you won't): brace yourself. . . .

(BENNETT:) hav u ever hear dat song dat go wut is luv baby dont hurt me no mo? u no dat sonf?

(ME:) Yes. It's called "What Is Love?" I think.

(BENNETT:) Kk

(ME:) Did you just say "Kk?" That's the girliest text message you've ever sent me.

(BENNETT:) nigga i speak da female language. i blend in like a ninja a kk text is a ninja star a :) is my sorde.

(BENNETT:) i got a black belt in bitches.

(ME:) Clearly.

(BENNETT:) it wrks nigga . bitchez luv me they bow 2 da kk.

(ME:) Haha. They bow to the Kk?

(BENNETT:) lol yup i speak 100 persent fluant bitch langauge my txt game is on sum pure playa shit. i say kk and they bow 2 me .

(ME:) Wow. You sound like Genghis Khan if he was a preteen text messaging his servants. "Bow to the Kk!"

(BENNETT:) ?

(BENNETT:) wat

(ME:) Nevermind.

(BENNETT:) im tellin u.. be a rushin spy wit bitches.sspeak jus like em

(BENNETT:) ya c? dats y bitches B gittin wit other bitches.cuz bitches kno wat bitches want.they all soft and sweet 2 eacJother .

BENNETT: so i let dem know hey im bennett.i know wat bitches want 2.

BENNETT: so i say shit like Hey sweety and Dats fabulus And Kk and O honney ur hair looks gr8 . an they think im sinstive

BENNETT: but den i go in fo da kill

ME: Okay, okay, I get it. Speak their language.

BENNETT: C..if u Wuz in mexico an u met a bitch who spoke mexacin and a bitch who spoke amercian which bitch wud u prafer 2 git wit ?

ME: Well, I'd rather get with the girl who spoke English.

BENNETT: england niggaz sound funny i recamend u dont sound wierd wen u talk to chix dem niggaz talk like da crocodiale hunter

ME: LOL. Bennett, in America, we speak English. And the Crocodile Hunter was Australian.

BENNETT: dis aint a scan tron test nigga shudup and rispect my pimpen

BENNETT: Bow 2 da Kk ha ha

For the past few days, my much younger cousin had been giving me dating advice. Yeah . . . more on that later.

BENNETT: R u comein home soon their iz a guy here sayen he need 2 hk up a kord or sum shit.want me 2 tell him 2 fuk off? My mom talken 2 him rite now

ME: Oh shit! I forgot. The WiFi is getting hooked up today. Fuck.

ME: No, I won't be done in the studio for a while. Let him in.

BENNETT: k

BENNETT: man my mom is nodden out off oxy wat shud i say 2 him..

BENNETT: hello

ME: Sorry, was mixing something. Tell him to do whatever he needs.

BENNETT: ok

BENNETT: dis guys hole ass crack is sticken out his britchez.he coo doe.we talken bout guns . his name is dan

BENNETT: hello . he need to use ur computater

> [BENNETT:] hey he need 2 use ur Laptop is dat ok.... to test da kinection
>
> [ME:] Password is BEERSNOB
>
> [BENNETT:] k

And I guess that's where my phone must have died. I was pretty busy in the studio and didn't have a charger there, so I didn't really think much about it at the time. However, it looked like Bennett proceeded to text me about the Wi-Fi several times while I was MIA.

> [BENNETT:] wat do u want him 2 call da net work
>
> [BENNETT:] u their..
>
> [BENNETT:] he asken wat we want 2 Call da wi fi. name it somethn eazy 2 remmber
>
> [BENNETT:] wat shud we call it he gatta go
>
> [BENNETT:] hey
>
> [BENNETT:] Ay fukr i jus call U no anser
>
> [BENNETT:] ?????????????
>
> [BENNETT:] he say we can name it watever u want
>
> [BENNETT:] yo im gna jus name da wifi thing he say i can pick da name
>
> [BENNETT:] ?

That was it. Bennett walked into the kitchen as I was finishing the texts, still dumbfounded. I glared at him as he filled a massive bowl of cereal for himself.

He chewed a minute, swallowed, took a thoughtful pause, took another scoop of cereal, chewed and swallowed again, then proceeded with, "To answer your question. I dunno why he wanna kill us. I ain't racist, my nigga. I'm more in tune with my black incesters than my white ones."

I knew he meant to say *ancestors*, but whatever. Bennett butchering the English language wasn't new, surprising, or important at this point.

However, the term *incesters* struck me as weirdly appropriate when I thought about Bennett's part of the family. Nevertheless, I had learned to pick my battles, language and otherwise, with him. Even though I've done extensive research on both sides of my family lineage, I had sworn to never engage Bennett in a discussion where we debate about whether we have African in our bloodline. Never again, that is.

"Okay, well, something happened. Did you leave the house today?"

"No."

"Did you listen to any loud rap music, with the *n* word, that he could have misinterpreted as being racist?"

"No."

"Did you, your mom, or Leshaun, do *anything* today that Mr. Cole could have perceived as racist, uhhh . . . offensive, or disrespectful?"

"Nah."

"What did you do today? Tell me your entire day," I said as he took a seat at the table.

"Okay. It go like this. I woke up and eated some cereal. I smoked a Newport out front. Then I watched TV in the basement. I watched some show named *MacGyver* about a white nigga who can make a bomb out of a watermelon and a vibrator battery. Then I jacked off to Rachael Ray's *30 Minute Meals* show. I ate cereal again. I rolled a blunt. I smoked it in the garage, since I'm not allowed to smoke weed out front no more. Then I smoked a Newport out front 'cause you never told me I couldn't smoke cigs out front no more. I rode my bike to the store to get more cigs. I rode back. Uh . . . I did some push-ups. The internet guy came to hook up your cordless internet. I smoked a Newport, then went downstairs and turned the TV off, then I came upstairs because *SpongeBob* is on the DVR up here. And right when I turn on *SpongeBob* I hear Mr. Cole yelling outside."

"And that's when you went outside?"

"Well, at first I ain't think he was yelling at me. But the more I looked at him, the more I noticed he was talkin' shit. So I ran outside to see what was up. We argued for a couple minutes, then you showed up."

I had nothing. I've learned to tell when Bennett is lying. Bennett is usually lying. But he was unwavering and stern, so I decided to chalk it up to Mr. Cole's being a loon. There are numerous elements of Mr. Cole's dossier that would point to him being a batshit crazy loon, like, for example, kidnapping a sixteen-year-old for driving like a sixteen-year-old.

"God, what a crazy fucker," I said to Bennett and patted him on the shoulder. He guffawed and took another bite of cereal. I sat down next to him at the table, and opened my laptop. I was just going to have Bennett listen to the new song I created in the studio today.

I right clicked on the Wi-Fi icon and the menu of neighborhood networks dropped down. I slowly scanned the list top to bottom. At first it didn't register. Maybe it was denial, maybe I just didn't notice it. But after adjusting my retinas and mouthing the words silently to myself, I caught it. I found it. My heart stopped. My life flashed before my eyes. My jaw was on the floor.

"Oh my fucking God, Bennett! What did you do?!"

Bennett was so startled that he slammed his hand into his bowl of cereal, flipping it over, drenching himself and the table with milk and soggy Frosted Flakes.

"What? What? *What?*" he barked as he squinted his untreated, astigmatic eyes at the screen. "What this stuff mean?"

"Look, dude." I pointed to the Wi-Fi menu. "This is why Milton thinks we're racists!"

"What? I don't get it!" he pled. Bennett was clueless.

PERRYBACON_NET
MCOLE_14707
NETGEAR_14817
NETGEAR_14811
PrietoWifi_14803
Bow_To_The_KKK_14808
CoffeeHouseWireless

I swear we both read it a good twenty times to make sure what we were seeing was real. I pushed my fist in front of my cousin and counted off his mistake on my fingers. "One K . . . two K's . . . and a third, *racist*, K."

"What do you mean 'racist K'? It was 'posed to be funny!" Bennett bellyached, perhaps close to tears.

He leaned back in his chair, covered in cereal and milk, with the eyes of a crushed little boy. He wanted to be black more than anything else in the world, and he had just committed a mistake that a highly skilled, white-haired, samurai warrior would commit seppuku over. Well, if the code of ethics that this particular samurai warrior lived by involved never saying anything racist, accident or not.

Also, accident or not, this was the third neighbor in three months who Bennett had infuriated to levels of disrepair. After all that had happened lately, I was a little shocked to realize that it had only been that long since Bennett and his family had been living with me and my life was changed forever.

At which point the thought occupying my mind was, *Just give him the money before something bad happens* . . .

But hang on. I can't start the story here, let's back up a bit to the beginning and the email that started it all.

Me and You, My Cousin, and His Mama Too

On Sep 7, at 2:53 AM, Lillian O. wrote:

Hi Macky..Auntie Lillian here.. How are u honey? I miss u so much and hope u are doing good whats going on with u Pookie ? Lily

On Sep 7, at 6:26 AM, David Sheldon <asklethal@gmail.com> wrote:

Wow! Hey, Aunt Lily—

It's so great to hear from you! Things are going wonderfully over here. My music is going better than ever. Touring is absolutely wonderful. Just bought a new house a few months ago! Getting settled in!

Also, I met a girl named Harper a while ago. She's really great, and I know it's probably moving too fast, but she's definitely the ONE. She graduated from the University of Vermont and comes from a pretty rich family back in Vermont—they're very educated and wealthy! But luckily, she's amazing and will be a wonderful mother to your nieces and nephews! Well, let's hope, haha.

I was shocked when I saw your email address in my inbox. How is everything? How's Bennett?

Mac

On Sep 7, at 4:02 PM, Lillian O. wrote:

Hi Macky.. Well not much here.. well the recession has hit Tim and me pretty hard and we are losing the house to foreclose.. We stopped paying those assholes and plan on sueing them. We tried to ask them for a break many times being that we were so good with pay ment for the yeers leading up but they just said no and our morgage was sold to a other bank..wellt he good news is i should be getting my settlement from the construnction company soon and will be able to rent an apartment.. Bennett is doing pretty good. Still popular with the girls, which is trouble..but he is looking cute as the dickens. Well good talking to you.. I hope your doing good !! So happy ur in love Pookie! Aunt Lily

p.s. WE LOVE U POOKIE :) :)

On Sep 7, at 9:35 PM, David Sheldon <asklethal@gmail.com> wrote:

Aunt Lily,

I don't understand. You guys are losing the house??? That's horrible. Is there any way I can help? I know you've been struggling with health issues, so I would feel absolutely horrible to know you were losing the house if it could be prevented.

Sorry for the brevity, I'm just very concerned. You already know I love and miss you.

Mac

p.s. Do you have a current # for Bennett?

On Sep 8, at 11:56 AM, Lillian O. wrote:

Well we are going to try to live at a motel here in KCK.. it isnt the best option but Tim has a friend who owns the American motel in KCK and well it will be a fresh start for us.

Well i dont think there is much you can do Pookie but we love you :).

Bennetts # is 913-588-****

A Beer-Stained Letter

Who's the greatest basketball player of all time?

Who's the most ferocious boxer of all time?

Think of a number between one and ten. Got it? Good.

Michael Jordan, Mike Tyson, and the number seven are all prime examples of a single entity being such a powerful, behemoth force in their respective industries that they erase whoever came before them from memory *and* are used as a constant measuring tool to compare and contrast whoever comes after them.

Now. Think of a few famous rappers. Got 'em? Who'd you come up with? 50 Cent? Jay-Z? Kanye West? 2Pac? Biggie? LL Cool J? Lil Wayne?

Good job. But what about white rappers? How many can you name? And no, Vanilla Ice doesn't count. He was a major record label experiment gone awry. I mean famous, certifiably talented, *white* rappers. Who'd you conjure up? Got him?

Eminem.

Eminem is an undeniable talent. He deserves every dollar and fan he has accrued over the last decade. However, the motherfucker kinda sorta casted a titanic eclipse over the hip-hop genre and type-casted every other melanin-deficient rapper as nothing more than an Eminem wannabe.

Well, at least on a mainstream level.

If I were to tell you that there are several hardworking, but not super famous, white rappers who began their careers before Eminem even existed in the public eye, and who currently make a decent-to-great living off modern rap music, would you believe me? And I don't mean white poseurs, drinking Moscato, throwing wads of cash around in their videos, acting like "stereotypical black rappers." I mean rappers who rap about day-to-day things people of all races go through. Authentic rappers, with skills and rhythm and a voice worth listening to. I'm one of those rappers.

I've gone by Mac my entire life, but my legal name is David McCleary Sheldon. I'm a thirtywhatever, full-blooded American male with grandparents from Kilkenny and Cork. I inherited the classic Irish temper; a pasty, outer layer of skin; and ginger facial hair that blends with the chalky black hair my Black Irish relatives always had.

A NOTE ON THOSE BLUE-EYED, DRACULA-LOOKIN' MOTHERFUCKERS

As I've explained to Bennett on at least ten different occasions, "Black Irish" is a term used to describe descendants of immigrants from the prehistoric Iberia and Basque regions who hybridized with Irish natives in 7000 BC. It's not referring to African American people with Irish names, e.g., my sixth-grade teacher Mrs. McCormick, and Eddie Murphy.

I was born in Kansas City, Missouri, during the Leo moon to Warren and Ruth Sheldon. My dad is a hardworking, blue-collar Ohio boy who has a problem being nice to waitresses and terrible road rage. My mom was an artsy, thoughtful, Saint Louis belle, who was always *very* nice to waitresses and drove too slow. My parents divorced when I was five years old, so I never really saw them married, but they lived only a few blocks away from each other, so I had a solid relationship with both of them while growing up. My mom died in 2004, but I still have my dad; my two sisters, Rose and Evelyn; and their great husbands, Greg and Henry.

I've loved Brazilian jujitsu, movies, and rap music for my entire life. I spent a majority of my formative years having vivid daydreams, staring into the distance, thinking about girls, and being completely disconnected from what was going on in the classroom. I was a space cadet, fully apathetic to the idea of success or work. School was so boring. I just wanted to sleep.

What might surprise people: my Kansas City high school was a third Caucasian, a third Latino, and a third African American. There were also a few Asian and Indian kids, a band of Russians, and one Lakota kid, who came to school on hallucinogenic mushrooms at least twice a week and whose legal name was Adam Little Elk Running Over the Enemy. (What up, Adam? Call me when you see this!) There were a lot of drugs, fights, and troubled kids at my school. There was also a nursery for the girls who had babies.

I wasn't necessarily a bad kid, especially compared to some. But I did have disciplinary issues. I skipped school a lot, got caught smoking pot in the parking lot a few times, and even got busted for having vodka mixed into a plastic bottle of Tropicana orange juice. I just wasn't stimulated by the stuff my teachers were teaching.

I tried to get my parents to let me attend an art school of some sort, where I could develop right-brain abilities like sketching, oil painting, and creative writing—but they declined. They didn't have the money to send me somewhere like that. So, instead, I just sat in decay, year after year, letting public schoolteachers cover my third eye with black spray paint.

One random, agonizingly boring day during sophomore year, having slept through my morning classes, I was quite refreshed after lunch and was sitting in study hall with nothing to do. Not unusual. That day, though, I borrowed a piece of paper from Letasha Tilman and wrote *MC Reptile* at the top of it (my first rapper alias).

I still remember the verse by heart:

My name is MC Reptile.
I weave words together like textiles.
I grab the microphone and smack the sheriff off his saddle.
I battle like a rattlesnake and make you all skidaddle.
Rappers fuck with me they get beaten like eggs.

You try to kick rhymes and I'm eatin' your legs.
I stay so fresh, cook rappers like gizzards.
Bitch I'm the wizard, the Reptile lizard.

It may not look like much, but the mere act of writing those eight lines permanently seared the cobwebs from my imagination and inspired me to never sleep during class again. Instead, I began nurturing my passion for rapping.

I'd heard the cliché: "You must spend ten thousand hours intensely practicing something to master it." So for the next six years, I did just that. I filled countless notebooks with rap lyrics, constantly challenging myself to parent my own, unique writing style. I read dictionaries and thesauri to expand my vocabulary, memorizing all sorts of exotic words and their definitions.

Borborygmus: the rumbling sound of gas passing through
     the intestine
Fuscoferuginous: having a dark, rusty color
Quomodocunquize: to make money by any means possible

I read every book I could find by William S. Burroughs, Jack Kerouac, Vladimir Nabokov, Ernest Hemingway, Mikhail Bulgakov, Kurt Vonnegut, and Cormac McCarthy to try and learn how to write with deliberate fluidity. I devoured every rap album I could find, picking apart each rapper's deficiencies, adopting my interpretation of their strengths. I would freestyle rap for hours in my bedroom into a handheld tape recorder, while doing jumping jacks and push-ups. This helped me simultaneously improvise new rap ideas *and* develop lungpower, projection, verbal articulation, enunciation, and breath control.

I was methodical. I drilled constantly, pushing myself to improve. I never set out to be famous, or even make a living off music. I just wanted to impress kids in the high school cafeteria with my freestyle raps, while I made fun of Margot Glasscock's last name, or rapped about sleeping with Miss Steele, the school's foxy, thirty-two-year-old algebra teacher.

After honing my rapping skills, I set up a makeshift studio in my mom's basement and recorded my first album, *Mixed Drinks*. The writing was funny, weird, and quirky. I made songs about not being able to find my car keys, and getting broken up with by a girl I didn't like in the first place but wanting to win her back just to have bragging rights on who broke up with whom. While it was lo-fi and sounded like crap, the people I passed it out to seemed to enjoy it for what it was. So I dropped out of high school and decided to pursue being a rapper full-time. Backup plans are for pussies

Touring seemed like the best way to expand my career, so I spent years networking with other independent artists, driving ten to fifteen hours every day, just to play free shows for crowds of fewer than fifty people. I passed out free tapes (and eventually CDs) that I assembled myself at Kinko's and slept on the beer-stained apartment floors of random weirdos my crew and I would meet at shows, to avoid paying for a hotel room. I could fill an entire book with tour stories from my early years, most of them unfortunate.

Touring and building a fan base from scratch is immensely hard, and most people don't even achieve moderate success doing it. Most people quit the first time they fall flat on their face. Believe me, you have to be partially nuts to endure the things that traveling, working entertainers endure.

Only 1 percent become megastars. The other 99 percent of us are on a daily grind, dreaming we can one day pay off our bills from music.

Luckily, my dreams started to come true. After giving a passionate decade of my life to being a rapper—I started to turn a profit. My tiny, scattered, local following had enveloped into a dedicated worldwide fan base. I could play just about any part of the world, and pull at least one hundred people—one thousand in some places.

I sold T-shirts, CDs, trucker hats, sweatshirts, dog bowls, backpacks, fanny packs, socks, girl panties, pint glasses, shot glasses, et cetera—all with my logo printed on them. I was a working, self-funded, independent rap artist, selling out shows, paying the bills, and living a dream that is oft never achieved by a majority of musicians, let alone rappers.

For once in my life, music was no longer a struggle. It was a highly lucrative roller-coaster ride that afforded me the ability to travel anywhere and purchase anything I wanted, which was new to me, and slightly unsettling. I knew there was no way this could last forever, so I decided to invest my money wisely while my chips were up. I found an amazing, albeit slightly gaudy, house in the Brookside area of Kansas City, Missouri, put down a giant down payment (since touring tends to lead to bad credit), and moved in.

I had my own home (I bought a house!), and it felt great.

(ME:) Hey fucker, guess who?

(BENNETT:) ?

(ME:) Guess who this is, you little-dicked twerp.

(BENNETT:) hoe i told u to stop texten me my girl gonna c dat shit

(BENNETT:) bcide u wuz luven my big dicc in da parkin lot da otha nite lol slut

(ME:) Lol, you think this is a girl.

(BENNETT:) dis is ashly duh

(BENNETT:) look.. u ever seen a tigger or a lion git married?

(BENNETT:) u ever seen a eagel wit a diamend ring on it"s finger?

(BENNETT:) no u havent dats bcuz men R not saposed 2 be wit 1 women. men R wild animels...... i fucc alot of hoez cuz men r saposed 2 spred there seed da bibel says we gatta evolve and fucc

(ME:) This isn't a girl!!!!!

(BENNETT:) wat

(BENNETT:) now u gunna try 2 say u were a guy da hole time?bitch i seen ur vaginna u a girl or u got a realy gud sex change

(ME:) LOL, STOP. This isn't fucking Ashley. Who's Ashley?

(BENNETT:) quit playn on my phone bitch who dis !!!

(ME:) It's Mac.

(ME:) Helllooooo???

BENNETT: mac my cuz??..

ME: Yes sir.

BENNETT: o shit lolz

BENNETT: wud up G

ME: Care to explain what's happening with your mom losing her house?

BENNETT: man.. it sux

BENNETT: basicly da punk ass govermant niggaz is kiccin us out da crib cuz day so broke dat even my mom bustid ass house is wort takin

ME: Is she not doing well? Why can't she pay the bills?

BENNETT: nigga my mom on Oxycotton 247365 times a day.

ME: Do you mean 24/7/365?

BENNETT: ya but im gittin sum pussy right now so i aint have time to type dat side ways / thing

ME: Liar. You said "times a day" which negates a / even working.

BENNETT: look pussy u alweys talk shit to me when we txt.. u probaly jellice from all da COCC i sell and da $$$ i get

ME: You make money selling cock?

BENNETT: na COCC... fuccin.. cocainn

A NOTE FOR THOSE LOOKING TO LEARN HOW TO SPEAK FLUENT CRIP

Members of the Crips do not ever put the letters C and K next to each other and just use two C's instead. CK stands for Crip Killer, so this is a very serious typographical issue.

ME: I'm fucking with you. WHY is your mom on OxyContin?

BENNETT: cuz she also sleep all day an stop payen da bills..

ME: Her back is fucked up still, right? But OxyContin? Does she need OxyContin?

BENNETT: ya she in pain alot. butt cmon playa n e 1 who take oxycotton does it for fun not bcuz they need it..nigga u ever try dat shit?it make u feel like ur 2pac in dat hot tub holden stax of cash pouren chammpane on a striperz head

ME: I see. Uh. Also, who's Tim?

BENNETT: dats my mom BF

ME: Yeah? You live with him? Why can't he help with the bills?

BENNETT: he wierd. he duz acid and smoke hella weed wit me but he a bum ass nigga 2.haha. he broke as fuk.

BENNETT: butt he smart like U doe.... .

BENNETT: he read sum wild ass books like U. sum crazy shit wit Da Illuminadi. he a wild ass nigga.

BENNETT: he show me a video on UTube of 911 an how da govermant planted dinamite in da billdings and blew dem up

ME: Do you believe that stuff, Bennett?

BENNETT: hell yea who doeznt.?da white house has a grave unda it wit gosts and shit

BENNETT: i dont beleive anything on Da news

ME: Right on, buddy. I'm going to call your mom. What's her number?

BENNETT: K hang on

BENNETT: 913-648-****

Now that I knew more of the scoop, I called Aunt Lillian and extended an invitation for them all to come stay with me for a few weeks. She was so intoxicated on painkillers that I couldn't understand a word she said, other than, "Thank you so much!"

This was spur of the moment, but I knew it was the right thing to do. Family is family. You're supposed to help family. Right? And all I wanted to do right then was help my aunt. Especially after hearing the pain and confusion in her voice over the phone.

Especially after what she did for me in 2002.

HARPER: You keep bringing up "the '02 thing."

HARPER: What happened in 2002 to make you feel obligated to do this?

ME: Well

ME: I needed a van in 2002 to go on my first tour.

ME: My mom wouldn't rent me one because i wasn't even 21 yet . . . which made sense. If I woulda wrecked it she woulda been fucked.

ME: But at the time I thought she was being difficult so I put up a bit of a fuss over it.

ME: Lucky for me in the middle of arguing with her over it Aunt Lillian called.

ME: My mom told her what was going on and Lillian offered us her conversion van that was sitting in her driveway.

ME: She wasn't using it. She had a string of surgeries and was out of work for a while.

HARPER: What kind of surgery?

ME: Not 100% sure. My aunt has some serious medical issues. Back problems, nerve damage etc. She takes lots of pills.

ME: Anyway . . .

ME: Yada yada yada she insisted and we took it.

ME: For 5-6 weeks it worked great.

ME: Until it completely died in Gainesville, FL on the highway.

ME: Just crapped out on us. We had to take a Greyhound cross-country back home. Luckily, the tour was two shows from being over when it happened.

ME: I was going to fly back to Florida to get it but the repairs were so expensive. The engine was shot. It was gonna cost like $2,000 to fix. But Aunt Lily said not to bother.

ME: She said she had another old car she could drive if she needed to.

ME: And was genuinely happy that she contributed to my tour. Didn't sweat me to pay her back at all.

HARPER: I get it. I guess. I mean that's very nice of her.

ME: Right.

HARPER: So who all would be moving in with us then?

ME: Aunt Lillian, her boyfriend Tim, and my cousin Bennett.

HARPER: Ok.

ME: They're good folks.

HARPER: Just to clarify: from what you've told me in the past, Aunt Lillian has a terrible OxyContin addiction, can barely pay her bills, and sleeps all day. Her boyfriend Tim is apparently a conspiracy theory nut who believes Barack Obama drinks human blood and "shapeshifts" into a reptile that lives underground. And Bennett is a 17 year old gangbanger who says he's partially black, when he's not. Amiright?

ME: Yes. You're right. Totally.

HARPER: K. So I think I get why you want to do this. But a gangbanger? That's scary.

ME: Yeah. Hmm. Bennett is a troubled kid. I'm just being honest. But he's got a good heart.

HARPER: Like . . .

HARPER: That's neat and all. But there's also a lot of people with good hearts in prison.

HARPER: I watch a show about it on A&E. They give kittens to prisoners to make them good people. They're still rapists and murderers though.

ME: I doubt Bennett will ever end up in prison.

HARPER: Hasn't he been to juvie like five times already?

ME: Twice.

HARPER: For what?

ME: He got into an argument with someone and kicked their car or something.

(HARPER:) He went to jail for kicking a car? That doesn't seem like it makes sense.

(HARPER:) It doesn't matter. I just don't feel comfortable with this, that's all.

(HARPER:) I've never really been around people like them. I do NOT say that disparagingly.

(ME:) I know you don't, honey. But I promise, Aunt Lillian is one of the nicest relatives I have.

(HARPER:) I see.

(HARPER:) Why can't she pay her bills again?

(ME:) Well . . . she's just a little irresponsible.

(ME:) My grandpa Mike, her dad, didn't exactly love her or put energy into raising her. He kind of hated her to be honest. She has mild Asperger's. You wouldn't be able to even notice.

(HARPER:) God. Who could hate someone with Asperger's? That seems uncool. Then again I guess I've never had a child with Asperger's.

(ME:) As a kid she had trouble learning and functioning. Grandpa Mike was very abusive and always drunk.

(ME:) He accused Kitty.

(ME:) My grandma/his wife . . .

(ME:) Of having an affair on him and said Lillian wasn't his, and that the night Kitty got pregnant with Lillian the mystery guy accidentally peed in her and contaminated the sperm cell causing it to not develop properly.

(HARPER:) That's hilarious. Did your grandma really have an affair?

(ME:) Nah, Lillian looks exactly like Mike. He was just an asshole.

(ME:) Btw that's really not "hilarious."

(HARPER:) Well? Did she act up a bunch as a child or something?

(ME:) No. She is seriously one of the sweetest people in the world.

(ME:) At my mom's funeral she sat with me and my sisters and just cried and hugged us.

ME: To see her feel that type of pain over my mom dying brought me closer to her.

ME: Hello?

ME: You there?

ME: Sorry. Nipples! Dinosaur cocks!

HARPER: Huh? . . . ?

ME: Because I'm getting all serious on you and want to be more lighthearted.

HARPER: Sorry, baby I didn't respond because my boss was making me help him with something.

ME: Do you get why I feel obligated to do this?

HARPER: Umm..

ME: Bennett can sleep in the basement. So we just need to let Lily and Tim use the guest room for a few weeks while they find a new apartment.

HARPER: You know what? It's your house. Your decision.

ME: Hey, stop that. I don't want you to feel that way. It's your home too.

HARPER: I don't want to feel this way either. But what choice are you giving me? It's like it's out of bounds for me to say what I feel.

ME: What do you feel? Honestly.

HARPER: I feel like you should tell Aunt Lillian to get off her ass and take care of her family like a big girl. But, again, I don't want to tell you what to do. I just know if it was my family I wouldn't want anything to do with it.

ME: Sheesh.

ME: I'm not trying to start a fight, I'm really not. But your entire family is Democrats. The whole basis of your politics is helping the poor. Assisting the lower class.

ME: But when its actually time to put that plan into effect you want nothing to do with it?

HARPER: *it's

(ME:) Huh?

(HARPER:) You mean "it's" as in "it is." Also "are Democrats," not "is."

(ME:) Seriously? Clever way to avoid the topic at hand.

(HARPER:) Baby, no. I'm not avoiding the topic. I just disagree.

(HARPER:) And you know how annoyed I get over bad grammar!

(HARPER:) By the way, we want to tax the rich and redistribute their money to the poor. What does that have to do with letting people freeload off us?

(ME:) Freeload huh?

(ME:) Unreal.

(ME:) You know what? I'm taking a nap. I don't want to say something unkind right now because I love you.

(HARPER:) Baby, wait.

(HARPER:) You know what I meant.

(HARPER:) I didn't mean it like that.

(HARPER:) Honey?

Granite
Countertops

4

My girlfriend, Harper, grew up in Manchester, Vermont, and was raised in a twelve-bedroom, white colonial house from the 1800s, replete with forest-green shutters, a driveway comprised of faded, black cobblestone and auburn bricks, and a front yard boasting 150-year-old shagbark hickory trees.

Due to the nature of this book, I couldn't obtain legal permission to disclose exactly who her father is, but to put it vaguely: he's a monstrously successful business magnate who birthed a very important, ahead of its time computer company and then a couple of other companies that also achieved great success. He was a pompous, liberal (but not really) prick. The kind of guy who enjoys homebrewing oatmeal stout beer but also names his four Brittany spaniels Tic, Tac, Toe, and Moe. Her mom was a philanthropist and college professor. Her siblings, both still in college. Let's just say they were a particularly influential piece of the elite Northeast liberal oligarchy.

I met Harper when she was in Kansas City, visiting one of her old roommates from college. This roommate was a mutual friend of ours, who dragged Harper out to see one of my local shows. After watching me perform, she approached me and said, "Touché."

Touché. That's the first thing she ever said to me. As if I proved her wrong on an argument we were having. Which, apparently, I did.

Originally, she assumed that since I was a rapper, I'd be an illiterate, materialistic misogynist. Her experience with hip-hop music was limited, I'd say. But after watching me, she admitted that my lyrics were "more like poetry than rap." I "surprised her a lot." Thus: "Touché."

I've classically had bad luck with women. They always found me too intense and overtly passionate. For example, I made Danielle Gamby, a cocktail waitress at Garozzo's Italian restaurant, an arts-and-crafts project out of old, repurposed shoe boxes to express my love for her. She enjoyed the ballet, so I created an auditorium and stage out of the boxes and inscribed a poem for her on the backdrop of the stage, full of romantic proclamations and fancy caesuras. She ended up fucking my friend Nate in his car the night I gave it to her.

Harper was a perfect match for me. Both of us had rocky romance histories. So much so that in social settings I didn't approach women just to avoid rejection, but she *did* approach men, to avoid being alone forever. She had a . . . how should I say it? *Strong* personality. Her approaching me wasn't a cosmic phenomenon. Jaded, lonely people instinctually find each other at bars, the same way alcoholics and cokeheads do.

After the show, we shared a couple pots of cheap coffee at a diner and talked, joked, swooned, and did things like exchange "Top 5 of All-Time Lists" about "Entertainment's Holy Trinity."

Until ten in the morning.

Mac's Top 5's

Films

1. *The Wild Bunch*
2. *Goodfellas*
3. *Pulp Fiction*
4. *Boyz N the Hood*
5. *Dazed and Confused*

Albums

1. Ice Cube's *Death Certificate*

2. Nas's *Illmatic*
3. Jay-Z's *The Blueprint*
4. Wu-Tang Clan's *Enter the Wu-Tang*
5. Scarface's *The Diary*

Books

1. John Kennedy Toole's *A Confederacy of Dunces*
2. Roald Dahl's *Charlie and the Chocolate Factory*
3. Christopher Moore's *Lamb*
4. Iceberg Slim's *Pimp*
5. Neil Strauss *The Dirt*

Harper's Top 5's

Films

1. *Edward Scissorhands*
2. *Buffalo '66*
3. *Synecdoche, New York*
4. *The Life Aquatic with Steve Zissou*
5. *I Heart Huckabees*

Albums

1. Radiohead's *OK Computer*
2. Sonic Youth's *Goo*
3. Patti Smith's *Horses*
4. Nick Drake's *Five Leaves Left*
5. Brian Eno's *Ambient 1: Music for Airports*

Books

1. Richard Bach's *Jonathan Livingston Seagull*
2. Dave Eggers's *A Heartbreaking Work of Staggering Genius*
3. Lucy Knisley's *French Milk*
4. Oscar Wilde's *The Picture of Dorian Gray*
5. Mark Z. Danielewski's *House of Leaves*

I was drawn to her intelligence (college graduate, articulate, critical thinker, smart with money, informed politically); the places she's traveled (England, Israel, Australia, Argentina, Iceland, Russia,

Mexico, New Zealand); her taste in hip art and obscure entertainment (see aforementioned Top 5's); her spunky way of dressing (up-and-coming designer and thrift-store fashion; Euro hairstyles; Louis Vuitton loafers on casual days); her athletic, healthy body (vegetarian); and her fierce independence.

We were inseparable for the rest of her trip, and even after she flew back home, we talked on the phone every single night for the next five months. After a lot of long-distance admiration, the pent-up, quixotic energy was too much to handle, so she came out for a weekend stay at my new house.

But . . . we fell in love and she never flew home.

Luckily, Harper had the deep, family-bestowed finances to be able to do something like that. I didn't fully grasp how loaded her family was until she found a job as the assistant to the regional director of a local computer company, for nothing more than "the socializing and the office gossip."

She never looked down on me for not being educated like her. Well, she tried not to anyway. She never judged my broken, dysfunctional family, our limited income, or our white-trash instincts. Well, she tried not to anyway.

It seemed like she was really ready to ditch the attitude she'd grown up with and begin the underrated, difficult journey into adulthood.

She had officially lived with me for only a couple of months when shit hit the fan.

ME: Why'd you go to jail last year?

BENNETT: why da fuck did U just put 'd at da end of why ? dum fuk

ME: It's an abbreviation. Why'd = why did

BENNETT: wats a abrevation

ME: Just tell me why you went to juvenile detention.

BENNETT: i cudnt sleep cuz this bitch was laughing so i filled her car with water

ME: Who was she?

BENNETT: she lived in da house next door. she a russian ho

ME: You filled your NEIGHBOR'S car with water?

BENNETT: yea nigga i told you bennett is a boss hog gangsta

BENNETT: basicly dis bitch standed out in her yard all day wit a hose waterring her grass... and she wud get mad at me and my homie loony for walken thru it

BENNETT: she wud always B trippin sayin GET OFF MY GRASS U LITTEL ASS HOLES

BENNETT: well i had to wake up early one mornin after she wuz on her bacc portch on da phone laughin talkin russia style all late at nite

ME: Russia style?

BENNETT: ya u know how they sound like they got hella loogys in there throat ? its wierd .

ME: That's Russian. Their language.

BENNETT: watever .. she sounded like she swallowd a porky pine

BENNETT: and i didnt appricate how loud she wuz bein bcuz i cudnt fall asleap .. i wuz starten my new job da next mornin at Taste Of India Buffay

BENNETT: so i waited til like 2 am she had her lites off for a cpl hours . and i seen dat her car window was open a lil . so i took da bitch hose and stucc it in da window and turnt da hose on all nite

BENNETT: Da very next day da cops showd up at da buffay and arrestid me .

BENNETT: i cant keep a job ITS really wacc

ME: Did the car have a lot of water in it?

BENNETT: O fucc ya !

BENNETT: i new i wuz gonna get in troubel wen i road by on my bike on da way to work da entire car wuz full of water . !

BENNETT: fishes and lobstars cud have lived in dis bitchez car . i got off my bike and took da hose out . i wuz nervus as fuk.. but i wuz like maybe she will think it rained all nite and shit

ME: What did they charge you with? How long were you in there exactly?

BENNETT: disordarly conduct and criminil damage to proparty . i had 2 serve some time in JUVY Bcuz of my priar record it wuz gay .

BENNETT: 90 dayZ

BENNETT: nigga im exited to live wit U we gon party like KRAZZY

ME: I'm an adult man. I don't party anymore.

BENNETT: Wat. nigga pleaz We gunna have stripers over ! quit acten like U got a rainbow design on ur butt hole

And just like that I was suddenly reminded of how disrespectful and high-maintenance this kid was. Was I potentially biting off way more than any logical human could ever chew?

Yet, the more I thought about it, the more I realized that he was at a *crucial* point in his life. Seventeen-year-old kids are wild and Bennett didn't really have anyone looking out for him—as much as I loved Aunt Lillian, she wasn't really helping him out.

I'm going to save the kid's life. I owe my aunt that much.

Overages 5

In order to maintain *some* privacy, Bennett did not want his legal first name disclosed in this writing. But that doesn't really matter. Bennett has always gone by Bennett. It's his middle name and is his birth father's first name . . . we *think*. There are two options as to who fertilized Lillian's egg.

One is Bennett ***, a former semitruck driver from Liberty, Missouri. The other is Juaquin ******, a carpet salesman from Peculiar, Missouri. Aunt Lillian was romantically involved with both of them simultaneously, but felt that Juaquin ****** would be a better choice for a father since he "made more money." However, once it was known that she was pregnant, neither man would ever be seen by her again, and family odds just fell on the truck driver.

Thus, Bennett grew up in a single-parent, low-income household, bouncing around from town to town and school to school. He grew up in trailer parks, skid-row apartment complexes, and around a lot of inner-city people. He dropped out of high school at age sixteen, has been to jail way more times than I was telling Harper, and represents the Crips, a predominantly black street gang that originated in South Central Los Angeles. People who meet him for the first time hear him dropping the n-bomb every other word and think he's just another privileged white kid, assimilating urban, black culture. But he's not.

He isn't your typical white kid who "acts black" with his other white friends on the way to varsity lacrosse practice. Bennett has no idea that saying the *n* word is something he isn't supposed to do. The way he acts is 100 percent natural to him. He doesn't know any better and honestly probably relates to the plight of black people more than he does white people.

Bennett represents America's white lower class. A very real, deeply threaded stitch in the fabric of our country.

(HARPER:) Baby

(HARPER:) I understand you want to help your family. I know you like your aunt.

(HARPER:) But it's not necessarily the right thing to do.

(HARPER:) Also, you don't even like having your friends over because they leave a couple of empty beer bottles in the living room. How could you possibly handle this?

Oh yeah. I didn't even think about that.

(ME:) I already thought about that. They won't be messy. I'll lay the law down if a single thing gets out of hand.

(ME:) As far as Bennett's concerned, he won't do anything bad. I promise. He's not a bad kid.

(ME:) He just grew up with no guidance, like a lot of kids like him.

(HARPER:) There are other kids like Bennett?

(ME:) Are you kidding? Tons.

(ME:) What are you doing right now? Am I distracting you from work?

(HARPER:) No, go ahead. I'm drinking bubble tea in my car.

(ME:) Ok, good. So there's a legendary story

(ME:) About Bennett.

(HARPER:) Tell me.

(ME:) Well, for example... I'm PRAYING he isn't still seeing Mercedes. Or they're in a fight or something.

HARPER: Who's Mercedes?

ME: His girlfriend. Maybe his ex? Not sure. I know he has a girlfriend. Hopefully it isn't Mercedes.

ME: She has a tattoo under her belly button that says "THUG BITCH". She has long, obnoxious acrylic fingernails that she paints weird colors.

HARPER: :-O

HARPER: Is she at least a nice person?

ME: Absolutely NOT.

ME: One time I was at the mall buying a new pair of dress shoes and I saw Bennett and Mercedes up there walking around. So I asked them if they want to get lunch at the cafeteria. Right?

HARPER: ...

ME: We're sitting at this table eating and Mercedes leans back in her chair, squinting at something in the distance.

ME: Then under her breath she starts saying "What's good, bitch? Wassup, bitch?"

ME: She looks at both me and Bennett and says, "Look like we gots a problem. I don't even know this ho and she's been staring at me since we sat down."

ME: So she gets up and bolts! I was like "OH SHIT." Out of nowhere she got up and RAN towards this chick.

HARPER: To fight her?

ME: Yeah but check this out.

ME: She is running towards this lady screaming, "WASSUP BITCH? YOU WANNA FUCK WITH A THOROUGHBRED GHETTO BITCH, BITCH?"

ME: Everyone in the food court is looking at her. Kids are hiding behind their parents. EVERYONE sees it.

HARPER: Omg

ME: She has her hands thrown up in the air with her fists clenched, looking like she's getting ready to swing any second. ANY SECOND.

ME: She gets about 10 feet away from her. About to throw a punch.

ME: And then she suddenly stops.

ME: She starts cracking up, turns around, and runs back to the table.

ME: Meanwhile I'm trying to figure out what happened.

HARPER: Wha?

ME: Because it was a mannequin.

HARPER: ?

HARPER: What???

ME: She can't see very well. She's supposed to wear glasses and doesn't. So she thought a fuckin mannequin posted outside of Nordstrom was a woman standing there staring at her. Bennett and her thought it was hilarious.

ME: But what kind of idiot starts a fight with a mannequin?

HARPER: Wow, she sounds terrifying.

ME: Oh, one time Mercedes had B E N N E T T S H O painted across her fingernails.

HARPER: Dear god.

HARPER: I'm very unsettled by that story.

ME: Really? I actually think it's kinda funny. It's just another classic from Bennett's life.

HARPER: Did your aunt at least try to parent Bennett? I mean Jesus.

ME: Mmmm not really. If Lillian wasn't at work she'd be asleep on the couch due to her "back injury," which caused her to develop a very heavy OxyContin dependency.

ME: So Bennett basically spent his entire life calling his own shots.

HARPER: Sigh.

HARPER: Anyhoo, that's cute and all, but I think I'm gonna just be honest here. I don't want to do this.

HARPER: At all.

ME: I know, but it's the right thing to do.

HARPER: I don't agree with you on that.

(HARPER:) Sometimes you have to let people deal with their own problems. We aren't a hotel. Maybe we could buy Lillian a used van or something to repay her.

(ME:) If you do this, I'll buy YOU something really nice.

(HARPER:) I can buy my own things.

(ME:) I know. But as we've discussed, you having tons of money is exactly the reason you value presents more than things you buy.

(HARPER:) A present, huh?

(ME:) Yes. A great one.

(HARPER:) Why are you so dead set on doing this, again?

(ME:) Because. I won't be able to sleep at night knowing my extremely sweet aunt and her family are living in a hooker motel.

(HARPER:) Yeah yeah yeah.

(HARPER:) I'm just a little nervous.

(ME:) Nervous about what?

(HARPER:) Well! In Vermont it's nice. The guys I went to school with went to their vacation homes, not jails.

(HARPER:) I'VE never been to jail.

(ME:) I have.

(HARPER:) I know. But a few nights after DUIs isn't the same really.

(ME:) I went for other things too.

(HARPER:) I know. You know what I mean though.

(ME:) I promise, nothing bad will happen.

(HARPER:) And if it does?

(ME:) Then they're outta here if anything goes wrong.

(HARPER:) Even if I say I'd like them to leave and you don't want them to?

(ME:) Ha. Yep.

(ME:) Ok?

(HARPER:) You'll buy me something nice, that makes me feel loved?

(ME:) Yep.

HARPER: Like what?

ME: :::::::Drumroll:::::::::

HARPER: Badadadadadadadadadadadadadadadadadadadada...

ME: Granite countertops for the house?

HARPER: !!!

HARPER: Really? I thought you said we couldn't get those!

HARPER: You drive a hard bargain.

HARPER: Asshole.

ME: :D

HARPER: Ugh.

HARPER: Wait--why would you buy me granite countertops for your horribly ugly kitchen?

ME: To soften the blow.

HARPER: Soften what blow?

A NOTE FOR SNEAKY NINJAS PLOTTING THINGS WITHOUT SPOUSAL CONSENT

Harper had no idea that I already told them they could move in for a few weeks. This was a done deal. So as long as I could get her to agree to it, everything would work out.

ME: The blow that I already committed to this and would rather buy you granite countertops than back out on my aunt!

HARPER: Ahhh, the plot thickens. Wow, you ass.

ME: It'll be good for ya.

HARPER: I'm sure it will. What will be even better: I'm going out with some girls after work. I'll be home pretty late.

ME: So are you saying you're okay with this all?

HARPER: Apparently, I'm going out for a drink aren't I?

ME: Now I feel bad.

HARPER: If I die in a car accident from drunk driving, you can feel bad.

e no mo? o

the girliest text messa

a female language i blen

nja star a :) is my sorde

it wrks luv me they bo

rsent fluant langauge

a i say kk and they bou

ushin spy wit. speak jus

B gittin wit other bit

soft and sweet 2 eacJo

ennett. i know wat wa

Dats fabulus And kk an

they think im sinstive

dat song dat g

Part 2

Mom's 5 Rules for Bennett

1. NO TAKING MONEY FROM MOM'S PURSE

2. WASH DISHES AFTER USING THEM

3. NO SMOKING POT IN THE HOUSE

4. NO SEX IN MOM'S BED

5. SNORT COCAINE AND ADDERALL IN YOUR OWN BATHROOM

The Pilgrimage

At first I thought an exterminator had pulled up to the wrong house. A rusty, chartreuse-yellow 1992 Chevrolet Astro van, with corroded side panels and the words *Thompkins Something-or-other* painted on the side, chugged down the block, pulled into my driveway, and seemed to deflate and shutter like a giant bug when the driver killed the engine.

It had been a lovely Saturday afternoon before that. Harper was lightly trimming the azalea shrubs, and I was sitting on the porch swing thinking about how awesome it would be to be able to shoot fire out of my eyeballs. Both of us looked at the van.

"Is that them? That's not them. Is it?" Harper asked.

"Uh. I don't know. No. It can't be. Who the fuck is that? Is that them?" I replied.

"You didn't tell me gypsies were moving in with us," Harper said.

"What?" I asked.

"The van. It's like what homeless people drive. I can't believe it's in our driveway. Hideous," Harper hissed.

"Homeless people don't drive, babe," I snooted.

The contraption's side door swung open with a loud, unpleasant squawk, revealing my cousin. He had a burning joint in his mouth that he was inhaling and exhaling, hands-free, as if it were normal oxygen. He was wearing black corduroy slippers folded down inward at the heels, white tube socks pulled up to his kneecaps, and baggy, oversize Charlotte Hornets basketball shorts that hung so low off his waist that his entire buttocks poked out the back of them. If he wasn't wearing boxer shorts with *The Godfather* logo tiled across them, his entire ass would have been exposed.

He was shirtless. His chest, arms, stomach, and neck were covered with poorly drawn and terribly executed jailhouse-caliber tattoos. He had a mustache that didn't quite connect in the middle— typical of sub-eighteen-year-old boys—so there were two strips of peach fuzz on either side of his nose. He had earrings in both ears, six lines shaved into his left eyebrow, and an extra-large, starched, steam-ironed Crips-blue bandana wrapped around his head from the rear and knotted in the front.

Bennett held the door open with his foot and, without an expression on his face, sat there scratching his penis while studying me and Harper both, before hopping out onto the driveway.

"My mothafuckin' nigga! Oh, shit!" he yelled.

Simultaneously, both of the front doors slowly creaked open. I tried to get a look at Lillian to say hello, but Bennett quickly ran over to me and put me in an affectionate headlock. He smelled like BO, cheap beer, cheap gas station cologne, cheap pot, and the cheap cigars the cheap pot was rolled up in.

"Hey, man! How are ya?" I said, hugging him, with a firm pattern of pats on his back.

"Dude, I'm so excited to move up in yo crib! It's about to be a *war zone* in this bitch. The party starts now, my niggas!" he yelled. "It's *Vietnam Two, Nigga! Hos better take cover!* We 'bout to film pornos with bitches and build a two-hundred-foot bong! *Nigga!*"

"Bennett, this is Harper," I said in reply, pointing to Harper, "my girlfriend."

"Ohhh. What up, boo!" He stuck his hand out to shake hers, while exhaling a cloud of blunt smoke in her face. "Damn, you fine as *hell*! I bet your body is amazing as fuck! You ever been a stripper? You could be one and easily make a hundred bucks *a night*!"

Harper's eyes pulsated in shock while she shook his hand back. Her eyebrows shot to the top of her head in bemusement. She smiled and politely said, "Uh. Well, than . . . ks. That's quite the . . . um . . . compliment." She was trying not to hug him very tightly.

"Is that my sweetest nephew?" Lillian yelled from the van, while her boyfriend, Tim, helped her start to crawl out. My entire family was notoriously loud, and she was no exception.

"Ohhh, it's him! It's my sweetest nephew!" she yelled.

"Hi, Aunt Lillian!" I said. She had a bright smile on her face as Tim guided her tiny, frumpy body to me to avoid her collapsing. She laboriously walked with a limp; her rickety skeletal frame would fall if she attempted to walk on her own. When she was close enough to hug, I embraced her.

She was shorter than I remembered and had a certain snuggly quality to her, probably beacuse she was soft and smelled like fabric softener. Between her plaid pajama top and oily, tangled gray hair, her pupils hovered at the size of needle points, a side effect of her being high on painkillers. Letting me go, she scanned the new house with curious eyes.

"Ohhh! I love the house! Isn't this house beautiful?" she yelled to the air while limping toward the front door. "Oh! I'm so proud of you! Tim, isn't this place great? It's our house now too!"

"Yes, Lillian, it's great," Tim said, veiled with irritation.

"Thank you—we love it!" I said.

Lillian spun around and gave me a look of deep sincerity. You could tell by her facial expression alone that she was impressed with the house and excited to stay with us.

"It's nice, isn't it?" Harper said, with forged enthusiasm. She was being a true champion.

"Hi! I'm Lillian! But you can just call me Lillian!" my aunt said.

Harper, with a natural inability not to be sarcastic in such a situation, however politely, responded with: "That's easy. I'm Harper. And . . . you can call me Harper!"

"Did you meet my son, Bennett, Harper? He's your age and could treat you right! Bennett, damn it. Son, put on a shirt and some perfume so Harper will like you better."

"What?" Bennett said, looking at Lillian crazily. "Mom . . . you off them Oxy pills like crazy right now!"

Harper shuffled over to the side of me and vaguely leaned against me to indicate our bond.

"Uh, yeah, Aunt Lillian, Harper is my girlfriend," I said.

"Ohhh. She is? Boy, you like 'em young! She looks like she's fifteen!" Lillian said.

> ### A NOTE FOR CHRIS HANSEN
> **Harper was twenty-seven. She looked twenty-seven, which is something I liked about her. She definitely didn't look fifteen. She looked like a woman! (!(!!))**

I stuck my hand out to shake Tim's, but he gave me a closed-fist dap in return.

"I don't exchange germs with strangers," he said.

"Oh. Okay," I said, giving him the fist bump back.

"Uh. Tim, this is Harper, she's my fian—"

"I heard you introduce her to Lily. No need to say it twice, now," he said, cutting me off. "It's bad enough that we're standin' outside where the CIA can film us and what not. So please, Harp, Haribou, Harpey, whatever . . . darlin', don't you try to shake my hand either. Let's just get ourselves inside," he smugly said to Harper in a heavily twanged hick draw before spitting his chewing tobacco onto our lawn. "Fancy lil' neighborhood like this . . . you know the CIA got freakin' billion-dollar flies that fly around with cameras in 'em, right? Lil' robots filmin' every move you make and sellin' the info to China. Your neighbors are probably investment bankers or members of the Skulls. Yeah. I prefer the indoors, but it's certainly nice to meet you folks."

It was then that I noticed that in addition to flawlessly quaffed hair with a shoulder-length mullet growing down the back of his neck, he wore a dingy, stain-covered T-shirt with that wonderful catchphrase of the nutty everywhere:

9/11 WAS AN INSIDE JOB

. . . in bright, metallic orange letters, which were sitting on top of a picture of George W. Bush and Osama Bin Laden superimposed to appear to be shaking hands, with sinister grins on their faces, and two burning World Trade Center buildings behind them. To top that off, Skoal-mouth wore reddish-crimson thrift-store slacks, a pair of high-end canvas-colored flip-flops, and purple-framed, glittery sunglasses on his face. *Hannah Montana* sunglasses. Yes. *With a* Hannah Montana *logo on them.*

All I could think of doing in the face of such a getup on such a man was ask, "Why Hannah Montana?"

To which he replied, "Hannah is a small town in Montana my grandfather grew up in. They export a lot of coal and cattle."

To which I concluded he was so full of shit and out of touch.

I had heard from other family members that he was a conspiracy theorist, but I had at least assumed his conspiracies had *some sort* of academic merit. Nope, nothing but tall tales with lacunae in the credibility. Tim definitely wasn't working with a full deck of cards.

Across the street, one house to the right, my Sudanese neighbor Edgard Amsalu, sat on the top step of his front porch, massaging the shoulders of his exotic, magnetically attractive wife, Mariam. Edgard had plenty of reason to rub Mariam's shoulders. She was a stunning African woman, with onyx-colored skin that visibly absorbed the day's glowing particles of sun and swirled them onto a cherrywood palette of skin complexion that mixed hues of obsidian, charcoal, hot magma, and ink-bottle blacks with the Earth tones of melted chocolate, spun gold, polished doubloons, and pungent cinnamon powder, and the textures of brushed suede, ripe mahogany, and crispy, burnt auburn. Her eyes were the color of gilded honey, and her lips lightly enveloped into an irresistible, swollen pucker.

Yeah, I'll admit, I thought she was pretty cute.

They were immigrants from the ruins of Juba, a war-torn village in the southern region of the Sudan. Once they met and fell in love, they decided to elope and fled to Senegal to avoid the seemingly endless genocide that had devastated the Sudan for so long.

Edgard worked on a tobacco farm while Mariam was allegedly a coquette of some kind and entertained a couple of powerful Senegalese politicians to supplement an attractive amount of income. This particular part of the story is murky and is largely based on neighborhood hearsay, so I can't confirm how much truth there is to it. However, I do know that Edgard and Mariam had been deeply passionate about saving enough money to move to America so they could start a family here.

The state of Kansas has the largest population of naturalized Sudanese people in the entire United States—a vast majority of whom are hardworking people who have, or should have, in my opinion, the *right* as human beings to aspire to experience the peaceful state of living they could find here in comparison to the Sudan. Which is something Edgard and Mariam wanted at any cost.

Edgard's brother Samir Amsalu had already moved here eleven years ago and attained citizenship by marrying his wife, Minoo— an American citizen of first-generation Sudanese lineage. All four of them lived in the tiny but cozy ranch across the street, one house to the right. Minoo was a registered nurse at Saint Luke's Hospital, Samir and Edgard both worked at a local nursing home, caring for elderly tenants, and Mariam stayed at home caring for her and Edgard's seven-year-old son, Jean Paul. The star of the neighborhood.

Jean Paul was a pure boy. Soft-spoken and gentle. Polite and allergic to bee pollen. He was slender, with a bony, unathletic frame, and wore khaki shorts pulled up to his belly button with a collared shirt tucked into them. He had thin-framed glasses and hyperextended his knees when he walked. He rarely played ball or ran around the neighborhood causing ruckus. Instead, he liked to draw and carried around with him a Big Chief paper tablet and a large box of assorted colored pencils. He drew exceptional pictures of suburban nature, clouds, and African wildlife.

Whenever I was outside, he loved to curiously stare at me from the edge of my driveway, quietly observing whatever I was doing. He always had a pocket full of Dum Dums, and gave me one every time I saw him, before showing me his newest drawings. Every person on the block loved him and would always honk and wave at him when driving by. He was unsurprisingly enrolled in gifted classes, which he only attended four days a week, so he was home with his mother a lot.

Currently, his parents were watching him attempt to ride his bike without training wheels.

"Look at dat young ghetto child, learnin' how ta ride his bike," Bennett said, full of compassion and warmth. "I bet dat lil' nigga gonna be a gangsta when he grow up!"

"Bennett, he's from the Sudan. He doesn't act like a 'gangsta,'" I said.

"What? You racist, huh? Don't even know yo own neighbors!" Bennett said, disgusted. "Dat kid is black. Can't you see the color of his skin? To know da lil' niggas struggle? And y'all wonder why so many black folk in prison."

He then cupped his hands over his mouth and yelled across the street.

"Keep hustlin' on dat bike, *young playa!* You'll make it out da hood one day. Smokin' weed helped me learn how to ride *my* bike, *young ni—*"

I slammed my hand over his mouth. He was seconds away from dropping an n-bomb to actual, real-life, Third-World-country Africans.

"Hey! Let's get your mom inside so she can relax! Here, Bennett, grab a suitcase!" I put Lillian's bag in Bennett's arms.

Harper stared at me, widely opened her eyes, rolled her eyeballs, then walked away. She was already over it.

The Gracie Family

While Bennett and I brought in his family's luggage and put it upstairs in the guest bedroom, Harper—bless her—sat down at the kitchen table, chatting to Lillian and Tim. We then took Bennett's gym bag and two milk crates of belongings down to the basement, where he would sleep while staying with us.

"Damn, you cold pimpin' now! Dis house is da shit! You could run a full-blown ghetto mafia operation out dis bitch!" Bennett screamed in awe of my finished basement.

"What exactly is 'a ghetto Mafia operation'?" I asked.

"I'm sayin', mane, you could, like, sell heron', coke, have hookers, machine guns, and shit. Some stripper poles, sell some crack, and what not, right? But since it's so nice and shit, if da cops fuck wichu, be like, 'Hello, officer, I'm a tooth doctor.' Haha!"

Bennett tried to give me five after saying that. I politely shook his hand instead.

"Uh. Yeah. I don't think we'll be hosting any 'ghetto mafia operations' anytime soon."

"C'mon, nigga! You rap, right?" Bennett said, collapsing onto the couch.

"Yeah. I rap," I replied.

"Homie, I'm glad we havin' this talk. Look, my nigga, rappers gotta glorify da streets and shit. You gotta be backhandin' hos and stealin' jewelry from Donald Trump! How you gonna have street cred when you rap 'bout global warnings? We want blood and Lamborghinis wif bullet holes in our music, my G! I could help you learn how to rap like dat."

"Do you mean 'global warming'?"

"See? A street nigga like me don't even know da name of it. But fuck naw. global warming, my ass! It's a cold world. It ain't warm. Bring dat street shit!"

"That's not my style. Nor do I want it to be."

"Mane . . . fuck!" Bennett said, frustrated. "Aiight, mane, look. Can I tell you a secret, Cuz?"

"Uh. Sure."

"Look. I ain't tryin' to dis you or no shit like dat. But . . . that's always been your problem, my nigga. You be makin' dat weirdo, art rap stuff. Rappin' bout Lord of Da Rings and puppies and all dat shit. You should own twenty houses like this! Makin' millions! Movin' Bolivian cocaine like all the famous rappers do. This house don't even got a stripper pole! Rappers 'posed to have stripper poles in their house!"

"Okay, yeah, some rappers. But that's just not *me*. I have an audience for what I do, full of respectable, intelligent adults who don't promote violence, materialism, or negativity."

Bennett quietly raised his eyebrows, contemplating what I just said. "Pfffffft!!! Hahaha! Mane . . . fuck dat. Violence make da world go 'round! You need to get like 50 Cent and Gucci Mane and make those ghetto, street anthems. Dat raw, gutta shit, for hustlas and thugs, with ambitions like 2Pac, who swim in bathtubs full of money."

He was impossible to connect with, and I was already losing patience with him, but I had an idea. I figured my newer material was so polished that it might be *somewhat* appealing to him. At least appealing enough. Grabbing a fresh copy of my latest album near the stereo, I popped it in the little system I kept in the basement.

"Okay, check this out," I said.

"Is this yo new shit?" Bennett asked.

"Yeah, this is new. I think you may like it."

"Bump dat shit den, nigga. I ain't heard yo shit in a good minute. Maybe it got better. It used to be *booty* though! You was rappin' 'bout granola bars and savin' panda bears and shit. Hahaha! Lemme hear dat hood flava! I don't wanna hear raps about how it's important to wash my hands and eat my five food groups! I wanna hear about you blastin' a shotgun at a bitch nigga and throwin' one million bucks at a stripper 'cause she pissed you off, my nigga. Like how real rappin' thugs do it up in the strip club, G."

I couldn't understand why he kept suggesting my music was about things like puppies and granola bars. I mean, no, it wasn't the edgy, street-driven stuff that someone like Waka Flocka Flame makes, but I certainly didn't talk about freeing Malomar or Myanmar or whatever. I made music about life as I knew it. About heartbreak, financial woes, blue-collar struggles, drug addiction, and loss.

He was quietly staring at me, waiting for me to press play. In that very moment, I noticed that he had the words *Tony Montana* with a picture of Al Pacino, aka Scarface, holding a machine gun, tattooed on his right pectoral muscle. I'd also like to point out that Scarface, in Bennett's tattoo, had angel wings.

He had what appeared to be a monster tattoo on his left pectoral muscle.

"Uh . . . why do you have a monster tattooed on one chest muscle and Scarface tattooed on your other chest muscle?"

"'Cause, like . . . nigga, you know how dem Messican stripper bitches get a angel and a devil tattooed on dem?"

"Uh. Sure? I guess."

"Can't you see, nigga? I'm not only a thug, I'm a genius. An artist. A hood scientist. You should prolly let me write yo raps for you. I could come up with tons of clever ghetto shit. Let's be honest, Cuz. Even you didn't notice who was in my tattoo. That's how clever a nigga like Bennett is. Dis nigga right here on my right chest muscle is Freddy Cooger."

"Krueger?"

"Yup. And he like . . . represent all da ugly thoughts I be havin' and shit. He's like da devil on my shoulder and shit. And den, Scarface right here on my left chest muscle, which is da only good movie I ever saw, my nigga Al Pacino . . . he's like da angel on my other shoulder. Tellin' me to kill deez niggaz and get money."

"Bennett, I'm not trying to sound like an asshole. But you got your lefts and rights backwards, buddy. Always remember, your left hand makes an *L*."

I have no idea why I decided to correct him. Maybe to change the subject? Either way, he didn't acknowledge his inability to differentiate between left and right. He just changed the subject.

"Hurry up and play dat shit, ya ol' fruitcake ass nigga!" he said. "I wanna kick you a rap I wrote after."

It didn't even occur to me that Bennett had decided to start rapping himself.

"You write rap music now?"

"Yep. My name is Bennett Gotti, aka Ciroc Obama, aka Pat Bennett Tar, aka One Man Gangbang, aka Steal Your Bike Tyson."

I looked at him for a moment and, to my credit, instead of laughing, I just pressed play on the stereo.

The inner guts of the CD player buzzed, clicked, pinged, and squeaked while loading the disc. I quickly skipped to the second track, which was a song of mine titled "War Drum." The beat began with an echo chamber of xylophones, syncopating in an awkward, staircasing rhythm for a few measures, then Southern rap–inspired 808 snares rolled and rattled before the thunderously pulsing bassline kicked in, with the rest of the beat in full bloom over top of it.

I was menacingly nodding my head, double time. Partially because I loved the song, partially because I was encouraging Bennett to love the song as well.

My first few stanzas came in:

And I remember back when I was twenty-five,
when I was still young, still tender, still passionate with
    sunny vibes,
before the rain, before the tragedies and bloody skies,
before my memories were massacred and mummified . . .

Bennett was staring at the ceiling. He rolled his eyes, the song visibly bothering him. My verse continued.

sippin on a rocks glass, warm Scotch, cold ice,
I like relaxing, don't mistake that for a dull life,
my whole life, it's been really hard to breathe,
I've been waiting for a person that could finally put my heart
    at ease,
I weave through the carbon freeze,
wind blows through the scarlet trees,
it's been years since I felt jealousy, since I felt this pressure,
hell-bent for leather, shedding felt tip letters,
so down-swill your beer,
you turn thirty just so you can realize that everything is
    downhill from here,
say good-bye to having party-time amongst friends,
and say hello to single mothers that don't trust men.
This is the life! This is paradise!
Feeling so incredible, my head is full of vice-es,
this is the light, living with no spite,
there is not a reason to be evil or divi-sive,
all my friends know, that my heart is like a drum,
that my heart is like a war drum,
all my friends know, that my heart is like a drum,
that my heart is like a war drum.

Harper appeared at the bottom of the basement staircase. She surveyed the room, grinned, and approached us.

"What are you guys up to? Are you playing Bennett the new record?" she asked while sitting down next to Bennett on the couch—reluctantly, he was shirtless after all—and looking up at me.

I turned the volume down on the song.

"Oh, you don't have to turn it down, honey. I just wanted to tell you boys that Lillian and Tim are laying down in the guest bedroom upstairs. I didn't mean to interrupt," she said.

"Nah, I'm kinda happy you did. Cuz, damn . . . dat shit was . . . dat shit waaaaas . . . wick wick WACK! Mothafuckin' weak!" Bennett said.

"You didn't even hear the whole song!" I protested.

"Don't gotta, doo. You still on dat lame, depressin' shit," Bennett said, disappointed.

"You don't like that one?" Harper asked, turning to Bennett.

"Not . . . really," Bennett said with a bratty nasally texture to his voice. "I mean damn, playboy. What da fuck does 'money fried' mean?" Bennett said.

"'Mummified' means, like, you know? A mummy?" I said.

"Nigga, a mummy? You rappin' about fuckin' mummies? Niggas wrapped in toilet paper for Halloween?" Bennett said.

"No. It's poetic, dude. It means like v—"

But Bennett cut me off. "I don't care what it mean, fool. I ain't feelin' it."

"I think it's good," Harper said.

"Well yeah 'cause y'all go steady and shit. You his bitch, so you hafta love his raps," Bennett said.

Harper's face was impatiently scrunching into a frustrated grimace of disgust. "Look, I know in the Compton ghettos or wherever you're from, women are called bitches. But in this house, I'm *no one's* bitch. *Do not* refer to me that way," Harper said. I could tell she attempted to hold that one in and not say it, but Harper doesn't hold her tongue. Ever. "Furthermore, no, I definitely don't *have to* love *anything* he does."

"If you don't gots to, den why you act like you does?" Bennett said.

"Because . . . I do enjoy it. I think he's a phenomenal writer," she said defensively. "I don't even like rap or hip-hop music outside of Mac's stuff."

"Damn, bitch, you know you don't gotta kiss his ass, right? He gonna love you no matter what 'cause he sensitive and shit."

"Yeah. I know I don't, thank you very much," she said, nodding her head condescendingly.

"Cool it on the 'bitch' stuff, man. Harper tells me when she doesn't like something. She's not like that." I tried to calm the obviously blooming friction between them by provoking some constructive criticism from him. "Okay, wait. Wait a minute . . . you didn't like *any* of the song? How about the beat?"

"Yeah. I guess da beat is coo'. But you was kickin' dat white-people-nerd shit over it," Bennett said.

The room quieted. I stared at the floor, I guess disappointed in my gut at Bennett's reaction to my music, but most of all, I was just embarrassed that Harper's first encounter with Bennett was going like it was.

I could feel a migraine approaching from the tension and stress The room was again silent for a few more clicks before Bennett postured forward, and, just at that point when a normal person would change the subject, maybe inject some positivity into the conversation, or even apologize he . . . continued to berate me.

"Alls I'm sayin' is . . . if you gonna make *rap*, den make *rap*. But your shit? You should start a band or somethin'. *Sing* dat shit. Do dat white-boy shit where you put on lipstick and leather tights and spikes and shit."

Bennett made devil horns out of his hands with his index and pinkie fingers extending.

"What's dat called? Where you dye yo hair black and be cuttin' yo'self and shit? Heavy metal? Punk rock?" Bennett said, while pulling a piece of paper from his pocket.

"I don't know, man, a lot of people are into the kind of song I just tried to play you," I said.

"Maybe some white hippie bitches like it. But I can help you sell millions of CDs, doo. I can help you feed deez streets!" Bennett said while unfolding the piece of paper. "If I wrote dat shit for you, I could help you get a bigger crowd and hella money. Den we could tour together."

A NOTE ABOUT LEECHES

Aaaaand, there it is. Every time Bennett disparaged my music, he always coupled it with a suggestion for me to involve him in my career somehow.

Harper quietly gazed at me with a look of frustration, disgust, impatience, and rage. I shrugged, shook my head, and closed my eyes.

"Aiight, check *dis* shit out," Bennett said. "*Dis* is da shit you need to be spittin' over dat beat. Check it. Dis one called 'Ghetto Terminator.'"

I'm da mothafuckin' boss, wit' a big-ass dick.
I make money every day and go hard on chicks.
You little fuck boy, you better duck, boy,
your wife at my crib, I'm about to get sucked boy.

His delivery was crap. He had no rhythm, no ability to project his vocals. His lyrics were full of exhausted gangster rap music clichés. I sat there hearing nothing more than amateur garbage but didn't say anything. What would criticizing him or trying to show him up do?

Fuck bitches every day eatin' lobster tail.
I'm a billionaire homie, on my yacht I sail.
I fucked Donald Trump's wife 'cause she paid me to.
I didn't even wanna do it though, she made me, foo'!
My Ferrari is big, my Lamborghini much bigga.
I'm the Ghetto Terminator, Bennett Schwarzenigga—

"Hang on! Hang on! Stop! Time-out. Time! Out!" Harper interjected.

Bennett stuttered, and didn't even finish closing his mouth. He just sat there surprised that Harper cut him off like that.

"You're a 'billionaire' all of the sudden? How could you sit here and disrespect Mac's music like you did, before reciting *that* rubbish?"

This was catastrophic. Fuck. How awkward. I appreciate a girl going up to bat for me, but this was just nothing even close to awesome. Nothing about the two of them meshed together. There wasn't even tension. It was more like two boulders, with rough edges and rigid surfaces, trying to quietly rub against each other.

"Da fuck you mean?!" Bennett exclaimed, with a deeply wounded look on his face.

"You don't own a fucking Ferrari! What the fuck are you talking about?" Harper snapped, with an almost amazed look on her face. "That sounded like a bunch of idiotic nonsense!"

She was *mad*.

"You said all of twenty seconds' worth of lyrics and still offended me multiple times! You *do* realize that women don't just get naked and give blow jobs all day? Seriously—do you?"

Bennett was shocked. He tried to swallow but his throat was jittery and nervous. He had puppy-dog eyes. I was shocked too. I tried to swallow, but I just sat there still. Wanting to hide.

"Damn . . ." Bennett said, looking down at the piece of paper.

"Go ahead, finish. I just . . . fuck. Maybe I just have no idea what I'm talking about," Harper said, looking into the distance, visibly irritated.

I felt like my parents were arguing. Bennett disliking my music didn't bother me that much, but the fact that these two were at each other's throats within minutes was horrible.

A few minutes of silence went by. Bennett stared at the sheet of paper, defeated. Harper and I stared into space. All was unsettling, until Bennett broke the silence.

"Mane. I gotta piss. Can I use da bafroom?" he asked.

"Uhhh. Yeah, dude, it's upstairs and right next to the refrigerator. You can't miss it," I said.

He stood up and quietly walked upstairs. It was obvious that he was rattled by what had just happened and appeared to be leaving the room out of overwhelming sadness and/or hurt.

Once I could hear his footsteps creaking in the ceiling above us, I turned and peered at Harper.

"Was that necessary?" I asked.

Her eyes popped open and she hung her lower jaw in a dramatic droop. She looked amazed by the apparent audacity of my question. "Was it *necessary*!? Are you fucking joking?" she snarled.

"I'm just saying."

"You're just saying what, exactly?"

"Whoa. Relax. You're really mad right now."

"Relax? *Relax?* I'm going to fucking kill someone. These people fucking smell. I can't even count on my fingers and toes how many fucking things they've collectively said that were inappropriate. *Relax?* And it's only been an hour!"

"Whoa, slow down. Babe, babe, babe."

I went over and sat next to her on the couch, then grabbed her hands and tried to console her.

"I didn't want to do this in the first place. But you basically made me. I feel like the walls are fucking caving in on me right now!" she angrily whispered.

"Okay, calm down, they're my family, remember? Not friends. Family."

"They're not *my* family, though!"

"I know. But I'm your family. Or I'm gonna be, soon. The fact that I love them should mean you love them, no?"

"You love these people?"

"Of course I do."

We sat in silence for a few more minutes. She cooled off a bit. Her temperament changed slightly. The venom in her voice had dissipated.

"These people are trash. You know that, right? They're not even white trash. They're just trash," she said.

I rapidly blinked and looked around the room, trying to absorb how those comments made me feel.

"Soooo. My mom's sister is trash?" I asked, deciding I was borderline offended.

"Yeah, kinda. She is. I'm not saying that your *mom* is."

"They grew up in the same house. They had the same parents. They're basically the same person."

We sat in silence for a few more minutes, longer than the few minutes we sat in silence a few silent minutes before that. She cooled off much more. I cooled off too.

"I'm sorry. I didn't mean that. That was a rude, shitty thing to say," she said apologetically.

"It's okay. I'm sorry you have to deal with this," I said apologetically.

"Can we at least do *one* thing?" she asked.

"What's that?" I asked.

"Can we try to get rid of them as quickly as humanly possible?"

"Definitley, yes."

"Like soon though?"

"That was the plan from the beginning. But, yes, I'll start encouraging them to leave soon and to think of this as a quick little pit stop on the way to their new place."

"Okay."

"But one thing. Will you do *one* thing then? For me?"

"What?"

"Please, *please,* go find Bennett and apologize. Not necessarily apologize, but just . . . try to get him to come downstairs and finish his rap song for us. You don't even have to listen."

"*Baby!?* Did you not hear all the shit he said about your music?" she exclaimed, startling me.

"Shhh. Yeah. I did. It's fine. He's just being a punk. Go say sorry. Even if it's a fake apology. Just go. Okay?"

She stood up.

"Okay. If it means we can go to Vancouver, I guess I can do that," she said, stretching. "I'll go find him."

She walked up the stairs. I could hear her footsteps creaking the floor through the ceiling above. I started getting a vision of Harper and Bennett bonding, and being cordial with each other. The relief of her not being upset anymore gave me a minor wave of euphoria, which I translated into the hope that her and Bennett would end up becoming the best of friends.

Slugger

I sat there relaxing on the couch, amazed by the way human beings interact with each other. Sometimes we are these amazingly complex creatures who communicate in powerfully abstract methods to help each other solve the mysteries of our infinitely expanding universe. Other times though, we're nothing more than highly evolved monkeys who scream and throw poop at each other. If it wasn't for us inventing the wheel, agriculture, language, and the Toyota Tundra, we'd be mid-foodchain, tops.

Harper stealthily walked back downstairs to the basement. She looked flustered. Concerned.

"Uh. Bennett has locked himself in the bathroom. And . . . it . . . it sounds like he's crying," she said, concerned. "Fuck. I really hurt his feelings. Oh my God."

"*What?*" I said.

"I was looking around for him and heard some tapping in the bathroom. So I walked over to the door and kinda eavesdropped for a second. Yeah, he's sniffling and breathing all heavy."

"You're kidding," I said.

"No. I'm not. Maybe you should talk to him," she said.

We followed each other up the basement stairs, through the hallway, and beyond the kitchen, to the door outside of the kitchen bathroom. I leaned my head toward the door and lightly suction-cupped my ear against it to listen.

I could hear Bennett deeply sniffling. It sounded like he was sobbing. This wasn't good. The level of guilt that began to over-take me was difficult to reckon with. I looked at Harper and silently raised my eyebrows, mouthing the words, *What the fuck?*

She stood there silently, confused.

Every thirty to forty-five seconds, Bennett would sniffle loudly. This went on for a few minutes before the toilet flushed and the door squeaked open.

"Whoa! Fuck!" Bennett yelped, completely startled. There was no sign of him crying at all.

"Uhhhh. Dude? Are you okay?" I asked.

"Uhhhh. Yeah?" he said, looking at Harper and me. "Fuck y'all niggas doin'? Listenin' to me take a shit? I was taking a shit!"

"Oh," I said. "OHHH!" I said again. I felt like we were encroach-ing his space, but I also wanted to apologize. I decided to mutually apologize for both myself and Harper, so she didn't have to say any-thing herself.

"Hey, man, we just wanted to both say sorr—"

"Wait a second, how were you taking a shit?" Harper asked, cutting me off, peeking her head inside the bathroom.

"Whatchu mean how? How else?" he said.

"Well, considering there isn't any toilet paper in this bathroom, I'd like to know. Did you shit and not wipe?" she said.

Oh yeah! Duh!

"And were you crying in here, dude?" I asked.

"What? Cryin'? Fuck naw, I wasn't cryin'! I never cried in my life, Cuz. Thugs don't cry homie; I seen it on National Geographic. Gangstas have no emotions, homie," he protested a little too much.

I got close and studied his face. His eyes were completely dry.

"Bennett, I hate to be nosey, but what did you wipe with? This bathroom doesn't have toilet paper," I asked.

"Yeah it do!" he said.

"No, it doesn't. I make sure none is in there, so no one poops in it," Harper said.

"Bennett, were you crying, man?" I asked again, with more intensity in my voice, but empathy to let him know it's okay if he was, in fact, crying.

"Nahhh! Quit actin' like I was cryin'! What da fuck, mane!" he exclaimed. "Homie, do you cry? Is you a thirteen-year-old girl faintin' over Justin Bieber, homie? Damn, loc!" He sniffled.

Harper walked into the bathroom and began investigating. She was a highly persnickety person who was extraordinarily difficult to lie to. When she smelled blood in the water, or had an inkling that a lie was being told, she turned the entire world upside down waiting for clues to fall from your pockets. It drove me mad when she did it to me.

Bennett stood there looking at the bathroom floor. Instead of acting weirded out by the whole situation though, he just stood there quietly. Something was off about his reaction.

Harper was staring into the toilet. It was full of clear water. She then looked at the floor for a few seconds. Nothing. She blinked a few times, and focused her eyes on the counter next to the bathroom sink. She leaned forward and closely studied its surface. She noticed something and increased her pace and purpose. She then wiped her fingers across it before studying her fingertips. I stood next to her. She showed me her fingertips. They were covered with bright bluish residue.

"What's up?" I said.

She didn't respond. She walked out of the bathroom and into the kitchen, where she picked up the Balenciaga purse I bought her and rummaged through it before pulling out a pill bottle. She opened the pill bottle and emptied its contents into her hands.

"One . . . two . . . three . . . four . . . five . . . six. Hmph." She counted the pills before funneling them back into the pill bottle and closing it.

"What?" I barked. "What's going on?"

"Well, you obviously didn't get them out of my purse. So that's good," she said, approaching Bennett.

Bennett stood there silently. Completely unresponsive.

"Were they yours?" she asked. "If they were yours, just tell me.

We aren't your parents or the police. I just want to make sure you didn't steal anything."

He didn't respond. He was standing in a hardened pose, with an emotionless face.

She stared at him for a few seconds, squinted her eyes, then walked back into the bathroom and opened the medicine cabinet. From the medicine cabinet she took out a tiny woven basket that she kept stocked full of pill bottles and other various medications, like extra amoxicillin, Nupercainal, Xanax, Percocet, Vicodin, Tamiflu, et cetera, in case we ever got sick and needed medicine. Harper always had various prescription drugs for various things. Her psychiatrist was nothing more than a drug dealer with a degree.

She used her fingers to dig through the various pill bottles, and finally pulled out the one she was searching for. She then held it up to the light and tried to count how many pills were inside of it.

It all made sense now. He had gone into our medicine cabinet and stolen some of Harper's extra Adderall.

A NOTE I FEEL THE NEED TO INJECT

Harper's Adderall prescription exists to "help her focus." I never found her ability to focus on minor, insignificant details to be inadequate though, so I'm not exactly sure she needs it.

"How many did you take?" she said.

He hesitated for a second, darting his eyes around, then reached into the pocket of his shorts, pulled out two tiny blue pills, and placed them into her hand.

"Is that it?" she inquired.

"Yeah . . . I swear. Dats it," he said.

"You stole from us, dude?" I said.

"Well, nah . . . I ain't steal nothin'," Bennett said.

"No, really, you stole from us," Harper said.

I took the pills from Harper and put them back into the extra pill bottle before sealing it shut.

"Go downstairs, Bennett. And when you get down there . . . don't move. Harper and I need to talk," I said.

Bennett hightailed it to the basement door and tiptoed down the stairs.

"Come talk to me upstairs," Harper said, motioning her finger for me to follow her to our bedroom. We trekked up to the top of the stairs. From the guest bedroom, I could hear deep snoring reverberating through the oak door. Tim and Lillian were out cold.

Harper dragged me by the hand into our bedroom and sat me on the bed. She then stripped to her underwear, exposing her tightly carved, featherweight body, wrapped in olive skin that was sticky with a layer of perspiration she expunged earlier while working in the yard. She put on highly cut, lime-green soccer sweatshorts with the number *88* on the right front leg and one of the heather-gray tank tops with spaghetti straps that she often wore around the house when relaxing.

She removed the metal dragonfly hair clip that she had used to position and hold her elegant, sandy-blond hair in a twisted bun. She then began to comb her hair out in the mirror until it was untangled and puffily frizzed, needing to be washed. She sat next to me on the bed.

"He stole pills from the medicine cabinet."

"Yeah. I know."

"And obviously, you're not going to kick them out?"

"Well, I mean. I don't know."

"Yep. That's what I thought."

"What the fuck is that supposed to mean? They've lived here for an hour."

"He stole my pills from the medicine cabinet. Within an hour!"

"Maybe he just assumed anyone could use those pills?"

"I love you, but you're not that naive."

"I'm not being naive."

"Yeah. You are. And let's be clear, this is the first offense for me."

"Ha! Okay . . . ? The first offense?"

"Yep! They don't even get three strikes. The next thing that bothers me, and I'm going to ask you to make them leave."

"Harper, calm down. How about you try to enjoy them living here? I mean geez, do you think this is easy for them either?"

"Yes, I do. They get a free place to live."

"I promise you, they don't. Okay? Besides, you knew Bennett was troubled. He might do a couple things wrong, but I'll talk to him. It sucks to see you have such hunger pains to make them leave."

"Hilarious. Okay. Well, we have an agreement. It's only a matter of time. And, babe, don't ever say 'hunger pains' again. You aren't stupid. At least, I think you aren't."

"What's wrong with saying 'hunger pains'?"

"I'm not trying to be a bitch. But it's hunger *pangs*. Pang. P-A-N-G."

"Well, I like 'hunger pains' better. It makes more sense."

I wasn't thrilled about Harper's malicious attitude. It felt alienating. I stood up and left the room without another word.

Then, after a few minutes of silently boiling in the hallway, I popped my head back into the room and said, "The only reason your ass takes Adderall is to get high. Don't think I don't know this." And left.

"Adderall doesn't get you high! They help you read!" she yelled, as I stumbled down the stairs.

"Then why are you mad that Bennett took them? If he reads, he'll be smarter, won't he?"

I walked downstairs to the basement to talk to Bennett. He didn't notice me enter the room, which was funny, because he was interviewing himself on imaginary late-night TV. He was talking to himself in the full-length mirror against the opposite wall.

"Damn, Bennett, what you been rappin' fo'—jus' a few months, huh? Damn, negro, you got a hussla's spirit. What you finely do with all da cheese you make?"

After asking himself the interview question in the mirror, he adjusted his body and stepped a few feet to the side, to give the pretend interviewer an answer.

"Damn, Conan O'Brien, you gotta excuse me, I'm a little amped up on pills right now. Anyway, my redheaded negro—I been watchin' you since I was sellin' heroin by the boatload, my dude. Here, have twenty thousand, nigga. Go buy a Lamborghini, playa. You welcome, homie. No, for real, don't thank me. I got you, playa!"

He began counting imaginary dollar bills out on the table. I hadn't seen anyone do something like this—interview themselves in the mirror, giving grandiose delusions as answers—since I did it at age seven. It was endearing. I smiled quietly.

"I'mma get a new Hummer and shit. Get dat bitch bulletproofed like Tony Montana in *Scarface* and shit. I'm *definitely* gonna hit da strip club and get a thick, bad bitch who can't talk. A fine-ass broad who was born wifout a mouth. And uh . . . oh! I almost forgot, check dis shit out, right? Hahaaa. I'mma get LeBron James painted on my Hummer. Jus' so da hood knows I'm bout bein' s'cessful. After sellin' fifty trillion CDs, Conan, I'm tryin' ta give back to da black community."

"Who do you equate your success to? Who helped you get here?"

"Well, Conan, my nigga. Prolly my mom. My mom taught me everythang I know. Plus, jus' bein' from da hood. Rags to riches man!"

"Hey," I said, interrupting. I figured if I was going to catch him playing pretend, I'd at least bust him on it during a high moment in his celebrity interview with "Conan O'Brien."

Bennett jumped and spun around.

"Oh shit. 'Sup?"

"I just wanted to tell you that you're getting a get-out-of-jail-free card with the Adderall. Okay? Don't take things without asking. Pills, money, alcohol . . . hell, even food. *Nothing.* You got it?" I said.

"Okay. I got you."

"If you fuck up again, you're gone. I'm not even kidding. Harper already wants you gone. Please, give me a reason to let you stay here. Prove me right."

"Okay."

"Enjoy your interview with Conan O'Brien."

"Uh, nah I was just . . ."

"Save it. I used to interview myself in the mirror too."

in like a ninja a kk
got a black belt in bit-
2 da kk lol yup i speak
y txt game is on sum pu
2 me wat im tellin u...
ike em ya c? dats y bit
ez. cuz kno wat want.
ner so i let dem know h
r 2 so i say like Hey sw
O honney ur hair looks
t den i go in fo da kill
wut is luv baby dont hu
you just say "Kk?" That
+ me. i spe

e no mo? u
the girliest text messa
a female language i ble
inja star a :) is my sord
it wrks luv me they b
ersent fluant langauge
a i say kk and they bo
rushin spy wit. speak ju
z B gittin wit other bit
soft and sweet 2 eac
bennett. i know wat wa
d Dats fabulus And Kk a
they think im sinstive
dat song dat g

do u still sleep with a stuffed animal???

No. I'm 30. What a bizarre question. Why?

mY friend Tremaine was making fun of my Bunny today and i almost whoop that niggaz ass

i dont sleep with him but i have him on my self as a reminder to keep me humble

What's its name?

HUSTLA DA RABBIT

Gogoplata

The rest of the weekend went pretty much without incident. Bennett and Harper avoided each other, and the rest of us settled into a rhythm. Harper and I decided to lay down a few house rules, and I made it very clear what would happen if they didn't follow them.

To help out with rent, Aunt Lillian told me she would contribute fifty-five dollars a month from her disability check. Tim insisted that the government would track him down and arrest him if he got a job because he had access to "highly confidential information about certain rogue members of Congress," so he was obviously going to be useless. I wasn't really expecting much out of either of them.

But for Bennett, and I didn't hesitate to send him on his bike, looking for a job the first Monday morning that rolled around. I figured witnessing firsthand that hard work puts money in his pocket would give him some structure and a sense of responsibility. He could buy some of his own things and realize you don't take people's stuff without asking. Plus it would get him out of the house.

When he went out looking at ten that morning, I went to the studio. Harper had already gone to work. Tim was still on the Xbox 360 from the night before. And Aunt Lillian was doing word searches and probably fantasizing about the naps she was going to take all day.

After the studio session was over late that afternoon, I pulled into the driveway of my new house and parked my car. The sprinkler was running on its preset programming, which made me feel rich and snobby.

For now, I owned a sprinkler system with preset settings.

A NOTE ON BEING A NEW HOMEOWNER

I loved feeling rich and snobby. Pulling into my first driveway, after living in dilapidated duplexes and mildewy apartment complexes my whole life, made me feel like a young billionaire computer prodigy, social media mogul whose face was on the covers of *Time*, *People*, and *Forbes*, respectively. A wet dream for gossip rags after I cheated on Jessica Alba—in front of her—with Jessica Biel. A boldly controversial high school dropout with $16 trillion in assets, including a private helicopter that teaches me Portuguese while I sleep in it and elephant-skin wallpaper in my living room. The next additions to my nouveau riche lifestyle would obviously be:

Ecuadorian butlers who ride tricycles while shooting pieces of fried unicorn meat into my mouth with crossbows.

A Porsche tank that I could use to flatten rush-hour traffic with when I was in a hurry.

A private golf lesson with the man, the myth, the legend himself: Burt Reynolds.

I walked inside and sat on the sofa behind Tim, who was sitting on the floor. "What's up Tim?"

"Yo."

"Where's Aunt Lillian?"

"Getting dressed."

"What are you doing?"

"Shhhh. I'm busy. Playing *Rainbow 6*."

What a dick. I texted Bennett to see how the other man of the house was faring.

ME: How's your first day of job hunting?

BENNETT: its gud i shud have sum money 2nite..gatta plan

ME: Really? Already?

BENNETT: yah

ME: That's great dude. Good work.

BENNETT: if dis shit work i might start my own bizness no 1 does this as a job

I heard a weird tap on my door. It wasn't a knock, but someone had been on the porch. I opened the front door and found a flyer taped to it.

MISSING CAT: SLUGGER
4 YEARS OLD // $100 REWARD
STRIPED WITH BLACK CIRCLE MARK
AROUND EYE
HAS SEPARATION ANXIETY
CALL TALLULAH, 913-###-####

Looking down the block, I could see that the same drawing was taped to every front door on the street. I sat on the couch reading it for twenty minutes, while a plan began to formulate in my head. With Bennett already finding a job, he was exhibiting to me that he was taking the situation seriously. I didn't want to overload him with things to do, but if he could pull this off, maybe it would send a rush of money-making euphoria through him. It could really make him value financial compensation for his hard work. I sent him a text to explain.

ME: Hey. I got a tip for you. A quick way to make $100.

BENNETT: 4 real ?

ME: Yep.

BENNETT: spit it out g

ME: Someone just taped a flyer to the door. Some neighborhood cat is missing and there's a reward if you find it.

ME: I know you're out looking for a job but if you found the cat, you could make some quick cash. $100

ME: I understand if you don't want to do it. I personally hate cats. No amount of money can make me want to deal with a missing cat.

BENNETT: o... .so da cat is missen an shit ?

ME: Yep. It's a cat from the block my house is on.

BENNETT: Ok by N E chants is his hole body brown ?

ME: Nope, doesn't look like it.

ME: You want the description?

BENNETT: chill hang on i mite not need it

BENNETT: duz he got a big blacc circle around his eye ?

ME: Uh. Actually yeah I think so.

BENNETT: is he a lil white and blacc stripped muthafuka who cry like a lil bitch all day ?

ME: Wtf. Yeah he is. How'd you know? Did you see the flyer?

BENNETT: i snatcht it out da nieghbers yard 2day

ME: I don't understand what that last text meant.

ME: I'm saying the cat is missing. You got the flyer from a neighbor's yard? Like off a fence?

ME: There's a reward if you find this cat.

BENNETT: nigga is ur IQ only 1400 or sumthin ? u dum or wat ?

BENNETT: i alredy got da cat... .i took it from dat blond chix bacc yard

BENNETT: it has sum fukin mental problems 2

ME: What? I don't understand.

BENNETT: i kidnappd da lil kittin from dat chix yard

ME: WHAT?!?!?!?!?! Who's yard????

BENNETT: i dont no her name..she drive dat dope ass B M W and has hair like Emanem all bleatched and shit

ME: Dude, stop fucking with me.

BENNETT: chill i aint gonna bring it in da house or nuthin... i wuz tryen to do sum bizness wit da cats earliar . i spent da mornin gittin a few

BENNETT: i took em up to dat chinese restrant Bo Lings down da street and tride to sell em

ME: ????????????

ME: PLEASE tell me you're fucking with me.

BENNETT: nah im 4 rill i walked up into Bo lings and said

BENNETT: Excusse me how much can i get for deez lil muthafuccas?

BENNETT: but they kicced me out . bitch said she wz gunna call da cops on me i wz like YO CHILL BITCH.

ME: OMFG

BENNETT: all da custamers wuz mean muggen me.i wuz like QUIT Haten, im jus a yung nigga tryn 2 git paid

I slumped over, burying my face into my lap and squeezing my head with my legs. I'm not even flexible enough to do that normally, but this was surreal.

ME: ARE YOU OUT OF YOUR FUCKING MIND?!!!!!!!!!!!!!!!!!!!!!!!!!!!!????? ???

BENNETT: why u care nigga i thot u hated cats ?

ME: Oh no.

ME: Where is the cat now? Take it back to her yard, dude! Seriously?!?!

BENNETT: im rollen a blunt . i wanna get da cat high agan bcuz it just sat here fuckin whinninG all day. but da blunt made it stop goin waaaa waaaa

BENNETT: i got em in a big cage i found at da creek.. wit a boll of water

ME: Please don't get the cat high. Please.

BENNETT: 2 late but itz all gud. 4 rill da cat is a much more plesant kitty now . da weed help it allot..

ME: No! Man take the cat back!!!

I called him seven times back-to-back. No answer.

ME: Hello? Why aren't you answering my calls?

ME: Please, man. You're going to get me arrested or removed from my home!!!

ME: Please, dude, take the cat back. And PLEASE don't tell her you tried to sell it to a Chinese restaurant either. Just give it back to her.

BENNETT: K

ME: Wait a second. I just reread this text. You said cats. You stole more than ONE cat!??!

BENNETT: ya i got 3 . but Yo! my nigga quit bein a lil bitch . i will take all da cats bacc to there yards

BENNETT: i just gadda remember which yard da other 2 cats balong in .

ME: Oh my god, Bennett. No, man. No no no.

BENNETT: i gadda questin Do u think da lady at Bo lings wuz mad bcuz chinese people eat dog and not cat ?

BENNETT: did i affind her?

BENNETT: did i get it wrong? dogs r cute as fucc who wud eat a dog?

BENNETT: hello u their

I couldn't speak to Bennett when he got home. Sans cat(s), I should add. I couldn't even look him in the eyes. I just told him to go to the basement and sit there quietly. I obviously wasn't going to tell Harper about this, even though she's a dog person and doesn't particularly care for cats. I'm a dog person too, though I actually like the concept of cats. They are independent and sleep all day.

I've been the owner of only two cats in my life. The first, Grizza-bella, was a huge, twenty-five- to thirty-pound cat that I had for my entire childhood. She was unlike most cats. She was so fat that she could sit on her butt, lick one paw, and use the other paw to hold her tummy up while she bathed her underbelly. She died at age eighteen. So it goes. RIP, Grizzy.

The other cat I owned was named Droors. He was smashed by my garage door the first night I owned him. My mother found his corpse, leaking blood, oozing its soft viscera onto the cement garage floor. I was twelve and very sad. Grizzy, on the other hand, was stoked. I think she's the one who pushed him under the door. So it goes.

Cats can be filthy, temperamental, and let's be honest . . . weird. But in my opini—

Wait a second. Why the fuck am I even talking about cats? Regard-less of whether I hate cats or not, trying to sell a cat to a Chinese res-taurant is unacceptable and probably punishable by some law.

Mom, if you can hear me, please save us. Please.

Ironically, all that talk about Chinese food had made me hungry for some honey-walnut shrimp. So I decided to drive up to Bo Lings that night to get some carryout Chinese food. More important, I wanted to make sure the proprietors didn't know that Bennett was related to me.

At first I was nervous. I have full tattoo sleeves and imagine most restaurateurs find me to be a little suspicious. So the staff immediately all begin staring at me, which freaked me out. But after standing there for a silent couple of seconds, everyone went back to work. The old lady with the limp, who runs the place with her husband, even smiled big and said, "Hello! Welcome to Bo Lings!"

I took a seat by the porcelain elephants and statues of old Chi-nese sages, with long beards and contemplative faces, while I waited for my order. My phone buzzed.

HARPER: Something weird just happened.

ME: What's up?

HARPER: You know our neighbor Tallulah? With the really blond hair?

HARPER: The rich girl?

ME: Yeah, the girl who lives kitty-cornered to us?

HARPER: *catty-cornered

ME: It's kitty-cornered.

HARPER: It's caddy-cornered.

ME: We've discussed this. I googled it. It's kitty-cornered.

HARPER: That doesn't even make any sense. That's like people who say crick instead of creek.

ME: I agree that "crick" is the wrong way to pronounce it. However in this particular case the term is KITTY-CORNERED.

HARPER: Wrong.

ME: ???

HARPER: Wrong. It's catty-cornered!

HARPER: Don't argue with me right now. Listen. She just randomly showed up here like 10 minutes ago.

ME: Who did?

HARPER: Tallulah.

HARPER: She brought $200 and a tray of brownies over for Bennett. She said she's so thankful that he risked his life by jumping in front of the truck and rescuing her cat.

HARPER: ...

HARPER: Hello? You there?

ME: I know you just typed that, and I could easily reread it. But I need you to just... repeat yourself. Send that text again. I think I'm hallucinating.

HARPER: You aren't. She said Bennett jumped in front of a truck and saved her cat.

HARPER: Apparently he also nursed it back to health and—

HARPER: Get ready for this one..

HARPER: Read it a story?????

HARPER: So she brought over a tray of brownies. An envelope of $200. And a letter personally written to Bennett.

HARPER: She had tears in her eyes. She said Bennett was an angel sent from heaven. She also said her cat Slugger was much more calm and that Bennett's presence relaxed him.

ME: What did Bennett say about it?

HARPER: I haven't showed him yet. I think he left on his bike, but he might be in the basement.

ME: Don't give it to him yet. I'll be right there.

After receiving my bag of carryout food, I opened and read the fortune cookie that was sent with it:

> You drown faster when you try to fight it.

I drove home with the food. Upon walking into the kitchen, Harper showed me the envelope and the tray of brownies. The bottom side of the tray felt warm, like she had just taken it out of the oven. I opened the letter and read it.

Dear Bennett,

Words can't describe how thankful I am that you rescued my Slugger from the middle of the highway. He must have been so scared! He's been purring all night, telling me how much of a hero you are. You are MY hero too.

Here's your $100 reward + a $100 donation for the dolphin benefit race you are running. It's amazing that you care for endangered animals enough to run 50 miles in the blistering African sun. I hope the brownies help fuel your training!

You are a beautiful neighbor. Congrats on buying the new house. Come over and say hi anytime, darling.

Kisses,
Tallulah

p.s. You being single is a true crime.
913-302-****

Omoplata

ME: Where are you? I just looked in the basement and you're not here.

BENNETT: im in line at da grocrey store and gotta stand wit my legs spread and rock side to side.. dis bitch in front of me think im tryin to dance wit her all creapy

ME: Huh? Why are you standing like that?

BENNETT: cuz i aint wipe my butt good enuff cuz i was in a hurry now it all oiley in my butt

BENNETT: man dis sux.. dis bitch think i want her. she look like a vacum cleaner

God, I know he spells like a moron and constantly degrades women, but he still made me laugh almost every time we texted.

ME: Why are you at the grocery store?

BENNETT: im gittin sum condoms got a new girl im gunna try 2 git wit

ME: Who?

BENNETT: telula da bitch dat live by U

ME: CAT GIRL?

BENNETT: ya her

ME: The girl you lied to? Who thinks you A. Own my house B. Rescued her cat from the middle of the highway and C. Are running a 50 mile run for dolphins in Africa?

BENNETT: YA

ME: Well she brought you some brownies and $200.

BENNETT: 200$ wat!.datz more then wat she sapossed to give me for a reward LoL damn dis bitch luv me

ME: Dude!

ME: You lied to my neighbor about saving her cat. If she knew the truth she'd probably try to kill you.

BENNETT: why u haten on a balla ?

ME: She's my neighbor! I LIVE here.

ME: Did you not gain anything from the conversation we had after you stole the Adderall?

BENNETT: yes i realy did dats why im like why u trippen i didnt steal nuthin

ME: YOU STOLE A FUCKING CAT!

BENNETT: i didnt steal nuthin from U doe

ME: You're a thief, dude.

BENNETT: i aint no thief i dont gatta steel shit i git hella chee$e

ME: Oh do you? Then why don't you have a job yet?

BENNETT: if u wud stop piccin on me i cud tell u sumthin

ME: What?

BENNETT: i got a job

BENNETT: 4 real i found a gig to work at

ME: Oh really?

BENNETT: yup

ME: Liar.

BENNETT: i sweir..100 precent tru

BENNETT: i got hired 2day

ME: Doing what?

BENNETT: daliverin pizza

ME: Delivering pizza?!

ME: ON YOUR BIKE???

BENNETT: i no but dats why i need Ur help wit da bitch acros da street.if i can make her fall in luv wit me she will let me use her car to daliver pizza..she drive a DOpe ride!

BENNETT: her dad died and left her tons of money so she a rich ass ho

ME: Wait wait wait...

ME: Your plan...

BENNETT: wat

ME: Let me get this straight. Your plan. Is to manipulate Tallulah into letting you drive her car... A BMW SUV... To deliver pizzas?

BENNETT: can git U ur money dis way

ME: What are you going to tell Tallulah?

BENNETT: wat do u mean

ME: Won't she get suspicious that a "house owner" needs to drive her car all the time? What about the fact it will smell like pizza?

BENNETT: peep game

BENNETT: heres wat i wuz thinken i will B like baby i want to pratect da enviranmint so we shud share a car i will stop driven my car and u can let me use urs

BENNETT: she luvs me i bet she say yes

ME: You don't own a car.

BENNETT: she dont kno dat..i pointed at ur bitch car an said it wuz mine

ME: No you didn't.

BENNETT: why da fucc it matta ? im jus maccin on her

ME: So who did you say the people that live in "your" house are?

BENNETT: i said yall my meth head cuzins

ME: WHAT?!?!

Fuck! Agghhhh!

I was so shocked by his behavior that I accidentally tripped and stubbed my toe on my dishwasher. Shouldn't pace around the house while texting.

ME: Oh my god! Come to the house immediately. You and I need to have a serious chat. I'm not fucking with you. Do NOT steal or fuck anything up. Just come here.

BENNETT: R u gonna tell talula da truth

BENNETT: dont snitch on me nigga rats sleep wif da fishes

ME: You're unbelievable.

ME: It's so embarrassing that I'm not going to tell her so I can avoid having my neighbors think my family is crazy.

BENNETT: R u gunna tell harper

ME: Maybe. Maybe not. Come to the house ASAP.

BENNETT: do u mind if i stop by talula house on da way their i"m stress out about dis hole thing and wont feel beter till i C her

That was the problem with Bennett. He had an innocent heart. His upbringing and the environments he grew up in were the reason he was so lost. Constantly lying. Pilfering pills and cats. Being crass and rude. The fact that he took the initiative to stop by Tallulah's on the way back made one thing clear though: he felt guilty and needed to confess. For Bennett to need to be absolved and cleansed of his wrongdoings to Tallulah, even though she didn't know one way or the other, was pretty big of him. I could see the sprouts of maturity starting to blossom from the soul of my young cousin's rich soil.

ME: That's big of you. Do you want to come pick the money up so you can give it back to her when you apologize?

BENNETT: wat

BENNETT: apalagize? nah . i jus wanna stop by her crib and try 2 git laid real quicc i jus buy condems dont wanna waist $

Never mind.

ME: No. Come here now. I'm going to go for a jog. I'll talk to you after I get showered.

I was majorly put off by the shit he was stirring. My aunt was in such a pill coma that she had said all of ten words to me since they had been there, and the words she did say were bizarre and completely nonsensical. Tim played Xbox and read weird books about secret government societies and the Illuminati and the Reptilians. He also never showered. Bennett was lying to my neighbors and trying to swindle them for their luxury vehicles. It was not a good way to kick off things between all of us.

I walked into the living room to say hi to Lillian and Tim. They had been so quiet that I began worrying about whether they felt welcome. When I got to the living room, Tim was sleeping on the floor with the looping intro of the Xbox game *Red Dead Redemption* playing on repeat. The music was irritating, so I shut it off. Tim didn't notice.

"Hello, Lillian," I said to my slumbering aunt as she snored and whistled away.

"Shhhhhhh," she responded.

"Lillian it's your nephew. Mac."

"Hi, sweetie. Come back another time. I'm sleeping to heal my brain."

She was a mystery, that's for sure.

I went for a jog that night to clear the clutter out of my head. Bennett wasn't home yet when I got back. I laid my sweaty frame overtop my king-size duvet on my bed and fell asleep for a while. I woke up at 11:00 p.m. It was a couple of hours later. Bennett's navy-blue combat boots were under the coatrack by the front door, so I knew he was in the house. I decided to go downstairs to the basement to seriously lay things out on the table.

I wanted to explain to him how important keeping a harmonious Zen between my neighbors was to me. And to explain that I was going to have to throw his family out onto the street if he did anything else wrong. I wasn't going to even blame Harper for it. By now, I wanted them gone just as badly as she did. The only reason I didn't boot them out onto the street was because Lillian, the person I was interested in helping, had barely even gotten to stay with us. I didn't want to hurt her because her son was an idiot.

He was asleep, sitting up on the new basement sofa, with his chin on his chest and his phone in his lap. The red light on the upper left corner of his phone was blinking to alert new text messages. I shook him to wake him up. His phone fell off his leg, onto the floor. He grumbled and stretched out on the couch in a deep pot-induced sleep.

I picked up his phone to make sure it hadn't cracked. It was a cheaply built flip phone, and it was showing in nearly eight-bit graphics:

1 new txt.

Intriguing. This kind of phone could store only fifteen to twenty text messages at a time, but I decided to read through them anyway, like a true asshole cousin. All of them were to/from Tallulah. I wasn't really sure how he'd gotten her number, but it seems the damage was already done.

(TALULA:) Please refrain from text messaging me. Thank you for finding my cat.

I scrolled to the earliest one left on his phone.

(BENNETT:) na like i said i luv anamels alot 2.i used to rescue rockwilders im one of da highest paid members of PITA

(TALULA:) Oh, well that's nice. Ur a very sweet boy.

BENNETT: i cry at nite wen dey play dem cammercials wit da homliss kittins i wish i cud adopt all of dem and play gatarr for dem

BENNETT: u their

BENNETT: hello

TALULA: Those commercials are SO sad. I wish I could adopt them all too! I donate a lot of money to animal rescue places.

BENNETT: U want me 2 cum over

BENNETT: i got some natral light beer we cud tell storys abut cats

TALULA: I don't think so.

BENNETT: ur body is fanaminal

BENNETT: i fanticized abut U all day in my office at PITA today i cant lie i want u so bad it hurts let me rub u down wit locion

TALULA: Ugh.

TALULA: U are bordering on inappropriate with ur texts.

BENNETT: r u their baby

BENNETT: hello i want to make love to U while i snuggel a kitten

BENNETT: hi

BENNETT: ??? i want to feel Ur body aginst mine lets git macthing kittin tatoos

BENNETT: send me pix of ur booty

I closed the phone, put it back on his lap, and walked to the chair adjacent to the sofa he was sleeping on. I grabbed the brown blanket from it and covered him up. I turned off the lights and went upstairs so I could have a glass of wine and stare at my aunt as she nodded in and out of consciousness on the couch.

She was now watching the Home Shopping Network, obviously in a painkiller haze. I had never grasped how childish and bizarre she was, but at this point precisely, seeing her doing . . . something . . . with a bowl of ice cream and her bare hands, I was beginning to understand why the family had treated her so different.

"Hi, Aunt Lillian. Whatcha doing?" I asked.

Not noticing what she was doing until I snapped her out of her pill coma and verbally pointed it out, she looked at me excitedly. "I'm making an ice-cream sculpture. It's George Clooney!" she said, pointing down at a bowl of strawberry ice cream she was playing in. She was using her bare hands, and they were covered in a sticky pink film.

"Oh, okay," I said, completely weirded out.

"Can you get me more ice cream so I can make Brad Pitt? I wanna make the cast from *Ocean's Eleven!*" she yelped.

"Uh, actually, let's stop making ice-cream sculptures. Okay? That strawberry ice-cream isn't even mine. It's Harper's, and she loves it. She gets really mad when anyone touches her food in the fridge. I'm gonna have to buy her a fresh container of strawberry ice cream now."

"Ohhhh!!!!" Aunt Lillian groaned.

Her eyes were tightly locked shut and her face was soured. She appeared to be feeling some sort of physical pain.

"What? Are you okay? Aunt Lily?" I rushed to help her.

"I think so," she said, adjusting her pajamas and dusting them off. "I just felt like you was a reprimandin' me, and it made me sting."

"I'm so sorry for that. It's honestly not a huge deal. Have as much ice cream as you want. Sorry, I'm tired and cranky."

"It's okay, dear. I'm fine. It just caused me to have the damnedest memory," she said, luckily no longer in pain but still with an awful tart facial expression.

"Memory? Of what?"

"Your mama," she said, as she simultaneously tilted her head to look me in the eyes.

"My mom?" I said.

"Oh, Macky. She was just the sweetest, most precious thing," she said, adjusting her body so she was sitting up straight and no longer slouching on the couch. "That's very special you have a girl who likes strawberry ice cream, dear. Very special."

I took a seat on the ottoman. I hadn't, at all, talked to Lillian about my mom since she'd been here. I hadn't really even talked to her that much.

"Mac, your mother and me . . . we used to have the funnest summers."

By the way she was smiling, I could tell that a film of blissful reminiscence was playing on the movie screen of her imagination. Her eyes were the size of silver dollars and absorbing the scenery from whatever decade she was wandering through. I'd never seen her so composed and articulate.

"Yeah? Why? What did you guys do that was so fun?" I asked, eager to hear what my aunt had to say.

A NOTE FROM THE BEREAVED

When a person is so important to you that his or her death, in turn, causes the residual death of a piece of you—you never quite find a way to heal from it. You try to blend different analgesics and numbing agents to block the pain signals from traveling to your endorphin receptors; you try to mix various medicines and elixirs to war with the immortal virii it leaves orphaned inside of you, coursing through your body's elaborate network of fragile arteries and throbbing vessels; but overall, it's a lifelong experience that has only one remedy: acceptance.

For me, this person was my mom. For you, it could have been your dad or a best friend or a child (God forbid) or someone who is breathing today, that, due to the tragic nature of the beast we call "life," will not be breathing tomorrow. You love these people so much that once in a great while, your dreams provide you the highly treasured, albeit brief moments where you can hug them. Not in the way dreams provide you opportunities to have sex free of stimuli or feeling, or get into fistfights where your punches inflict 0 percent damage, and something in the mechanics of it all goes tragically wrong, causing you to wake up unfulfilled, or defeated.

No. I mean, you actually get to hug them. Well, kinda. This person sneaks into your dreams without proper credentials, affectionately burrows into every crevice of your tightly constricted muscle tissue, and with a body squeeze, reduces your existence to a warm ocean, where the grains of your molecule sand cover the floor's surface, and the monsoons of your own saltwater-taffy tears slap and collide into the docks of your orbital bones, submerging the beachside forests of your eyelashes and drenching every ridge and ravine of your facial structure . . . until the alarm clock goes off. Then, as the qualia dwindles into a more standard breadth of earthly consciousness, your cortisol levels begin to regulate back to normal, and you climb from the frosty, dark-blue grave plot of the scientific phenomena known as "morning sadness," you dry your cheeks, and realize you were hugging a feather-stuffed pillow the entire time. Which for me, is close enough to real to be considered real.

ANOTHER NOTE FROM THE BEREAVED

Basically what I'm saying in the previous paragraphs is if someone you love a whole bunch dies, sometimes you have very realistic dreams about hugging them.

A FINAL NOTE FROM THE BEREAVED

When you get a chance to hear new stories about your cherished loved ones that are no longer here, you unselfishly listen, hoping every charming, funny petal of ambrosial detail falls into your butterfly net, for you to savor forever.

"Your mom didn't have to attend school in the summer, but I did. I had to attend a summer school to help me read and do school-work good," Lillian said. Her words were no longer slurring, she had life in her face, and her posture was near perfect.

"Well, it was a big pie on my face, for me. See, back then we didn't have air conditioners, so it was really stuffy and hot, and the summer-school teacher was rotten to us kids. Wouldn't even let us get a bottle of Coke to cool off with! I was in class with mostly simple kids. Kids who couldn't tie their shoes or do arithmetic. How should I say it?"

My aunt, suddenly impish, looked both ways to make sure no

one could see her, cupped her hands over her mouth, and whispered, "slow kids."

She straightened back up slowly. "Ya see, I hated it like anyone would. I wanted to be out at the swimmin' pool, doin' cannonballs with my friends. I didn't wanna wear saddle shoes and a skirt all day till my mama come get me after work. 'Cause she always finish her flask of Scotch on the way to pick me up, so she'd be hollerin' at me about how I was just the worst damned thing ever happen to her. Time I get home from summer school, I'd have to go to my room grounded."

"Were you grounded every day of summer?" I asked.

She stared into space as if she were attempting to mentally play back every summer day she could ever remember, to take inventory and check to see if she was grounded or not, so she could provide the most honest answer possible to my question.

"Yeah," she said.

I can't describe to you how childlike and innocent her face and voice were when she said that. There was no fight in her voice. Her face slightly bubbled up into a morose melting pot of immature expressions.

"Why?" I asked, defensively.

"Well, my dad ain't like me too much. I just come out that way when I was born I guess. People don't like me around much, so I spend most of the time in a bedroom."

"Did you just lie in your bed all day?"

"No. I didn't have a bed."

"You didn't have a bed?"

"No. I used the couch or the hammock in the backyard when it was nice out."

"You slept on a hammock?"

"Yeah," she said with the same innocence as before. "But it was comfy. Who needs a bed when it's nice outside? You can talk to the frogs and the stars."

I reached forward and held both of her brittle hands in my palms. They felt stiff and stubborn. It was either from the sticky remnants of the George Clooney ice-cream sculpture that she'd created and flattened in the bowl. Or it was a genuine surge of fear over what-ever narrative was going on in her imagination. I could tell my grab-bing her hands comforted her a bit. Which is good, because I had some difficult questions for her.

"So wait, whose bedroom did you go into if you didn't have one and were sleeping outside?"

"Whoever ain't usin' their bedroom, I go in there and sit on the floor and draw pictures. Then if they want their room, I go to some-one else room, or the laundry room mostly."

"I see. What did you do in the laundry room?"

"Play with my pet bird, Hattie Pearl. Had her five years. She would chirp and sing songs about Vietnam with me. We stayed in the laundry room most days together. She was nice to me. Prolly the nicest friend of mine beside your mom. Until Daddy decided he hated my bird."

"Wait, huh? What do you mean?"

"My daddy gave most of our pets the death penalty."

"Huh?"

"Besides his mini-Chihuahua, Chili, he hated animals."

"And what did that have to do with your bird?"

"Well, Daddy . . ." She popped up her eyebrows as if to say, *Hello? What do you think happened, genius?*

"Oh boy."

"Daddy think she was bothersome to me and what not. I annoy him a bunch 'cause it took me a little longer to get my times tables remembered than most students. One day he—"

I realized that I already knew the story. My mom had told me it over the years, and I didn't know if knowing what was coming would make it easier to hear Lily's version of events, or harder. I always knew the story took place in the laundry room, but what I didn't know was that Lillian was essentially *exiled* to the laundry room.

The Rise and Fall of Hattie Pearl

Grandpa Mike was the fountainhead of our family's cruel and unusual alcoholic dysfunction, and just about every seedling and grand-seedling that sprouted from his loins grew up with several of his urban legends already firmly implanted into their archive of memories and family tales. Unfortunately, all of this made you want to leave the theater before you even saw the ending.

The way I had always recalled this particular story was relatively soft-core in comparison to the other Grandpa Mike anecdotes.

The story goes: Grandpa Mike was grilling a couple of slabs of ribs out in the backyard for the family (himself) on a Sunday afternoon. It was a swelteringly hot July day, and a bout of cloudbursts and torrential rains had soaked the city a few days prior to that, so the humidity was miserable at levels that only Midwesterners can understand. The weathercock planted on the house's pointed roof was hardly moving, if at all. It was horrid outside. The breeze was hot.

Grandpa Mike started getting drunk before the sun even rose that day. By afternoon, he was a violent sack of bones and booze. Lillian was secluded in the laundry room and ordered to study her multiplication tables. Upon hearing Grandpa Mike fumbling around and cursing in the kitchen, she stuck her head out and asked him if she could come play in the backyard with everyone else and have some tasty ribs.

Grandpa Mike stumbled into the laundry room and said, "Sure, kid. You can come have some ribs. But you gotta recite your times tables. Every single one from one times one up to twelve times twelve. If you get 'em all right, you can come have some ribs and play. Hell, I'll even let you play in the hose. But if you miss one . . . if you miss just one . . . you get flicked in the forehead."

"Okay, Daddy, here I go. Ready, Daddy? One, two, three, go!"

She looked down at her math book and started reading from the multiplication grid.

"One times one equals one, one times two equals two, one times three—"

"*Why are you reading from your book, Lillian?*" he screamed, smacking the book out of her hands onto the floor.

Kitty (my grandmother) and Lillian's three sisters, including my mom, heard the commotion from the lawn and ran into the house. When they got to the laundry room, Lillian was trembling with fear.

"Start again. No books. Same rules. Now! Go!" Grandpa Mike commanded.

"Uhhhhhhhm." Lillian swallowed nervously. "One times one is two—"

"*One times one is two?!*" Grandpa Mike screamed. "*One times one is two?!*"

He flicked her in the forehead. She held her hands over her face and buried it into the corner behind her.

"Michael, you leave her alone. God damn it. *You hear me?*" Kitty, also drunk, was yelling at Grandpa Mike.

"Quiet! Fuckin' pig tell me what to do in my house! She needs to learn! She's stupid! She's *no good,*" Grandpa Mike yelled, then grabbed Lillian's arm and spun her around to face him again.

"*Again.* Do it right this time!"

"It's okay, Daddy. I missed one. I better do my homework in the laundry room instead of play."

"Again. *Now.*"

The sisters left the laundry room and quietly sat outside trying not to listen. They knew that trying to intervene would only make it worse for Lillian. Kitty knew it too. All they could do was hope he'd lose interest and leave her be.

"Okay, Daddy. I'mma try now," Lillian said. She began mouthing the equations in her head and using her fingers to keep track of the numbers. "Okay . . . here comes. One times one is one. . . . I know that, silly me from before! One times two is—"

"Stop using your fingers to count!" he screamed, and slapped her on the top side of both hands.

Lillian's bottom lip was shaking terribly. She was mortified of even speaking again and was on the verge of bawling.

"I don't want yummy ribs, Daddy, I'll just go ni-night now. I'm tired," Lillian pleaded while trying to force a yawn.

"Again. Do it right. You're not going to be an idiot under my roof. *You hear me?* How can you make it in the world as an idiot? Now, twelve times twelve. Do twelve times twelve and you can have barbecue with us," Grandpa Mike said.

"*Stop picking on your daughter, you heartless bastard!*" Kitty screamed, before taking the flask of vodka she was holding and chucking it at Grandpa Mike's head. The bottle somersaulted through the air, missed Grandpa Mike by three feet, and crashed into Hattie Pearl's birdcage, busting its thin wooden frame into pieces.

The bird floated out of the twisted, broken frame of cage remnants and began nervously circling around the laundry room. Lillian was still a little kid and too short to reach Hattie Pearl's flight radius. Even when she tried jumping up and down with her arms stretched into the sky, saying, "Come here, bird! Come to me, birdie!" she couldn't reach Hattie Pearl.

Grandpa Mike, however, took matters into his own hands. No pun intended. He saw his daughter desperately jumping and reaching for the bird.

"Well, shit. I see why you're so damn dumb. You spend all day playing with a stupid fuckin' bird instead of studying."

He backhanded the tiny bird into the wall, instantly killing it.

Now, Lillian's version of the story stops right there: Hattie Pearl dies. Beyond that, all Lillian can conjure up are vague, scattered memories due to justifiably blocking out 90 percent of her life. My mom's version of the story, however, while factually identical, and much easier to swallow due to the natural, inadvertent, emotional verve of Lillian's version of the story, extends one beat longer. And when Lillian abruptly quit telling me her version of the story, my mom's version of the story continued on in my head, and the image that was permanently lasered into my mind as a child, every time my mom told her version of the story, displayed itself in full color and high resolution.

After Grandpa Mike backhanded Hattie Pearl into the wall, Lillian looked up at him, and with her bottom lip positioned into a lumpy frown, cried, "If you love me, then how come you kilt my bird? I love you and wouldn't kill your bird!"

I stood up to leave the room for some fresh air, or something to shake the sullen blob of goop I had morphed into. The only thing I felt but pure sadness was a weird sense of joy. I just wanted to hug Lillian and tell her I was happy she was on my couch, safe with me.

My physical composure had become fragile. I felt so much hurt for her. Of course Bennett turned out how he did. Of course she ended up dating a guy like Tim. Instead of acknowledging that she was a baby birthed from a damaged pneuma, who needed parental patience, special understanding, and deeply therapeutic massaging of her frontal and parietal lobes, they neglected, and eventually, abandoned her.

"I'm shaken up right now," I said to my aunt, who seemed to be back to staring through a pharmaceutical narcosis. "No one should have to go through that. No one. You're such a nice person. You shouldn't have had to experience such bad summers."

Suddenly, her muscle fibers tightened as she snapped out of the pill haze completely. Her irises reengaged her surroundings. Her face went from a vampiric pale to a golden clay tone. She was operating at full physical, mental, and cognitive potential again.

"Wait, Macky! You didn't let me tell mah story. I loved the summertime. Did I say summer was bad? I loved summer."

"Oh. Well, no, I guess not. You started to talk about my mom and the schoolhouse a bit, but I thought you were done."

"No, I'm not done!" she said and pulled me back onto the couch. "See, your mom. She was the littlest sister, but all of us loved her so much. She was my best friend. She knew how hot it get up in that damn schoolhouse. So she take twenty-five cents from Daddy's change cup. Then she sneak her lil' behind out the house while Daddy sleepin'. And she go to Mr.Lou's ice-cream stand and get a strawberry cone and bring it to the schoolhouse! Every single day unless she was runnin' errands about town with Mama."

"You're kidding?" I said, wide-eyed. "Really?"

"Well, I had to get permission to use the latrine. And she would wait outside the window till I open it and say, 'One strawberry cone for Ms. Lily!' Sometimes it would melt by the time she gave it to me, 'cause the teacher ain't give me the hall pass till I threaten to pee my britches. But not always. Sometimes it be nice and cold and ready to munch! I ate it right there in the bathroom. Never got caught!"

I missed my mom. Not entirely because of Aunt Lillian's stories. I just felt like my mom passed away when I was too young to truly cherish how good our relationship was. Aunt Lillian didn't have a mean bone in her body, and after really conversing with her, and absorbing so many of the similarities she had and still has with my mother, I was very relieved that we were under the same ceiling.

Aunt Lillian slipped back into an opioid stupor and began slurring her words again. It was equal parts breathtaking and bizarre to see how telling narratives about emotionally volcanic memories could bring a sharp, serene, completely sensical person out of Aunt Lillian.

She wasn't quite making sense to me, but she definitely wasn't confusing me anymore.

Thug Passion: One Part Alize, One Part Cristal

12

I drank too much that night and woke up submerged in a post-wine katzenjammer the next morning. My head was buzzing, and every fiber of my body slowly shriveled and wilted as the alcohol exited it. My body was uncomfortable. So quite appropriately, as any dehydrated, hungover lush would spontaneously do at 7 o'clock in the morning: I decided to mow my lawn. I had just gotten a lawn mower for my birthday from my dad.

Harper was still asleep, so I flipped her arm off of me, snuck out of bed, threw on some old clothes, and ninja-prowled downstairs to the garage. I wasn't sure if it was too early to start mowing my lawn or not, but I at least wanted to make sure my new lawn mower was going to function properly. I didn't have a backyard as a kid, so I'd never actually mowed a lawn before, and I knew absolutely nothing about my lawn mower. I wheeled it out onto the driveway and gave it a top-to-bottom examination.

"Do I like . . . push a button to start it?" I whispered to myself. There were no buttons on it.

Seconds later my motivation was out the window. I always commit to shit, then hate myself for it twenty minutes later. What the fuck was I up so early for? Mowing the lawn sounded dreadful. The morning sun wasn't even fully showing and was still dark orange and rustic. The grass was damp with a moist layer of fog and drops of sticky dew. It was still chilly outside. And if it's still chilly outside in August: it's too early. Ostensibly, no one was awake in the entire subdivision.

A NOTE FOR THOSE WEIRDOS WHO ARE IMPERVIOUS TO PRESSING SNOOZE

Some people universally hate waking up at 7:00 a.m. No one in history has ever been excited that it was 7:00 a.m. If there was a swanky restaurant called Bill Johnson's Fuck 7:00 a.m. Lounge and Grill, it would be impossible to get a table there because of how busy it would be. I'd become Jewish if they changed the name of Hanukkah to "Fuck 7amukkah."

Suddenly, my neighbor Tallulah, Bennett's new flame, materialized from her garage. She had whitish-blond hair, a warped frame, and was wearing a tank top and sweatpants cut at capris length. She didn't wear makeup, and had a purple hue to her face that resembled a raw London broil slab. Her cheeks seemed puffy from a vigorous night of sleeping, and she had pillow creases indented into her face. There was purpose in her step. She locked eyes with mine and smiled with closed lips. I wasn't sure of how to handle this conversation, but I was eager to have it.

"Hi. Matt, right?" she asked, extending her hand to shake mine. I returned the shake. Her grip was hard. I hate when chicks shake hands harder than me. There's a very masculine quality to shaking hands too hard. For some odd reason it makes me wonder if the girl is secretly a transvestite.

I looked at her (or him), while shaking, and said, "It's actually Mac."

"Oh, sorry. My mistake."

"No no. Happens all the time. How's your morning?"

"Not bad. And yours? I see you got out the lawn mower."

"Yep, yep. Gonna give my yard a haircut. Sorry it's gotten a little long. I just had relatives move in, and it's been pretty chaotic over here. I know it's not fun to look at."

"Ohhh. It's been a nice break. The two guys who lived in this house before you cut it like every other day. It was really loud and annoying."

"Well that will definitely not be us. So what's going on?"

She opened her mouth to say something, but the words weren't there. Silence. She quietly smiled and nodded her head. Some internal shift in how she wanted to approach this talk completed, her face and posture went from polite to blunt in a snap.

"So, you own this house, right?" she asked, in a tone that assumed the answer to be yes.

"Mmhmm," I said, delivering a smile to imply the door was open to sound off about her concerns and/or experiences with Bennett.

"Yeah, I thought so. Well, I'm sure you know that your cousin Bennett found my cat the other day and returned him to me."

"I'm aware."

"Yeah, well . . . are you *aware* of everything *else* that happened?"

I couldn't tell if she was mocking me, or if she was really that disturbed by it. "Nah. What's going on?"

She furiously gazed into my eyes as she rummaged through her right sweatpants pocket and pulled out her iPhone. She was mumbling under her breath something to the effect of, "Bennett, he's an asshole. The kid's a pervert." Which would have been an applicable phrase to say, but I couldn't confirm that she indeed said it. I suppose she could have said, "Bennett needs a tassel and delicious sherbet." But that phrase would have only made sense if she was planning on throwing a graduation party for Bennett at a yogurt shop.

"Here, start at the beginning." She handed me the phone to read her open text conversation with Bennett.

MR. B: geuss who .

TALULA: Hello?

MR. B: its Ur new husbind

TALULA: Huh? Who is this?

MR. B: its bennett da cat saviar

TALULA: Ohh! Hey! I was just thinking about u! :D :D

MR. B: sup baby

TALULA: Not much! You?

MR. B: smoken a blizzy U

TALULA: Ahh. I don't smoke pot.. But i suppose i can forgive u for smoking cuz ur the greatest man I've ever met.

TALULA: I was sooo worried about my Slugger. He has seperation anxiety and yes this sounds rediculous but he also has suicidal tendencys. He's tried to kill himself a few times, which is why he jumped in front of the truck.

"Agh! Pet peeve! Never spell *ridiculous* with an *e*!" I said, looking up and smiling.

Tallulah was not amused.

> ## A NOTE FROM THE GRAMMAR-NAZI ASSOCIATION OF AMERICA
> It was truly uncalled for, but I didn't care. I'd interrupt my own wedding to correct someone's juvenile misspelling and/or misusage of the following words: *definitely, ridiculous, beautiful, you're, your, their, they're, there, we're, where, wear, weird,* and (for some strange reason): *parsimonious.*

TALULA: I didn't think u'd text, I figured u'd be out saving the world.. lol =op Your truly amazing.

MR. B: your amazon to..im always saven da wrld its my job

TALULA: It is? What did u say your vocation was again? Earlier on the porch? :) Sorry I vaguely remember.

MR. B: nah i dont take vocations baby im always husslin no time to relax gadda save deez yung anamiels

TALULA: Lololol. Ur funny. Doesn't hurt that ur cute too! :-*

TALULA: Are u typing like that on purpose?

MR. B: typin like wat

TALULA: Um... an illiterate? Haha.

(MR. B:) haha

(TALULA:) Lmao good... I love a man with a sense of humor.

(TALULA:) U were telling me that ur cousin and his gf are living with you. Right?

(MR. B:) yes

(MR. B:) dey r basicly bums adictid 2 meth..i let dem move N2 my house wile dey figa out a new place to live and get sobber..

(TALULA:) Seems like ur doing the right thing...

(TALULA:) Or should I say...

(TALULA:) Seamz like ur doin da rite thang hahaha.

(MR. B:) na fuk dat dey drive me krazzy

(TALULA:) Be nice... be nice...

(TALULA:) Seriously... text me the real way. I want to know more about u. :o*

(MR. B:) k

(TALULA:) So u really don't have a gf? >=oD

(MR. B:) na. im singel im waiten for da rite girl to luv me but i can only love a girl if she lets my 34 cats sleep in bed with us

(TALULA:) Ahahaha whoaa u have 34 cats???!!!

(MR. B:) yes i take a bathe with dem and watch moviez wit dem i luv cats so much i mite buy my cats a cell phone so i can call dem

(TALULA:) Haha i'm so gullible. Damn u!

(MR. B:) wat

(TALULA:) Hehe type the real way... I'm getting a migraine. :o/

(TALULA:) What's ur job though, Mr. B? Srsly?

(TALULA:) Oh i just saved ur name in my phone as Mr. B haha

(MR. B:) i preform charaty work i"m a human rites actavator

(TALULA:) Really? Me too! I'm a huge philanthropist!

(TALULA:) Are we like a match made in Heaven or something? Could it be? I'm already kinda crushin on u. :-X

MR. B: yes jesus made u from a Angle fether..u got wingz and a gold hoola hoop over yer head.OMG! u r my Angle talula Omg

TALULA: As annoying as ur being with this text style, that was actually very sweet.

MR. B: im good at writting potery

TALULA: I'll be the judge of that when u decide to text like an adult. But I can't lie... even with ur intentionally bad grammar my pupils are dilating

TALULA: U definately got me swooning, Mr. B.

TALULA: Heh. It's like I meet so many guys but none of them share my passion for animals and charity... except u... <333

MR. B: i mite get tha wordz animiels r so cute tattood on me

TALULA: I have a better idea. Tell me more sweet things! :) Pwease?

MR. B: k like wat

TALULA: I dunno. I thought it was sweet how u said Jesus made me from an angel feather. Tell me more stuff like that? Pwetty pwease? With a cherry on top?

Okay, this chick is pathetic.

This was really starting to gross me out. I stared at her silently, implying that she was quite pathetic. But then I realized that she had no idea what part of the text I was reading, so I continued reading.

MR. B: k

MR. B: jesus turnt a bottle of water into u

MR. B: like dat or diffrant

TALULA: Haha uh... I think that was sweet? How bout no more Jesus ones. Make up a new one. Pwease.

MR. B: send me sum pix of ur booty in A hot thong OMG mm send

TALULA: Excuse me? Whoa.

TALULA: Slow down, buddy. I'm not like that.

MR. B: k

TALULA: Ur gonna have to earn that :) Try again. Come on be sweet again!

MR. B: i wud loose my virginitty 2 u

MR. B: wanna no why?cuz u have sexy eye balls

TALULA: Errr...

MR. B: did dat 1 make u want me

TALULA: =/ The joke is getting old, Mr. B!

MR. B: k want a diff 1 ?

MR. B: hey u their ???

TALULA: Sorry phone died.

TALULA: So... how old are u again?

MR. B: 38

TALULA: Hmm. When's ur bday?

MR. B: i will tell U if U send me pix in ur Bra and pantiez

TALULA: Sigh. One day my prince charming will scoop me off my feet. I was hoping it would be u but u seem to be like all the rest of them. Only interested in 1 thing... :(

MR. B: sorry babby im jus so hot 4 U

TALULA: :-O Well... I think i kinda like u too? But come on, Mr. B, will u pwease type like a grown up. For me?

MR. B: K srry

MR. B: i do hella volantier work i was on da commity to save Tookie Williams da leader of da Cripz i also snuggel kittys for money at PEDA

TALULA: I see.

TALULA: Are u screwing w me or something?

MR. B: wat

TALULA: You keep typing like that and saying wierd stuff.

TALULA: When is ur bday?

MR. B: like march 1973 we think but my birth certifakit was burnt in a fire

TALULA: 1973 huh?

MR. B: yep

TALULA: You're definately lying...

MR. B: nope i aint lyen baby let me karess u wile i look n2 ur eyes. u will kno im not lyen when i kiss Ur brestz pashinitly

TALULA: So are you really like 19 or something? Did u just like find my cat and see there was a reward for him?

MR. B: na like i said i luv anamels alot 2.i used to rescue rockwilders im one of da highest paid members of peda

I had seen all the texts beyond that point. I gave her the phone back. Bennett was outclassed and outsmarted. His game, if that's what you'd call it, wouldn't work on a girl like this.

"As you can see, my cousin's a bit of a fibber," I said. "He's only seventeen and can be a heathen at times."

"He's only *seventeen*?" she snapped.

"Yeah? I mean no disrespect, but I don't understand how you didn't notice how young he was when he brought the cat back over to you."

"I guess I didn't pay attention. I was so excited to see my kitty. I really love cats. They are my life. Are you a big cat person? Cats are such majestic creatures. I have no shame in saying that I like them more than most human beings."

"Cats?"

"Yes. So anyway . . ."

[Fast-forward seven hundred to seven hundred and fifty para-graphs of bullshit about how fantastic cats are, trust me, you don't want to read it . . .]

". . . and that's why starting a tabby rescue is my calling. I think it should be pretty amazing."

At first I was sympathetic and apologetic to her for how Bennett acted, but after fifteen minutes of listening to her pine away at all sorts of nutty, hippie, catsexual propaganda: I no longer cared.

Especially after she revealed to me that she inherited her house and a hefty life-insurance sum when her father died. She really didn't count as a neighbor whose respect I wanted to earn. Her whole plan was to donate every dime she inherited to animal charity, then use her late father's very nice five-bedroom house for her cat rescue.

I apologized multiple times for my cousin and for suddenly having to "attend to something" in the kitchen and exited the conversation. I don't care if you started doing meth the moment you woke up, there is *never* a justifiable reason for being as energetic as Tallulah was that early in the morning.

I went up to my bedroom, stripped to my boxer briefs, and texted Bennett from my bed.

ME: I don't want to wake you up but here's the deal:

BENNETT: im up

ME: You're up?

BENNETT: yes i got a job inerview at popeyes chikln

ME: Really?

BENNETT: yes they R hireing im gnna ride my bike and talk 2 da manger he call me last night

ME: Good. GOOD.

ME: Well shit. I won't keep you then. But...

ME: Your girlfriend Tallulah came over to complain about you. She showed me all the texts you sent her.

BENNETT: did u tell her N E thing ?

ME: Nothing she didn't already know.

ME: You really struck out with that one.

BENNETT: i like getto bitchez not yuppyz wat can i say

BENNETT: dat bitch drinkz green Tee and feeds her cat wit da same fork she eats with why da fucc wud i try hard

ME: Don't make me laugh. Hahaha.

BENNETT: i bet she wud make out wit a cat at da moviez

BENNETT: i bet she givs lap dances to Sluger

BENNETT: i just wanted 2 C her tittys cuz i can get pix on my fone now

ME: So you purposely offended her?

BENNETT: no i jus didnt want to put 4th da efert

ME: Why?

BENNETT: i basicly said Hi bitch im bennett lemme get sum loven

BENNETT: she said no and i wuz like watever

BENNETT: bcides she wuz talken shit abt da way i type i aint no english prafesser bitch i wanna study ur tittys all nite not vocabalarry wurdz

ME: So you didn't want to spend the energy on trying to make her like you?

BENNETT: make her like me ?

BENNETT: nigga U aint followen me i dont even like her why da fucc wud i cared if she liked me

ME: Um.

BENNETT: she wud cheat on a dood with a cat..she wierd as fucc . sumtims U gadda see what a persen has 2 offer u and try 2 get it

ME: Right. I thought you were going to use her car to deliver pizzas?

BENNETT: u said i cudnt so i had no reson 2 macc on her she alredy gave me money it wuz titty time or goodbye on 2 da nex one

ME: Fair enough. Honestly she seems like a nutjob. So I really don't care.

BENNETT: were r u

ME: I'm in bed about to go back to sleep. Here's the deal. Read this out loud to yourself if you have to.

ME: Do not fuck up one more time. NOT ONE MORE TIME. I'm dead serious. I've told you this a few times, but I mean it. I'm not gonna tell Harper or anything. No one. Just stay on point. Okay?

ME: Nail this fucking job interview and give me a reason to let you stay here.

ME: No more bullshit. I am really enjoying your mom's presence, so don't fuck it up.

BENNETT: Ok..my mom is a gr8 lady i wont fucc it up

ME: I'm serious.

BENNETT: me 2...

ME: I hope so.

Cutting-Edge Innovation 13

Somewhat to my amazement, Bennett was hired on the spot. He started the next morning. By that first afternoon, and then every single day after that, he was blowing off his responsibilities and texting me instead of working.

BENNETT: How do chikin fingers get so big? thier hands are way smaller.. i bet its really da chikins penis and they lie for markiting

ME: I think my question would be, "Why do they call them chicken fingers?" Chickens have claws.

BENNETT: i know..my girl got claws to.i wish i cud drive sticc. if i cud id locc my girl in a cage to stop her from clawin me..

BENNETT: but her car is sticc n i can drive sticc..so if i locc her in a cage i wont have a ride to da arcade my nigga :(shes a Wearwolf man

in like a ninja a kk
got a black belt in bit-
2 da kk lol yup i speak
txt game is on sum puk
me wat im tellin u...
ike em ya c? dats y bit
ez. cuz kno wat want. t
ner so i let dem know h
2 so i say like Hey sw
O honney ur hair looks
den i go in fo da kill
wut is luv baby dont hu
you just say "kk?" That
me. i spe

me no mo?
the girliest text messa
a female language i ble
inja star a :) is my sord
it wrks luv me they b
ersent fluant langauge
a i say kk and they bo
rushin spy wit. speak ju
z B gittin wit other bit
soft and sweet 2 eac
bennett. i know wat w
d Dats fabulus And kk a
they think im sinstive
dat song dat g

i was jaken off this mornin and my mom yell "BENnet wats dat loud gruntiNG noise ! "

Grunting?

fuk yea cuz i go hard when i jakk off. so i tell her "im watchin transformers 2 and a bad guy just die"

(but den i put lotion on my dik and my mom yell "son wuts dat clapping noise tell me at once..." so i say

"im clapping cuz transformers is so good !"

December

14

It was late morning and I had just pulled into town from a short, two-day show run to Iowa City, Iowa, and Chicago, Illinois. The shows went well, so the drive home was a breeze. I dropped my DJ, Astroblack, aka Patric, off at his house and headed home. Luckily, the couple of days I was gone were pretty tame. Harper gave me reports every few hours, and while she seemed detached and brief, during her conversations with me, she seemed to be getting used to Lillian et al being around the house.

> **ME:** I just got home. Please, man, don't smoke weed in the front anymore. Smoke in the garage where Harper's car used to be.

> **BENNETT:** Ok will du how was da shows

> **ME:** Great, actually.

> **BENNETT:** well hey

> **BENNETT:** i no u jus got home but man..can u cum up hear i gadda talk to u abut sumthin

> **BENNETT:** im off work

> **BENNETT:** if u hungry u can come git sum free food my manajer lets us hav wat we want

> **BENNETT:** i gadda talk 2 u abut sum crazzy shit

BENNETT: come up for lunch it free

ME: Yeah? That sounds amazing. Popeyes chicken is great.

BENNETT: come allone its improtant

ME: Is everything ok?

BENNETT: i dunno..i need 2 talk 2 u doe

ME: Okay. I'll be there shortly.

BENNETT: K

I had never had Bennett tell me something was "improtant" before. I imagined it was going to be about the financial situation he and his family were in. Under all the hoodlum lingo and idiocy, a sliver of him was starting to appear responsible enough to realize this was a serious issue.

I went inside and unpacked my show merchandise in the unfinished section of my basement, putting everything back on the wooden shelves I built some time ago. Except for the sleeping bag and pillows on the couch, Bennett's area of the basement was surprisingly really clean and smelled like perfume. There was a pair of high heels on the floor, which, seeing them, gave me a brief sensation of annoyance that Harper didn't keep them with the rest of the shoes she kept in the storage area of my basement.

I walked upstairs and found Harper ironing her work clothes in our bedroom.

"Hello, my love," I said.

"Hey," she said, without breaking concentration.

"I'm home!" I announced.

"Welcome home, baby," Harper said quickly, kissing me but distracted by something else.

"Okay. Um. You wanna go with me to Popeyes and eat lunch? I gotta talk to Bennett about something."

"Ehhh . . . no. No thanks. But you go ahead."

I kissed her a few more times, attempting to stare into her eyes so we could intimately lock irises. She still wouldn't look at me for some reason.

"Are you okay, Harper?"

"Yes. Fine." Nope. Nothing. She didn't tilt her head upward to even make eye contact.

When I got to Popeyes, Bennett was outside smoking a Newport cigarette. He flicked it upon seeing me and gave me a high-five and hug. I followed him inside.

He ordered us some crispy chicken leg and breast combos, with Cajun rice, mashed potatoes and gravy, and New Orleans–style pecan pies. His boss, Ned, a skinny, gray-haired Latino in his forties, told us to eat in the back corner, "away from the general population of customers." I tried to introduce myself to him, but he seemed very uninterested and acted as if shaking my hand was completely beneath his station. This, from the day manager at Popeyes, mind you.

The food was delectable, but Bennett seemed tired. Bothered by something. He'd been really quiet this whole time. I figured the early work shift must have made him lethargic. He was exercising work muscles that he probably had never known he even had.

Entranced by his phone, he sat still, rapidly text messaging someone, his lower jaw hanging wide open and slightly moving as he mouthed the words he was reading. Drool would ooze out of his mouth any second. He was covered in a layer of kitchen sweat, which caused the homemade EATIDE tattoo on his inner arm to glisten on his pink epidermis. His forearms were covered with scrapes, cuts, burns, and scratch marks. I knew the signs from many a friend's arms: he had been making fries all day.

"So what's going on?" I asked.

"Man . . ." he said, shaking his head.

"What?"

He didn't respond and didn't want to look me directly in the eyes.

"What, dude? What did you want to talk to me about?"

"Aw, man . . . nigga . . . did you see da video I shot?"

"What video?"

He stared at me blankly.

"What video, Bennett?"

"I shot it with your phone da other night."

"Huh?"

"Lemme see yo' phone, nigga. I'll show you."

"Uh . . . hang on, I've gotta go get it."

I had left my phone in my car, charging. Puzzled by where he was going with this, I decided to grab it so he could show me whatever moronic thing he was talking about, and also so afterward, I could peruse the news websites and music blogs I checked on a daily basis. I ran out to the parking lot and, as I unplugged the phone, noticed I had four missed calls and eleven missed texts. *All* from Harper.

I read them with growing concern while walking back inside to our table.

[HARPER:] HEY

[HARPER:] Answer your fucking phone!!!!

[HARPER:] Hello? Answer!!!!! I think a burglar is here.

[HARPER:] Some strange girl was in our basement. She just kicked open the basement door and started cussing really loud, my Magritte print fell off the wall and shattered!

[HARPER:] Motherfucker, please answer!!!!!!!

[HARPER:] ??????????????????????????????????

[HARPER:] OH MY GOD!!!! I'm calling the cops!!!

[HARPER:] She's screaming at Lily.

[HARPER:] GET HERE NOW WHERE THE FUCK ARE YOU

[HARPER:] ??????

[HARPER:] HELLO!!!!

She didn't answer repeated, back-to-back calls. I left a voice mail: "Hello? Are you okay? Hello? What's going on? Call me back, damn it! Is everything okay?"

I hung up the phone, then immediately dialed again but ended up disconnecting when I once again got Harper's voice mail.

In a frenzy, I ran inside of Popeyes and found Bennett sitting alone at the table.

"We gotta go, dude. Something's happening at the house. Someone broke in!" I yelled at Bennett.

"Should I ride my bike?" he said.

"No, leave it here, let's go! We'll come back to get it."

"Wait, man. Let's talk about somethin' right quick."

[ME:] I'm on the way home. What the fuck is going on? Why aren't you answering my calls? Bennett is with me we are on the way call the cops im driving right now

Bennett and I piled into my car. I flipped the ignition and fishtailed out of the parking lot onto the street. Bennett was still quiet. He seemed sick to his stomach.

My phone finally rang. It was Harper. I could hear a nasally loud voice screaming in the ambient background of the other end of the phone.

"Hello? Harper? Hello?" I yelled.

I could hear the phone on her end ruffling and rubbing against fabric or furniture or something. Finally, Harper's voice surged through my phone's speaker and ricocheted off my eardrum. I was in such a state of shock from what she said that I about ran the red traffic light.

"Mercedes is here."

Sylvia Plath and Young Jeezy Sitting in a Tree

"Why is Mercedes at my house right now?!" I yelled directly into Bennett's face as I drove. It sounded like a sonic boom in my car.

I don't even know if that's a proper usage for the term *sonic boom*, but it looks cool when I write it, and I was really fucking stressed, so I'm keeping it in. Basically, I yelled really loud at Bennett, who was staring straight ahead, his pale, bloodless face damp with sweat from a cocktail of the humid summer day and some unstated internal friction over something mysterious he wasn't speaking about. The expression on his face was ill and full of discomfort. It looked like he had food poisoning, or a sour stomach.

In either event, he wasn't responding.

I had recently discovered a shortcut home from Popeye that twisted and burrowed through residential streets and school zones. I was going no less than 60 mph driving through it, rolling through stop signs, making turns without signaling, getting so close to the rear bumper of slower cars in front of me that I could see the color of my own eyes in their rearview mirrors.

I was impatiently pushing my way home when my phone suddenly started playing "It's Raining Men" by the Weather Girls.

"Hello?" I answered.

"Where the fuck are you?" Harper said.

"I'm almost there."

A NOTE ON BEING NON-APROPOS

A few months ago, I was lounging in my house's new breezeway, drinking pinot noir and downloading ringtones onto my cell phone. I had just recently gotten a new phone, so I wanted to utilize all the cool features it had. I tried to download "Make It Rain" by Fat Joe, a bouncy, club rap song, as a first choice. I planned on getting several ringtones, so this would be a fun place to start. I typed "Rain" into the search bar under the ringtones section. I figured it was a popular enough song that I wouldn't have to type the entire name out, right? About a tenth of a second after the results popped up, my inebriated equilibrium caused me to lose balance and spill my glass of wine all over myself and my phone. My slippery hands fumbled and dropped the phone in a twirling, flipping motion until it smacked, face-first, onto the Spanish tile. The facade of the phone was completely shattered, but after tinkering with it for a few minutes, and drying it off, I found that it was still 100 percent operable. The only problem, however, was the collision popped the mute switch out of the side of it, rendering it unable to be silenced or turned down. It also mistakenly downloaded "It's Raining Men" by the Weather Girls instead of "Make It Rain" by Fat Joe, and automatically set it as the default ringtone for all incoming calls and text messages. Wonderfully, this was unable to be changed. It was very embarrassing. Most people in public would stare at me. Some would smile.

"*Hurry!*" she yelled, then hung up on me.

"*Why is Mercedes at my house right now?*" I yelled at Bennett, again.

He remained looking forward but finally responded. "She crashed in the basement with me last night."

"Why?"

"She said she was gonna fuck Lil Juan from Twelfth Street if I ain't let her come over."

"I thought I made it abundantly clear that I didn't want people coming over. Girls, your friends. Anybody."

"I know, but she my girl, mane. You didn't say I ain't allowed to have my girl over."

"Dude! Why are you such an idiot?"

"What if Harper told you she was gon' fuck Lil Juan from Twelfth Street?"

"*Harper wouldn't fuck Lil Juan from Twelfth Street,* idiot."

"Yeah, dats what you think. Dat nigga drive a Benz and sell hella coke. Don't be quick to judge, nigga. Lil Juan fuck everybody girlfriend."

"Lil Juan wou—" I realized how ridiculous the conversation we were having was and changed the subject. "Well, she's freaking out about something at the house right now."

"Yeah, I know."

"You know? Whaddya mean *you know*? What is it? What's the matter? Why didn't you say something to me to warn me?"

Quite appropriate to the urgent nature of my need to get home immediately, right after saying that, I tried to take a sharp turn, was probably going a little too fast, curb-checked, and completely blew out my front *and* rear passenger-side tires. My car was rumbling loudly and rattling loose, scratched-up CDs, stray lighters, and gummed-up coins in the door and middle console. The top of my head vibrated as the car came to a grinding halt.

"Fuuuuuuuck!"

We were a five-minute drive or a thirty-minute walk from my house. One long, stretch of road, with two stop signs and nothing else. I started punching my steering wheel. It felt good to punch, but my aim inadvertently shifted to the middle of it, so my punches did nothing but honk the horn after a few times. Once I realized my windows were rolled down, I casually said sorry at a modest tone to nobody in particular.

For the octogenarian watering his rose garden in his front yard, the three kids playing basketball in a driveway, and the reverse pear-shaped woman speed-walking up the sidewalk, the twenty-five-second interval that just took place sounded something like this:

Vroom!!! **Kerplunk, kerplunk!!!** Psssssssssst. **Grrrrumble.** "Fuck!!!!!!!!!!!" *Bang—Bang— Bang—Bang.* **HONK! HONK! HONK! HONK!**
"Sorry."

"This is absolutely fucking motherfucking wonder-fucking-ful. Now what are we gonna do?" I said quietly, with impatience and venom in my voice.

I called Harper. No answer.

"Should we push it?" asked Bennett.

"We're at least two miles from the house. It takes like thirty seconds to drive there. Probably twenty-five to thirty minutes to walk. You want to push the car for two miles?"

"Man . . . yeah. Kinda. We need to get there. I can't even lie. Who know what da fuck my girl is doin' at da house," Bennett said, scrunching his face and shaking his head.

"Okay, dude! You know what?" I snapped, shutting the ignition off. The idling, grumbling car engine went quiet. All that could be heard now were the neighborhood kids playing basketball and the distant chirps of bobwhites, cardinals, and sparrows. "Tell me now. What's up? What's the problem?"

He inhaled a giant breath through his nose, slapped his thighs, reached into his pocket, grabbed his flip phone, opened up his text messages, and showed me the conversation with Mercedes he was having back at Popeyes.

[MERCEDES:] SO WHY BITCHES WRITING U LUV LETTERS? U GIVIN DA QUEENS DICK OUT? «QuèenMerceDe$»

[BENNETT:] fucc u talken abot im at wrk

[MERCEDES:] DONT PLAY W ME NUKKA I FOUND SUM BITCH LUV LETER N UR DRAR «QuèenMerceDe$»

[BENNETT:] wat ?? CHILL im at wrk

[MERCEDES:] SUM BITCH WIT A WEIRD MOSLAM NAME TALADEGA OR SUM SHIT GIVIN U HER NUMBER TALKIN ABOUT UR SINGLE «QuèenMerceDe$»

[MERCEDES:] YOU CHEATIN? ILL CUT UR DICK OFF U LIL PUNK ASS FUCKBOY DONT EVEN TEST ME BENNY «QuèenMerceDe$»

[BENNETT:] man dat girl wuz thanken me 4 saven her cat quit bein jelus u fuccin ideiot i hate when u ack this way god dam

> **MERCEDES:** O I BET U DO.. & UR GUNNA HATE WUT I DEW NEXT IM ABOUT THA LAST BITCH U WANTED TO PLAY W TO DAY HOMIE «QuèenMerceDe$»

> **MERCEDES:** BITCH ASS NUKKA «QuèenMerceDe$»

> **BENNETT:** chill out mercedes dont git me kicced out da house u so insacure sum times im at work fucc

> **BENNETT:** my mom is sik dont start shit i promis i dont even like that bitch

> **MERCEDES:** FUCK ALL DA PPL U LIV WIT THEY GILLTY FOR HELPIN U CHEAT IMA MOBB ON UR HOLE FAMLY 2..YOU LIL HOE ASS PUSSY «QuèenMerceDe$»

> **MERCEDES:** U A PUSSY.. COWERD «QuèenMerceDe$»

"That's it? That's how you left it?"

"Yeah. I ain't respond to her. She crazy."

"Dude, she was in the basement, wasn't she? The perfume smell . . . W-w-w-w-ait. You let me come up to Popeyes to eat. And just sat there saying nothing? Knowing she was at my house starting shit?"

"She ain't gonna start shit. Don't trip. She always acts like this. I just don't want her to yell at anybody. Don't trip though."

"Don't *trip?*"

I sat there looking at Bennett, contemplating how hard I wanted to sucker punch him in the chin without warning, but I had no time to waste.

A NOTE FOR THOSE INTERESTED IN LEARNING THE D'ARCE CHOKE FROM SIDE MOUNT

I jog or do an hour-plus of Brazilian jujitsu training five times a week. I'm in great shape. Not trying to be bumptious or self-aggrandizing, just pointing out why I didn't sit there and let another grain of sand fall to the bottom of the hourglass. Why I did this . . .

I reached over Bennett's lap and opened the passenger-side door. We had to get somewhere immediately, and I wasn't interested in going at his pace. I used my foot to push him out of the car.

"Let's go!" I commanded, clapping my hands at Bennett as I emerged from the vehicle, before I took off in a fast-paced jog up the street.

Instead of following me, he just stood there; I imagine, asking himself, *Is this really about to happen?*

But much to my cousin's chagrin, I had internally boiled over with rage and frustration, so without losing a step in my rhythm, I circled around, jogged back to the car where he was standing—and openhandedly slapped him in the mouth.

It was straight out of a cartoon. You could see the spread of my handprint on his cheek in a dark-pink hue.

"*Keep up with me, or I'm going to kick your fucking ass. I don't care how much of a gang member you think you are. I'll beat your ass. Now let's go!*" I said, jogging in place.

We both hit it, clipping at a comfortable, sub-seven-minute-mile pace. For the first twenty-five to thirty yards, Bennett was angrily running his mouth, which wasn't exactly smart considering how out of shape he was. I thought about warning him not to overexert himself, but fuck it. He deserved the punishment.

After one hundred yards, his scrawny lungs were wheezing and squeaking. He sounded like a pawnshop accordion trying to insult someone in gang slang, while pausing to violently suck in air between every few words.

"Why *::cough, cough::* you gotta smack me *::eeerrrgghhh::* man? Why? I'm"—volcanic bursts of phlegm bursting through his chest tube—"a G. Respect me! *::wheeze, wheeze::* I *::sigh::* I respect *::wheeze::* you. Fuck."

"Stop talking while you run, idiot, focus on breathing slowly. In through your nose, out through your mouth."

Bennett's face was burgundy. He wasn't even breathing, just clenching his abs and grunting. He had no grasp on how to pace himself or how to maintain a slow, steady flow of oxygen to his lungs. He was also wearing combat boots that were spray-painted blue. He dropped his hands to his sides and began walking.

I couldn't wait. I increased the pace and yelled, "Hurry the fuck up!"

I was almost sprinting, which requires a slightly different type of conditioning than I'm used to. I could feel a tightening in my lungs and capillaries. Mind over matter. I cut through a few rows of housing sprawl and hopped a couple of backyard fences. One of my subdivision neighbors was unloading mulch from his truck when I zipped by him. He saluted me and said, "Howdy!"

Without making eye contact I yelled, "Sorry, I gotta run through your yard, it's an emergency!" and sprinted on.

I slowed down and mentally processed where I was for a few seconds. I was close. My internal navigation clicked into gear, I drove my feet into the asphalt, and finally heaved by throbbing legs over the steep hill that was blocking my view of my house.

That cleared, I kept running but began surveying the area to see if any mayhem had transpired in the front lawn, no longer focusing simply on getting there fast so much as scoping out the situation.

And there she was.

I stopped at the edge of my driveway.

Mercedes.

Mercedes.

Mercedes, standing on Tallulah's driveway . . . laughing? Tallulah was . . . smiling? Everything was . . . merry?

What in the actual fuck was actually happening?

I figured Harper was inside and safe, so I wasn't too worried about her for the time being. I just wanted to figure out what was going on with Mercedes. I walked up to the two girls, who were blinking airily and making faces painted with feigned comradery. I was winded, slowing my patterns of inhaling and exhaling, trying to catch my breath.

Mercedes was nineteen. As much of a psycho, moonstruck, screwball that she was, it was impossible to deny the fact that she was attractive. Or it was at least impossible to deny that by age twenty-five she'd *end up* attractive. If she could tighten all the loose screws in her head and refrain from going to prison on a felony assault charge, she could end up being quite a tantalizing woman.

However, the nineteen-year-old version of her had on hoop earrings that were the size of a baby's head. She had a white wifebeater layered overtop a white tank top undershirt, both with homemade slits cut about five inches down the front, intentionally exposing her cleavage. She had long, fake gold necklaces dangling down to her stomach, and a belly-button ring with a cloudy cubic zirconia stud reflecting violet shades of sunlight off it. Her jean shorts constricted her juicy, corn-fed thighs and were cut so high that the inner pockets were exposed, hanging lower than the bottom of the shorts themselves. She had on shiny, bright-yellow platform heels that were obviously made of Tupperware or plastic or some other cheap material that only strippers seemed to know about.

Those were the shoes I saw in the basement. If I'd noticed they were plastic, I would have known *they weren't Harper's.*

Her hair was tightly pulled back, and she had about three full cans of hair spray hardening and adhering her side locks to her cheeks. She had on a liberal amount of concealer and eye shadow, and her lips had a blackish outline lightly drawn around them to accentuate the sparkling brown lipstick she was wearing. Her acrylic nails were plastered with a dark-red background, various white dots, and thin white lines. From a distance, it seemed that she had domino designs on her fingernails. Her fake eyelashes were unnaturally long. They looked like wings more than eyelashes. She was obnoxiously chewing a piece of gum, blowing bubbles, and nodding her head in agreement to whatever rant Tallulah was midair with when I interrupted them.

"Girl, I know! I love cats. They're so pretty!" Mercedes exclaimed, looking at me and winking. "Not as pretty as you though, T." She rubbed her fingers through a thatch of Tallulah's bleached hair like they were best friends.

"Wow, thanks, Sarah. I appreciate that. You're basically like . . . so much prettier though, your shoes are so cute," Tallulah replied. "It's so cool that you found my house through the missing cat flyer.

I'm excited to work with you. This is my neighbor, Mac," she said, pointing at me, while I walked up.

"What's up, Mac?" Mercedes said, reaching for my hand.

"Yo, what? Dude, what the hell, Mercedes?" I said, drawing my hand into my armpit to avoid shaking. I was confused.

"Geez, Mac, rude much? This is Sarah, she's going to help me rescue cats," Tallulah said.

Before I even had a chance to process the peculiar fact that Tallulah was calling Mercedes "Sarah," our future felon withdrew her hand from the catsexual's hair, took two steps back, firmly planted her heel spikes into the ground, squared her legs up inline with her shoulders, corkscrewed her upper half back forty-five degrees, tightened her legs to act as antennas probing the ground for kinetic energy, tensed her entire physique from the toes up, whiplashed her torso, applied the equation that momentum equals mass plus velocity, torqued her waist with a snap, and with a devastating right hook punched my neighbor square in the nose with terrifyingly perfect aim and flawless form. It sounded like a drunk, blind, fastly flying bald eagle smacking into the side of a barn.

Tallulah's knees buckled under her, collapsing her body to the ground. Her nose began spouting blood from both nostrils. Her eyes rolled into the back of her head. She shriveled into a ball, screaming and squealing a cacophony of panicked expressions at the highest octave her vocal cords could register.

"Oggghhhhhhh! Sarah, where are you? Agggh! Sarah? Mac punched me! Call an ambulance!"

I didn't make a peep. I was so shocked by what had happened that my ability to react was derailed and frozen in a trance. After nine or ten seconds, I snapped out of it, grabbed Mercedes, and pulled her away from Tallulah, throwing myself in between them.

"Whoa! Whoa! Whoa! Stop punching her! What the fuck are you doing?!"

"I ain't punchin' that ho no more, dummy. Look at her. She's a wrap." Mercedes snarled and coolly walked away. "Woo! That's better than sex! I gave that bitch the hand of God!"

She didn't even have the courtesy to look at Tallulah, the girl she'd just blindsided, who was on the ground, sobbing and bleeding uncontrollably. In fact, she instantly disconnected from it all and began typing a text message while walking across the street, as if nothing even happened.

Once she was completely across the street to my driveway, she yelled out, "Don't ever try to fuck my man again, bitch!" then got into her Hyundai and sped off with Chamillionaire's newest CD blasting from its half-busted stereo.

Silkworm

"Harper?! Baby?!"

Her name echoed and reverberated through the vacant hallways and staircases. No response.

I ran upstairs and scavenged through each of the rooms, unable to locate her. Finally, it occurred to me to check in the most obvious place: our master bedroom.

"Honey?" I said with confusion and curiosity. "Darling? Baby?"

"I'm in here."

I heard a muffled voice in our walk-in closet. The door opened slowly, by itself.

"Is she gone?"

"Yeah, she's gone. Are you all right—what are you doing in here, honey?"

Walking in, I saw she was hiding under a pile of coats and a couple of bathrobes.

"What am I doing in here?! Uh, hello? That psychotic, white-trash bitch threatened to kill me!" she snapped, throwing aside the clothes.

"What—she tried to kill you?"

"She told me she was going to! She was going through all our stuff! I was *so* scared!"

I knelt next to her, lightly putting the back of her neck into a gentle Thai plum, wanting to make her—my precious, harmless girlfriend—feel safe.

"Baby, are you okay?"

"No. No! *No! I'm not okay! That was horrible!*" She pushed my arms off her.

"Oh my God, baby, I'm *so* sorry. I'm here. I'm right here. Nothing will happen to you."

She was trembling.

"That girl is so scary. She ran in here and threatened to beat me up! I was so scared! I was so scared!" Tears were swelling from her eyes. "Make them leave—make them fucking leave!"

"Shhhh. Okay. They're gone," I said. I tried hugging her, but she constricted her muscles and stiffened her bones, so it was an awkward, one-sided embrace.

"Shhh. Shhhh. They're leaving right now. Okay? They're outta here," I assured her. "Calm down. Relax. It's okay. Shhh," I said.

I wasn't fucking around anymore. I didn't care if they had to sleep in a motel for the rest of their lives. The line had been crossed. Harper, a woman who couldn't hurt a person if her life depended on it, was scared shitless, in my home—in *our* home.

I walked outside to find Bennett so I could bring him in to discuss it in front of the entire family. He hadn't even made it to the house yet.

I looked across the street. I'd helped Tallulah to a sitting position to catch her bearings while I ran inside, but now she was gone. A puddle of blood appeared to have accumulated on her driveway where she'd fallen. The neighborhood was quiet. You could hear wind chimes and the white noise of distant traffic a few miles away. I sat down on my front porch. The last hour had gone by so fastly and strangely that sitting down made me realize how out of breath I was. I needed a second to gather my thoughts.

At the house across the street and one to the right, a garage door opened. Out of the cavernous, dark pit of a garage emerged Jean Paul and his bicycle. His gorgeous African mother, Mariam, soon followed.

"'Allo, Mac!" he said, in his British-like accent, while waving.

"Hey, Jean Paul!" I replied. "Ridin' your bike, dude?"

"Yes!" He looked very focused on keeping his balance. "Look at this wheely, Mac!" he yelled before popping the bike's front tire, no more than three inches off the ground, for no more than a single second.

"Ohhhh! Very good!" I said. Being anything but supportive when it came to Jean Paul meant your heart was on a milk carton.

Mariam began speaking to Jean Paul, but it was inaudible from where I was sitting. He dismounted from his bike and went to speak to her up close.

From somewhere nearby, a muffled subwoofer started rattling. Seconds later, the music having grown clearer and louder, Mercedes's Hyundai sailed over the hill, scraping its belly on the hill's curvy peak before its worn-down brake pads screeched against its rusty rotors, grinding it to a stop in front of my house. Mercedes and Bennett both got out of the car. Bennett, yelling at her, was holding a medium-size object in his hands as they approached where I was sitting.

"Fuckin' crackhead bitch. Always trying to get me in trouble. What the fuck is wrong with you?" Bennett quipped.

"Oh shut up, pussy. You know half a dis shit is yo' mothafuckin' fault, okay?" Mercedes replied.

They stopped square in front of me. Bennett stared Mercedes dead with a side glance, but she was unphased and obnoxiously chewed her gum to prove that exact point.

"Well? You plan on saying something, you fuckin' dirtball ass hoe?" Bennett said.

"Slow down, Bennett. I'll shove my fist up yo skinny ass and pull yo mothafuckin' lunch out. Don't talk to me like I ain't your pimp, because I is! I'mma bust yo' nose open like that Tostito bitch across the street, ya keep talkin' dat shit. Don't even act like I ain't beat yo' ass before, lil' nigga. Don't."

Bennett shook his head and handed me what appeared to be a DVD player.

"This is yours. Mercedes stole it," he said as I took it from his hands.

"Huh? You stole my DVD player?" I asked Mercedes, befuddled.

"Wait, mothafucka, you told me this was a Blu-ray player or

whatever and that it wouldn't play my DVDs!" Mercedes erupted at Bennett.

"Yeah, I lied. You don't take shit that don't belong to you, dumbass. I had to tell you something so you'd bring it back."

"Damn, Bennett! You fuckin' hatin' ass lil' bitch!" Mercedes said, absolute disgust in her eyes as she eyeballed him. "So I could play my Madea DVDs in that thing this whole time?" She fumed with injustice.

"Yeah, skank, you can play normal DVDs in a Blu-ray player. You just can't play Blu-rays in a normal DVD player. I learnt that shit when I worked at Walmart. Stupid, get a job and sophistimicate your life," Bennett said.

They began calling each other names and yelling over each other. It was unintelligible.

"Wait! Wait! Wait! I'm confused. You *stole* my DVD player?" I asked again, with growing rage.

"First off, bitch nigga, it ain't a DVD player. It's a Blu-ray player. Second of all, does it look like I stole it? You holding it ain't you?" Mercedes barked, without hesitation.

"How the fuck does that matter? You still stole it!" I said.

"I ain't steal shit. You holding it in your hands, ain't you? Well, calm down, bitch ass nigga." Mercedes raised her left eyebrow, sizing me up from head to toe.

"If you took it from my house, that means you—"

"Dat ain't even da worsest part," Bennett interrupted. "Give him the other thing. Now. I never hit a bitch before but I swear on East Avalon Crip, I'll bust your whole melon open if you don't give my cousin his shit back. Bitch, I swear on the six-pointed star. *Give it back to him!*"

Whoa, Bennett was dead serious. But what was he talking about?

"Sadie, give him his shit back! I ain't tryin' to get kicked out of the house because you fucked up. You my girl, but this nigga is my family. *Give it back!*" he spat.

Mercedes shoved Bennett's head back, knocking him, and herself, off balance momentarily. Once she was resituated, she reached into her pocket and pulled out a watch with green and red stripes. I focused closely on it. It was the $2,500 Gucci watch that I bought Harper as a moving-in present. I felt sick.

"*You stole my girl's Gucci watch?!*" I yelled, snatching it out of her hand.

"Again, you fuckin' stupid mothafuckas. I didn't *steal* a Got damn thing. I just *tried* to steal it. You got it back didn't cha? Well all right then. Let's go get some food," Mercedes snipped.

"You stupid bitch! You stupid fucking piece of trash! How dare you? *How dare you?*" I yelled. "Get the fuck off my porch. Now. Go!" I screamed. "You're banned from my house. Go wait for Bennett in your car, you fucking moron."

"Fuck you, homo. I gave it back didn't I? You should give me a reward for it or somethin'—"

"Mercedes, get yo ho ass off this man's property and wait in the damn car," Bennett said, shoving his nose in her face.

"You ain't comin'?" was all she said to him.

"*Go!*" he snapped.

She marched across the grass to her car, her posterior jiggling . . . defiantly?

A NOTE TO HELP WOMEN UNDERSTAND THE AFFLICTION THAT MEN DEAL WITH ON A DAY-TO-DAY BASIS

I was furious. Devastated from anger. Taken advantage of. All of those things. But I still couldn't hesitate to notice how great Mercedes's ass looked in her shorts. Ladies, stop giving us guys shit for being the way we are. We can't help it. Sexual attraction vetoes any and all logic, in any and all situations. On this you cannot relate.

As she passed Jean Paul, who was parked on his bike at the edge of my driveway, watching the entire time, she stopped and studied him for a few seconds. I began to prepare myself to tackle her in case she tried to mess with him.

"You cute!" she finally said in a jubilant tone, alleviating the suspense of the moment. "Damn, I love black kids. So mothafuckin' beautiful," she said, opening her car door.

Before she got in her car, she elevated herself on her tiptoes, gazing at Bennett and me over its roof. She lifted both hands, flipped us off, and plopped down into the driver's seat. She then lit a cigarette and rolled her car windows down.

Fucking Mercedes.

Young Trill

Little Jean Paul had only known this neighborhood to be Norman Rockwellian and enamored with him, so it must have been strange to see us all so angry. Still, he didn't seem too bothered by it and before I knew it, he'd ridden a few houses up the block talking to Ralph, an old, retired, gray-haired cop. Ralph sprayed a hose at Jean Paul, who was giggling as he tried to evade the mist.

"Come inside, you stupid fuck," I said, grabbing Bennett by the collar of his shirt. "We're going to have a nice little house meeting. I hope you're happy. Your poor mother deserves someone who respects and loves her. Move your ass."

Completely compliant, he walked to the living room ahead of me.

"*House meeting!*" I yelled. "*Harper, come downstairs, babe!*"

Lillian wiped the cold out of her eyes and hunched forward, putting her bifocals on. Tim continued playing Xbox 360 and didn't even act like the house meeting applied to him.

"*Harper? Come downstairs, babe!*" I yelled again.

After a few seconds, I could hear the floor upstairs creaking from her footsteps, and she finally materialized and took a seat.

"Tim, turn the Xbox off," Bennett said.

"You don't have power over me. You're a teenager—shut it," Tim quipped.

"Okay. Fine. Tim, I'm telling you to turn the Xbox off," I said. "Not only that, but hey, here's a 'pretty please, with a conspiracy theory on top,' turn the fuckin' Xbox off."

"Why?"

I had no patience left. I walked up to the entertainment center that the television and Xbox 360 were located on and kicked the fuck out of the Xbox a couple times until it turned off. Or maybe it broke—who cared. It had a red light circling around the on/off button, which (hopefully) meant it was broken.

Tim gave me a look of hatred and disgust, then left the room and walked upstairs. Bennett took a seat near the fireplace; his sweaty skin colored magenta from the run.

"Look. Guys. Aunt Lillian. Lily, I love you. But you guys gotta go. This just isn't working," I said.

Lillian was sitting upright on the couch she frequently napped on. "Did that succubus cause problems again?" she asked. "Because I'll have you know, I don't like that little rat!"

"Yeah, she did. But it's more than that. This is just . . . too much," I said.

"She tried to kill me," Harper chimed in.

"What?" Aunt Lillian said.

"Yeah, she threatened to attack me," Harper said.

"Oh, heavens!" Aunt Lillian said, gasping. "Why was she here?"

Harper glowered at her. "Oh, I'm envious of the genius you possess," she condescended. "Do you think *we* invited her here? Your degenerate son—who you don't parent—had her here."

I gave Harper a scowl. Her assault on Lillian was uncalled for. For her part, my aunt raised her eyebrows, then stared at the floor in disappointment. She was always predictably quick at blaming herself for the problems happening in other people's lives.

"Relax, Harper. Aunt Lillian has a valid question. We didn't know she was here either."

"I didn't mean . . . I meant why was she so angry? She went off on me too, but I was just waking up and couldn't understand the little tramp," Lillian explained.

"Good for you. I'm sure you're used to it. But I'm not. And to answer your question, she threatened to kill me for not telling her that Bennett was cheating on her!" Harper yelled. "She said Bennett had been 'creepin' with mutts!'" she said, making air quotes with her fingers. "Whatever that means."

"Well, I didn't know that he was," Aunt Lillian said.

"Couldn't you imagine that he was? All he does is lie to people and cause trouble!" Harper snapped. She began sucking her teeth and sarcastically laughing under her breath. "You know? It begs the question: Have you ever parented this kid one day in his entire life? Jesus Christ—he's a fucking criminal. He has no manners. Steals medication from us. Are you even the slightest bit worried that he's going to end up in prison? What kind of shitty mom are you?"

"I would appreciate if you didn't speak to me that way." Lillian said with an austere tone.

"If you give me a good enough reason not to, I won't—but maybe you need to hear this—"

"The first reason is, it's rude. The second reason, is you misused the phrase 'begs the question.' And as stuck-up as you are about how people talk, maybe you shouldn't be talkin' wrong," Lillian said.

Damn! Lillian with the slam dunk!

"Ha! How do you figure I misused that phrase? You of all people?" Harper retorted.

"'Cause I seen it on one of my favorite morning shows yesterday. They say most people don't use that phrase right. It don't mean to raise the question, it means somethin' else," Lillian said.

Hey, that's good enough for me.

Bennett turned his head to look at me. We met eyes for a brief moment before he shook his head, looking the other way. Harper didn't appreciate the gesture.

"Oh, is something bothering *you*, Bennett?" she ask-yelled. "Do you have a *problem*? Are you going to correct me on something too, you little shit?"

"Nope," Bennett said.

"I'd like to think not. We gave you a chance. You guys moved in here, completely mooched off our food, and haven't paid us a dime. I'm sorry, but that's a pretty lowlife existence if you ask me."

I raised my hand at Harper to insist she diminish the nasty tone in her voice. I then took a deep sigh and addressed Lily and Bennett. "To put it nicely, we just don't have the energy or the space to do this anymore. We are becoming increasingly more and more worried every time we leave the house. Every d—"

"To *put it nicely?*" Harper interjected. "Fine, if you're going to dance around the issue, I'll be the man of the house for you. You guys are—I'll say this in the most polite way possible—total white trash. Leeches, if you will. None of you work. None of you have a job. And you, Lillian. I know it's not an easy thing to admit, but you're addicted to drugs. You're basically a bum! How are you *not* a bum?"

"Yo, bitch. Watch yo fuckin' mouth talkin' to my mama like dat!" Bennett yelled, as he stood up, aggressively walking toward Harper.

"Hey, hey, hey, dude, relax!" I yelled, grabbing him and pulling him back. "Stop it! *Stop it!*" I was screaming at all of them—everyone in the room. Not that Harper realized that.

"See? No tact or manners at all! And you people are who the wealthy, hardworking families of America have to support. Do you know what taxes are, Lillian? You ever paid them before? Oh, no, that's right, you haven't. You use the ones I pay to buy drugs and weird stuff off the Home Shopping Network," Harper continued on.

"Quit bein' mean to my mama, bitch! Don't make me expose you!" Bennett yelled, shoving himself out of my grasp. "Don't make me expose da whole shit!"

"Hahaha. I'm sorry, Bennett? The 'whole shit'?" Harper said, mocking him. "What, exactly, is the 'whole shit'? Huh? How you lied to Tallulah and told her you owned our house? Huh? How you've stolen almost all of my pills, even after we told you not to? Hmm? Is that the 'whole shit'?"

"I didn't steal yo' damn pills, bitch. I been tryin' to do good," Bennett said.

"Oh, you didn't? Then where did the entire bottle of Percocet go? It was a full prescription I got when I had surgery. I took *one*, and it made me puke. Where did the other fifty-nine go, *homie*?"

"Harp, honey, I have those," Lillian said, digging through the nylon medicine pouch she kept on the end table.

I was pretty shocked. But also, I didn't care. Bigger fish to fry.

"Wait, what? *You* stole all my Percocets? *You?* Jesus. Go. Fucking. Figure."

"You can have them back. I only took a few, honey." Lillian reached out to hand Harper the prescription bottle back.

My girlfriend didn't extend her arm to take it.

"Lillian. You're a grown woman who steals people's prescription medication? That's fucking ridiculous," she said.

"I didn't steal them. They were in the medicine cabinet when I went pee . . ."

"*Of course* you stole them! They're not yours, are they?" Harper said.

"Well, I didn't put them there. My name isn't on them. . . ." My aunt was starting to look really upset now, more angry than I'd ever really seen her.

"I know you need help understanding stuff sometimes. So I'll make this simple for you: if you take something that isn't yours, it's—"

"I'm not finished Harper. You keep talking during other people's turns to talk—now it's my turn," Lillian interjected. Taking off her glasses and fogging one of the lenses with her mouth, before wiping it off with the lapel of her robe, she waited to confirm that Harper would remain quiet before proceeding.

"If you don't want people taking those pills, then why did you put them in the medicine cabinet?" Lillian said at last.

To which Harper condescendingly shrugged. "Ya know? I don't . . . I really don't know, Lillian."

"I agree witchu, Mom. Y'all niggas put medicine in da medicine cabinet, den get mad when niggas use da medicine? It don't make no type of sense."

"Okay, just because it's in the medicine cabinet, doesn't mean it's medicine for *everyone*! How is that concept hard for you retards to grasp?"

A NOTE FOR AMERICA
Stop using the word *retarded* to describe things derogatorally.

"I guess we just see things a different way, darlin'. At my house, the medicine cabinet has medicine for our friends who visit. Need a pill? Grab one, sweetie. Need some ointment? It's in the medicine cabinet, babe. It may not be much, but if it's in there, help yourself," Lillian said.

"Interesting," Harper began, and at first she seemed almost calm. But I knew this was just the next phase in her anger. "First of all, you don't have a house. Second of all, you couldn't keep prescription medication in a medicine cabinet for longer than two days if your life depended on it. But, I'll say this. It's honestly the perfect analogy. See, there are people out there I'd give all that Percocet to in a second. Because they *need* it. But you don't *need* a fucking thing. You're a freeloader—a drug addict. You know, Lillian? There are people on disability because they are disabled. You're n—"

"Chill. I'm dead serious. Chill," I said, cutting Harper off.

Harper turned on me and scoffed. "*You* fuckin' chill."

"Child, I know I'm not the brightest. Not the best. Not the richest. I know all that—" Lillian started.

"That's good. Not being sarcastic. Not trying to disrespect you, Lillian. I know we aren't having a pleasant moment right now. But, I gotta say, it's good you know that about yourself. It's good to see your weaknesses so you can work on fixing them. Because I'd hate to have to be the one to tell you all the things that are wrong with you."

Lillian swallowed a mouthful of excess saliva and momentarily postured herself against the back of the couch, straightening her spine, before letting the tension loose and sliding back down the couch. She then proceeded: "It stinks to tell someone things that are bad about them, Harper. A lot of people have done it to me in my life. I don't like it. It stinks. And it stinks for me to tell you that I hope you're working on learning how to share your strawberry ice cream. Because a person who keeps their fridge off-limits to friends, doesn't have real friends."

I don't know if Lillian meant to be profound with that statement, or if she meant something else and was inadvertently wise, but I have to admit being a little blown away by her telling Harper that.

I fucking *hated* how selfish Harper was with her food. Especially at restaurants. She never asked me if I wanted a bite of her food.

> ## EXAMPLE OF HARPER'S INABILITY TO SHARE
> **"Can I have a bite of your truffle macaroni and cheese, Harper?"**
> **"Mac, if you wanted a bite of truffle macaroni and cheese, why didn't you order truffle macaroni and cheese? I didn't want a bite of braised beef ribs, so I didn't order them."**

"What a bizarre thing to say. If you want some strawberry ice cream, you can fuckin' have it, Lillian. Okay? Jesus, keep the Percocet. Want my clothes too? Look—it's not my fault you guys are fuck-ups!" Harper snapped.

Looking over at my cousin, I noted that Bennett had started punching his hand and grunting. He locked eyes with me, then shook his head in frustration.

"Bitch, what I tell you about dissin' my mama? I swear. I'mma tell this nigga Mac the whole shit. The *whooole* shit."

"Son, do *not* call her the b word!" Lillian said. "I mean it. Talk like a gentleman."

"I'll expose the whole shit," Bennett said calmly, and my aunt seemed mollified.

I stood in between them, partly because I didn't know what any of these people were capable of right now. Bennett was mouthing words I couldn't understand, trying to tell me something to no avail. Harper had moved to sitting in the klismos chair behind me and up against the living room wall, positioned in direct alignment to the Banksy *Monkey Parliament* oil painting replica.

"Yes, the 'whole shit.' Is it how you tell me not to disrespect your mother, while calling me a 'bitch' fifty times a minute? Is that the 'whole shit'?" Harper continued. "Or wait. Is it how your girlfriend assaulted our harmless neighbor and is sitting in front of our house like an idiot, waiting for the police to take her to jail?"

"You lucky she ain't whoop yo' ass," Bennett said.

I was about to drag him out of the house by his shirt collar and pummel him on the driveway. At that specific moment, I was kind of glad him living with me was coming to an end the way it was. I knew I'd feel no guilt about it when I remembered how disrespectful the little fuck was to my girl.

For her part, Harper stared into the distance after that comment. The thought of Mercedes beating up Tallulah and threatening her was visibly disturbing her.

Then I noticed she had begun giggling . . . almost sinisterly.

Her inhibitions crumbled into a pile of carbon powder. After socioeconomically soaking in utero for twenty-seven breezy years in a protective sac of Democratic amniotic fluid, while feeding on a nutrient-rich diet of opulent, New England liberalism, adorable theories on the importance of racial equality, piles of unreported cash, washed clean and hidden inside poverty-fighting nonprofit organizations, and riveting fantasies about saving, interacting with, and understanding the minorities her family doesn't actually want to save, interact with, or understand, Harper was abruptly severed from her umbilical cord, toweled off, and kicked out of the nest.

I was always suspicious of those who had passionate beliefs about things they had never actually experienced, and this was all the confirmation I needed.

Harper dropped the atom bomb.

"Or is the 'whole shit' how your mom pretends to be a retard and you pretend to be a *nigger*?"

My heart stopped. My eyes popped out of my head. I couldn't believe she said that.

"Whoa—whoa—whoa—whoa—whoa!" I said, panicking. "That's eghhhh. Bleeeergghhh." Argh—I was unable to formulate any actual words.

"*What?* He says *nigger* all the time. Why can't I?" she demanded.

"Dude. He doesn't say it like thhh . . . aaat," I said animatedly. "What the Ffff . . . this is my family! How could you say blaaaaarghh? No!"

"Because it's true! He pretends to be a nigger and Lillian pretends to be a retard. How else can I explain it to you so that you'll finally see what's going on?" she said. "Or is it even possible to? After all, you did swim out of the same gene pool as these cretins, apparently you don't get it either."

"Well . . . I'm just . . . hmph!" Lillian said, shocked.

I closed my eyes.

There was an impenetrable, nearly deafening cloud of tension suffocating the entire room. For the first time in my life, I asked whatever God was listening, whatever God I doubted might be out there, to wake me up from the nightmare that I was lost inside of.

"What about the nigga you was kissin' in the car the other night?" Bennett asked, with a bomb of his own.

My Style Is Impetuous, My Defense Is Impregnable, and I'm Just Ferocious. I Want Your Heart! I Want to Eat His Children! Praise Be to Allah! (~Mike Tyson)

I opened my eyes. Was this a cruel joke? Was I on some candid camera TV show where your own friends and family destroy your life for a national TV audience? Because there's no way this was real.

"Ha! Sure!" Harper said in an abnormally high-pitched voice. "No, seriously, answer the question. Why do you act like a—"

"Wait, what?" I interrupted, looking at Bennett.

"I tried to tell you at Popeyes, homie. I was tryin' to tell you, but we had to leave 'cause Mercedes was trippin' 'n' what not," he said, looking embarrassed for both me and himself somehow.

Harper stood up and walked around me, just inches from Bennett. She put her hand on his shoulder as if to console him and said, "Don't say things like that. Don't be an asshole. It's bad enough that you've caused this much trouble; don't lie like a jerk."

"Bitch, I ain't lyin' 'bout shit! And you know dat!" he snapped.

"What the fuck are you talking about Bennett?" I said.

"I tried to tell you at my job. I tried to show you the video," he said.

"What video?" I asked.

"It's on yo phone. Get out yo phone."

"Mac, this is ridiculous. Can we make them leave already? Seriously?" Harper said.

"No. Hold on. I want to know what he's talking about," I said, pulling my phone from my pocket.

"I'm sure it's a video of him stealing drugs or shooting somebody in Compton. Come on—let's focus on the issue here," Harper said.

Going to my media page, the last video was something I had filmed weeks ago as a demo recording reference for a song I was working on.

"There's nothing on here, dude." I looked at my cousin hard. "What are you trying to pull here?"

"I ain't lyin', Cuz! I seen her kissin' another nigga in his car da other night!"

I looked at Harper. She shook her head.

"You fuck. You little wigger piece of shit," she growled.

"Nah, fuck dat! Nigga, Mac. Your phone was in da garage. Hangin' with da gardenin' stuff. Da hos and da shovels and shit! I swear on CRIP, nigga!" Bennett pleaded.

"Wait, what?" I said. "My phone was in the 'gardening stuff'? You mean the tools?"

"Yeah, yeah! In da garage! I put it back dere after I took da video."

I looked at Harper's face. She swallowed to alleviate the lump in her throat that had instantly enveloped. She took off, in a very fast-paced walk, toward the garage. I instantly followed.

"What's he talking about Harper?" I said, running after her.

"I don't know. He's full of . . ." she said, not finishing her sentence, running through the kitchen.

Bennett followed the two of us. By the time Harper was opening the garage door, we had all caught up to her. She walked into the garage and ran to a pile of gardening supplies she had kept in the corner.

"Where do you see a phone, you little lying faggot wigger?" Harper yelled, sorting through the tools. "I don't seem to see one! Huh—I wonder why!" she said, sarcastically.

"Because dat's not where it is!" He climbed up on a wooden workbench on the other side of the garage and stretched up at a pile of things on a shelf. "I meant *deez* garden tools," he said.

"Dude, those are kerosene lanterns. What are you doing up there?" I said.

"Whatever, mane. Here."

Opening a hard-to-reach cabinet, he grabbed a phone that looked similar to mine from an acrylic paint–stained Kansas City Royals cup. Honestly, my first thought had been that the cup and the phone must have been leftovers from the house's previous owners.

"*Give me that!*" Harper ran toward us.

Bennett swiftly jumped down from the workbench and gave me the phone, right as she made it to where we stood. I dodged her grasp.

"Wait. What the fuck is this?" My eyes were the size of chocolate chip cookies.

Again, Harper tried to grab the phone, I evaded her until she stopped and stood in silence, breathing heavily. She spat in Bennett's face, then walked inside, slamming the door behind her so hard that one of the kerosene lamps fell from the tackboard it was hanging from and cracked.

"Dude . . . no. What is this Bennett?"

I pressed a button on the phone and its screen lit up. There were several missed texts — all from a Wichita, Kansas, area code. Harper didn't know anyone from Wichita, Kansas.

1-316-915-####: can i c u?

1-316-915-####: got a cpl bttles of 1970s napa wine u have to try. delish.

1-316-915-####: u check the phone today? gna go 2 jazz fest can u cum

1-316-915-####: good c ing u. yummy

1-316-915-####: can u get away tonite?

1-316-915-####: u checkin the phone 2day

1-316-915-####: is he back in town, babe?

"What is this Bennett?"

"I was lookin' fo' a place to hide some 'shrooms one day and found dat shit. Da otha night when you was outta town fo dat show, I seen Harper kissin' on some nigga in his car out front of da crib at like four a.m."

I kept reading and rereading and rereading the texts as my cousin spoke. Just moments ago, my reality was a much happier one. Somehow.

"Yeah, homie. What's worser den dat is I videotaped it all with dat phone. I thought dat was yo phone—I was wonderin' why you kept it up on da shelf. Thought you was hidin' it from me or somethin'." Bennett paused, like he had to say something he didn't want to. "She was out there kissin' him for like a hour, late as fuck. I jumped up an got da phone and videotaped it."

"I've . . . never seen this . . . phone in my life," I mumbled.

"Yea. Because it's her secret phone, ain't it? Look at da video."

I opened the media content folder. One video was on it, like a challenge. I tapped it with my thumb.

Bennett's face, in very low light, popped up. . . . Not what I was expecting.

My cousin was grimacing, his eyes flicking around as he repeatedly said, "Bitch. This dirty-ass bitch. Slutty bitch. You dirty bitch. Ohhh, you dirty-ass bitch." This went on for a good six minutes before stopping on an awkward still that looked up his nostrils.

I looked at him confused. "It's just your face, Bennett."

"Nah! Where's da other side of da video? I was pointin' da thing right at 'em!" he protested.

"The 'other side' of the video?"

"Yeah! It was filmin' me mad as fuck, and also filmin' Harper kissin' some dude. I ain't know how to watch the video though—my phone don't got da split screen video feature thingy! I promise I ain't lyin'. On Crip!"

I sighed.

"You were filming yourself the entire time, dude."

Bennett needed a few seconds to compute the misfortune of the situation.

Then he needed a few more.

He picked his nose a bit, which helped him finally get it.

"Awwww. I was?"

"Yep." I tossed the phone onto the table, then walked into the house, with my heart seconds away from melting to liquid and oozing out of my tear ducts.

I found Harper in our (now *my*) bedroom. She was standing and leaning back against the bed, looking at the floor.

"So who is he?" I said.

She was silent.

"Wow. You're going to just fuck some other dude while I'm out of town, doing a show?" I said.

"No. I didn't have sex with him. I wasn't kissing him. We just kissed good-bye."

"Bitch, quit lyin'! You was sittin' on his fuckin' lap!" Bennett yelled from the staircase.

"*Shut the fuck up!*" Harper screamed.

"Bennett, shut up, man," I said.

"Who is he?"

"Please . . ."

"Who? Who were you kissing?"

"Please, baby."

"Stop calling me baby. Tell me. Who is it?"

"A friend. But I wasn't kissing him."

"A *friend*?"

"Yeah . . . a, uh, a . . . guy I'm friends w . . . ith."

"A guy you're friends with, huh? Elaborate a bit."

"A guy . . . from . . . a guy I work with." She was looking at the ground.

"In front of my house? You kissed another man, in front of *my* house?"

"I didn't kiss him! Why do you believe that white-trash piece of shit over me?"

"Stop calling them names! You hipster . . . *fucking* . . . hipster *bitch*."

I kicked the lamp off of my nightstand. It fell to the ground, bending the lampshade, but remained lit. I was hoping it would shatter into a trillion pieces and make a super badass point, but all it did was emanate a very bright, unobstructed light from the bottom of the shade, so I leaned over and picked it up and put it back on the nightstand.

Bennett was eavesdropping from the bottom of the staircase and started sending me text commentary while we argued, which, thankfully I only saw later.

BENNETT: she lyen

BENNETT: u mite wanna git a aids test

BENNETT: or tell her 2 git 1 and see if she got aids

BENNETT: she wud prolly lie doe so u mite wnna git won

BENNETT: or fucc a girl and tell her 2 git one den see if she has aids so u dont gadda git a aids test

Harper gazed at the ground for a few minutes, unresponsive. Finally, she closed her eyes and fought back tears.

"I'm so sorry. I kind of . . . kissed him." She was full-on crying now, trying to hug me.

"Don't touch me!" I yelled, swatting her arm away from me.

"Just come here. I can make this better."

"Stop touching me, you fucking jerk!" I screamed.

I hesitated for a split second, before lunging from the mattress and landing on my feet, with my arms flying from behind me. Without thinking, I telegraphed a right overhand cross into the wall adjacent to the bed, punching a fist-size hole through the mocha-colored drywall. Harper was bawling.

"I'm sorrrrrrry. I'm sorrrrrrrrrrrry!" She was sobbing and gargling her own saliva. Desperate torment filled her voice.

"Were you fucking him?"

"No! No! I swear!"

"Then what's the phone for?"

"What?"

"Why do you have an extra phone? To sneak around fucking other guys?"

"No. It's . . . it's my work phone."

"Why didn't you tell me you had a work phone?"

"Uh . . . what? I just got it. I . . . dunno."

"Who is it? Who's the guy? Stop lying now and . . . stop lying. Stop lying and I might forgive you."

"Why does it matter?"

"Because it matters. Who was it? Do I know him?"

[BENNETT:] i seen him.he drive a nice car

[BENNETT:] hE look like da type of dood dat wud B best frendz wit a girl he cudnt have sex wit..

[BENNETT:] type of nigga who wud sleep in da same bed as a girl but not take there cloths off..thinken dat mean sumthin

[BENNETT:] u no dem type of bitchez? i fuccd a girl like dat once.. for da first 15 minits her guy friend was layen in bed wit us tellin da girl dat she wuz maken a big mistake

[BENNETT:] finaly her boobys came out and he left da room sayen he had a stomech ake LoL

She was silent and unresponsive again. I asked her to identify him nine or ten more times before she finally broke her silence and answered.

"Chad."

Now *I* was silent.

"Chad?"

"Chad. From work."

I had met Chad before. He drove an Audi A5 and dressed like a pompous prick with an indispensable surplus of trust-fund money. He wore Gucci high-tops and Prada turtlenecks. He vacationed in Cabo and ordered $435 magnum champagne bottles at clubs from his VIP table. His conversations were full of tall tales about his celebutante friends and posh taradiddle about trivial art pieces he planned on purchasing. He was one of the superiors at Harper's company. He was younger than the other bosses but older than me and Harper. He listened to really cheesy dance music, like Tiësto and the Black Eyed Peas, and bought front-row seats to the ballet and other obscure performance-art shows. He had two dogs, both Weimaraners, which he referred to as his kids. And he sent them to a high-end, and very expensive per day, dog daycare, whenever he'd leave town.

"Chad. Chad. Chad? Of all people? Chad. Jerk off, turtleneck Chad. Organic soy beer Chad. Vegan Chad. Wow. You fucking idiot wwwwwhore. Thanks."

"I was just . . . just mad . . . at you."

"Mad at me?"

"Yes, over them"—she pointed at the floor toward where Lillian slept in the living room—"staying here. I was . . . frustrated."

"So you *fucked another guy*?"

"Yes . . . wait. *No.* No, I didn't . . . I didn't f—"

"You fucked him, didn't you—didn't you? Stop lying!"

She rolled her suddenly dry eyes and slapped her hands against her thighs, as if the whole conversation was a huge inconvenience to her. "Aw, geez. You know? This is getting stupid," she said with an irritated tone.

"Don't even try to act like this is some burden on you. You cheated on me—in my front yard. I thought you were a loyal person. I thought you'd never cheated on someone."

Silence until: "I don't usually cheat."

"No, you told me you *never* cheat!"

"Hehe, well . . . I never *usually* cheat," Harper said, trying to lighten up the situation, as she put her hand on my back.

"Harper, get your fuuuucking hand off me. If you think I'm going to have a sense of humor about this, you're wrong."

"I'm sorry. God, I'm just trying to lighten up the mood. What do you want me to say?"

"Say something honest. I won't break up with you if you're honest. If you're honest, I at . . . I at least know how to try to work on things with you. Where to rebuild things from."

I crouched down and looked her in the eyes. "Now," I said. "Please be honest. Okay? Did you sleep with him?"

She looked away, covering her mouth with her hand.

"What's your answer?"

"My answer is . . . I've just been . . . unhappy."

"That wasn't the question."

"But yes, it is, baby! That's the answer!"

"Okay. So you fucked him?"

"Stop. . . . It's just . . . I just . . . I don't understand you sometimes."

"How so?"

"You're not like I am. And I want to understand you. I want to love you. But you grew up without money. You grew up uneducated."

"So the fuck what?!"

"I just . . . I need time to understand your level of people."

"My level? My level? The fuck does that mean? My *level* of . . . people?"

"That's *not* how I meant it!"

"Hang on. Stop changing the subject. Did you fuck him?"

Silent again.

"Have you had sex? With Chad? Since we've been together?"

"Mac . . ."

"No. Let me rephrase: have you had sex, with Chad, a guy you met because you moved here to be with me, a Kansas guy, since we've been together?"

"Forget about that. Let's focus on the real issue. We've moved very fast into this relationship and need to establish a common ground. I just don't understand you. The way you grew u—"

"Okay, just stop." I cut her off. "Why did we even do this? Who the fuck moves in with someone after seven months?"

I stood up and entered her side of our walk-in closet. I then bear-hugged all the clothes of hers I could grab and pulled as much of them off the hanger pole as I could, then threw them on the bed.

"Why are you doing that? Why are you throwing my clothes—?"

"You know why." I went back and grabbed another load. "Because, you're an asshole. You're a closet racist, an elitist, a bitch. Okay? I mean— Jesus! My family may not be wealthy and politically influential. But they at least have loyalty. They at least understand pain and hardship."

"Please, honey. I—"

"Stop calling me honey. You're a *bad* person."

"No. Baby. I'm not a bad person; I'm just very confused right now."

I threw more clothes on the bed. I began emptying her sock and underwear drawers.

"Yes, you are."

"No! I'm not! I'm a good person!"

"Okay, then you're a bad person for me."

"We can fix this."

"No, we definitely can't fix this."

"What are you trying to say? Are you ending things with me?" She sat and covered her face with her hands. "Mac? You're going to give up this soon?"

"Yeah. I am."

"No, I want to hear you say you're ending things with me. I don't think you can. I think you know we can fix this and want me to beg for you to take me back. If you really think I'm a bad person, then ask me. Ask me to leave."

"Ha! 'Ask' you to leave? You aren't understanding me. There's no 'asking' going on here. Your daddy's name isn't on this mortgage. *My* name is on the mortgage. This isn't a request. This is an order: *Get your things and get the fuck out of my house!*"

She collapsed onto the ground screaming.

And I? I just walked out.

God, Politics, and Jay-Z versus Nas

I drove around for hours by myself, listening to Mexican polka on the radio. For some reason, the accordions and Spanish language that I couldn't understand a word of helped lessen the sting of finding out that Harper cheated on me with turtleneck-wearing vegan Chad. I pulled over to the liquor store and bought a six-pack of Founders Red's Rye PA. I didn't have a bottle opener in the car, so I had to bite off the bottle caps with my rear molars—a practice I had been using since ninth grade.

My phone was on the passenger seat. I had no idea if anyone was calling or texting. I didn't care. I was stewing in my own self-pity. After a beer was finished, I'd throw its empty bottle onto the street, hoping a person who had recently cheated on their spouse would trip and fall on it. Then I'd open another one. They were getting progressively warmer.

I hadn't felt this type of sadness—the gambler's uncertainty, the feeling that I was doomed to be forever alone—since I was a little fifth-grade lad and Katie Stanford (a seventh grader!) dumped me at Skateland South. She said I "wore dorky shoes" and was "too shy," and she broke up with me just like that.

Wait, no. Scratch that. Beer memory. She didn't actually say anything. She had her friend Lynn come over and break up with me *for* her. I remember trying to instantly heal the abrasions Katie left on my heart by rebounding with the first girl in sight. Which was Lynn, by default. I had such a cheesy, skewed, Disney-movie grasp on attraction and love that when Lynn asked me, "Are you going to be okay?" I read the flickering light from the Coke machine that was reflecting in Lynn's eye as a supernatural twinkle, so I responded with, "Your eyes are glowing. I can sense your love so deeply. Go steady with me, Lynn. Go steady with me." And I took her hand.

With perhaps outsize pity, Lynn patted me on the head and declined. It was devastating. But I soldiered on . . . and ended up being spurned by three other girls that same night. To extrapolate on that, I literally skated up to a group of three *other* girls who were playing pinball, and one by one, in order of cutest to least cute, asked them all to go steady with me. They all said no.

After another particularly otherworldly polka rendition by Los Banditos Milagros of all things, and a few more crushed bottles, I realized that, indeed, my phone had been vibrating.

(HARPER:) Baby, please.

(HARPER:) Baby? Lover?

(HARPER:) Honey?

(HARPER:) You are my life. My dream man.

(ME:) Shut up, bitch.

(HARPER:) It kills me to see you say that. Baby, no.

(ME:) Go back to Vermont, you racist.

(ME:) I'm coming home soon and if your stuff is there I'm going to let Mercedes have it.

(HARPER:) *[Very long text about how she's sorry, and how I'm her everything, and she will regret this till the day she dies, and all this other drivel that you don't want to read, because it's a bunch of bullshit.]*

(ME:) Yeah, that's nice. You should have thought of that before fucking Chad.

(ME:) This is the last text I'm going to send you. I vow to you if you aren't gone by the time I get home in 2 hrs I'm going to let Bennett and Mercedes have your stuff. You don't have that much shit at my house. Take all you can. The rest I'll get to you soon. Good-bye and fuck you.

[HARPER:] I love you, David McCleary Sheldon.

[ME:] 1 hour 59 minutes and counting. Try me.

I ended up an hour away in Topeka, which is Kansas's state capital. (Most people get that wrong.) I parked my car at a high school that had a twilight baseball game going on under the school's fluorescent stadium lights. I remained in my car and studied every single player who stepped up to take bat at home plate, evaluating their physical characteristics and trying to imagine if he would end up getting cheated on or not.

After a half hour, the game ended, the parking lot emptied, car by car, and the stadium lights shut off. I remained where I was, the windows rolled down, breathing in the khamsin of the pitch-black Topeka summer. Famished mosquitoes feasted on my arms, and I didn't bother to swat them away. I was rotting in my car, seeping out gusts of rancid fumes and mare's tail clouds of black smoke, as I felt Harper incinerating the deepest dimensions of my existence.

I made it home three hours later.

Bennett found me standing silently in the kitchen. He was shirtless, eating a dry, syrupless waffle with his bare hands. His Freddy Krueger tattoo looked somehow sadder than usual. His pants hung off his ass, and his *South Park* boxer shorts puffed out of them. His facial expression was that of someone who just punted his puppy over a fence. It was guilty and burdened with hurting someone he loved. He had a huge welt under his eyeball.

"Bennett, what happened to your eye?"

"I broke up with Mercedes, and she punched me."

"Jesus."

"Nigga. I got really bad news."

"What?"

"Uh . . . Cuz. I was jus' tryin' to be a good cousin by tellin' you what she did, and shit. And . . . it sucks dat I gots to tell you dis shit too. But uh . . . man. Harper took her stuff and left."

Hearing her name, I'll admit I was tempted to call her and tell her to come back. But I couldn't. Too much pride. Too much fear of enabling it to happen again. I'd been cheated on once before, years ago, and infidelity always has been, and always will be, the one unforgivable offense for me. Other than eating in our bed. Gross.

"I know she did, man. I told her to. I broke up with her and kicked her out."

"Yeah, I heard. But uh . . . I thought y'all would do like me and Mercedes do."

"Dude. She cheated on me. What do you, or would you do, if Mercedes cheated on you?"

"Uh . . . yeah, mane, like, Mercedes cheats on me all the time, homie."

"How do you live with that?"

"I cheat on her back."

"Geez. So . . . you guys constantly one-up each other, trying to out-cheat the other person?"

"Uh . . . well. Mercedes cheats on me 'cause I cheat on her."

"Why don't you stop cheating on her?"

"Because she's fuckin' crazy!"

He removed his navy-blue bandana and unfolded it on the kitchen counter. He flattened it with his hands and began to refold it with fresh creases.

"Uh, also, mane," Bennett said.

"Yeah?"

"Nigga, Tim took his luggage and moved out too."

"Huh? He did?"

"Yeah."

"Why?"

"I think because you broke the Xbox."

Well, at least something positive was coming out of this. I seldom played video games and hated Tim. Small price to pay.

"Well, fuck," I said.

"Yup."

"Wait, is your mom mad that Tim left?"

"Hahahaha. What?"

"Is that funny? Sorry. I just, wasn't sure if she was mad that Tim left."

"Doo, my mom hate that mothafucka. Nigga always fussin' about somethin'. She just use him for his nice van."

"Ah. Yeah, a twenty-year-old Astro is a great vehicle."

"Fuck yeah it is. But that ain't the point, G. Is we good?"

"What do you mean?"

"Well like . . . I know a nigga got mad at yo' girl earlier and shit. But, like, you was sayin' we had to leave earlier and shit. And . . ."

"Oh. Do you guys have to leave still?"

"Yeah."

"No, Bennett. You guys have to *stay* now. I'm gonna need help with these bills."

I didn't need help with the bills. I just had an urgent level of paranoia burgeoning in my stomach and wanted someone to sit there next to me while I sorted this all out inside.

"Word? For real?"

"Yeah, now you guys can't leave. I had it all set up with Harper to work a certain way, and well . . . yeah. Now it won't work. I need as much money as you can bring in."

"But how? What should I do?"

"Get another job."

"*Another* job?"

"Yeah, *another* job. Get *a few* jobs. Bring in some dough, man. I got a lot of shows coming up this week. That will bring in some good money. I need you to stay busy working too. Every dollar you make comes to me, okay? I'll get us tons of groceries, pay the bills, get you cigarettes. All that."

"Okay. I think I can do dat."

"Yeah?"

"Yeah. I don't wanna get all, like . . . bitch made on you and shit . . . but, like . . ."

Bennett was having trouble articulating his thoughts. He was biting his lips and trying to find the right words to say.

"I dunno, my nigga, I jus', like . . . I don't want you to think I'm just this, like . . . thug nigga. I wanna be like . . . a good nigga. Dat don't always get in trouble and shit. Like . . . I want you to see me and be like, 'Dat's my cousin Bennett. He'd never go to jail. He gonna start his own business mowin' lawns and shit. . . . He like . . . like a business . . . professional nigga . . . nigga."

Bennett had a burning desire to prove himself to me. It was endearing. Someone reforming themselves from a hard-core hoodlum to even a mere semi-hard-core hoodlum is quite impressive.

"You can do it, man."

"Aiight, mane. Fa sho. I'll try to find another job."

I don't know if I was just emotionally beaten to shit, but I really liked Bennett right then. He was acquiescing to a logical and beneficial arrangement. Even though I was lying and just wanted to be codependent on him and Lillian for a while, I was proud of his willingness to help out.

"Let's do it!"

"Gangsta shit, homie. We gon' get dis money."

Bennett pounded my fist with his, and that was that. That started it all.

For the next few weeks, Bennett busted his ass at Popeyes, sold weed and the rest of Harper's pills, and looked around for other jobs. For the next few weeks, I toured around America doing shows, sold instrumentals to aspiring rappers online, and attempted to mend my severely broken heart.

I hate being melodramatic, but I can genuinely say that the only things that made me smile throughout those days were Bennett's warped and accidentally brilliant text messages. Though I did have to sift through a lot of really stupid ones to get to the good ones.

ne no mo.
the girliest text messa
a female langauge i ble
inja star a :) is my sord
it wrks luv me they b
ersent fluant langauge
a i say kk and they bo
rushin spy wit. speak ju
z B gittin wit other bit
soft and sweet 2 eac
bennett. i know wat wa
d Dats fabulus And Kk a
they think im sinstive
hear dat song dat g

da sandwitch theary is simpel.. when u talk 2 a girl sandwitch sumthin kinda rude in batween 2 complimates

dont flat out diss da bitch.. but say sumthin nice, den a kinda playfull insult,, den sumthin nice agin.. be like

wow u r very pretty

i think u cud put on sum cuter shoez next time ur arnd gr8niss like me but watever

i luv ur outfit

u can make up ur own... jus make sure its a sandwitch.. she will like da complimlts an wanna proove herself 2 u afta da disses

Smoking DMT with Tom Waits

BENNETT: how tour goin

ME: Good, man, had a nice crowd tonight.

BENNETT: wat city R u in rt now?

ME: Boston.

BENNETT: ah.fucc boston nigga fucc da red sox

ME: Huh?

ME: Why do you dislike the Boston Red Sox?

BENNETT: U ack like u Dont no wat gang i reprazent ? Ea$t Side Avalon Crip gang homie i bang da Blue flag fucc da bitch ass Red sox

ME: Let me get this straight, you dislike the Boston Red Sox because "Red" is in their name?

BENNETT: well thnk abt it gang bangen is a unaversal thang playa im sure Dat back in da sival war days wen baseball startid their was bloodz an cripz

BENNETT: dats my point.niggaz been part of da gang war for hundrids of decades

ME:] Wow. You sound very high. How often do you get high? Why are you awake?

BENNETT:] shit it depend on how much scrilla i got.. a nigga cant sleep cuz im going thru weed withdralls !

ME:] Do you need money to buy some weed?

BENNETT:] nah im gud. today i knocced on an old ladys door and told her i was a jahovas witnesses and needed 20$ for jesus

ME:] I'm in tears.

ME:] Hahahaha!!!!

ME:] Did she give it to you? That's horrible, I shouldn't laugh.

BENNETT:] na she said i cud help her around da house doe

BENNETT:] so i got a new job its pretty coo

ME:] Oh yeah? Doing what?

BENNETT:] taken care of da old ladys house

BENNETT:] Yo !! she keep her teith in a glass itz so nasty

ME:] Really? You work for the old lady who thinks you're a Jehovah's Witness?

BENNETT:] ya

ME:] Wow. I'm suddenly scared.

BENNETT:] nah she my homegirl we jus chill all day

BENNETT:] i make her lunch and kicc it at her crib and help her

BENNETT:] we wuz lisanin to 2PAC today an she cudnt even hear it she just sat their sleepin wit her mouth open

BENNETT:] wanna buy sum vicadin ? she also got sum shit called blood thiner

ME:] Dude, don't you DARE sell her medication. You're kidding right?

BENNETT:] naa she coo man she dont even ramember my name she always like hello son want a buttar scotch

BENNETT:] she talk about dis nigga Rudy she went to prom wit all dam day sayin Rudy gnna cum git her for prom

[BENNETT:] im like relax girl Rudy aint cummen its yung Bennett eat your salid

[BENNETT:] she was born in 1742

[ME:] What's her name?

[BENNETT:] uhhhh

[BENNETT:] valdessa.i just call her V

[ME:] How old is she?

[BENNETT:] 81

[ME:] Ha. Ok. Does she have family?

[BENNETT:] ya her son... . dis fat nigga name steve

[BENNETT:] he bug me . he cum to her house evaryday sayen shit .

[BENNETT:] he always like Benjimin do da dishes and landry . 1st off my nigga da name aint benjimin its Bennett aka Money Baggz Bennett

[BENNETT:] 2nd i cant even do no landry ! i dont no how

[BENNETT:] So i gatta hide her dirty cloths under her bed

[ME:] What if she runs out of clothes because you put them all under her bed?

[BENNETT:] ill quit

[BENNETT:] or tell steve mexicins did it

[BENNETT:] I hate him.but its coo wen steve aint their i party with her

[BENNETT:] 2day i put shadez on her and a bandanna and made heR say funny shit

[ME:] Don't be cruel. Lol. I can't believe I'm laughing.

[ME:] Seriously, don't be cruel.

[BENNETT:] she was laffin 2 i swear .

[BENNETT:] she thinxs it fun to kicc it wit me

[BENNETT:] nigga ladys of all type luv me old new black wite im so charmming

[BENNETT:] we jus party da hole time

BENNETT: 2day i wuz makin her say shit like

BENNETT: brake yoself U bitch ass nigga !

BENNETT: and

BENNETT: east side ridaz !

BENNETT: i tryed to make her throw up the east side E with her hand but she said she cudnt bcuz of a painfull diseez in her hand called art ritus

ME: Arthritis?

BENNETT: ya wat is dat?

BENNETT: i was saprised to lern dat their r diseezes dat pravint u from throwin up gang signs . sciense is fuccd up

Grilled Pineapple

ME: When do you get paid next? I need to pay the electric bill asap.

BENNETT: i gat sum cash in da basment at home U can grab it if U need it im gng out with my nigga Leshaun afta wrk

ME: It's all good. Can you give it to me by tomorrow morning?

BENNETT: fa sho

BENNETT: were u at u shud cum get high wit us

ME: Ha, you go ahead. I don't really like smoking weed, sir.

BENNETT: why

ME: It honestly makes me kind of paranoid. Smoking pot makes life feel fragile for me.

ME: I have stuff going on in my life right now and getting high would make it a lot worse.

BENNETT: U sound like a lil girl scout who didnt git a pony for her birth day.!

BENNETT: man smoken weed make evarythin better.its like medasin for Ur mind..

BENNETT: Gorge Washingten smokd weed evary day , da Whitehouse has a speshil room Jus 4 smoken da lovly herb

BENNETT: plus da constatushan was wrote on hemp paper

ME: So that's where the George Washington pot-smoking tall tale is these days? Haha, it's evolved over the years.

BENNETT: it's a conspieresy negro

BENNETT: how cum weed is allegal?

ME: Honestly? I don't know.

BENNETT: da problem is dat all da polaticains dat made weed allegal are all in2 god an shit. but god made weed.

BENNETT: why da goverment cockblockin my nigga God? he want us to hav weed let us smoke!

BENNETT: i bet if i smoke at church God will give me miracels

BENNETT: 4 real imma go 2 church an smoke in da back of da sanctiary den try to walk a cross a pool an see if i can walk on water dat wud be da shit

ME: You do that.

ME: In the meantime, I have a date.

BENNETT: U gat a date ? is she dope?

ME: She's ok. Kinda boring and clingy. Luckily, I'm in Seattle, so it won't really matter.

BENNETT: duz she got nice tittys

ME: I don't know. Or care. I give up.

ME: I think I'm gonna just get married. I've realized all women are pretty much the same.

BENNETT: U jus now realizen dis? havent i ever tolld u da ass theary?

ME: No, what is the ass theory?

BENNETT: no matta how perfict and nice an ass looks. poop comes out of it evary day. jus like bitches. no matta how pretty a bitch is she still annoyeng as FUK.

ME: Ha. That's kinda true.

BENNETT: dam rt its tru dats why im da super bowl champien of gittin pussy i got 10 trofys

[ME:] Who would've guessed that you would have an accurate philosophy on something?

[BENNETT:] i got billans of dem hommie.i have a 11 commandmints list for bitchez dats commandmint 5

[BENNETT:] i no ur older den me but im gnna tell U dem n e wayz mayby dey cud help U

[BENNETT:] let me tell dem 2 u

[BENNETT:] k ?

[ME:] You have an 11 commandments list? Like... one you wrote?

[BENNETT:] ya

[ME:] And the list is about pulling girls?

[BENNETT:] ya i spent all sophmor yr mastering how to git chiccs. Let me give u my list..it will help Ur broken heartd ass

This seemed far from plausible and close to bizarre. Bennett can't even spell the word commandments. Literally. How could he have an eleven commandments list for getting women? Seemed hokey.

[ME:] Okay, give me ONE. Not two, not ten. ONE. Let me read one.

[BENNETT:] witch 1 ?

[ME:] Uh... lol... pick one?

[BENNETT:] hear cums

[BENNETT:] 5. Thou shalt alweys take a shit before goin out

[ME:] What?

[BENNETT:] have u ever weighted urself b4 u took a poop

[BENNETT:] poopd.den weighted urself after da poop ?

[ME:] Have I ever stood on a scale and weighed myself before taking a shit, took the shit, then weighed myself after taking that same shit?

[BENNETT:] yes

ME: Haha. Actually, yes. I have.

BENNETT: an u didnt weight as much huh?

ME: Lol. Nope. I weighed 187 before and 186 after. It was astounding.

BENNETT: K peep dis

BENNETT: b4 u took dat shit, da scale SAID U weighted more, but dat actuly wasnt tru. 187 wasnt da real U. 186 was..

BENNETT: Da real U weighted less U just had 2 get sum shit out first

BENNETT: da scale made u sumthin u wernt

ME: Ok.

BENNETT: c

BENNETT: ..u neva go out when u need to take a shit.u wont feel comfterble... rt?

ME: I guess, but what does needing to poop have to do with meeting women?

BENNETT: always poop b4 u go meet bitches.

BENNETT: bitches like thangs lite.doods who act all heavy freek a girl out

BENNETT: if u meet a bitch when u got a bunch of shit inside U dat U need to git out she gunna think ur sumthin dat u arnt.

BENNETT: if U all sad about ur life and have hella shit inside dat needs to cum out U r gnna gross a girl out.Ur gunna feel too heavy and end up shittin ur pants At da house party when u shud be pimpen her

ME: But what if my shit doesn't smell that bad? I find women like talking about my problems with me. It makes me feel good too.

BENNETT: nigga ALL shit smell bad

BENNETT: U may feel gud when U poop but a girl dont .

BENNETT: no 1 is botherd by the smell of there own shit

BENNETT: dat duznt mean Ur shit smells gud

BENNETT: Jus like ur problams.u cud sit their and talk abot ur own problams all day but dats rude and will gross ppl out

ME: Haha. I get it. I'm following you. Wait though. What does the scale have to do with it?

BENNETT: its a figeur of speech

BENNETT: jus look incide urself an make sure U got a gud attatuid b4 u leave da house

BENNETT: if u feel like ur full of sad problams and sadness. shit it all out. vent... call a friend,,,, leve it all bahind

BENNETT: take a poop first.go out with a empty butt so bitches meet da real U

BENNETT: an neva take a shit in front of a girl u wanna fuk

BENNETT: dats obvias

Calliope

BENNETT: r u comein home today

ME: Yep, I'm sitting down on the plane right now.

BENNETT: coo how was da showz

ME: Great, actually. All of them had good crowds.

BENNETT: coo

ME: Is the thing with the older lady still working out?

BENNETT: na

BENNETT: na she is bein moved 2 a nursing home by her son

ME: That sucks. That was fast.

BENNETT: ya her son is a fucccin h8r.got mad at me for jaccin Ambien.but V said i cud have it!

ME: No comment. Okay. What about other job prospects?

BENNETT: im tryen but popeyez is so wak man

BENNETT: i dont no how much longer im gng 2 have dis job

BENNETT: hello u their

ME: Yes, sorry. Was putting my bag in the top compartment thing.

ME: Wait... Why?

BENNETT: my boss Ned is fukin tripen

ME: Why? What's the matter?

BENNETT: i told him dat i must have a set scedule bcuz im tryen 2 find a Xtra job but he keep sceduling me 2 wrk on dayz i need off

BENNETT: i am sapposed to have a 2nd interview diss week at dat grocary store Hyvee but i also gatta work now

BENNETT: it like he tryen to keep me from haven another job

BENNETT: im sorry cuz im tryin man

BENNETT: but he such a assfuk.nigga

BENNETT: its rlly strssn me out

Over the plane's loudspeaker, a bubbly flight attendant said, "Folks, I'm going to need you to stow all portable electronic devices in just a couple of moments!"

BENNETT: man im tryen so hard to help out i dont wanna let u down. it really sux dat i have such bad lucc

But my cousin was sending me incessant text messages. I could barely stop my phone from vibrating long enough to respond to him.

BENNETT: da mthafcca toll me it was coo if i did it too.den he snaked me like a scandilis bitch

I had only a few minutes but wanted to calm him down, so I decided to call him . . . which I'd later find out was a horrible decision.

"Hello?"

"Hey, my plane is departing in like two minutes, I have only a couple seconds."

"Yeah."

"Your boss is a dick. You really told him you needed the day off for a job interview?"

"Yeah! And he goes 'Well, it looks like you'll have to reschedule the job interview. I need you on milk shakes and beverages.'"

"Geez. He said that?"

"Yeah, man! This the second time he done this shit! And I know I can get this job—but I *gots* to be at this fuckin' second interview."

"Hmm . . ."

"What should I do? I'm not bullshittin'. I want to work. You know I ain't tryin' to piss you off."

"I know you aren't, man. It sounds like you need to hit him with an ultimatum. That usually works. It will probably make him respect you more."

"A what?"

"An ultimatum. Sorry, the plane's loud."

I had an aisle seat on the plane, but unfortunately, the two people next to me were both staring at me, visibly perturbed by the volume of my talking. Not to mention the fact that Bennett was talking so loud, people within the five to six rows of seats that surrounded me could probably hear him.

"How the fuck I do that?"

"Just go down to the job. Pull him aside, and do it. Make sure you say 'I need a set schedule, or I need to quit.' It should work."

"Hahaha. Nah, Cuz, that's dumb. That's gonna get me fired."

"If you get fired for it, at least you had dignity and acted like a man. I won't be mad at you. If anything, you switch to the job at Hy-Vee now."

"Really? Mothafuckas do shit like that?"

"Well, yeah. Of course they do! It's the best way to make someone take you seriously. It's a classic, customary thing to do when someone is fucking with you and needs to stop."

"That's funny. I just hope I don't get fired for it. I need this job, my nigga."

"I doubt he will fire you over it."

"You really think I should do this? I can't believe I never heard about this before."

"You're still young, man. Still learning how to take charge."

"Sounds like it could get pretty messy."

"What do you mean?"

"Just runnin' up in there and blastin' him like that."

"Nah, it won't. Just be direct and stern. If putting him on blast hurts him, he's a huge pussy."

"Haha, true, there's no way it would hurt him, right?"

"I'd hope not. He's the manager, his skin should be pretty thick."

"Pssssttt. Damn. Okay, fuck it. I'mma try it. If you say it's a custom and shit. You the successfullest nigga in da family, so you prolly right."

"Like I said. If it doesn't work, for whatever reason, then you don't want that job anyway. Luckily, my merchandise has been picking up online lately. So if you need to switch jobs, or lose the job, it's fine. I can handle things right now. Just *try not to*."

"No, no, no. I want to have both. I don't mind workin', G."

"Well, yeah, because you just sit there and text girls all day."

"Whatever, nigga, I get paid, that's all that matters. *Hahaha!*"

"Okay, I gotta go, Bennett. Be home in three, four hours."

"Bet. Peace!"

"Bye. Remember, direct and stern. Lay it the fuck on him. Be respectful, but don't be afraid to man up."

I turned off the phone and put it in the storage fold attached to the seat directly in front of me. A baby boy was looking back at me through the seats, so I put my hands over my face, waited for a second, then split them, making a funny face. He just stared at me.

What a dickhead. Babies have no grasp of social contract. If he did it to me, I'd go "Hahaha!" even if he was an ugly little cuss. It's polite. But nooo, he's a little baby who thinks he has carte blanche, so he gets to make me feel like a jerk.

The flight attendant came by after we were airborne and gave me some chocolate chip cookies. She had sunken eyes and a tired face, her hair tangled and pulled back in a sloppy cinnamon bun of brown and golden hair. But beneath it all, she was pretty cute. She was obviously just uninterested in using her looks to impress the day-to-day cunts she deals with thirty thousand feet in the air, I thought as I dozed off.

I woke up two hours into the flight, the same flight attendant hovering over me. I was sweaty and thirsty. She asked me if I wanted some water, and I nodded my head. Once she returned with the tiny plastic cup of water, I drank it down.

"Wow, you're thirsty, mister!" she said, pushing the artificial enthusiasm a half notch too high.

For some reason, when you're a single guy, and your confidence isn't 100 percent, you think every simple, platonic interaction with a woman might end up with you having sex with her. It's just the way it works. Women should probably never smile at guys, and they should *definitely* never compliment them. Even if it's in regards to how much water they just drank in a short span of time.

"Want some more water, honey?"

Ohhh, she called me honey! The next step is sex in the lavatory.

"Please . . ." I said, slurping in a deep breath.

She walked back to the plane's galley and returned a few seconds later with a tall bottle of water and refilled my cup.

"Here ya go, baby. Drink up."

"Thank you, baby," I said, taking a sip of my water.

She smiled and watched me chug the second cup in a row.

Time to go in for the kill!

"So, what do you usually do when you land?" I asked.

"Huh? When I land?" she said, smiling but with a confused look on her face.

"Yeah, like. When the plane lands. What happens for the rest of the night?"

"Uhhh. This plane will go through inspection and tune-ups, then we start the route again in the morning."

Trying to hit on women was always difficult for me. It's not that I lacked the confidence to walk up to a girl and talk to her. Hell, I'd walk up to the hottest girl in the entire world. That didn't scare me. The problem was that the things I said to women never seemed to interest them. I always hoped being a creative conversationalist would win me points, but it didn't. Mostly it seemed to creep them out.

Morons get women, and I never learned how to be a moron. I didn't know how to make small, mindless talk to attract a female. Asking things like, "Do you like the movie *Amélie*?" or "If you could be reborn as a historical figure, who would it be?" at a loud club, full of drunk people, is a horrible idea. Therefore, I was always doomed with delivering awkward conversations. A girl would seem luke-warm to the idea of dating me as it was, so I'd put nails in the cof-fin with my way of approaching them. Unfortunately, I was always delusional enough to think the girl I was trying to hit on would be one of the special ones and dig the way I conversed.

Thus I scored a few hot, intelligent girls in my day with those types of conversations. But the slew of women I had to be rejected by in order to meet them was huge.

"No, I mean you. What do you do when you land? Are you stay-ing in Kansas City? Do you go out at all?"

"Um, yeah, I'm staying in Kansas City. Um . . . yeah, actually, sometimes I go out."

"That's cool. Well, hey, do you want to maybe get together or something tonight? We could drive out to the country where there isn't any light pollution and lay on the hood of my car, trying to find constellations."

Bam. I did it. I asked her out. There was an amplified rush through my body. But, of course, the guy in the seat next to mine, who had three empty bottles of Absolut Citron on his tray, interrupted our conversation.

"Haha, the country? Why, so you can *kidnap her and kill her*? Hahahaha! Can you say . . . *creepy*?'" he said, loud enough for everyone within five rows of us to hear.

"Hahahaha, no joke. Sorry, bud, maybe ask her for a drink next time? Something normal?" a guy in a Tampa Bay Buccaneers hat said from diagonally behind me.

"Hahaha!" Four or five other random people started laughing.

Time froze. I analyzed this highly embarrassing situation and came to the conclusion that there were only two possible outcomes. She would either think I was being sweet and accept, telling the hecklers to fuck off. Or she would laugh at me with them, which would make her look like a huge bitch. And no girl ever wants to look like a huge bitch. Time unfroze.

C'mon, honey. Door one or door two? Look like an angel or look like a bitch? Which will it be? You got two choices here.

Oh. She went for door number three. She didn't acknowledge me at all. She didn't acknowledge the hecklers. She didn't laugh. Didn't smile. Didn't anything. She walked away, fastidiously tending to each passenger—helping them adjust their seats, grabbing their garbage, passing them blankets.

I surmised that she thought I was joking. Who would do something like that? Now it was war. Now it was time to get an answer. Yeah, I didn't really know her. No, we didn't have a moment or anything. But I wanted a date. I waited a few minutes until she came back by. She was walking fast, but I put my hand out to slow her down and she looked down at me with an expressionless face.

"Hey, maybe we could get a drink? I'm thirsty as you've seen. Haha," I said.

"What?" she said. Leaning in, opening her eyes wider to focus on me clearly, "A drink?"

"Yeah, a drink."

She nodded her head.

"Okay, honey. I think I can do that," she said.

Oh, shit! It worked!

"Hell yeah, bro. She's going to write the digits down. Nice work!" said Tampa Bay, leaning forward to give me a fist dap.

"Hell yeah!" I mouthed to him, nodding my head. He nodded back.

"I'm impressed, I'm impressed," said the drunk guy next to me.

I smiled and stared forward. I was elated. I just pulled a flight attendant's number out of thin air!

When Captain Christian Van Matre's slow, lilting voice gave us the descent speech over the loudspeaker, I adjusted my seat forward. I looked outside the window at the Kansan farmland and rural, grassy sprawl that surrounds the Kansas City International Airport. I yawned. The flight attendant approached from behind, leaning over every few seats, to tell people what everyone knows: belts need to be buckled and seatbacks put forward.

I intentionally kept the tray attached to the seat in front of me extended down. There was an anxious knot in my gut. I was imagining what her name was. What her handwriting would look like. If she wrote a heart on the napkin, giving me a sign that she thought I was cute. I stared forward so it didn't look like I was desperately waiting for her to give me the number. I wanted to appear patient and aloof. I'd raise my eyebrows when she put the number on my tray and act like I half-forgot about it. I'd say, "Oh, cool. Yeah, I'll give you a buzz after I make a few business calls." She'd wait in her hotel room for hours, hoping I'd call. I'd take my sweet-ass time and call *right* when she gave up hope and started feeling unwanted.

::Thunk::

Thunk. That was the noise a water bottle makes when set on a tray. Not the noise of a napkin with handwriting on it.

I looked down at the bottle's odd shape. It was lightly wobbling on the tray, finding its balance. I stared at it for a second, then looked up to see if she was still there. She had already advanced a dozen rows forward and was not looking back at me at all.

Was there a phone number on this? I picked it up and studied it, looking at the label, top, and bottom. Nope.

I felt like a failure of catastrophic proportions. Guys behind me were giggling and the one even shook my seat a little.

In desparation, I opened the bottle and guzzled from it before yelling, "Thanks! I was super thirsty." When I saw that the flight attendant was definitely out of hearing range, I said, "Call you tonight, Lindsey!"

No idea what her real name was.

While the plane was slowly deboarding, I turned my phone back on. It began to vibrate uncontrollably. Bennett was going apeshit in my text messages . . . again.

[BENNETT:] fucc !

[BENNETT:] why u tell me to do dat man wat da fucc

[BENNETT:] yo

[BENNETT:] i got fuccin fired !!

(BENNETT:) plz hit me up wen u land

(BENNETT:) dammit fuccccc

I was holding a heavy bag of luggage, so I could text him with only one free hand.

(ME:) Hello?

(BENNETT:) ay

(ME:) Yeah what's up? What happened?

(BENNETT:) i got fired !!

(ME:) What do you mean? Why?

(BENNETT:) man i dont even no wat i did wrong but i made dat mothafucca mad as fuk.he almos calld da cops on me Cuz!

(ME:) Wait wait wait... what?

(BENNETT:) he startid cussin at me an shit.Sayin he gonna call da Po Po on me if i dont get da fuk off of da proparty

(ME:) Dude, what did you do?

(BENNETT:) i did wat u told me 2 do !

(BENNETT:) i went up to Ned

(BENNETT:) i said we need 2 talk

(BENNETT:) he said talk rt here im busy

(BENNETT:) so i told my homie manny who wrk n da kitchin to move out da way

(BENNETT:) i said to Ned cant keep da job If u dont let me go to my inteview i will hav 2 quit if u dont let me

(BENNETT:) he said Bennett we talk about dis alredy

(BENNETT:) so then like a asshole he stop payin attn to me

(BENNETT:) so i reach in da bag and grab da tomato

(BENNETT:) an i said Ned u need 2 respect me plz dont take dis da rong way

(BENNETT:) and i threw da tomato at him hard as fuk

ME: WHAT????

BENNETT: and it xplod all over his bacc

BENNETT: it got on da counter

ME: WHY DIDddd

ME: Why did you do that!

BENNETT: it got on sheila da chik who do drive thru

BENNETT: huh

BENNETT: u told me 2!!!!!

ME: Why would you throw a tomato at him???!!!

BENNETT: see man ! u gnna act like u didnt tell me 2 do dat! u fuken ass hole i new it

BENNETT: U jus want a excus 2 kik me and my mom out huh ? u fuken assfuk

ME: DUDE, WHY DID YOU

ME: Throw a Toma

ME: Throw a tomato at him?

BENNETT: Nigga u told me to hit him wit a old tomato ! Dat was UR idea!!!

BENNETT: U Said it

BENNETT: ya an it wasnt even old i had 2 usE a new 1

ME: AN OLD TOMATO?

BENNETT: yea pussy u said it.go up in da kitchin and hit Ned wit a old tomato

ME: Bennett

ME: Bennett

BENNETT: ?

ME: Bennett

ME: I said ULTIMATUM

ME: NOT OLD TOMATO

ME: ULTIMATUM

BENNETT: ?

ME: Oh fuck

ME: An ultimatum is where you make someone decide between 2 choices!

ME: YOU HIT YOUR BOSS WITH A TOMATO?

BENNETT: Wat da fuk is dat

ME: Oh no

ME: Hello?

Terror Birds

I didn't hurry home. I didn't care about Bennett losing his job. I didn't care about paying the mortgage, or bills, or even keeping the house. I didn't care. For some reason, the flight attendant's apathy toward me depleted every ounce of confidence that I had left inside.

Everyone feels like an unwanted loser sometimes. It's the only way to have those other times where you feel like the high-exalted king of the universe. The flight attendant wasn't even that cute, I told myself. But that only made it worse because of the caste system in dating that states one is only as hot as the person they're fucking.

I drove home, stewing in despair, feeling hopeless and awful. When I pulled up to the house, there was a car in the driveway. Its engine was running, and its exhaust pipe was grumbling, spewing puffs of toxic smoke. It was a vomit-yellow station wagon, with wood-grain side paneling and a bumper sticker on the back that read, VOTE FOR DUKAKIS '88.

The front door of the house swung open, and Bennett bursted out behind it. He started to run to the station wagon but skidded in his tracks when he saw me pulling up into the driveway. I stopped my car parallel to the station wagon and rolled down my window.

"What up, Cuzzo!" he yelled, nodding his head at me.

"What are you doing, dude?" I replied. "You going somewhere?"

The driver side window manually rolled down in jerks and fits.

A head popped out of it. It was a teenage kid in a Kansas City Royals hat, with sunglasses on at 9:30 p.m. on a Sunday night.

"Man, ain't you a rapper, my nigga?" the unidentified kid said.

"Huh?" I said, having no idea who was talking to me.

"Rappers is s'posed to be ballin' heavy as fuck, nigga! You drivin' that bitch-ass Nissan Sentra—hahaha!" another unidentified kid, deeper in the car, said.

Great, a carful of teenage boys, all of them laughing at me and my car.

"I got other things to spend my money on, boys. Cars depreciate in value," I retorted, and activated the garage door opener.

"*Pussy* don't depreciate in value though, old man! And bitches love nice cars!" one of the boys yelled.

Okay, good point.

Bennett walked to the passenger side of my car and peeked his head in through the window. I could hear the station wagon doors open. Within a few seconds, three other boys were standing alongside him. One was his friend Leshaun, but the other two I'd never met before. I've known Leshaun since he was a little kid. He's Bennett's very animated, extremely loud best friend and the de facto leader of the gang. He's also a bona fide hoodlum.

I got out of my car and walked back to greet the crew. "What's up, dickhead?" I said to Leshaun, sticking my hand out. He shook it flimsily. Gangsters like Leshaun have a weird phobia when it comes to giving solid handshakes. Either that, or no one ever showed them how to properly shake hands, which was feasible. Leshaun's dad has been in prison since he was five months old.

I hadn't seen him in a couple of years. He was taller than me by three or four inches now, and burn marks, knife cuts, and homemade tattoos covered his exposed skin. He was honestly pretty intimidating. A bandana gently perched atop his head, positioned at a delicate angle, cleverly resembling a king's crown. Under it was a full head of straightened, chin-length hair, tightly pulled back in a ponytail. He had another bandana hanging from his rear left pocket (like any Crip would insist upon). Both of the bandanas were heavily starched and flawlessly ironed. He had on a very large white T-shirt, with an unbuttoned navy-blue Dickies shirt over it, also heavily starched and flawlessly ironed. Likewise his blue jeans.

In fact, all of them were dressed in various combinations of the blue bandana, button-up Dickies shirts, khaki pants, sunglasses, gold teeth, and earrings. Each had a slight variation to his outfit, but I had to hand it to them all. They certainly looked like four people you wouldn't want to run into in a dark alley.

A NOTE FOR MIDDLE-AGED WHITE WOMEN WALKING THE MAIN STREETS AT MIDNIGHT IN FEAR OF BEING ROBBED

What's the obsession with running into people in dark alleys? That's the universal location people use to attach a fearsome aura to someone. It's useless. Running into a terrifying person at a racquetball court doesn't make the person any less scary. And Bennett's friends looked like they'd scare every last overweight salesman, retired brain surgeon, and real estate investor asshole straight off the racquetball court. Even on Saturday afternoon during peak hours.

When Leshaun shifted the cigarette in his mouth, I noticed that he appeared to have seven to eight stitches in his eyebrow.

"Let me guess—you got into a huge gang fight and someone hit you with a brick?" I asked, pointing to his eye.

"Nah, nigga, that's racist!" he said, scrunching his face.

"That's racist?" I asked.

"Hell yeah, it is. I didn't fight nobody. I fell off a horse. I went horseback riding and hit my head. I'm offended as fuck!"

Everything was silent. You could hear the sleeping cicadas quietly buzzing in the bushes. I studied Leshaun's face. He looked me dead in the eyes and took a long drag from his cigarette. His face was starting to appear weathered and aged. He wasn't the young boy he used to be. Life had gone a few rounds with him and effectively worked its jab.

"Are you lying?" I said, raising an eyebrow.

"Nah, bitch!" Leshaun punched me in the arm.

"Leshaun, chill, nigga! Chill!" One of the guys behind him grabbed his arm.

Everyone's face was filthy with panic.

"*Baaaaaahaha!* Aiight, yeah . . . I'm lying! Haha, you was all scared! I thought y'all was s'posed to be gangstas! Haha!" he said.

"Uh. So what did happen to your eye?" I asked.

"I got in a fight. Duh, nigga. I scrapped with a security guard. C'mon, Mac, black people don't ride horses—ain't you see what happened to Superman? That nigga fell off a horse and became a quadrapleznic! Nigga had to dookie in a bag for da rest of his life, and he never got no pussy again, just so he could say some gay shit like, 'Giddy up, horsie!' *Hahahaha!*"

Leshaun had the habit of cracking himself up.

"Ay, cuz. What the fuck is a quadrapleznic? Stupid ass nigga. Don't you know it's called a paralegal? Superman couldn't walk 'cause he was a paralegal. At least get the name right, dummy," said a short, half-white, half-Latino-looking kid with slicked-back hair and a giant spider tattooed on his neck.

Leshaun looked back at him, mouth half-open, eyes squinting into space, deeply ruminating, processing the new information he was given.

What anticipation led me to believe would be Leshaun's witty retort simply came out as: "Aw, shit. It *is* paralegal, huh? My bad. Damn."

I took a glance around the neighborhood, hoping nobody heard this ridiculous conversation. Nothing is worse than someone who is wrong, being corrected by someone else who is wrong, and just conceding.

> **Person A: Babies come from a woman's nostril.**
> **Person B: No, babies come from a woman's butt hole.**
> **Person A: Oh yeah. You're right. Touché.**

"This playa here is Kino," Leshaun said, pointing to the kid with the spider tattoo. "And this fat mothafucka is Bolo," he said, pointing to a chubby black kid, no older than sixteen, who promptly gave me a closefisted pound.

Leshaun leaned against the hood of the station wagon, with his pants sagging off his waist, blowing big clouds of menthol smoke into the sky. There was a tracking device of some sort wrapped around his ankle. I didn't ask. I'm sure he was breaking the law.

"What are you guys doing tonight?" I asked.

Leshaun whispered into Bennett's ear. Bennett shook his head in declination and looked at my shoes.

"Nothin' much," Bennett said.

"What's up? Why did you shake your head no?" I said.

"Come on!" Leshaun said, looking at my cousin. "Just ask him, Bino!"

"Ask me what?"

Bennett shrugged his shoulders. Leshaun looked at me, then Bennett, then me, then Bennett. "Man, fine. I'll ask him. Buncha pussy-ass mothafuckas. Daaayumn!" he finally snapped.

"Ask me what?" I repeated.

Bennett reached into the hatchback of the station wagon and pulled out what appeared to be a silver beer keg shell.

"Is that a keg?" I asked.

"Yup," Leshaun answered. "We dressed up like cops and confiscated it from a high school party down the street."

I began laughing uncontrollably. "You what?" I said.

"Yeah, we put on cop costumes and rolled up into a house party. Them white kids was so scared and cryin' and shit. We said, 'Give us the keg of beer and we won't tell yo mothafuckin' parents.' And they did."

"Yeah, but fat fuck over there got the wrong keg. This one is fuckin' empty!" Bennett said, pointing to the Mexican kid.

I started laughing even harder.

Picking up on this, Leshaun pressed on. "Yeah, nigga. I'm Officer Spicoli. I'm named after that white nigga Sean Penn in *Fast Times at Ridgemont High*."

I started laughing harder than I had ever laughed in my life.

"Yo, Mac, so will you buy us beer? We tryn' to kick it tonight for real. This lil' buster got fired, so we goin' in tonight!" Leshaun said. "We gonna celebrate his first morning off in weeks. We just don't got beer 'cause our heist got all fucked up."

Ahh, the good ole days of finding adults to buy you beer. It took me back . . .

A NOTE FOR UNDERAGE DRINKERS

When my friends and I were in our teens, we would sit in our cars in the grocery store parking lot, asking people to buy us beer. Most would say no—but one in every four or five people would end up saying yes. Usually Mexicans were the best choice. The theory was: they didn't know we were underage. Apparently they just thought we needed them to grab the beer for us because we were lazy and didn't want to get out of the car and physically go into the store. Which was fine with them. Mexicans are better people than Americans are.

"Hmmm. Where would you guys drink this at?" I asked.

"We just gonna go up to the park," said Bennett. "We ain't gonna cause no trouble."

"At the park? Yes you are. You're going to get arrested like a bunch of idiots."

"Nigga, I'll beat a cop's ass," said Bennett.

"No, you *won't*," I said, quietly staring at the boys. I was tempted to just crawl into bed, sober and heartbroken, so I could go to sleep early and numb the current emotional trauma I was afflicted with through deep, depressed slumber. But, I also knew that hanging around friends, especially wild friends, who lack the ability to be polite, rational, or intelligent, even, could inspire an enthusiastically spirited version of me to emerge. And I needed that shit!

"You guys are drinking with me tonight," I proclaimed. "I should be intelligent and go to sleep, but the fact that you guys dressed up like police just to get beer is fucking amazing. Plus, I hate all the yuppies in this school district. "

"The bitches was hot as fuck, nigga! I tried to holla at some blond cutie but she was all scurred of me and shit," Leshaun said.

"My only question is . . . did they not notice you were in a station wagon?" I asked.

"Nope," the boys all answered in unison.

"Okay, well let's get fucked up," I said, excitedly.

"Damn, Mac is gonna buy us beer *and* parlay! It's about time your old ass got fucked up with us!" Leshaun said.

I really wasn't thinking this out. I was tired and had no desire to party with these guys. But for some reason, in that particular span of four seconds, while my whims were throbbing and I was ignoring my need for sleep and relaxation, it sounded like something fun that could take my mind off things. Plus, you had to commend them. That shit is genius.

"What do you guys want? I'll shoot up to the store and get it," I said.

"Nah, just hop in, holmes," Kino said, opening the passenger-side door of the station wagon. "I'll drive."

I got into Kino's station wagon and the other four boys piled in the back. Kino turned the keys and backed out of my driveway, scraping his front bumper on the curb. The inside of the station wagon had a colorful stack of approximately fifty assorted air fresheners hanging off the automatic gearshift. There were Zig-Zag rolling papers, condom wrappers, beer cans, empty cigarette packages, and a picture of the Virgin Mary hanging off the rearview mirror.

We drove a few blocks away to Royal Liquor, one of the only places that stays open late on Sunday night. I grabbed us a couple thirty packs of beer and a liter of crappy vodka. The boys sat in the car arguing about which Hostess snack was gayer, Twinkies or Cup-Cakes, and on the way back home, the night took a very big turn.

"Ay, Mac!" Leshaun said from the backseat.

"Yo?" I replied.

"Can we have some bitches over to your crib tonight?" Leshaun asked.

"Yeah! Let's have bitches over!" Bennett said.

"Hell the fuck yeah!" Bolo said, slapping fives with Leshaun in the backseat.

"Come on, folk! Let us have some girls over!" Leshaun said.

"What girls?" I asked.

Bennett leaned his head over the seat. "Ever since Mercedes and me broke up, I got this new bitch," he said. "Her name is Krystal. But she goes by Pistol Krystal."

"Pistol Krystal?!?!" I gasped.

"Ay, dude! Tell Krystal to bring her boss. She Mac's age. That bitch finer than a mothafucka!" Leshaun said.

Now, as a man, when another man, in any capacity, says to you that a girl is good-looking, by default you ultimately think she is too. You start to envision all of these attractive characteristics about her. So when Leshaun said, "That bitch finer than a mothafucka!" with enthusiasm and umph in his voice, I started to imagine an extremely good-looking female—a picture-perfect one who would love me, be loyal to me, and have incredible sex with me. I instantly went from torn and ambivalent about the evening to optimistic and excited.

"So she's cute, Leshaun?" I said.

"Dude, I think she *bangin'*. She your age too. She their manager," Leshaun said.

"Yeah, she sexy," Bennett said, "She used to date one of them Chiefs players. They was together for a while and shit."

Damn. This girl used to date a Kansas City Chiefs player? Those guys are professional football players. They get the best-looking women in the world. Could it be? Are my ignoramus cousin and his friends about to connect me with my first rebound from Harper?

"Look," Bennett said, pulling his phone from his front pocket. "Krystal just texted me saying, 'What are you doin' tonight?'" Bennett declared.

"Ask if she's with her boss," I said.

"She is. They all just got off work and wanna kick it," Bennett said.

Instantly my adrenaline levels spiked through the ceiling. I had a tight knot in my stomach. I couldn't wait to meet this chick.

"Okay, give them directions. But let me make sure I like her manager before you try to hook me up!" I said. "Just tell her I'm single and wanna mingle."

"Shut up, you old R-and-B-ass homo. Mothafucka said, 'I'm single and wanna mingle.' Fool you sound like a chubby secretary bitch drinkin' a tiramisu martini at Applebee's," Leshaun said.

"Okay, I want to have sex. How's that?"

"Better. Bennett, get it done," Leshaun replied.

Bennett called and relayed the plan, and like that three girls were coming over. Two were teenagers, one was my age. This was fun. My spirit was thriving. There was so much mystery and so many good vibes in the air. I felt young again. We were going to have girls over, drink alcohol, and party.

We got to the house and went outside to my back patio to avoid bothering Lillian, who was asleep on the couch. I grabbed everyone a beer and tossed it to them. The night air was humid. Lightning bugs blinked and flew around. Moths smacked into the backyard's lamp.

"God, you guys get a lot of girls, huh?" I asked.

Leshaun and Bennett both nodded. "Yeah, it's all we do for real," Leshaun said.

"I'm single now and can't even get a date," I said, half-laughing.

"How can't you get girls being related to this bitch-ass nigga?" Leshaun said, pointing to Bennett.

"What do you mean?" I said.

"Dude, this nigga is the fuckin' *king* of pullin' bitches," Leshaun screamed!

"Girls love this lil' dude, G. He get all type of girls. Eighteen-year-olds. Eighty-nine-year-old bitches. They all love him!" Kino said.

"He wrote a list of rules, man!" Leshaun said.

Leshaun reached over to Bennett and slapped him on the back of his neck.

"So I heard," I said. "It's honestly kinda shocking. A kid half my age has an entire list of rules on how to date women."

"Ain't he showed them to you?" Leshaun asked.

"No. Well, he showed me a tiny bit of them. I haven't had a chance to try them out," I said.

"Nigga, show your fuckin' heart-broke-ass cousin the list so he can stop mopin' around like a lil' bitch all the time!" Leshaun said and pounded his beer.

"So who's Pistol Krystal?" I asked, refocusing the subject away from me.

"She bad as fuck," Bennett said. "She work over there at Sonic."

"Wait, what? Sonic? This girl works at Sonic?" I said. Suddenly, I was worried.

"Yeah, man. She a waitress," Bennett said.

"No. Not Krystal. This other girl! You guys are setting me up with the manager of a Sonic?"

"Fuck is wrong with Sonic, nigga? Sonic got good-ass Coney dogs!" Leshaun said.

"Yeah. You racist against Sonic, mothafucka?" Bennett said.

Kino was so high that all he could come up with was, "Yeah! Sonic is . . . fuck . . . damn."

I didn't respond. For the next fifteen to twenty minutes, I sat there watching the boys pass around a grape Swisher Sweets Cigarillo stuffed to the edges with pot, while laughing and discussing highly informative topics like guns, writing to friends in jail, and robbing banks. Every one of the boys was covered finger to toe in homemade ghetto tattoos. None of them opened their eyes very much, and they all possessed a bitter, mean scowl on their faces. They were getting ready to try to impress the girls.

Bennett's flip phone rang. "Wassup?" he said, answering it. "Aiight, coo. Be right there."

From the backyard I could hear car doors slam and girls laughing in the front yard as Bennett got up and went into the house. The suspense was eating at me, but I took a few drinks and sat back, relaxing. This was *my* house. That had to count for something, right? Hopefully this girl wasn't hideous.

The back door opened. Bennett walked out first, holding his beer. Behind him were three ladies.

"Hey, y'all!" said the first one. "I'm Krystal."

"*Pistol Krystal!* What up, girl!" said Leshaun.

"Hey, boo, how are you!" said Krystal, kissing Leshaun on his cheek.

Krystal was about nineteen, tall, slender, and had dirty-blond hair. She had on a white T-shirt and black sweatpants, with flip-flops on her feet. Post-work attire. She was cute. Her face was innocent even through the dark eye shadow and glittery lipstick. She shook my hand and sat on Bennett's lap. I had no idea why her nickname was Pistol Krystal.

The next girl walked out and waved. She was holding a forty-ounce of St. Ides beer. She was a short Latina girl in overalls, with black hair pulled back in a bun. "I'm Angel," she announced to nobody, really.

Leshaun grabbed her hand and pulled her close to him to sit in the empty chair next to him. "What up, love, I'm Leshaun aka Loony." Leshaun made his hand into a letter C, yup, to signify that he was a Crip. He literally introduced himself to this girl with a gang sign. She smiled and seemed to enjoy it, for whatever reason.

And then there *she* was. Female number three: about five foot five, with curly blond hair, tightened close to her head by a headband. Her body was *stacked*. She was in jeans and a halter top. Her skin was buttery and tan. She smelled like lotion and a subtle spritz of citrusy perfume. "Hey, I'm Sabrina," she said.

She was way prettier than expected.

At first.

Cloistress

24

"Have a seat!" I said, pulling a chair out for her. I was so cynical about what I was going to end up thinking of her that my expectations seemed to sink to unnaturally low levels, which she effortlessly exceeded.

"Awww. Thanks, baby!" she said, leaning against me, thigh to thigh under the table. I tuned the rest of the guys out and looked at Sabrina. There was a sexual buzz already pulsing through us.

"Welcome to my house!"

"Thank you, boo! It's so pretty."

Every single person Bennett knew talked in a ghetto twang. Sabrina was no exception. She had cheap black eye shadow sluttily painted across her eyelids. She kept her lips tightly pursed and close together when she talked. As she introduced herself to the other guys, I detected a jagged front tooth that slightly slid over the other front tooth next to it. Her bottom jaw was a cemetery of crooked, chipped canines and curved, discolored incisors that zigzagged and intertwined like stalagmites growing from the bottom of a limestone cave.

All of which I discounted, because it's easy to disregard "physical flaws" when you are attracted—or *want* to be attracted—to someone. Which felt right at the time, I mean, not everyone's parents could get their children braces, right?

She put her hand on my thigh and leaned in close enough to have a quiet conversation. "You're the one and only Mac Lethal, huh?"

"Yes. Yes I am."

"That's so tight! I used to work with a kid who loved you so much. He used to always rap your lyrics to me."

"Oh, really? Ha. That's cool. What was his name?"

"His name is Byron."

"Cool, cool."

"I was his boss at Sonic. He wrote me a poem of your lyrics and pretended it was his one time! He used to have the biggest crush on me."

"He wrote you a poem? With my lyrics?"

"Yeah. But I knew he didn't write it, it was too good. So I was like, 'C'mon, dude, quit lyin', who wrote that shit?' And he was like 'You,'" she said, pointing to me.

"Ha—what were the words?"

"Huh? Oh . . . uh . . ." she said, nervously. Her eyes were darting around, focusing back and forth from the sky to the ground, "It was like, umm . . . 'Baby, you're my somethin' somethin'. My angel . . . uh . . . something. I wanna hit that booty all night long. Get money!' It was like . . . really sweet. If I heard it I'd know. It was one of your older songs."

I'd never written a single thing that sounded like that. She was actually, absolutely full of actual, absolute shit.

But . . .

I did not care. The instant attention and admiration she so generously provided me with was practically medicinal. She was a radiant sylph, inspiring my overlabored, underappreciated, and out-of-sick-days heart to put on its boots and head to work. At that point, it felt like anything about her that wasn't compatible with me (which was probably a lot), wouldn't even matter. I'd *make* it work.

"So, are you like, the next Eminem?"

"Everyone seems to ask that question. Haha. No, I'm the first *me*. The only thing we really have in common is that we're both white."

"That's cool, baby. Eminem is super sexy. Mmm. You have that in common too!"

"Thanks. I guess. The stuff we rap about is a lot different. I'm more cerebral."

"Oh, cool. So you do stuff for mentally slow people."

"Huh?"

"Cerebral palsy? You rap about that?"

"Ahh. No. I meant, my content is a little more . . . deep. I guess. Make sense?"

"Helly yeah—I love deep lyrics! Like that jam by Nelly and Kelly Rowland, 'Dilemma.' It's about how they wanna fuck but don't wanna date. That shit makes you think, you know?"

"Yeah. Yep. I know. I love thinking. Hehe."

I was on autopilot. I had zero judgments to pass. All I wanted was primal love and companionship. At this point, all I had to do was figure out how to introduce her to my family without getting weird looks, and I'd be set. Maybe I'd just move away with her instead.

"So did you buy this house with money from rappin'?"

"Yes. Sure did."

"Mmm. All you need is a down-ass bitch to cook you dinner."

"Cook? Wait! Can you cook? I love a woman who can cook."

Harper's cooking abilities were second to none. One of my biggest fears had become never being able to replace how it felt to have someone cook like that for me. Homemade lemon meringue pie on Sunday afternoons for no reason, Copper River salmon, home-broiled lobster tails, garlic-butter-slathered filet mignons, bouillabaisse. You name it.

Did I just find her replacement? Holy shit.

"Hell yeah. I cook every day."

"What's your number one recipe?"

"Prolly blue box macaroni 'n' cheese. I put hot dogs in it too. Makes it so dank!"

I had not tried Kraft Macaroni & Cheese with pieces of hot dog in it and wondered why Harper had never bothered to make it for me.

"Yum. Sounds great!"

Sabrina leaned forward and brushed the tip of her nose against my cheek. This girl had a serious bout of promiscuity circulating through her. And I needed female companionship of some sort. Validation. Ego-stroking. *Any* stroking. Sorry for being crass, but when her nose touched me, it was like an eyedropper of grain alcohol squeezed over a fresh exit wound. It caused my body to shrivel and sent a frighteningly orgasmic sensation through my body. She noticed.

"Awww, boo, it looks like we're a match! Mac, baby, what's your sign?"

"I'm a Leo."

"Ooo—I'm a Gemini. I'm a great communicator. We're a match. Our sex life is the best too."

Krystal stopped tonguing Bennett and looked over at us. "Awww. Are you guys gonna get married?" she said.

"It looks like I might have found the one!" Sabrina said, rubbing my thigh and smiling before pressing her lips to my neck and making airtight, compressed slurping noises.

I had no qualms with any of this. Broken logic is a side effect of a broken heart.

"So . . . you work at Sonic?" I said.

"Yeppers. I'm the manager. It sucks. But, I gotta raise mah kids! *Haha!*"

Ohh. She has kids. "Ohh. You have kids. Uh. How many kids do you have?"

"Six." She smiled.

"Haha. Oh, really?" I joked back.

Instead of telling me the real answer, Sabrina looked over the table at the other guys. "Hey, someone pass some herb over here! I'm trying to smoke!"

Bolo leaned across the table and gave her the burning cigarello. Taking it, she rocked back in the chair, putting her legs on top of mine. I had no idea why she was being so frisky with me, but I didn't care. She babysat the spliff for a few minutes and pulled out an unopened flask of gin from her purse. She broke the seal, twisted off the lid, and took an enormous swig from it. She offered it to me, but I declined with a wave.

"You smoke, baby?" she said, wrapping her lips around the blunt with sexual savagery.

"Um. Not really. I'm not really a big fan of getting high."

"Awwww, baby, get high with me!" She put the jay in my face.

God damn it. I hated getting high. I've smoked pot thousands of times, but it always ended up creating the same feeling for me. I'd smoke once and enjoy it a lot. Then I'd decide the missing piece in my life was regularly smoking weed. So I'd buy an ounce and some papers and go at it daily for a few weeks, and I'd be relaxed, sleep better, be all therapeutic.

Then, after accepting it as my favorite vice for a few weeks, it would change on me. I'd start becoming paranoid. Anxiety-ridden. Completely zapped of motivation. Lethargic. Everything became fragile. My judgment became that of a nine-year-old, and even though I was finding it challenging to connect thoughts, I'd become very analytical of people and things. When I was high, I thought everyone knew something about me that I didn't. I'd sit there in social situations, convinced that people thought I was a weirdo. It had been years since I smoked. This had disaster written all over it.

I took the cigarello from Sabrina and pulled a hit from it.

"Damn, my cousin Mac is smokin' that cheeba with them Avalon Crip gangstas tonight! *Hell yeah!*" Bennett said.

"Hit that shit again, baby!" yelled Leshaun.

Now everyone was looking at me. Now there was social pressure.

I took a *huge* hit from the blunt. The smoke burrowed deeply into my chest, sneaking into my capillaries. I felt it torching the cilia of my lung tissue. It was infernally hot. I instantly started coughing and felt compression in my face and throat.

"Oh, shit! Careful, dog! Weed is way better now than it used to be in the 1980s, homie!" Bolo said, very, *very* concerned.

I crouched down, violently hacking, over and over. A yellow mucus-filled loogie flew out of my chest tube, completely surpassing my mouth, and landed on the back of Sabrina's pant leg. Fortunately, she didn't even notice.

Once my body stopped freaking out about the smoke, I felt very light-headed and floaty. I was soooooooooo high. Fuck.

Bennett and Krystal were kissing. Leshaun and Angel were talking nose to nose. These girls wasted no time. Unrestricted, irresponsible, adolescent sexual energy is very discomforting when you're high. Kino and Bolo stood up and started slap-boxing in the grass. They were so fierce and agile. Combative, masculine strength—also very discomforting when you're high. What if someone gets hurt? But at the same time, I was enamored with their physical ability and graceful footwork. If I was sober, they would have looked like two teenage idiots slap-boxing. But right then, they were well-polished pugilists, employing the sweet science of boxing and human-chess trickery of Brazilian jujitsu.

No one ever depicts getting high correctly. In the movies, people always have visual hallucinations and imagine themselves possessing supernatural abilities (e.g., flying, shooting lasers from their eyeballs). This is very inaccurate. Weed just turns the volume up on every single facet of your life. If you were hungry, you're suddenly famished. Music is so good that it weakens you. Insecurities become full-on panic attacks. Things that are semifunny shatter the bounds of comedic genius. It can become mentally and emotionally messy if you don't take charge of it, aren't accustomed to it, or haven't smoked in years.

"There ya go, boo. Now you'll feel nice and relaxed," Sabrina said, interrupting my thoughts by putting her hand on my thigh. Her fingernails were cut short and had red polish chipping off them. They felt great. She rubbed my thigh and the back of my neck. I wanted to scream. The female touch was fantastic.

"You never told me how many kids you have," I said.

"Yeah I did, baby. Six."

"Six?"

"Six."

"Really?"

"Yep."

". . . Six? You *have six* kids?"

"She *does*," Krystal snapped, coming up for air from Bennett's mouth.

"Yeah, I know, it's a lot."

"Wow. Okay. . . . What are their names?" I said.

"Why you wanna know their names?"

"Just tell me. I don't believe you have six kids."

Sabrina sighed. Her face became very serious. She leaned forward and began. "Katia, G.G., Latrell, Misty, Denzel, and Lil' Nevaeh."

"I *love* the name Nevaeh," Krystal said.

"It's *heaven* spelled backwards," Sabrina explained.

"*Heaven* spelled backwards?" I asked.

"Yes, baby. My lil' Nene. She's my angel."

"And you named her after heaven?"

"Yeah?"

"And spelled it backwards?"

"Yeah?"

"Why didn't you just name her Heaven?" I asked. "Why spell it backwards?"

"I dunno," Sabrina said, shrugging. A woman with tremendously low self-esteem suddenly manifested herself within the look she was giving me.

The weed was engaging my brain on full blast. I was hyper-analyzing Sabrina. Who the fuck names her kid Nevaeh aka heaven spelled backwards?" Why not name her Unicorn, or even better, 432836, which spells out *H-E-A-V-E-N* on a phone's keypad. *What the super, ultimate, actual, absolute fuck?*

"How many kids do you really have?" I said, trying to have a very serious, stop-fucking-with-me tone in my voice.

"Okay, I'm lying, three."

"Oh, okay. Only three?"

"No, I have *six* kids."

"All with the same guy?"

Sabrina made a notable break in the eye contact she had been making with me the entire night and took another pull from the joint.

"Nah. Not with the same guy," Angel replied for her, which was the first thing she had said loud enough for everyone to hear since she got there. She had been showing pictures of her own child to Leshaun on her cell phone while he licked her neck.

Instantly, the feeling of Sabrina alleviating my desperation completely vanished. I started scratching the knuckles on my left hand, one of my ticks from childhood. Holy shit, these were *Bennett's* friends, not mine. Bennett, my troubled, gangbanger cousin who wasn't even old enough to buy cigarettes, had set me up with a girl who had *six* kids. And wait a second. . . .

"How old are you?" Now I was definitely interrogating Sabrina, not just being curious. "I never got your age."

She blew a huge puff of smoke and stood. "Come inside with me, I wanna show you something."

She grabbed my hand and led me behind her into the house, guiding me through the dark, main-level hallway, into the foyer where the stairs were.

Leading me upstairs and into the guest bedroom that Lillian was supposed to sleep in but where really she just kept her luggage, Sabrina fumbled around for the light switch. I heard the sound of the coffee mug I used to keep pens and pencils in tipping over.

"Where's a lamp, boo?" she said finally.

I reached over and turned on the light. She smiled at that and walked toward me. Grabbing the bottom seam of my shirt, she started to lift it over my head. I attempted to resist, not wanting anything to do with this woman, but when I felt her stubby-edged nails graze my ribs, my hormones kicked in—betrayal—and I helped her slide the shirt off me, exposing my full deepwater-themed sleeve tattoos on my arms and various other pieces of skin ink on my chest and ribs.

"*Wow!* Oh, baby, those are hot tats!"

"Ha. Thanks."

With the nails and the compliment, my ego was almost fully hydrated and my reservations about this girl had all but vanished.

Sabrina removed her shirt in a melodramatically seductive

manner, though even through my haze I could tell it was more absurd than anything else.

Standing there in her bra, she asked, "Do you think my tattoos are sexy, daddy?" and began rubbing my chest and kissing my neck. I kissed her on her bottom lip and had full intentions of doing whatever she wanted, but I was very high at that moment, so her question actually distracted me. I returned a few more kisses, and tilted my head inward so I could look at these tattoos of which she spoke. Before, her halter top had completely hidden her ink. But once she was topless, it was a much different story.

I stepped back and gently pushed her hands off me. I examined her upper body.

She had a faded, sloppily drawn hummingbird-type thing on her left hip.

Chinese lettering adorned her left breast. It probably stood for *peace* spelled backwards or something.

Next to her belly button, a pot leaf, which I was betting she did herself with a paper clip, a mirror, and some Indian ink.

All atrocious. There was no calculated aesthetic for how they were positioned. They looked like they were done by a guy behind a truck stop who traded such scars for meth.

"Do you like them?" she asked.

"Wait. What's the Chinese one mean?" I asked, to be polite and to dodge the question.

She bit her bottom lip and giggled a very harsh, nasally giggle. "I don't remember. I just thought it looked cool, so I picked it off the wall."

She tried to start kissing me again, but I dodged my head out of the way. To which she turned around and pressed her butt against me.

"Whoa!" I yelled. Her back—it was *covered*.

She had the word *Sabrina* on her upper back and across her shoulders, in horrible cursive letters.

She had very shitty angel wings, or butterfly wings, or whatever, covering the majority of her middle back.

Six different dates, undecipherable in terms of the actual numbers, ran down her side. Her kids' birthdays . . . I hoped.

And finally, last but not least, she had a *giant* heart on the small of her back, with a thick XXXXXXX^{x}X XXX inside of it, covering something else up.

"What does this heart mean?"

"Aw, baby, don't worry about that, lemme—" She tried to unbutton my jeans.

"Stop," I said, pushing her hand away. "Just explain it, I'm not going to make fun of you."

"I got it when I was young and dumb. Don't we all make mistakes? Now please—" She tried grabbing my package.

"Sabrina. *Stop.*"

"Oh Jesus. Okay. Fuck. Uh . . . Okay. It used to say 'Garrett's Ass.'"

"Garrett's Ass?"

"Yeah. It used to say 'Garrett's Ass.'"

"Why did it used to say 'Garrett's Ass'?"

"Because, this used to be Garrett's Ass."

"Who's Garrett?"

"Baby, you're ruinin' the mood. Come on, lemme please you—" She tried to unbutton my jeans again, I grabbed her arm and held it away from me.

"*Stop doing that,*" I commanded.

She let out a big sigh. "Who do you think Garrett is? One of the fathers."

"How old are you?"

"Thirty-eight. And you're thirty—so don't act like I'm all old and shit."

"No, no. I just thought you were younger. . . ."

All of a sudden Sabrina looked pretty old. Her face was leathery and aged. She smelled like fast food now. She was covered in mistakes, lowbrow disasters, and the words *Garrett's Ass*—no matter how badly she wished they were covered up.

"Come here, baby, lemme satisfy you."

"Why'd you cross Garrett's name out?"

"Because, he's not my daddy no more. But you. *You*. You could be if you want to!" she said, in a cloying baby voice. She started sucking my index finger and I yanked my hand away.

The thoughts occupying my mind at this point were as batshit as it comes. I was grossed out. I didn't feel like I was on a higher level of humanity than her necessarily, but her tattoos, her backstory, her ability to just produce random children with who knows how many different men, at such an irresponsible rate, really dipped my dynamite stick in rainwater. I was weak and would have given anything to have an even low-rent sexual encounter at that point, but I found myself literally fighting this girl off me.

As bad as I felt about projecting my disapproval and judgmental attitude on her, I needed a way to get the fuck out of there. I was desperate for an excuse that wouldn't hurt her but would still liberate me from the situation. A way to let her down easy. I decided to throw a Hail Mary.

Time to pretend that I'm megafamous.

"Put your shirt on, honey. I need to go do something," I said.

"What! Come on. Baby, please. Let me make your wildest dreams come true," she said.

"Sorry, not tonight."

"What did I do? Why you change all of the sudden?"

"Sabrina, my angel, we've had a moment here, and I feel like I want to marry you and have even *more* children with you. But to do that we shouldn't have sex right now. Let's fall in love, and I can meet your children! You're so beautiful. I feel like you complete me in a lot of ways."

"What? Really?"

"Yes, truly. Not sure if Bennett told you, but I have to be somewhere in about thirty minutes. Gotta hit the studio—recording with Eminem and Alicia Keys tonight. But give me your number, and we can get together."

"See?" She started grinning.

"What?"

"I knew somethin' was special about you! My mom the other day, she said, 'Sabs, why don't you find a rich rockstar and marry him?'"

"Sounds like your mom was right!" *I was definitely going to hell.*

"And you like kids? You promise not to whip them?"

"What? Of course! Write your number down; I gotta go!"

"Wait. You're gonna call me right? You promise?" she said.

"Yes, I'm falling for you," I replied, then added, "Boo."

"I'm falling for you too. I forgot to ask! How many rooms is this house? Can all the babies have a room?" she peeked out into the hallway.

"It's four bedrooms, but we'll figure something out. I'm in a hurry, honey."

"Well, wait. I think Nene should sleep with us. She wets the bed sometimes."

"No, Nene will sleep in her own room."

What the fuck! Why didn't I just agree? I'd never see this woman again in my life, but I was so high that I couldn't even agree to letting a child with bed-wetting tendencies sleep in the same bed as me in my *pretend* life. Apparently my stance on the subject only reinforced the genuineness of my proclamations, because Sabrina stood there staring at me in pure awe.

Creepy, creepy awe.

I grabbed her and kissed her passionately. It was the only thing I could think of to shut her the fuck up. I then left her standing in the guest bedroom and ran downstairs. I bolted outside to the back patio. Angel was straddling Leshaun, kissing him. Both of them looked back at me.

"Where did everyone go?" I said.

"Bennett and Krystal went downstairs. The other niggas left. You need a condom, cuz?"

"No," I said very definitively, and closed the door.

I heard Leshaun yell "Mac!" from outside. I opened the door back up and leaned out. "Yo?"

"Can I post up here tonight? I ain't got no ride."

"Yeah, yeah, whatever. Sleep upstairs in the guest bedroom."

"Aiight, thanks, cuz."

I stood there, with the screen door propped open in front of me, envisioning how not awesome it would be if I returned to the house later and Sabrina was still there plotting ways to renovate my home into a daycare. It was time to give Leshaun an assignment.

"Hey, Leshaun, make sure no one but *you* and *Bennett* stay here tonight. Okay? *No females.* Okay?"

"Aiight, I got you, playa. It'll just be me and him."

"Okay."

I slammed the door and ran back through the main level of the house. Sabrina was walking down the stairs and tried to touch me, but I juked out of the way, enacted a 360 spin, and yelled, "Gotta go!" She said something. I don't know what. For all I know she spelled the word *Czechoslovakia*. Who cares? I was going to drive up the street to the park and pass out in my car.

I grabbed my keys from the mail table and ran to the garage and pressed the garage door opener. Right before I opened the car door, right before I was to make my escape, right before I would be transported to find safety, I looked down my driveway to where the gutter marries the black asphalt . . . and saw the worst possible person who could've been standing there.

Mercedes.

"God damn it!" I whisper-yelled under my breath.

The Infamous Harry Houdini

25

SIZE *DOES* MATTER. That's what Mercedes's tank top read. She also wore baggy gray sweatpants and had a mess of hair that looked damp from a recent shower. She looked like she'd been harboring heartbreak for weeks and probably hadn't done much on a social level in just as long.

I would've pretended to not see her and attempted to just drive off, but I instantly worried about Mercedes beating up Pistol Krystal or something ratchet and ignorant. The last thing I needed was a girl brawl in my new house. I walked down to the edge of the driveway to see what she wanted.

"What do you want, Mercedes?" I said, walking up to where she leaned against her car.

"Damn. Nigga, you on the monthly bleedin' cycle or somethin'? I ain't here tryin' to start no shit," she said. "I'm a changed girl. I just wanted to bring this to Bennett."

She handed me a crusty stuffed brown bunny rabbit, all the while fighting back tears. The bunny had a tiny collar with a dark-blue pet identification tag attached to it.

It simply read HUSTLA.

"Is this the infamous Hustla Da Rabbit?" I asked.

"Yeah. I washed him in the washing machine. He smell good now and not all fonky like before. Please give it to him and tell him I'm sorry."

"Okay. I will." I turned back to my car.

"Wait, mothfucka, damn!" she yelled.

"Yes? What's up?" I said, facing her again.

She reached back through the open passenger-side window and pulled out another stuffed animal. "Will you give this to him too?"

She handed me a plush bumble bee.

"And this would be . . ."

"Queen Bee."

"Queen Bee?"

"Yeah. Queen Bee. The Queen Bitch."

"Okay, I'll give Bennett Hustla Da Rabbit and his friend Queen Bitch the Queen Bee."

"Ugh!" Mercedes gasped. Her pupils dilated and her eyebrows raised. "*It's Queen Bee the Queen Bitch!* It ain't Hustla Da Rabbit's friend! It's his girlfriend! Queen Bee hold daddy *down!*"

The petite psychotic inhaled deeply through her nose—to prevent herself from crying, I think—did an about-face, and went around her car. Opening the door, she stuck one leg in but then paused and looked over the roof at me and yelled, "Ay . . . Is she cute?"

"Is who cute?"

"His new girl."

"What new girl?"

"Don't fuck with me. The girl up in your crib right now suckin' Bennett's little ass dick. Is she cute?"

"Oh. I don't know. No, not really."

"See? *::sniffle::* I'm the baddest bitch he ever had. *::sniffle::* Why he don't want me no more?"

I try to pick my battles. If I can avoid saying something that will cause commotion, I will, normally. But I couldn't avoid it.

"Do you want me to answer that? Because I will if you want to hear some truth."

"Truth? What? You know why he don't want me?"

"Of course I do."

"Tell me."

"Uhhh . . . okay. Mercedes, you're fuckin' crazy. You steal shit from people. You beat girls up. In fact, I'm kinda worried you're going to burst up into my house and beat a girl up right now. You make me that nervous."

"Chill. I ain't trying to go to jail over some hooker who wishes she was as good as me at freakin' down Bennett."

"Right. Okay. Can I give you some advice, Mercedes?"

"Yup. I guess so."

I positioned myself parallel to her and leaned against her car with her, so I could demonstrate both tenderness and sincerity in my voice without raising it. She brushed the nomadic lock of hair out of her eyes, exposing the retinas of a furiously wounded young lass. There was so much suppressed anger incarcerated inside of her that her eyes ravenously transformed colors like the four-hundred-year-old anticyclonic storm on the surface of Jupiter. I cupped my palm around her cheek to endear her.

"Mercedes, if you want people to like you, be a likable person. It's that easy."

She disconnected her eyes from mine and stared into the distance. Eventually, she said, "I think I'm too crazy to be likable, homie. . . . But I'll try. I will."

"Okay . . . well, I'll give this stuff to him," I said, heading to the garage.

"Ay, also I wanted to say sorry for somethin'."

"Yeah? What? Sorry for what?"

"Uhh . . . I forgot. It was gonna make you like me though. I thought it up on my own before you even said dat jus now."

She was snapping her fingers repeatedly, trying to remember something.

"Um. Excuse me?"

"I been smokin' hella weed man, fuck I'm 'posed to do? I had a apologation planded out for you, but now I don't remember it for real."

"Was it in regards to stealing my girl's watch, beating up my neighbor Tallulah, or anything along those lines?"

"Ohhh, yeah! Yeah . . . yeah that's right. Sorry for jackin' that shit from your crib."

"It's okay, Mercedes. I'm sure you were just emotional and not thinking straight."

"Nah, man." She smacked the roof of her car. "I just wanted that shit and ain't got that type of money. So I took it."

"Okay . . . well . . . I appreciate your apology and that you at least feel badly about it."

"I don't feel ba—"

"Okay, okay. Never mind. Just thanks for the apology."

"Yup. That's what I'm here for." She glared at something up the street, then over at me again. "By the way. You look good man. Real fit and healthy. You'll find a new bad bitch, soon."

And with that, she got into her car and sped off.

When Mercedes broke Tallulah's nose, it was because whatever clever plan she originally laid out before going to her house had completely flown out the window. She probably had daydreamed something elaborate wherein she would give Tallulah a fake name, penetrate her cat rescue, and blindside her when she least expected it . . . and then forgot it because of the copious amounts of marijuana she smokes. Or equally plausibly, she never actually thought out a plan that went further than pretending her name was Sarah and then punching Tallulah by surprise.

The girl just ran on a different type of fuel than most human beings, incapable of sugarcoating her thoughts or mincing her words. She's so blunt that she's homicidal with honesty. So, when she pays you a flagrant compliment, you feel like it's dipped in gold.

Driving a few blocks until I found a tiny neighborhood park, I parked my car, cracked the windows, and leaned my seat back. Warmed by Mercedes's quasi-goodwill, I closed my eyes and drifted off to sleep.

Hours later, it was blue outside even if the sun hadn't quite showed its face yet. I awoke to a fog that packed tightly into every artery of the park, wrapping around the jungle gyms, slowly traveling through the wooden teepee kids could play in. An early-morning train rumbled and clanked over the iron tracks in the far distance. The whole scene was hypnotizing.

I started my car and smeared the frosty condensation across the windshield with the wipers. Autumn was coming.

I drove home, to no cars outside. The girls must've left. I walked in to find Lillian watching TV, of course.

"Good morning, Macky," she said sleepily.

"Morning," I replied, "Whatcha watching?"

"Home Shopping Network. Oh! I wish I could afford this. I want this so bad!" She pointed to the TV screen.

Which showed a $1500 taxidermied wolf.

"Why?" I asked.

"Because I love wolves!"

"But what would you do with it?"

"I'd put it on top of the television."

"You'd put it on top of my television?"

"It's *our* television, Mac! Don't be selfish. It could be a good way to add some life into the living room too."

"You'd put a stuffed, dead wolf on 'our' television to add life to the living room?"

"Yes, and to help us all get in touch with our animal spirit."

The guy on the television screen, in the studio selling this wolf, had yellow teeth with infinitesimal spaces in between them and a gravelly voice that was so rough it was almost visual.

"Imagine the happiness you'll feel when this one-of-a-kind wolf is protecting your living room from evil spirits!"

He was acting like this fucking wolf was the end all be all to life or something.

"Go to sleep, Aunt Lillian. I love you."

"I was asleep, but I woke up from a good dream because I heard them talking about this beautiful, one-of-a-kind, magnificent timberwolf."

She was a puzzle I'd never solve.

Going into the basement, I found Bennett asleep on the couch and Leshaun sitting on the floor in front of him, trying to unscrew his house-arrest anklet with a butter knife.

"Is that a good idea?" I asked.

"I don't give a fuck," Leshaun said, without breaking concentration.

"What if they catch you?"

"They ain't gonna catch me. I ain't goin' back home. Fuck this shit."

"I don't get it. Are you on house arrest?"

"Yeah. For four more months. Only time a nigga can leave the fuckin' crib is when I need to get a haircut or when I go to work. And I ain't got no fuckin' job, so I never get to do shit."

"Why are you out right now?"

"I just left. A nigga wanted some pussy, G."

"Fair enough. Speaking of which. That girl, did you just meet her right then and there?"

"Yeah. I don't know her. Her name was Angel or somethin'. She was a suuupa freak. I'm gonna try to get her to tattoo my name on her ass cheek."

"Haha! What? So you had sex with her, right?"

"Yup."

"Where—not in my bed, right?"

"Nah. Outside."

"Outside? In her car?"

"Nah. On the back patio."

"What the fuck? Dude, that's my back patio! I don't want sex residue all over it."

Leshaun looked up at me like I was the lamest, dumbest old person ever. "Nigga, we was on the ground. There was a slug crawling a few feet away from us."

"Oh . . . yeah . . . okay. Touché. I guess it's outside and doesn't matter."

"Yeah, plus I been on lockdown for a minute. I had to get some kitty kat, baby. I needed that."

"So you didn't know that girl? At all?" I clarified.

"Nope. But check this out, G. Dat bitch tried to stop fuckin' 'cause she seen a rollie pollie walkin' by on the ground. I was like, 'Chill, if you see rollie pollies walking during sex, it makes orgasms better'—and bitch believed me, *haha!*"

"God damn it. I'm fuckin' thirty years old and can't even do shit like that."

"Shit like what?"

"You just took her and made her fall in love with you at the snap of a finger. I know it's confidence and stuff, but I'm crushed inside. I don't have the gas in my tank right now."

"You just gotta have that swagger, bro. Your ex made you turn soft. Did you grow some boobs, nigga? Where's your swagger?"

"I have a mortgage and a retirement fund. I don't have swagger."

"Exactly though! You own a house. You got money in the bank. How you gonna let a broke-ass nigga like me pull a bitch before you?"

"Yeah, but, like, how do I tell a girl I own a house without sounding like a dick?"

"Uhhh? Just be like, ''Sup, bitches? I own a house. Come over with a friend; let's get in the hot tub.'"

"I don't own a hot tub."

"Right. So when they get here be like, 'Please accept my apology, bitches. But the hot tub is temporarily out of service. Looks like we gotta take a bath.' Truss me, nigga, it'll work! Bitches love lyin'-ass niggas. They hate the truth."

"Okay. That's not going to happen. I could never say that to a woman."

"Nah? Well, fuck. Can't you just be like, 'I'm a famous rapper, gimme some booty'?"

"Well, no. Of course not. Besides . . . I'm not famous *enough*. I have a complex with the girls who like my music. I'd rather just let them be fans. I can't just take advantage of them!"

Leshaun stopped picking at the anklet with the knife and looked up at me. "Man, fuck all that. If I was you I'd fuck every single girl who liked my shit. I'd make music strictly for gettin' bitches. I'd be the first nigga rappin' bout saving dolphins, and weaving baskets, and sugar-free fudge recipes for chubby bitches, and how it's okay to cry and shit."

"See, that's the stuff Bennett says I need to *stop* doing with my music, and you seem to think the opposite."

"Obviously. Hang on though, it's a meth'ology—I'd be super in touch with their feelings. They would think I was a sensitive nigga, but I'd turn around and lay pipe on 'em like a grown man!"

"Dude, you're only seventeen!"

"Eighteen."

"Okay. You're only eighteen."

"Yep. So now if I bone a teacher, she won't get locked up. *Haha!*"

A NOTE FOR THE TEACHER-STUDENT LOVEFEST

Leshaun was a part of a minor statutory rape scandal. When he was sixteen, he fornicated with a teacher's aide at the high school he attended. She was only twenty, so it wasn't necessarily pedo-gross. Well, not completely. I mean, it wasn't like she was molesting a child. However, the judge disagreed and off she went to a women's sanction house for six months.

I threw my arms out. "Man. I don't know. Lately when I'm around women, my confidence is super low. Every time I've ever had a breakup, I've ended up spending the next nine to ten months directly after it being a pussy around chicks."

"Wait though. I thought you hit Sabrina last night?"

"No. I bailed out and slept in my car. She *really* grossed me out."

"So you had a girl who openly wanted to fuck you, but still say no girls wanna fuck you?"

"Well . . . that's different. And besides, it helps if I find a girl actually *attractive. You* told me she was hot. Dickhead."

"Haha. I just wanted you to let us have hos over, cuz. Ha!"

"Well it worked. But, like, remind me: How do I get a *cute* girl the way you did? How do you have that confidence?"

"What confidence, playa?"

"Where you just grab a stranger's hand and guide her to sit next to you."

Leshaun took a thoughtful pause and stared into space, gathering his thoughts. "I dunno. I mean, for real? Honestly? I think it come down to the fact that I ain't no bitch."

How profound.

"I think it's a little more elaborate than you not being a quote-unquote bitch, Leshaun."

"Nah this is kinda somethin' Bennett put me up on. Okay, like, you ever rode a skateboard? Or stole somethin' from QuikTrip?"

"Uh. Yeah."

"That feelin' you get before you do dat shit. It kinda scary and shit and most niggas punk out. Dats what happens with you and bitches. You get scurred and bitch out. Me? I just go for it."

When you're eighteen, eighteen-year-olds look like grown men to you. When you're thirty, eighteen-year-olds look like babies. Leshaun's skull wasn't fully grown yet. He looked young, albeit weathered. I studied his barely grown mustache and boyish characteristics. They were hidden among the scars and darkness of his skin, but they were there. Another wave of anxiety breezed through me as I realized I was receiving dating tips from an eighteen-year-old.

"Man, how you ain't know this shit bein' this dude's cousin?" Leshaun said, pointing at Bennett.

Popped a Molly, I'm Sweatin'!

Looking over at my cousin, sleeping with his mouth not just open but absolutely *agape,* and him not just drooling but full-on water-logging his pillow, all I could think to ask Leshaun was, "Why the fuck do you keep saying that to me?"

"Bennett is like . . . the master of gettin' girls, cuz! If he could pull his dick outta Mercedes for a few minutes, he'd have twenty-five girlfriends, man."

"No way. Bennett is a knucklehead. Not a chance."

Leshaun silently contemplated his next words. He looked down at the anklet and moved the butter knife to the other bolt he hadn't tried yet.

"Homie, Bennett is a lot of real dumb shit. He think he can fight but can't. He dress bummy as fuck. He can't roll blunts. He always broke. He lies like a scandalous bitch do. He think he a rapper and always disses yo music, but he listens to it and worships you."

"Wait, wait, wait . . ."

"Ha. Homie. Bennett wishes he was you. He has got drunk and fessed up to me. His dream is to have you make music wit him and take him on tour."

"It's hard to believe, because he always talks shit on my music."

"Yeah. He a bitch. He just won't admit it. But, nigga, anyways, listen. Bennett figured some like . . . scientific way of pullin' hos. That nigga got a whole list. Like these, eleven commandments to gettin' bitches. I swear."

"This keeps coming up. It sounds like a joke you all are playing on me."

"No. They're real. Real as fuck. They's the only thing Bennett has ever accomplished in his life."

"It's real? Like a full-on, written-out, thought-out piece of literature?"

"One hundred percent real. Dis nigga Bennett was in detention almost every day after school last year. And he couldn't skip because skipping detention gets you out-of-school suspended, which woulda been a violation to his probation."

"Yeah."

"So basically, he would sit there bored as fuck, thinkin' up ways to talk to bitches. He got sick of gettin' dissed by chicks, so he decided to start runnin' game on 'em. At first it didn't work, and he almost got his ass whooped by some hatin'-ass boyfriends."

"Lemme guess, you're the reason he never did?"

"As long as I'm around, nigga—and I'm *always* around, lurkin' in da shadows—y'all will be safe. They call me Nigga Ninja, nigga. Creepin', plottin', watchin' my boy's back."

"You're a good friend."

"Mac, shut up, homie. So Bennett kept experimentin' and shit. And he finally started figurin' it out."

"Yeah? Started getting cute chicks at school?"

"Homie, when news broke around school that Eva Fazio sucked Bennett's dick under da bleachers during a school football game, the whole game changed. Eva was one of da finest hos at school."

"Wow."

"Yeah. But shit didn't get real till he dated Eva Fazio *and* Mercedes at the same time. Mercedes was never popular, but every nigga at school wanted to fuck her. He dated the two baddest chicks at school at one time."

"What ended up happening to Eva?"

"Mercedes Frisbeed a pre-algebra textbook at her face and knocked one of her teeth loose."

"I'm shocked she isn't in prison."

"Someone must be prayin' for dat bitch, cuz she would'a got da death penalty by now."

"Speaking of praying . . . what are these commandments? And why do they work?"

"The main idea and shit, homie, is you gotta just be . . . just full of *thug* charisma. It's all in how you talk to girls and how you let 'em talk to you. I got 'em wrote down myself. But they at my grandma Onion's crib. Ask him, nigga."

"Eh. I might."

"Nigga, don't be a hardhead. Let him show you his tricks. He showed me, and I'm black."

"Err . . . Okay. What's that mean?"

"Girls like black dudes. Some white girls date black dudes just to make their dad wanna kill hisself. But girls of *all* races like Bennett better than black dudes. Truth be told, nigga, if Bennett *was* a black dude he'd have 248 baby mamas, nigga! *On Crip,* nigga!"

"Wow."

"The only problem is . . . I mean . . . you know who . . ."

"Mercedes?"

"Exactly, my nigga. Mercedes the devil. She a big Ziploc bag of Kryptonite. Bennett even look at a girl at the mall, 'Cedes'll beat that ass. Doo! This bitch dropped a bitch in fronta her son once, then looked at the kid and said, 'If you start crying, I'mma cut your wee-wee off. You lil' pussy.'"

"Wow."

"Bennett ain't stop her. That nigga turn into Peter Parker around Mercedes."

"Wait, Leshaun. Peter Parker was Spider-Man. Clark Kent was Superman."

"Whatever, nigga, it's the Kryptonite hurting them I meant."

"No, no, no, it just hurts Superman."

"Word? Kryptonite don't work on all superheroes?"

"Nah. Just Superman."

Leshaun dropped the knife and gave me a fascinated look. His mind was blown in five different directions. "Errrghh. That crazy. See everythang a conspiracy, G. Teachers be lyin' and shit."

"Your teacher lied to you about Spider-Man and Superman?"

"Prolly. They say all sorts of crazy shit. You know them math problems is a lie. I ain't even pay attention in school 'cause I know they lyin'. But fuck nah. Look, forget Spider-man an' 'em. You need to get a new bitch, cuzzo!"

"I agree. You're right. I need to get back in the game."

"Ask him. Bennett can help you, nigga."

"Okay. I'll ask him. I'm just curious. I'll check it out."

"Ask him right now."

"No, no. I'll ask him when he wakes up. I'm gonna go pass out in my bed for a little bit. I gotta drive out later tonight for a show."

"Where to?"

"Saint Louis tonight. Columbia tomorrow night."

"Straight up, G. I'd go, but I'm on house arrest. I'd get in trouble for leavin'."

"But you're not at your house right now, bro. Remember?"

Leshaun's eyes were heavy. He was trying to stay awake. My logic escaped him.

"Anyway, word, Leshaun," I said. "Good talk, buddy. Good luck getting your anklet off."

"Ay, man . . ."

"What's up?"

"You think I could chill here for a few days?"

"Geez. I dunno. What if the cops find out you're here?"

"They won't, G."

As awful of an idea as this was, I really enjoyed having Leshaun around. He was humble and had an old soul. He wasn't overzealous and in constant need of attention like most teenagers are. It was highly illegal for me to let him stay at my house, but it was also highly good for my spirit.

"Yeah. But swear that you won't do anything to get in trouble. You won't leave the house. You won't tell anyone you're here. Nothing.

Swear to me. I don't want to come home to you in prison—and then *me* in prison. If you *swear* you'll stay out of trouble, you can stay here for a week or so."

"I swear! I do. I swear!"

"Hmmm. No. Not good enough. Swear on something important."

"Like what?"

"You know what."

"I do?"

"Swear on the most important thing to you. That you won't get caught."

"Okay. I swear on smokin' weed that I won't get caught."

"No. I'm talking about something you *love*."

"I love smoking weed a lot, nigga."

"Okay, but I mean something special to *you*. Swear on it."

"Uh. I swear on my grandma Onion that I won't get caught."

"Nah, not your grandma Onion. Swear on the *big* thing. Come on."

"My dick?"

"Shut up. The *biggest* thing in your life. It's over your head as we speak."

"Uh. I swear to God I won't get caught."

"No, everyone says that. This is special to *you* only. Not God. Come on. Don't make me say it. You know, the *one* thing that will make me believe you. Swear on it."

"Hmm. Okay. I swear on gettin' pussy I won't get caught."

"Nope."

"Uh. I swear on gettin' . . . white . . . girl pussy?"

"Leshaun."

"Yeah?"

"Come on."

"Man . . . okay. I swear on . . . Uhh . . ."

"Dude, you say this every time you want someone to take you serious!"

"I swear on my niggas? . . . No. Okay. I swear on the . . . *Oh!* I swear on Crip!"

"Bingo. There we go. Now you're good."

"Yeah! I'mma be quiet as fuck. If you don't mind I might read a book from your bookshelf. Tryin' to enhance my life an' not be a dumb nigga all day."

"Do it. Make yourself at home."

"Got any books with like . . . stripper bitches and Italian Mafia niggas holdin' machine guns?"

"Yeah, it's called *Atlas Shrugged* by Ayn Rand."

"Hell yeah. I'mma read that shit. Get some of this knowledge."

Ratchet as Fucc

27

I had a show the next night in Columbia, Missouri, which is a two hour drive from Kansas City. Cities that are an easy drive are good for one-off shows during slower months, so I can pull in a little extra cash. A little over three hundred fans paid at ten dollars a ticket. Technically the turnout didn't matter, because I received an $1,800 guarantee, but it was still a good turnout, considering the music industry climate. After I paid my agent 10 percent of the total gross and paid gas expenses, I walked away with $1,550. Not bad for ninety minutes of work. That's seventeen dollars per minute, which sounds super cool until you find out I didn't have another show for like three weeks.

Since Columbia is so close to home, I decided to drive back immediately after the show. I hopped into the driver's seat and pulled my cell phone from the front right pocket of my sweat-drenched jeans. Dead. I plugged it into the car charger, tossed it on the passenger seat, and began driving. I spent the first twenty minutes navigating myself back to the highway in silence, but once I found I-70 West, I popped in *Rant in E-Minor*, an old comedy album by Bill Hicks, one of my prime influences. The man was a truly ahead-of-his-time, controversial, stand-up comedian and thinker who died at age thirty-two from pancreatic cancer.

I had skipped a few tracks ahead into the album to get deeper into the show when my phone lit up, apparently having taken enough of a charge to turn on.

(BENNETT:) NIGGA where u at

(BENNETT:) hey

(ME:) I just got done performing. Pulled over to get some gas and read the texts. What's up?

(BENNETT:) Wat da fuck I picked up a 46 year old bitch with wet hair and no shoes on and she askin If I got bath salts to smoke?!

(ME:) That's that new drug that's been all over the news.

(BENNETT:) I got Sexy bath salts thats supposed to make you relaxed and horny

(BENNETT:) u think if we smoke them she will suck my dick

(ME:) Bennett she's homeless.

(BENNETT:) She can sleep in da garage

(ME:) QUit fucking with me. Is everything good at the house?

(BENNETT:) ya jus tryen to get head from this bitch

(ME:) DUDE

(ME:) Do not tell me you're serious.

(BENNETT:) ?

(ME:) You seriously have a fuckin homeless person in the house??

(BENNETT:) how do u no she is homeless

(BENNETT:) She dont no my dad

(BENNETT:) she got a missen front tooth tho

I grinned lightly. Bennett had stirred up so much shit by this point, that I was completely gullible and believed him too readily, even when he was clearly fucking with me.

(ME:) Enjoy smoking bath salts with your new friend. I'll be home in a couple hours. Driving.

(ME:) Don't let her eat your face off.

I threw my phone back onto the passenger seat. The drive was boring. It was getting cold outside, which caused my sweaty T-shirt to adhere to my clammy skin. Fall was fully erect, fucking my life in every orifice.

Finally, I pulled up to my house at around five. My grass looked plastic, which felt good. In really nice suburbs, the grass looks clean and new. Like each blade is artificial.

Leaving my merch in the car until morning, I went inside, where I found Bennett rolling a spliff on my kitchen table and giggling with a strange-looking meth head. She had an emaciated face, decrepit skin, and a ramshackled frame. Easily in her forties, she sat across from Bennett, her filthy, peeling bare feet up on the table. Looking up at me, she squeaked out of her cigarette-damaged voice box, "Hey! Your house is purdy fuckin' cool, man!"

I approached the table slowly. Neither Bennett nor his lady friend even noticed that my face had gone from a look of contentment to confused upset.

Bennett took his eyes off the joint momentarily. "What up, you old-ass nigga? How was the concert? You get some groupie love?" He refocused on the joint.

"Hey there," I said, extending my hand to the woman, "I'm Mac. Welcome to my home. . . ."

"I'm Cindy," she said, shaking my hand. Her hair was oily and matted and she smelled like a dog that'd been left out in the rain for a month. Which maybe was appropriate, since her clothes appeared soaked.

"Ma'am?" I inquired. "Why are your clothes wet?"

"Oh, man!" she said before bursting into a shrill of laughter. "Hehehehe."

Her feet came off the table and she leaned forward, exposing a maroon-and-peach-colored farmer's tan.

"I was walkin'—and seent dis little boy's folks threw him a pool party in his backyard. His name was fuckin' uh . . . fuckin' . . . Justin. So I walk into their yard. And ask for a beer. Fuck it—it's a party— ain't it? Well they start yellin' at me, 'Get off my property' and what not—so I yell, 'It's a free country, motherfucker!' and jump in that pool. Hehehehehehe. . . ."

Bennett began laughing with her. I glared at him, which, of course, he didn't notice.

"Luckily, Benjy was nice enough to pick me up and get me some smoke."

She reached into her damp jeans pocket and pulled out a gold foil sack. On the top of it, in bright-purple bubble letters, it read: SOOTHING BATH SALTS.

She threw the package on the table toward me. I picked it up and examined it.

"Bennett did you smoke bath salts tonight?" I asked bluntly.

"Naw, playa, I hear dat shit makes people go stupid dumb crazy. I heard dis one dude crashed his car into a grocery store, high off dat shit. They found him on the side of the highway trying to cut his dick off with a knife or some shit. Shit make you go ratchet as fuck," he responded casually.

I was furious.

"Well, has your friend Cindy smoked any bath salts tonight?" I asked.

Before I could even get an answer from my clueless cousin, Cindy shot up to her feet, slamming her chair into the newly granite-topped island behind it.

"I smoked a *whole* packet to the fuckin' head, man!" she yelled, then burst into hysterical laughter. Which would have been pretty creepy had it not been followed by a half minute of deep-lung coughing most likely caused by a cigarette habit nursed since the tender age of nine.

"Bennett, come talk to me for a second," I said, motioning to the dark, vacant dining room next to the kitchen.

Once he had followed me in there, I turned, put my hands on his shoulders, leaned forward, and whispered with furious anger, "Are you out of your fucking mind? You brought a fucking homeless woman into my house. A fucking homeless woman *who's on meth!*"

I took a step back and gazed at him with choleric eyes. His eyes were plump and harmless as he looked into mine. He took a thoughtful pause to process what I had just barked at him, and to conjure up what I assumed, or perhaps desperately hoped would be, something along the lines of, "I'll get rid of her immediately. I'm so sorry. I wasn't thinking. Tomorrow I'll graduate college and dedicate the rest of my life to speaking publicly about the evils associated with crossing someone's personal boundaries while you and your family are freeloading in their house."

Because my cousin had something for me to hear, an important psychological nugget, an apology more genuine and convincing than any before in history, he connected with me eye to eye, pulled back his lips, poked out his tongue, and confidently articulated, "She isn't on meth, nigga. She's on bath salts. They ain't illegal."

Oh right, this was Bennett.

"Follow me," I said sternly. Apparently I needed to boot her myself, so I walked back into the kitchen while clearing my throat.

"Listen, Cindy, we appreciate your company. But we are all tired and need to—"

I stopped midsentence. No one was at the table. Cindy was gone.

"Where the fuck is she, Bennett?"

For his part, Bennett looked under the table: nothing. He then lifted up a few magazines off the table and looked under those: nothing. He then vaguely glanced over toward the refrigerator. "Oh, shit, I don't know where dat bitch went, mane!"

"*Well you better fucking find her,*" I snapped.

I ran into the living room; nothing but Aunt Lillian on the couch, watching Home Shopping Network and completely unaffected by anything that was happening. Swiftly I sprinted from room to room on the main floor to find Cindy. I ran upstairs and through each room there. She wasn't in my office, wasn't in the guest bedroom. Worried, I opened my bedroom door and turned on the lights. Thankfully, she wasn't in there. I bolted downstairs, where I nearly ran into Bennett.

He immediately began defending himself. "She seemed coo'. She let me bum a few cigarettes for the ride, ya know. So I wuz jus bein' polite and shit. I was gonna try to get her to suck my dick up in your bed but she is all high off those drugs and all th—"

::Thud:: went something in the vents. Being that this was the only thing that kept me from manslaughter charges, I focused intently on the other reverberating sounds coming from it. I heard twists and dials, then a large machine breathing out hot air. The laundry room.

"The dryer!" I yelled.

I ran down the basement stairs and collided with the half-open laundry room door, slamming it open to find Cindy there, naked, shriveled, and sunburned, standing in front of the dryer, shivering.

"Yo, bitch, why you stealin' our laundry services?" Bennett barked.

I motioned for him to stop talking, but it was too late. She turned around with black, drug-induced eyes and a pale face, crunching and spasming.

"Cindy, put on your clothes, please. You need to go," I requested, with my hands over my face, to avoid looking at her disgusting physique.

"What, man? I'm fuckin' nekkid, man, leave me alone—I'm dryin' my clothes!"

Without hesitation, I reached my hand out to turn off the dryer, but Cindy thought I was reaching for her. She dodged my hand and charged past me, barely grazing my fingertips. Her skin felt like what I imagine a moldy alien would feel like. I nearly gagged.

"Don't touch me! Don't touch me—don' touch me! Donntuchme—I just need to dry my clothes and go to sleep!" she yelled, as she ran up the stairs.

Bennett and I looked at each other briefly and peeled off after her.

"Stop running! You're going to wake my neighbors!" I screamed after her.

Man, meth heads can run *fast*. I didn't want to touch her, so I was running behind her trying to, like, corral her with my yelling, hoping I could just get her to stop. "Cindy, stop running—you're completely naked—my neighbors will see you!"

She slammed open the front door of my house and ran out onto the front yard. I heard the garage door opening. Sounded like Bennett had taken an alternate route.

Cindy bolted halfway across my front yard and stopped, dug her feet into the ground, and juked away from me. I really didn't want to touch her, but I played along, hoping she'd stop running or fall over or maybe die from cardiac arrest. We ran in circles for what seemed like forty-five minutes. I was totally winded. She was high on drugs, so she had the stamina of a Greek battle horse, pulling a chariot.

We switched to a figure-eight shape, with me yelling "Cindy! Stop running!"

"*Lemme dry my clothes and get some food and sleep. Be a good American, man!*" she snarled.

Circles upon circles we ran. It baffles me to this day that meth heads aren't triathletes. They have tireless stamina. And while Cindy's body could've gone another three hours running around, she seemed to be slowing down a bit due to being sleepy. I was completely exhausted and could barely breathe. I planted my feet into the ground and put my hands on my knees. She was a good ten feet away from me, juking and twisting, hoping I couldn't grab her.

When I stopped suddenly, she stopped suddenly and focused her eyes on me. She was breathing heavy. I could hear chunks of lung particle squeezing through her chest tube.

"Cindy . . . why are you making me chase you? Can we stop running? Please?"

Her back was to my house, her front adjacent to me. The street was directly behind me. It was approaching dawn. The most subtle blue began bleeding through the black sky. It was past six.

Both of us were in a stalemate on the driveway. Panting. My meth-guest dropped to her knees from exhaustion. Across the street and one house to the left, the garage door lifted open and Jean Paul zipped out on his bike. If you're up early enough, you can catch him practicing wheelies and bunny hops in the driveway before his mom takes him to school.

"Good morning, Mac! Pleasant morning!" Jean Paul called out.

"Hey, buddy, stay out of the street!" I said back with concern in my voice, wanting to keep a ton of distance between him and Cindy.

Cindy's eyes turned yellow like she was a rabid werewolf. Thick ribbons of mucus and saliva dripped from her top teeth to her bottom teeth. She began salivating, staring at Jean Paul, as if she were plotting a stealth velociraptor ambush on him.

"Well, ain't that little boy cute? I think I'm gonna adopt the little fucker," Cindy said as she rose up from her knees and began gently walking toward him. I instantly froze with panic.

"Cindy, don't go over there!" I said.

"Oh I'm goin'. I'm going."

However, before she could take another step toward our little neighborhood all-star, Leshaun, like a steroid-enhanced Super Bowl linebacker, came charging at full speed from the garage directly behind Cindy and *slammed* into her back with pulverizing impact, levitating her body a good three feet in the air, causing her hair to zap in all directions like her head was a Tesla coil surging shafts of purple electric current, knocking the wind out of her lungs, flipping her forward one and a half times, and dropping her to the ground with a loud, face-first smack on the driveway's edge.

Cindy groaned from pain, and curled into a naked, white-trash ball. I cringed and looked away, but while she was lying on the ground in a drug-induced stupor, heaving for oxygen, Leshaun hovered over her yelling, "Yeah! Bitch! Don't fuck with the East Avalon Crips. We turnt all the way up, ho!"

He then leaned over and picked up what appeared to be her front tooth. He showed it to me and began cracking up. "That shit was fuckin' gangsta! I hit that bitch like Ray Lewis, my nigga! Whooaaaa! I should play football or work for the cops as a bitch tackler. Hahaha."

I scanned and surveyed my neighborhood. Thankfully, no one saw a thing. Not even Jean Paul, he was trying to do wheelies in his garage, where his father's car is usually parked.

"Make sure she doesn't leave . . . and is still breathing," I said to Leshaun.

I then walked inside, got her clothes from the dryer, and called the police. Back outside, I saw that Bennett had materialized from wherever the fuck he was and tied a green garden hose around her to restrain her. I sent Leshaun to the basement to hide from the police, since he would easily end up in jail if they looked up who he was—we could just say I'd tackled Cindy.

Forty-five minutes later, Officer Paul Gray of the Kansas City Police Department was on my driveway telling me all about Cindy: "Oh, yes, this one. She's a bipolar meth addict who sometimes gets so high that she ends up in various suburbs of Kansas City, wandering the neighborhoods, howling at the moon, jumping in people's cars, trying to hitch rides. She gets arrested a few times a month, but has never really committed a crime that could keep her in jail. It's a shame. She'll probably end up eating a puppy or something. If we're lucky, she'll get eighteen months for animal cruelty. Not sure if that counts as cannibalism. Haha! Oh well, have a good night."

I walked into the house to find Leshaun and Bennett both eating bowls of cereal at the table. Bennett stood too fast for the sticky chair-leg bottoms to catch a smooth wave of inertia, which tripped the chair, smacking it into the blinds behind him.

"Cuz. I'm so sorry, Cuz. Oh nigga—" he started to say, approaching me with his hand out to shake my hand. "She just seemed c—"

"How do you get women to like you like that?" I cut him off.

Bennett looked back over his shoulder at Leshaun, who out of confusion at my response, squeezed his eyebrows together and halfway opened his mouth, with no words escaping it.

"Uh . . . huh?" he said.

"You heard me," I said, sitting down. "Bennett, at this point, I don't care if my house catches fire and burns down. My life is fucked."

"Uh . . ." Bennett was perplexed. I wasn't angry like he assumed I was going to be.

I picked up this shitty olive-green clay vase that Harper had bought for my kitchen table and studied the miniscule designer cracks veining through it.

"My life is fucked!" I said, heaving it across the table between them into the refrigerator . . . where it didn't break.

"Hahahaha!" Leshaun began laughing.

I looked at him, alarmed.

"Nigga, I ain't laughin' at you. I just know how it feel. Throw that bitch-ass vase!" he said empathetically, standing up and grabbing the vase from the floor himself. "I'm probably going to fuckin' jail because I ditched my house arrest to get some pussy! Why can't I get it right? Why can't I make the right decisions?"

He slammed the vase down, also not breaking it. Watching it for a second, he picked it up again, set it back in the center of the table, then sat back in his chair and gazed at it.

"Damn, that vase is badass," he said.

Trying to punch the vase, Bennett overthrew his arm and hit it with his pinkie knuckle, eliciting a small *::ding!::* and not even moving it an inch.

"Huh," he said.

"How do you get chicks to like you like that?" I said again quickly. "I used to be able to get cute girls, but this whole thing with Harper tore out my heart. How am I supposed to ever walk again?" I asked, alternating between which of the two of them I was looking at.

"See?" Leshaun said, looking at Bennett.

"Man . . ." Bennett said, standing up. "I gotta go to work. I ain't even fuckin' sleep." And like that I thought my little fuck-up cousin had given up on *me*. Until he said over his shoulder, "But I'm gonna show you my commandments, my G. You actin' hurt in da booty hole right now, so I'mma show you da playa's rule book."

Pulling up his pants a little, he barrelled downstairs into the basement.

"Ohhhh, shit," Leshaun said, excitedly taking a milky bite of cereal. "You 'bout to get your whole game back, homie."

"Wait—it's like seven o'clock in the morning. And wait . . . I thought you got fired?" I yelled down the stairs.

"I start at da grocery store today. Gotta get dis money, mane! I'm a workin' mane!"

"Wait, when did you get hired?" I said.

"Uh, a few days ago? Why?" he said.

"No. Nothing. That's just . . . great," I said optimistically.

"I got bills to pay, homie! Gotta help Mama pay you."

I was proud of the kid. He hadn't even announced that he got the job.

"Cuz, you gotta understand somethin'. This is the *only* thing Bino cares about. He had so much trouble gettin' girls at house parties that he started workin' on this list. He would sit in school all day, workin' on it and not studyin'. Use it, playa. It works," Leshaun said.

"I swear on Crip, I hope it does," I said jokingly.

Leshaun raised one spooky eyebrow. "It will. Ay though, you my nigga and shit. But don't swear on Crip. Don't take the gang's name in vain. I'm s'posed to shank you over that shit, but I'm hella tired."

"Sorry."

"It's coo', man. Hey. I tried to read that Ann Rand book or whatever? Atlas Shrugs?"

"Yeah?"

"Yeah. I dunno, man. I read kinda slow and shit. But damn . . . my nigga John Galt got some peeps lookin' for him. He owe someone money or somethin'?"

I will love Leshaun until I die.

ne no mo? J ho

the girliest text messag

a female language i blew

inja star a :) is my sord

it wrks luv me they bo

ersent fluant langauge

a i say kk and they bo

rushin spy wit. speak jus

z B gittin wit other bit

soft and sweet 2 eacJo

bennett. i know wat wa

d Dats fabulus And Kk ar

they think im sinstive

dat song dat g

Part 6

BENNETT DA BOSS HOGGZ 11 COMMANDMINTS OF GITTIN' BITCHEZ

1. BE DA HOMIE B4 ANYTHING ELSE

2. DIS AINT A JOB INTARVIEW

3. IF SHE WANTID A GIRLFRIEND SHE WUD JUST FUCC HER GIRL-FRIEND

4. T.H.U.G.L.I.F.E. [TEITH HAIR UNDAARMS GWAP LANDRY ITCHERZ FEET ERB]

5. ALWEYS TAKE A SHIT B4 MACCIN ON HOEZ

6. KILL DA HATAZ BY SHOWEN EM LUV

7. KISS SEX GOODBYE

8. U R STILL IN LUV WIT LEAH

9. JACK OFF NOW SO U CAN FUCC L8ER

10. IF SHE WANT U TO HAVE HER NUMBA SHE WILL MAKE U TAKE IT

11. SEE COMMANDMINT 1 IF SUMTHIN GITS FUCCED UP

Charlamagne: The God Particle

Ten minutes later, Bennett reappeared from the basement, dressed in his work clothes and with a name tag that read #####—his legal first name.

"You gonna be awake, my G?" Bennett said.

"Yep," I said.

"Aiight, gimme just a few to get thangs coo' at work," Bennett said and handed me a folded piece of paper. I watched him lumber out the front door and waited for Leshaun to go downstairs to sleep before opening it.

BENNETT DA BOSS HOGGZ 11 COMMANDMINTS OF GITTIN' BITCHEZ it said at the top in the most gangster font I had ever seen.

I couldn't believe I was at this point. I was now my degenerate, troubled cousin's pupil as he schooled me on how to properly attract women. It was official: I was officially desperate, and Professor Bennett's class was about to start.

Reading it once, I laid back in bed to ponder my fate and wonder if this was a class one really wants a passing grade in.

BENNETT: k u stil up

BENNETT: Cuzo

ME: I'm up.

[BENNETT:] k u got da paper ?

[ME:] Yes. I don't understand what any of it means.

[BENNETT:] im gunna xplain

[ME:] Ok. Let's go. Get me a woman, young cousin.

Lying in bed, having been unable to fall asleep and feeling blue since I read the list, I was morose. Exhausted. Heartbroken all over again.

As much as I was hoping Bennett would have good advice to give, he was only seventeen. Telling me to "dress like a gangsta" wasn't going to cut it.

Bennett gave me a lot of advice through text. My phone was hot, my eyes hurt from staring at the screen, I was overwhelmed with information—but I was intrigued. Somehow he managed to spend his entire double shift—his entire first day—at the grocery store telling me how to pull chicks.

[BENNETT:] k hear go Bennett Da Boss Hoggz 11 commandmints of gittin' bitchez

[BENNETT:] u their

[ME:] Yes. Shoot.

[ME:] Wait. Why are their 11 and not 10?

[BENNETT:] i will tell u in a sec. read da 1st one off da page

[ME:] Uhh. #1. BE DA HOMIE B4 ANYTHING ELSE

[BENNETT:] 1. B da homie b4 anythin else..

[BENNETT:] Dis meanz dat no matta wat

[BENNETT:] alweys B a bitch best friend

[BENNETT:] if u talken 2 a girl an she thinks dat u want 2 fucc her

[BENNETT:] even if u do

[BENNETT:] she wont wanna git wit u

[BENNETT:] if u go at her like u wanna fucc her she will think dats da onley thing u want . u cant even act like Ur atractid 2 her for real

BENNETT: but if Ur just her friend..if U dont talk about daten her and aint afraid 2 opanly talk about fuccin otha chix in front of her she will think u dont want her dat much

BENNETT: and will like u.U gaDDA make her feel like u balong 2 her.!

BENNETT: if she hears abt all da hot girls U git wit she will think ur a gud catch cuz otha bitches want u

BENNETT: she will wanna hang wit u all da time cuz ur so funny and cool but mostley 2 keep u frum gittin wit N E otha bitchez

BENNETT: den u can try to git wit her

ME: What if you try to get with her and she rejects you? Won't she know you were faking the friendship?

BENNETT: na

BENNETT: first of all.. dont fake da friendship.. neva be a fake ass nigga. im sayen ReaLLy b friends wit her.. jus keep ur dazire 2 fucc her secrete

BENNETT: secind of all... if u try 2 git wit her and she says no jus be like

BENNETT: its ok..are friendship cums first i just luv bein around U

BENNETT: i luv it so much dat i worry if i meet anotha girl i cant see U as much

BENNETT: but ok no problam lets jus be friends

BENNETT: no matta wat she says...... i jus wanna be friends,,, i dont like u like dat,,, ur not my type

BENNETT: dont take it 2 ur head.she just talken shit..it jus means u havent made her like u enuff 2 get rommantic but dats OK it will happan

BENNETT: IF u dont act like a bitch dat iz

BENNETT: dont EVA b like i dont wanna b jus friendz i luv u i wanna buy u 200 roses dippt in choclit an shit

BENNETT: u gadda be supa coo wit it... u gadda proove dat ur da type of nigga she can fall in luv wit

BENNETT: B a real friend 2 her..and all her friends 2 for mo options =)

[ME:] Wow. That's... actually kinda smart.

[ME:] Because you can disarm her that way.

[BENNETT:] i wudnt disarm her she wudnt be able to giv u a hand job with no arms LoL

[BENNETT:] da coo thing is.sumtimes bein da homie is da only thing U need to do

[BENNETT:] if Ur jus nice and friendley 2 a girl but dont focas on sex... ..sumtimes she will B ready 2 fucc da same day

[BENNETT:] sumtimes da day u meet.sumtimes 4 or 5 bizniss dayz..if she a asain bitch it take up to 3 wks da point iz..bitches LUV a nigga who claims 2 be her homie..

[BENNETT:] dont hit on a bitch

[BENNETT:] dont tell a bitch u wanna go on a date

[BENNETT:] jus be her buddy

[BENNETT:] O also U can have like 8 diff chix at 1 time an use dem 2 make eachotha jellis.

[BENNETT:] U cant get drunk wit out a 40

[BENNETT:] U cant get free grosheriez wit out a WIC card

[BENNETT:] U cant git a bitch wit out bein her friend

[ME:] Okay. Got it. I'm actually glad you're texting me this stuff, because I can save it all and read it a few times.

[BENNETT:] well since u asked i will tell u also

[BENNETT:] numba 1 is so importint

[BENNETT:] dat numba 11 says to start ova at numba 1 if shit git fuccd up.we will talk abt dat soon

#2 This Ain't a Job Interview

ME: DIS AIN'T A JOB INTERVIEW

BENNETT: aint dat numba 3

ME: Nope. #2.

BENNETT: k Dis aint a job inteview is a imporint 1

ME: I don't get it.

BENNETT: ya cuz i didnt xplain it yet silly nigga

BENNETT: ok dis is when U first gittin to kno a chicc when u talken 2 her

BENNETT: Do not ask her fuccin questins dat makes her borred

BENNETT: da most borring fuccin ppl in da world are bosses given u job interviewz

BENNETT: maccin on a girl isnt saposed 2 be Boring it saposed to be excsiting , da girl shud think U r da coolist nigga she ever met..

BENNETT: she shud think ur cooler den Harrie potter dats fer sure

BENNETT: wats da next 1 ?

ME: Wait. Hang on. You didn't explain that one enough.

BENNETT: wat

(ME:) I mean I think I get it. But in your much less experienced life than mine, what have you found bores girls?

(ME:) What questions work and what don't work?

(BENNETT:) man dont ask NO questins if u dont haff to

(ME:) Really?

(BENNETT:) ya 4 real

(ME:) Not even her name?

(BENNETT:) nah...... if u wanna git her name tell her UR name

(BENNETT:) be like waddup im mac

(BENNETT:) she will giv u her name

(BENNETT:) sumtimes u can ask her questins 2 keep da convarsatin gng but dont be sittin their quizin da girl

(BENNETT:) u shud b abel 2 hav a connvarsation wit out evar asking a questin

(BENNETT:) tell her shit dont ask her shit

(BENNETT:) wat kinda muzic do u like

(BENNETT:) wat skool do u go 2

(BENNETT:) do u like kittins

(BENNETT:) hav u evar benn 2 canadia

(BENNETT:) dont ask none of dat shit TELL her dat shit

(ME:) Dude people have been getting to know each other by asking questions for millions of years.

(BENNETT:) i no and dats why dis is imporint Bcuz she will notice dat u dont act like all da niggaz dat have hit on her for milianz of years

(ME:) What the fuck do I say then? "Hi, I'm Mac, I like hip-hop music, I don't go to school because I'm 30, I hate kittens, I've been to Canada, and my favorite TV show is *Louie*."

(BENNETT:) Yeah! dats pretty gud !

(BENNETT:) datz funny i mite try dat LoL haha

(BENNETT:) try dat i bet it work betta den if u askd all dem questins you ask haha

(ME:) Shut up. You have no idea what you're talking about.

(BENNETT:) no nigga really think abt it

(BENNETT:) ill giv u a few ideaz 2 say but thinK abt it

(BENNETT:) Brb i gadda take a shit

(BENNETT:) Wooo better... U thar?

(ME:) Yeah, and I've thought about it and can't believe how well that would actually work.

(BENNETT:) ya it isnt like a picc up line.. it just helps u git da talk gng

(BENNETT:) picc up lines dont wrk on dope chiccs ne wayz..

(BENNETT:) ne wayz here go 2 i like to use

(BENNETT:) da first is waddup im bennett

(BENNETT:) im not da type to interup a pretty girl

(BENNETT:) but their is sumthin about u. sumthin abt ur style dat im tryen 2 figure out

(BENNETT:) she will go wat?

(BENNETT:) den i give her 2 things abt her to chose from dat are awsim

(BENNETT:) i say

(BENNETT:) U r either a girl who has incredabal dreams dat r supa intensce

(BENNETT:) and dey give u da abilaty 2 be vary styleish

(BENNETT:) or u C colors difrantly den most peopel.u c dem in a deep way dats hela deep and ur betta at dresseing den most hoes r

(BENNETT:) both of dem are bull shit she aint speshial

(BENNETT:) but bitchez wanna think dey are speshail so she will picc 1 and start talken abt her self.. den u builld on that and keep makeing her feel like a alien dat has speshil shit about her... ..

(BENNETT:) da sekond 1

BENNETT: hi im bennett.. i notice u hav sumthin speshial abt u most girls dont have

BENNETT: she says wat

BENNETT: u have wat r called prinncess cheeks and dis is wat dat means

BENNETT: 99 % of girls have normall cheeks but a vary small numba of girls hav prinnscess cheeks.u get cheeks like dat bcuz u smile in a real way not like most fake chix do.. it means ur a vary real persen who is genuwin and many ppl can truss u also u cum from a line of royalty

ME: Dude. Has that ever worked?

BENNETT: it works evry single time all girls want to be a prinscess

#3 If She Wanted a Girlfriend, She Would Just Fuck Her Girlfriend

ME: #3 IF SHE WANTED A GIRLFRIEND, SHE'D FUCK HER GIRL FRIEND.

ME: This one makes sense without even seeing an explanation.

BENNETT: *fucc

BENNETT: basicly dont be a guy she lables as one of da girlfriends

BENNETT: dont be a push ova.. dont be a sweety pie..dont gossip and be all sencitive and shit.dont be afraid 2 ignore her and tell her ur busy

BENNETT: da less u say da betta.. da more busy u r da more she will want u

BENNETT: if a girl calls u and says OMG wat r u doin lets talk abt how awsim i am and how pretty i am

BENNETT: b like No im watchen da game wit my niggaz

ME: What if a game isn't on?

BENNETT: how da fucc wud she no ? girls dont watch games

ME: What if it's 10 pm, when no games are on?

BENNETT: b like da game is in canadia its da aftarnoon their

ME: Lmao.

ME: So even if it's 3 am say I'm watching a game and gotta go?

BENNETT: well no if its 3 am she is callin cuz she wants 2 worship ur stachew of luv.. but N E thing b4 1130 u watchin da game

So far, what I had gathered was above all else: focus on and develop a friendship with the girl. A real one, where if she acts uninterested in dating you, you are unfazed by it because the friendship is that important to you. Don't ask her tons of boring and predictable questions, because you'll come off as boring and predictable. And don't act like a girl she shops and mingles with. Because you'll end up in the friend zone. Women want men. Men who say little and represent strength, loyalty, and being unafraid of taking control of a situation.

The sad part was I already knew all of this but was just missing something.

#4 T.H.U.G.L.I.F.E.

ME: Okay. #4 is THUGLIFE. Teeth hair etc. etc.

BENNETT: dis 1 is abt da hoW U CARRY URSELF AND APEAR

BENNETT: in order 4 u 2 pull dime bitchez u gadda live dat thug life

BENNETT: each leter stand 4 sumthin importint

BENNETT: T is Teith..brush ur teith. i mean hello . U dont want nasty ass yelow teith dat smell like u ate a frozzen fart... ..Have a fre$h mouth so u can kiss and talk to bitchez w no problam

BENNETT: H is for hair.u gadda have a hair cut..chix want a guy who isnt shaggy and keeps his hair trimed and clean... duh dats obvias

BENNETT: U is for Unda arms Dis is importint bcuz u will think im gunna say make sure u wear d.Odarent but im not. DONT Wear d.Odarent u hav wats called farramones in ur body i seent it on animiel planet

BENNETT: o also da smell of colon makes girls not wana fucc so dont where N E

ME: The smell of colon?

BENNETT: ya colon! its expencive and masks ur farramones

BENNETT: dogs smell eachother butt bcuz theirs farramones dat make dem wanna fucc and da smell of colon wud ruin it

ME: Lol. Not trying to laugh, I'm just a little confused. There's no real difference between a dog's butt and a dog's colon.

BENNETT: wat.?

BENNETT: dogs dont have colon idiet..only people spray dat stuff

ME: LMAO. Nah, dude, not "colon." The word you're looking for is "cologne."

BENNETT: ahh

BENNETT: O... .my falt. ya

BENNETT: cologne yep..man i no i aint da best typer but dis hole silent g shit is confussing 2 me

BENNETT: maybe u cud show me how 2 be a betta writer next

ME: Yeah? You really want me to?

BENNETT: hell ya i wanna b gud wit words like u

ME: I thought you hated my writing/rapping?

BENNETT: ehh. Ur rapin is purdy gud to be honess

BENNETT: i dont hate ur rapin. i jus wish i cud under stand it betta... u use crazzy words and shit when u b rapin dat i cant evan folow it

BENNETT: i jus feel kinda dum when i here u

BENNETT: maybe u cud show me how 2 be a betta raper which cud make ur shit easy 2 follow

ME: It would be a pleasure, dude. Especially because you taught me not to smell like colon when I take a girl out.

BENNETT: haha.Poop! insted of Joop! LoL

ME: Tip #1. Is use 2 p's when referring to rapping or being a rapper.

BENNETT: ok im not dat gud at spellin but ill try

ME: It's just because being a RAPER or good at RAPING has to do with hurting women, not making music.

ME: You following me? As in "rape?"

BENNETT: oooo man FUCC dat. i fuccin hate rape.

BENNETT: ill kill sum 1 who is gud at raping.

ME: Me too, Bennett, me too.

BENNETT: K so da g is for gwap

BENNETT: gwap is money cha ching $$$

BENNETT: chix git called gold diggaz alot which i think is stupid

BENNETT: bcuz they like niggaz wit $$

BENNETT: well so wat

BENNETT: chix want life to feel gud and EZ. a girl wanna no dat she aint gunna be payen 4 da movie ticcets all da time.she wanna no dat if u guyz wanna smoke weed she dont gadda spend her hole alowence on da sacc of herb

ME: Haha. True, but some girls are obsessed with finding a dude with money.

BENNETT: so wat sum dudes R obsesed with findin a chicc wit a nice booty.sum dudes only go stedy wit mexican chiccs.u cant be mad at sum1 for noing wat dey want

BENNETT: jus make sure u got ur own $. dont spend it tryen 2 make her happy. dont buy her a xtra slice of pizza at skool evary day at lunch... especily if U aint fuccin her

BENNETT: but jus in case she likes u its gud 2 have gwap u can spend on fun shit

ME: Makes sense.

ME: Keep it coming. I love this and really appreciate it.

BENNETT: L is lanry

BENNETT: Landry

BENNETT: u have gud style as it is..so dis aint dat serias.but jus to say it so i dont 4get nuthin.. chix luv a guy who can dress fly.dont dress like a jocc.dont dress like a prep..have ur own style..

ME: Bennett you wear all navy-blue boots, blue bandanas, Dickies outfits, and sunglasses indoors. You have gold teeth.

ME: Girls like that?

BENNETT: ya bcuz they C it and think damn dis lil nigga is a gangsta

BENNETT: dey go oh dam he got dat thug dicc

BENNETT: but dats da getto chix dat i like..

BENNETT: if its a rich prepy girl i jus pull my pantz up and try 2 talk like im a rich kid named Jeffry who no how to play tennis

ME: What the Hell is the letter I? Itcherz? Huh?

BENNETT: O. yea itcherz. finger nails.. dont be leavin da house with dirty ass finger nails man chix hate dat shit..shower an wash em

ME: Yeah, I know.

BENNETT: also clip em short so u dont cut ur girl's vajina at da movies

BENNETT: F is for feet.. man dont wear dirty shoes.. u got tons of nice shoes witch is gud chix Luv nice shoes.. make sure dey clean and make a statmint..

BENNETT: no spots or dirt on em.. if u cant clean em gud enuf jus git new ones.. u cud have da dopest outfit on but if ur shoes are lame or dirty ur pretty much a big skrub and no cute chix will git w u

ME: I agree.

BENNETT: dats like havin a lambergeeny with bicycle wheelz

BENNETT: E is for Erb..

BENNETT: hoez luv a nigga who got gud da erb 2 smoke

ME: Girls my age don't smoke as much as girls your age. The type of women I like think smoking too much pot makes you lazy.

BENNETT: well maybe u shud date chix dat R my age den bcuz i cud neva go out wit a girl who didnt smoke da heavanly green leaf omg fucc no

ME: Yeah, uh. Dating girls your age is illegal for me, bro.

BENNETT: crossin da street when da yelow hand is up is illegal 2 nigga but u still do it all da time.. sumtimes breaken stupid laws makes life a funner place

ME: Ok... so T.H.U.G.L.I.F.E. it is. I get it. Thank you. Makes a lot of sense.

#5. Always Take a Shit Before Macking on Hos

ME: Okay, now how about #6 KILL DA HATERZ BY SHOWING EM LOVE

BENNETT: aint it numba 5 doe ?

ME: Nah that's the TAKE A SHIT BEFORE GOING OUT one. You already told me that one.

BENNETT: my boss iz yellen at me so i cant respond for a bit.but dont think u done.. u aint a sammer eye waroir yet da lessens iz jus starten

BENNETT: ill txt u bacc in a littel bit i gadda go help stocc sum shit in da bacc

Hydra

I felt a certain sense of euphoria while reading Bennett's dating tactics. Part of it was from enjoying merely talking to my cousin and being fascinated by his logic. The other part of it was from feeling the first sliver of optimism I'd felt in several anguishing weeks.

Despite the long drive and our run-in with the soggy meth head, I couldn't sleep until I put my phone down and inadvertently closed my eyes while waiting for Bennett to text me back on number six. I ended up having weird dreams about Katt Williams selling tilapia fillets in televised infomercials, and the strangest thoughts.

Bennett had his own extremely developed level of intelligence. And sharing with me his theories and strategies on getting girls, while also displaying his humility and interest in developing his writing skills, not only made me realize that he was just as bright as anyone I'd ever met, but it brought me closer to him than ever.

I woke up damp with clammy sweat when I heard the front door slam at 6:19 p.m.

I checked my phone. I had two missed texts. Both from my friend Seven, both about throwing back a few beers tonight. Seven was responsible for all of the beats I recorded my songs to and was married. But he was always fun to go out with and grab a table with at a local microbrewery, so I texted him to invite JoJo and Alvie too.

A NOTE FOR CREATIONISTS

The human species is the most evolved species on our planet because of one specific reason: our ability to communicate abstract thought and complex emotion with each other. We have a deeper understanding and appreciation for each other than (most) other animals are capable of. This is largely due to our supreme intellect when it comes to communicating and our ability to create memories based on profound, emotional exchanges. Good or bad. I'm not suggesting other animals are shitty. I'm just saying we are better. Fact.

How did we become Earth's finest species? It's hypothesized that 7 million years ago, our distant Hominid ancestors had hit the evolutionary ceiling and were not advancing at a very rapid pace. In fact, other animals were kicking our asses. We needed a solution. That solution came from our brains.

One poor ape accidentally ate psilocybin mushrooms (that I'm guessing were picked right off a pile of cow shit) and began imagining bizarre concepts of problem solving and nuanced communication. Since there was no moralist society afflicting its citizens with egregious rules at this time, the hominid ape and its Hominidae relatives began eating these psychoactive mushrooms *all the time*.

The more psychoactive mushrooms these apes ate, the more they pursued these weird, trip-induced ideas. Making noises to represent feelings, carving shapes into the walls of caves to tell stories, and using their fingertips to draw symbols in the sand that represented letters and eventually words. Thus, speaking, drawing, and writing were born. I imagine these three prime forms of communicating were quite simplistic in their initial incarnations. But over the course of seven million years, they have not only developed and become much more sophisticated in their engineering, but they have also considerably expanded our ability to understand and adapt to our surroundings.

Humans are equal parts brilliant as we are gullible. We're brilliant enough to create an entire grid of numbers that are infallible in problem solving, organization, and counting. Yet we're gullible enough to believe there's a significance to things that happen within these numbers that we created ourselves.

Once the simple concept of mathematics was developed, we were off to the races.

Example: every 10, 100, 1,000 and (I'm guessing) 10,000 years, a chunk of Earth's general population begins to worry that the Universe is going to abruptly end. How could the year 2000 have been birthed without rampageous dragons spewing fire and vomiting goat blood all over Los Angeles? I mean, 10 is the first double digit, after all, right? And 10 times 10 times 10 is 1,000. And 1,000 years is a millennium. And 2,000 years is two millennia. How could someone be dumb enough to not see significance in that?

Simple: the year 2000 wasn't significant. The year 3000 won't be either. Why? Because numbers in the multiples of 10 aren't significant. Why? Because numbers aren't significant. Why? Because humans created numbers, and when humans created numbers we based them on how many fingers we had: 10. That's as high as we could count at that point. Well, I guess 20 if we removed our shoes. If we had 12 fingers, our number grid would be based on quantities in the multiples of 12, 144, 1,728, etc.

But what fun is that? What fun is realizing all the fear, mystery, destruction, and chaos that humans are enraptured in is nothing more than the by-product of a few apes who had a revolutionary idea on 'shrooms? What fun is considering the idea that our current world's civilization of humans, mutated life-forms, and soccer moms, is the second one this Earth has permitted to live here? What fun is entertaining the idea that our current civilization has only been present for about 0.000005 percent of Earth's existence.

My point in all of this is our level of intelligence has nothing to do with how many expensive words we know, or how well we speak. Our level of intelligence doesn't revolve around how well we can do calculus. (Well, unless you're Isaac Newton, who created calculus in six weeks when he was twenty-five. That's a motherfucker who just . . . *got it*. Sorry, Leibniz. I'm rolling with Big Isaac.) Those are all things that can be learned with enough practice and memorizing.

Bennett wasn't the most eloquent person. Showing him a function of differential calculus and wanting him to understand it was really no different than showing a dalmatian a page of Chopin's sheet music and expecting him to understand it. (Yes, the dalmatian puppy is a boy, you fuckin' feminazi.)

I rose and walked to the edge of the stairs to see who had come in.

Bennett was standing at the coatrack, on one foot, removing his navy-blue Dr. Martens combat boots. He stopped and looked up at me, exhausted from pulling the double.

He stared at me for a few seconds. "My phone died," he eventually said.

"Oh, it's all good man. I needed to sleep anyway."

I walked down the stairs, yawning, stretching, and feeling my tingling body start to fluctuate and reengage. I gave Bennett a handshake-turned-hug.

It was quiet in the house and when I walked into the living room, Aunt Lillian was sitting at an angle, nodding out as usual. Apparently sensing my presence, she opened her eyes and smiled.

"Hi, honey," she said.

"Hi, Auntie Lillian. Get some rest, sweetheart, sorry to wake you," I said.

"Oh, okay," she said, as she laid down.

Bennett walked past me, through the kitchen, and to the basement door. Opening it, he took a step down before cocking his head back and motioning for me to follow.

In the basement, Leshaun was down doing push-ups and crunches, shirtless and in black withered basketball shorts. He was glistening with sweat.

"Wassup, niggas?" Leshaun said, enacting an intricate Crip handshake with Bennett and giving me a regular handshake-hug-type thing. "You been workin' on your pimp hand, O.G.?"

"Yeah. All day. I might go meet a few friends tonight at the bar. So . . . we'll see how it works," I said.

At this, Bennett seemed to regain some energy. Quickly changing out of his work uniform and into a baggy T-shirt and some cutoff Tar Heels sweatpants. "Have a seat, mothafuckas. Loony, help me explain da rest of dis shit to him."

We all powwowed on the basement floor in front of the couch Bennett slept on and proceeded to discuss the rest of Bennett's dating tactics. Bennett's passion for them was inspirational, but the truly mind-blowing thing for me was how well-versed Leshaun was in them as well. Watching how fearless and unbridled the two boys were lit a fire under my ass, and soon I had an outrageous sense of self-confidence.

I just sat with my mouth closed, absorbing it all. Like performance art.

#6 Kill the Haters by Showing Them Love

BENNETT: *Girls always roll in packs. They got friends who dey look out for, and friends who look out for dem. Girls make decisions together, homie. They go to the bathroom together. They sleep together at sleepovers until they fuckin' ninety-two years old. They always need to ask each other opinions and shit before doin' anythaaang. Like "Should I wear this bathing suit? Is my ass fat?" Yeah, bitch, your ass is fat 'cause you eat too many Twinkies. Bitch.*

LESHAUN: The hataz *ain't the mark-ass dudes who talk shit on you or act like jealous ole bitches. Those niggas actually help you get pussy. If a dude talks shit on you to a girl he like, chances are, that girl gonna wonder why he hatin' on you so hard. What does he know that she don't? Dudes help you get pussy. Even if they say some foul-ass rumors about you (most commonly that you roofie girls drinks), don't trip. The girl gonna think you a piece of shit. Fear not though, boss nigga. When you go talk to her and she sees how cool you is, she gonna know it was all lies. Only bitch-ass niggas roofie girls drinks. In fact, next time I get cockblocked by a bitch-ass nigga I'mma roofie his drink and let my Rottweiler, Big Dracula, fuck his mom. On Crip!*

BENNETT: *Haha! You should write a book about that. Dat's crazy smart, young Leshaun. Da hataz are a chick's friends. Her chubby homegirl who don't approve of you 'cause you took da last hot dog on da rack at da skatin' rink. The hot-ass snobby bitch she hang wit who sound like she got jizz in her nose and don't want you stealin' all of da attention from her friend. A girl's homegirls is one of da biggest thangs you gotta deal with when mackin'. They her defensive line. But . . . there a real easy way to deal wit' deez bitches.*

LESHAUN: *Show 'em love, man. You ain't tryin' to fuck 'em. You don't gotta worry about a girl's friend thinkin' you too nice. In fact, the nicer you are to her friends, the more her friends are gonna ride for you. When the girl you wanna fuck asks her homegirl, "What do you think of this nigga Mac?" her homegirl gonna say, "He's so cool! Get wit' him!" One thing I will say though. Is if one of her fat friends likes you, and you don't gotta worry about gettin' caught, let her give you head. Fat girls appreciate the opportunity and go above and beyond with their skills.*

#7 Kiss Sex Good-bye

35

BENNETT: *I gotta say, y'all, my dick grew a few inches when I thought dis one up.*

LESHAUN: *Do you wanna have sex with the girl? Hell yeah you do. But don't even think about that shit for the time bein'. Girls you just met ain't tryin' to just give up the ass all fast and shit. They already assume you a playa. They already assume you tryin' to fuck. And you is. But, don't let it even be the goal. If they ask, tell 'em, "Nah. I just want a kiss." Be like "Do I look like a asshole who treats girls bad? Bitch, my favorite movie is Wall-E. I'm sensitive, ho."*

BENNETT: *Not only dat, but when you kiss a girl it activates her fuck organs. So you on the right path anyways. So when you go out tonight, don't even take no condoms. Don't even plan on havin' sex. And if a girl be down to have sex right away, she ain't really dat hot anyways. Tonight, my G, aim for a kiss. A kiss and nothin' more. Kiss sex good-bye.*

LESHAUN: *Hos think sex is hella serious. But they loooove kissin'. So if you say, "Look, I would never degrade a bitch like you, like some pervert who only wants one thing. You such a bad bitch that I would wait till we got married if thats whatchu wanted. But one thing I gotta confess to you, boo, is your lips are perfect as fuck. A nigga could* have sex with any girl right now and it wouldn't mean shit. But with you . . . I'd remember just a simple kiss witchu for tha rest of my thug-ass life." Then lean in and kiss that bitch all romantic as fuck, like in the movie Twilight.

BENNETT: *Hell yeah. Robert Pattinson that bitch. Make sure y'all got good chemistry and shit before you say dat doe, 'cause she might be offended if you call her Boo.*

#8 You're Still in Love with Leah

"Aiight. Let's do number eight. The Leah one," Bennett said.

"I don't like this one, my nigga," Leshaun said, leaning back against the couch, crossing his arms.

"Why?" Bennett asked.

"It's wrong. I'm a playa for life, but damn. Ain't the reason we do this 'cause we tryin' to show bitches we the best dudes in the world to ride with?" Leshaun said.

"Yeah? So?" Bennett said.

"Well, I think it's fucked up, cuz. You explain it. I need some more grape juice anyways."

Leshaun stood up and walked upstairs with his empty glass, leaving me intrigued to know what could possibly offend *his* sensibilities.

BENNETT: *Man sometimes you hang out wit a girl who seems like she gonna be hard to crack. Like she ain't really seemin' like she wants to get with you. You runnin' hella grade A Crip game on her. All dat shit. And she ain't actin' into it. Well, you gotta start talkin' about Leah. Leah is your ex dat got hit by a ice-cream truck and killt. You still in love wit' her so much and will never fall in love wit' another bitch. You can fake cry a little too. Just bring up Leah a couple times a day to remind da new bitch dat you ain't in love with her. As fucked up as it sound, da best way to make a chick jealous is by makin' her compete wit' a dead bitch. Dead bitches make da best wingmen.*

#9 Jack Off Now So You Can Fuck Later

Leshaun reentered the room. He looked enthused. Bennett began to lean back with hesitation in his confidence. This obviously wasn't the first time the eighth commandment had been the matter of friendly controversy between the two boys.

LESHAUN: *I made this one up. This one is kinda like the one about taking a shit, mixed with the one about trying to kiss instead of fuck, so you can actually fuck, because you tried to kiss instead of fuck, but not really. Well, kinda. The whole point with this one is to always jack yo dick off before you go meet a fine-ass chick. Just empty it out. Blast until the clip is empty, homie. This way, when you hangin' with the girl, you don't fuck up and say hella sexual shit to her like a hornball-ass nigga. I've been horny as fuck when I left the crib before and almost ruined my chances like a stupid ass. A nigga was helpin' a girl pick out art supplies and I kept sayin' shit like, "I wanna rub yo titties with watercolors," and "Mmm yeah, baby, let's make folk art, girl." She was like, "Leshaun, chill with that shit." So I went to the bathroom and jacked off. After 6.6 seconds I was fine. Then I could see clearly and get back to mackin' and tellin' her how much I love paintings by Claudia Money or whatever that dude's name is. Claude Money.*

#10 If She Wants You to Have Her Number She Will Make You Take It

BENNETT: *Don't ever ask for a girl's number. Just focus on yo game, focus on makin' her love you like a mothafucka, focus on . . . like . . .*

LESHAUN: *Nigga, focus on givin' her a experience she ain't never gonna forget. Fuck you gonna do wit her number? Call her and say some genius shit you ain't say when you first met the ho? If you can't make her love you then, her number ain't gonna help shit now. Don't even worry 'bout her number. Too many niggas try to get a girl number so they can bail out and not put in the work. If y'all talkin' and shit, and you runnin' game on her for a while, tryin' to be a super-cool nigga, that's super nice and ain't like them other buster-ass mothafuckas, but also a G. A man. Who is ruthless with his game. If you do all that shit and she don't make you take her number. Well, you done fucked up the whole shit anyway.*

BENNETT: *And never give yo number to a chick. If she say some bullshit like, "Lemme get yo number." Say what bitches have been sayin' to us fellas for millions of years, "Sorry. I don't give my number out."*

#11 See Commadment #1 if Something Gets Fucked Up

LESHAUN: *Yup. Most importantly. As gangsta as we are. As wrong as we are to talk about girls like this. The truth is, we love hos. And the friendship is the realest thing to us. This one is gonna be a more important one then you thank, cuz. Along the way to makin' a girl fall in love wit you, there are gonna be some days where you just say the wrong shit. One time I had just lost to my brother Tyshaun at Madden NFL on Xbox and shit, and my new chick called, and I spent fifteen minutes talkin' about how unfair the game was and how it hurt my feelings that Tyshaun got to practice Madden more 'cause Mama got him a Xbox and not me. Man, this bitch was like, "Nigga, is you serious? You sound like my little sister. I gots to go." So, I had to start from the beginning. She called to have sex, heard me whinin' about the Green Bay Packers and shit, and then didn't wanna have sex no more. So I had to remind her I was a great friend who would never leave her side. Then she remembered my beautiful chocolate baby arm on her own, and I was right back to it.*

BENNETT: *Good story. Makes you think and shit. The reason I added this one again is because like Loony said, bein' the best friend a bitch ever had is da most important thing to her. You gotta prove that you will always be there for the bitch, through hard times and, uh. Damn, I'm kinda high, what's the opposite of hard? Uh. Fun times. If you* *fuck up, start over as friends. Unless you take a shit in her underwear drawer, a girl will always give you another chance as friends, my nigga. The more you show you wanna be friends, the more she will be like, "Damn, how come dis nigga didn't stop talkin' to me when I didn't fuck him?" And, as long as you friends wit a girl, she can't tell you not to fuck other bitches. So as much as she wanna pretend to only wanna be friends and shit, when she see you with a bad bitch with a fat booty, she gonna be like, "Damn she like him like dat? Hell nah, he mine, not hers. Fuck her."*

The Riot Room

After hearing all their crazy, wild rules, I was itching to go out and meet some girls. Their game was so transcendent that it in all honesty wasn't a game. As vile as they spoke, and as crude as their language was, the general principles they employed with talking to women felt flawless. I wouldn't even be spewing out lame pickup lines or dumb routines. I'd just be being friendly. I had only one or two questions left.

"I gotta be honest. I'm twice y'all's age and am blown away by how intricate and perfect this is. You guys are going to have some serious women trouble when you get older," I said, shaking Bennett's and Leshaun's hands, in respective over.

"Go get you a new bitch, big homie," Leshaun said. "I got a new one I'm workin' on tonight too. She live pretty close to here. Fine as fuck."

"Nice man. Well enjoy that!" I said.

I stood up and brushed myself off. The next stop was my shower and closet to get cleaned up and pick out the night's attire.

I took an awesome shower. I clipped my fingernails and toenails. Trimmed my hair and face. Splashed on some Drakkar Noir cologne (wanted to get in that seventh-grade spirit). Threw on my expensive Calvin Klein boxer briefs and my nicest pair of 7 For All Mankind jeans overtop them. I slid into a dark-green Penguin button-up collared shirt. Clasped my gorgeous ceramic Nixon watch to my wrist. I even wore some stylish, artificial glasses with wood-grain frames and a vintage baseball cap, slightly tilted to the side. I was humming "Eye of the Tiger," trying to psych myself up. I felt attractive. I felt ready to get back out there.

I was ready to make a friend.

As I gave myself a once-over in my full-length bathroom mirror, Bennett walked in cautiously. I'd never seen him with this magnitude of innocence in his eyes. And then I realized: he was unsure of himself. After all that guruing, he was insecure about something.

"Ey, mane. I just wanted to ask you a question right quick if you don't mind. Nothin' major and shit." He leaned against the vanity in my bathroom.

"Shoot."

"Well, like, you know, I don't for real know how to talk dat good. Which I kinda guess makes my raps not dat great and shit. You smell me?"

"I think so, sure. But what's your question?"

"How do I learn some bigger words and shit? Just like . . . some of da shit you be sayin' sound smart. I don't wanna sound like an idiot-ass nigga, you know?"

"Okay. So, you want a bigger vocabulary? So you have more options when you write lyrics?"

"Yeah dat. And I jus' . . . well, I feel like I helped teach you some cool shit with hos. Maybe you could show me how to sound smart when I talk? Like . . . 'Cause I don't wanna sound stupid. Everyone always think I sound stupid and shit."

I turned off the light in the bathroom, brushing past Bennett, and motioned for him to follow me. We walked down the hall and down the stairs to where my main bookshelf was. I leaned down and scanned my finger over the spines sticking out. After some slow, focused searching, I found it.

"Here you go, dude. Start here," I said, handing Bennett a thesaurus. "I stole this from the high school library when I was about your age and forced myself to learn every single word in the book."

"What is dis, playa?" Bennett asked, flipping through a few pages.

"It's a thesaurus. Basically, it helps you find other, bigger words to say in place of smaller words. You look up a word, and it tells you alternate definitions and stuff."

"Damn! Dat's dope!" he said, turning individual pages, apparently looking for something specific. He stopped at the G section and squinted his eyes at the page.

"What did you look up?"

"Oh, fuck, nigga! Look at all da cool ways you can say *gangsta*! Fuckin' *mafioso*, *criminal*, *bandit*, *crook* . . . fuckin' *hoodlum*, *ruffian*? Damn, nigga, I'm already smart as fuck! I'm Bennett da Criminal Ruffian Thug Hoodlum now, haha! Yeah!"

"Uhm, maybe try to look up some words that don't revolve around violence and stuff too. Maybe you could rap about getting girls, instead of killing people and dealing drugs? Or maybe tell us some personal stories about your life?"

He took a second to contemplate the persona change.

"Nah, fuck dat. Haha. I'mma be a gangsta for life. I start rappin' about chicks and love and committin' suicide like yo' ass, I'mma end up wit' a bitch like Harper. Haha. Fuck dat."

"Okay. Well here's something I do want you to consider. That will make you sound like less of an idiot."

"What's dat?"

I closed the thesaurus in his hands, put my hands on each of his opposing shoulders, and looked into his baby-blue eyes.

"Bennett, you gotta stop saying the *n* word, dude."

"The *n* word?"

"Yes."

"*Nigga*?"

"Yes."

"Why? I'm a gangsta."

"You're also white."

"Mostly, but, homie, I have black in my blo—"

"No, we don't. Stop it. You've been saying that your whole life, and it's absolutely not true. You have no black in you at all. And even if you were *somehow* thirteen percent black, you still shouldn't say the *n* word."

"Why?"

"Because. That word comes from a place of pain. Black people are treated as unequals. At best made to be sycophants. They were whipped and chained up. They still have a harder time getting jobs. They still have a hard time getting into good schools, because they are discriminated against by white people. And you're way whiter than you are black. "

"But I'm way poorer den I am rich."

"So? You still have white privilege."

"Nah, nigga, *you* got white privligis. I got *black* privligis. And it don't gotta do with my skin color."

"Of course it has to do with your skin color. Skin color is the difference here. The American government took black people from their homes and made them slaves."

"Nigga . . . do you see us livin' in yo' house? Da American government took us from our home too. And our home was *in* America."

"But you don't get it, dude, black people aren't treated as equals. Do you grasp that?"

"I ain't treated equal either doe."

"Oh, really? How's that?"

"I can't get a job very easy."

"That's because you dress like you've been drunk since you were nine years old, and have no desire to work."

"Yeah? So? Dat's true. I *have* been drunk since I was nine years old, and I hate workin'. Who da fuck cares? Bosses always trip on employees for dat shit. Not actin' excited about workin'. Not dressin' nice enough. Fuck dat shit. Do dey really think employees wanna be at work? I mean shit, nigga. If we wanted to be at work you wouldn't have to pay us to be there."

I nodded my head to signify being surprised at my agreement with his point.

"I dress nice when I go get pussy, 'cause I wanna go get pussy. You don't gotta pay me to go get pussy. Work doe? Pay me and shut da fuck up."

I had no response to that. The kid was, is, and always will be a genius. That's my opinion, and I'm sticking to it. Still, I said, "I'll tell you what. Go across the street to Jean Paul's house and ask his parents to tell you how different your life is from theirs. Then tell me you feel like you're unequal."

"Why? Dey black people like me. Dey just more black den me. Dey can say *nigga* all dey want."

"Go. If you still want to say the *n* word after, I'll never give you shit about it again."

"Maybe I will, doo. Maybe."

I smiled at him then, happy that maybe I'd planted a seed of change in his young mind. "You're a good kid, Bennett. I'm glad you moved into my house, man."

"Fa sho."

"I'm outta here, man. How do I look?"

"You look good, Cuz. You look like you ready to start your life over."

"Thanks, man. I appreciate that. What are you doing tonight?"

"I dunno. I wanna read dis book and work on some raps. I gotta go meet Mercedes up da street. She gonna give me a ride to sell some more of Harper's Xanax. I found a full bottle in yo' dresser drawer in yo' room! Gonna have some cash for you tonight too."

Bennett looking through my things no longer bothered me. I didn't particularly enjoy it, but it was going to happen whether I wanted it to or not. And oddly enough, it's caused more good things to happen than bad things.

"Nice. But what's up the street?"

"Da park."

"Why the park?"

"Because you said I can't have her over, duh. Remember dat? She gotta pick me up."

I replayed Mercedes's moment of humanity with Hustla Da Rabbit in my head from the other night on the driveway. I also considered how difficult dating Bennett must have been for her. She was a firecracker, no doubt, but she was nothing more than a girl scorned by a boy she loved.

But . . . yeah.

"Yeah, it's probably best if you go meet her at the park. I'd tell you to have her over but wouldn't be comfortable with it. Sorry."

"It's okay, Cuz. You got it, nigga."

"Stop saying *nigga*."

"You just said *nigga*, doe."

"Bah! Enjoy your vocabulary building."

"Right on. Welp. I'm leavin', bro, see ya! I'm back on the scene, baby! Hopefully when I wake up tomorrow to get the new Wi-Fi installed I'll be with a nice lady!"

I gave Bennett a hard five and a strong hug.

I met Seven, Alvie, and JoJo up at the Riot Room, a bar in the Westport area of Kansas City. Seven, who I explained earlier, had an athletic frame, dirty-blond hair, and a soft-spoken demeanor. Alvie and JoJo didn't make music; they were just friends of mine. Alvie stood over six feet tall, was emaciated and lanky and had dark-brown receding hair. JoJo was a darkish, black-haired, Colombian-Caucasian hybrid, with a lean, muscular frame and a beautiful jab. He was my sparring partner five nights a week at the gym.

All my friends were covered in artistic, colorful tattoos, and we all dressed stylishly; tonight's objective was to meet some ladies. All three of them laughed hysterically at Bennett's eleven "commandmints," which I had brought along, and his handwriting, but they were blown away by his aptitude.

There were lots of girls at various tables and booths at the Riot Room. For a warm-up, I introduced myself to a few of the more attractive ones and shot the shit with 'em for a bit. The one thing I instantly noticed about Bennett's "Be the Homie" commandment, was you could have fifty-three different girls you were working on developing something with, all at once.

Well, if you wanted to, that is.

Not a single female was rude to me, and, more important, I was actually having a lot of fun. I met: Emily and Amanda, sisters who moonlighted as bartenders and enjoyed drinking Pabst Blue Ribbon and listening to Johnny Cash. Gabby, a personal trainer at a local gym, who had curly hair, tan skin, and a scatalogical sense of humor. Spencer and Bailey, younger girls new to the bar scene, who liked dancing and taking photographs of themselves. Alicia, Sammie, Kat, Cassie, Molly, Katie, Kate, Alana, Tuesday, Annie, Mary, and some Persian girl whose name I would never remember, sadly. Tia, Tasha, Naomi, and Pearl. Oh, and Jayden, who seemed consumed by the heartbreak men had inflicted on her and was offended that I didn't ask for her phone number. So she gave me her's, which completely validated commandment ten.

Over the course of three different bars in four hours with my friends, I conversed with every single one of the aforementioned girls, a few more girls who I couldn't even remember, and one man who was pretending to be a girl.

The weird thing though was that I wasn't inspired to try to push harder with any of them. All of them were pleasant (as most women are). All of them smelled good (as most women do). And all of them were attractive (as, well, some of them can be). But none of them inspired me to attempt anything beyond a bar-time conversation.

I was having a good time but was pretty anxious to try to meet someone I could create a moment with. Even if it didn't last beyond that night.

And then I saw her.

Tiger Style

41

She had artfully layered red hair, that ginger complexion, and a curvy, gym-toned physique. She had mint-chocolate-chip-colored eyes and red hair that uprooted the tree of my entire Irish lineage from the depths of my soul and shook every red-hair-colored apple loose. Her hair. I couldn't stop looking at, thinking about, or talking about: her hair.

A FIFTY-SHADED NOTE

Women kvetch a lot about being objectified by men. And while I think a huge element of their complaints are warranted, I definitely feel the need to provide some understanding as to why it happens. Ladies, we aren't trying to treat you like valueless sexual objects, we're just deeply affected by our burning desire to mate with you. From the DNA on up, this isn't a conscious decision. It's evolution. And before you try to psychoanalyze how we feel—*halt!* Once again, you cannot understand it. Just like we can't understand why the movie *Steel Magnolias* reduces you to tears, you can't understand what it's like to have physical pain in your body from just looking at an attractive woman. Yes, you read that right, *physical pain*. It hurts to see a hot girl sometimes.

I felt physical pain. She was intimidating. Buttery skin. French-manicured tips. Clothes that were one millionth of 1 percent too tight, so her chiseled body left impressions of its definition in them. I decided to say hello. No rejection would hurt worse than Harper having sex with Tofu-eating, soy-product drinking, fair-trade-coffee enthusiast Chad—Chad of the turtleneck and the pet Weimaraners he referred to as his children.

"Hi," I said, sliding onto the stool next to this red vision.

Facing forward, she kept her right arm as a shield between me and her but did say, "Hey."

"I saw you from over there."

"Uh huh."

"And couldn't help but notice your hair."

"Yep, it's bright. Pretty hard to miss."

Okay. Cold and guarded, but rightfully so.

"It's beautiful. It reminds me of autumn."

"Oh, well thanks."

"But . . . uh . . . it's gotta be a wig. It can't be real."

"What?" She turned toward me with a shocked expression on her face. Instead of focusing on the playful insult, I finished feeding her the Bennett compliment-insult-compliment sandwich.

"It's just too gorgeous."

She clenched her fist as a sullen, disturbed look brushed over her face. She then very lightly play-punched me in the arm.

"Of course it's not fake! Jerk! Hahahaha!" She laughed. Hard. Her laugh was . . . interesting. It sounded like someone threw a robot down a stairwell.

"Well, I like it."

"Thank you . . . I'm Rosemary, by the way."

"I'm Mac." I raised my glass in salute.

"Mac? Like Mac-a-roni? Hahahaha!"

Oh man. That laugh. It sounded like a dog whistle. Well, wait. Pretend like you're able to hear a dog whistle and then imagine how much it hurts like a bitch, right? That's how her laugh pierced me. Plus she made the *macaroni-name joke*.

> ## A NOTE FOR THOSE CLEVER NICKNAMES OF YOURS
> **There is no greater cardinal sin than referring to someone named Mac as "Macaroni," "Big Mac," "Little Mac," or "Mack the Knife." Do. Not. Do. This.**

"Uhh. Yeah. Like macaroni. Hehe." I fake laughed.

From afar, this girl was an ethereal angel. Up close, she was still an ethereal angel. Then her personality started to seep out a bit. Which can make an ethereal angel so . . . human. My crush on her faded fast.

Things she said: "So what do you do?" "Are you gonna be the next Eminem?" (Love that one, each and every time.) "So what kind of music do you listen to?" "I don't really care what kind of music I listen to. Anything on the radio is good." "Hahahahaha!" "I get so sick of people always correcting my spelling. Or telling me the difference between 'good' and 'well.' Or 'your.' That's the worst. You know what I mean? Who cares how I spell *your*?"

She was interviewing me. She was saying uninteresting stuff. Her laugh was making me homicidal.

After far too long, she *finally* told me she had to go home.

I asked for her number, hoping she'd be turned off and not want to give me it. Of course, that didn't work. She wrote Rosemary with five hearts, a few xo's, and a kiss mark on a napkin and tucked it into my pocket shirt in a gesture that I guess some might call sexy . . . ish. If a guy wanted to hook up with her, all he'd have to do would be call her hair fake, then sit there listening to her talk for twenty minutes, and he was in.

After she got up and left, I smacked my head against the bar. Was I seriously going to be unable to date women now because I knew too much about how to attract them?

"Careful," a voice said. A nice voice. I sat up and looked to my left. "I don't want you to break the bar. I come here a lot."

She was sitting at the table behind my stool with some friends. She was a tan, Asian-mixed dainty girl, with hypnotic black hair and a flawless face. I mean a *flawless* face. Her eyes morphed into different shapes when she blinked, and she had an absence of a facial expression. This was a paradox. Negative beauty. An overflowing void of gorgeousness.

"What about my head?" I asked.

"That? I guess I'll have to put my drink on it if you break the bar," she said.

She had on a faded V-neck T-shirt with stripes on the sleeves, fly blue jeans, and Chuck Taylors with Jolly Roger patterns visible on the tongue. She was on the outer edge of her group of friends, who were distracted by drunken mischief at the opposite of the two tables they had occupied.

"I'm going to sit next to you," I said.

"Then I suppose I'm going to sit next to you," she said.

"Well, how though? Because I'm the one who's going to be moving to sit next to you."

"I know. But by default if you sit next to me, I'll be sitting next to you."

She had brownish-hazel irises and an hourglass torso that indented just below her ribs and contoured back out down her hips.

"Mac," I said, sticking my hand out. I slid into the empty chair next to her.

"Christina," she said, shaking my hand.

"Well, Christina, I was cracking my skull because I'm freshly broken up with and came out to meet girls using all these tactics my seventeen-year-old cousin taught me. The funny thing is that now that I know them and have this crazy level of confidence, I'm not really into any of the ones I meet."

"Oh. You didn't like the red-haired girl with the horrible witch laugh?"

"No. I didn't like that girl very much."

"I don't blame you. So what are these tactics you speak of? I've recently decided to turn lesbian, so it'd be nice to know how to get chicks."

She was drinking a beautifully colored IPA.

"Why are you turning lesbian?"

"Because I dated a very mean guy recently. Who said some very mean things to me."

"Yeah?"

"Yeah."

"What did he say?"

"Tell me some tactics first. Fair trade or no deal."

She was so beautiful. She smelled like lavender and winter rain.

"Okay. One of them is to focus on being a girl's friend more than anything. Because being a girl's friend is the most important thing."

"Okay, yeah, but that's boring. Give me something good."

"Why is that boring?"

"Because it doesn't take a genius to know that couples are best friends first. Unless guys think married couples have sex, raise kids, and live with each other but never interact or do things as friends."

I felt physical pain looking at her.

"Okay. Uh. A better one is to never ask girls questions. Because it's like a job interview. To tell them statements about me, but never ask about them."

"That's ridiculous."

"It is?"

"Yes. How will you ever get to know them?"

"I don't really know. . . ." I took a sip of beer. "I think the idea is that over time more stuff will be revealed? About her?"

"Sounds to me like these guys like to get with girls who like to be treated like crap. There's nothing wrong with asking a girl what she likes."

"Hmm. Do you like 2Pac?"

"Yeah, I love 2Pac. But my favorite rapper is Bun B from UGK."

She was the most beautiful girl in the city. And she loved UGK—Underground Kingz. The greatest Texas rap duo of all time.

"UGK is my favorite group too," I said.

"Really?"

"Yeah. But let's not talk about music yet. I like where this is go—"

"I'd really like to find an awesome guy who would put headphones on my pregnant tummy while he played UGK to our progeny. You seem into that. By the way, so I don't sound egotistical, I am too. You're interesting. And I'm drunk. "

She was the most beautiful girl I've met in years.

Drunkenly, she just assumed that I liked her, and drunkenly just admitted that she liked me. Well, was intrigued by me. We accidentally found out that we love the same music. She wanted kids too.

"Okay, so I'm curious about what you think about this one. Pretend that you have a dead ex-girlfriend named Leah. So if a girl acts like she doesn't like you, you can make her jealous with your long-lost dead love."

"That's horrible!"

"Yeah?"

"Do people not have respect for death anymore? Death isn't something to joke about."

"It's not a joke. It's just a way to draw attention. But I guess I see what you're—"

"Okay, so the guy who I was dating? That I told you about?"

"Yeah?"

"He was such a dick. He joked about death. Something personal to me. And it really offended me. And he did it because he felt like I wasn't into him enough."

"What did he say?"

"I'd rather not actually repeat it."

"Okay . . . uh . . . well, why did it upset you? What was it about?"

"Just someone close to me."

"Who died?"

"Yep."

"Who?"

"My mom."

She was the most beautiful woman I'd ever met in my entire life.

"Your mom is dead?"

"Yep."

"Wow."

"What?"

"So is mine. She died in 2004. I watched it happen. It's the worst thing I've ever gone through and apparently the worst thing you've ever gone through too."

She studied my face for a second and lifted her beer to toast.

"Well, sorry for your loss, Mac."

"I'm sorry for your loss too, Christina," I toasted back in return.

She surveyed the room to give herself a moment of settling into the new information. I watched her body submit to the stings and bites of painful emotions she was neutralizing. The only reason I knew her body was doing this was because mine had done it so many times.

"So uh . . ." she said, then awkwardly sustained the "uh" because she didn't know what to say next.

"You know, I have all these new dating tactics and theories, and there's a bunch of social conventions I've had beat into me in the past, but, for some reason, I think I either just kinda fell in love with you in a totally just-met-you kinda way, or maybe just became a close friend of yours, or both. And I didn't even use any of the tactics."

"Haha. That's funny. I understand what you mean. Death is a weird thing to have in common with someone."

"Especially when you are entranced by the other person's beauty."

"You're making me blush. I'm starting to wonder if this is just a tactic of yours." She squinted her eyes just slightly and leaned back a little.

"Definitely not."

"Well, good. But let's not fall in love just yet. Let's fall in like."

"How do we do that?"

"The normal way. Get to know each other."

"Okay. Are you normally this easy to attract?"

"Who said I was attracted to you? I just said you could hold headphones up to my stomach, not that I liked you." She smiled. I couldn't tell if she was being sarcastic or not.

To make it worse, her thin brunette friend interrupted from the other table: "I thought we—"

"We're leaving. Gotta go meet Paula and Vani," said another friend.

"Okay. Give me a second," Christina said, scooting out of her chair and taking the last gulp of her beer.

I was in a terrible pickle. How was I going to get her phone number? I didn't want to turn her off.

She hugged a couple of people, then pulled her purse out of her wallet and counted out a few dollars onto the table. Her friends began exiting the tabled area. She approached me and stood directly in front of me.

"So uh . . ." she said.

"Um. Yeah," I said. I had no idea what to say or do. A voice in my head was telling me, *Wait through the suspense. Make her give me her number. Don't fuck this up.*

"It was nice to meet you, Mac."

"Yeah, hey. It was nice to meet you too." I was saying arbitrary shit, just waiting.

She stood and looked at me silently.

"Well, hopefully next time we'll have more time to talk?" she ask-said.

What the fuck do I do? Think, think, think. Tactics, Bennett, Leshaun. Think. Game, players, pimps. Think. Don't break your posture.

She wasn't reaching for a pen or anything.

Think. Think. Think.

"Yeah, definitely. Have a great night," I said.

"All right, see ya," she said as she turned around. She began walking toward the door. My stomach sank and tied itself into a million knots. She was almost to the door.

"Christina, wait!" I blurted out.

"Yeah?" she said, turning around.

I got out of my chair and approached her.

"There's another tactic I forgot to tell you about."

"Oh, really?" She smiled at me, like I was going to grace her with one last absurdity. "What's that one?"

"It says to never ask for a girl's number. Wait it out. If she wants you to have it, she'll give it to you."

She walked back to where I was sitting and leaned against the bar looking at me.

"Well that's pretty stupid."

"It is?"

"Of course. Especially because it's unladylike to force your number upon someone. Especially a boy."

"Oh, okay. . . ."

"Is that all?"

"Yeah. I guess so."

She turned around and walked to the door. Was I supposed to ask now?

"Uh, wait," I said.

"Yes?" she said.

"So do you have plans tomorrow?"

"Not that I know of."

"Do you want to come to my house and . . . uhhhhh . . . dude. I have no idea what to say."

"Haha. No tactics for this situation, eh?"

"I'm starting to maybe realize I drank a little too much of my cousin's Kool-Aid. Well, other than the fact that he reminded me to just be honest and not overthink it. I dunno, I'm brokenhearted. Or was. So I'm kinda repairing my life. My cousin has some good ideas, but he's also like fifteen years younger than I am. I don't kn—"

She put her index finger on my mouth to quiet me.

"Mac," she said.

"Yeah?" I mumbled through my lips that were sealed by her index finger.

"Ask me for my number." She dropped her hand.

"Can I get your number? And then take you out tomorrow? Somewhere awesome? While we listen to UGK? And miss our moms? And you won't say racist shit about black people? And you won't call my aunt a 'retard'? And you won't make fun of my cousin who lies and says he's thirteen percent black and in the Crips? And you won't judge me for being a high school dropout?"

She looked up into the corner of her eye, humming, playfully contemplating the question, then refocused her eyes on me.

"Maybe. Do you promise to use it? And take me out tomorrow? Somewhere awesome? While we listen to UGK? And miss our moms? And you won't crack jokes about the fact that I hug my pillow in my sleep, pretending to hug my mom? And you won't make Asian jokes? And you won't be an asshole?"

This Gets Its Own Chapter Due to How Hard Her Last Statement Made Me Fall For Her

Yes!

Yes

"Yes."

"Then, yes. Of course you can have it."

She was the most beautiful girl that's ever existed in the universe.

ne no mo!
the girliest text messa
a female language i blev
inja star a :) is my sord
it wrks luv me they b
ersent fluant langauge
a i say kk and they bo
rushin spy wit. speak ju
z B gittin wit other bit
soft and sweet 2 eacJ
bennett. i know wat wa
d Dats fabulus And Kk av
they think im sinstive
ear dat song dat q

Part 7

Wanna go to the gym today?

fuk nah! da jim is gay..niggaz walken aroudn in tights sayin shit like Hi im Todd

i hate doods named Todd

So you're too tough for the gym?

yep

Bennett I walked in on you peeing sitting down once.

I wuz drunk! gangstaz piss sitten down so we dont stain da nicE floor..idieot

Big Mama Cole

Okay, and that catches us back up to where this little book began, with Mr. Cole irate, my Wi-Fi quite possibly set for a call from the NAACP, and me pondering what to do about Bennett and Lillian.

"Okay. House meeting! Come on, guys! Gather round!" I yelled, moving into the living room near Lillian's couch.

"Does that mean me?" Leshaun said.

"Yeah, dude," I said.

Bennett and Leshaun both came into the living room. Aunt Lillian sat forward on the couch.

"Leshaun, where the fuck were you an hour ago when we almost got pummeled by Mr. Cole, my crazy-ass neighbor?" I said.

"I was watchin'. On Crip," Leshaun said.

"He was. He always is. You can just never see him," Bennett said.

"He was? You were?" I said, looking at Bennett, then Leshaun.

"Yeah, homie. If shit goes down, I'm there to bang. But most of the time, shit don't go down. And I hate . . . fuckin' *hate* listenin' to niggas argue. I don't make my presence known unless I have to. On Crip, I'm like Spider-Man, fool. All in da shadows and shit."

"No, man, Batman was the one in the shadows," I said.

"Mac, fuck you and your fuckin' comic book undwears. I'm like all them Bat, Cat, Spider, one-half animal, one-half man, niggas. I'm in the shadows, ready to fuck shit up, and I'm ghost after I do it," Leshaun proclaimed.

Visions of Bath Salt Cindy somersaulting midair occupied my mind. Made sense.

"Okay, so I have some good news and some bad news, my sweet family," I said.

They all looked at me silently, clearly unsure what to expect.

"It's time for you guys to move out. That includes you, Leshaun."

All three of them looked at the ground with hurt, puppy-dog eyes. Not a single one of them could've even been fathoming an argument against it. They had to know this day would eventually come.

"Yeah . . . well . . . that sucks," Bennett said.

"Now, now, my precious cousin. You didn't even hear the good news!" I said.

All three of them looked up at me, with optimistic eyes, but still had frowns on their faces.

"Guys, I'm not *kicking you out,*" I explained. "I mean, you can't stay here, but don't think I'm kicking you out. I can't thank any of you enough. The pain I went through with the Harper breakup . . . you guys all being here for me. Telling me amazing stories about my mom. It healed me. Made me a better person," I said.

I pulled my checkbook and a pen out of the end-table drawer next to the couch. "What I'm getting at is that it's just time for you guys to get your own place. You know? Before you overstay your welcome. Does that make sense?" I said.

"No," Bennett said.

"Yeah, we give you all our Southern Baptist pimp wisdom and you boot us out? Damn, homie, I see how it is," Leshaun said, clearly hurt.

"Guys, listen. I actually met a new girl last night! Because of you! We've been texting all day today. This wouldn't have happened without you guys! I'm realizing you're my friends now. Not just my family. But my friends. And I don't want to ruin that friendship. Does that not make sense, guys?"

"Yes it does, Pookie," Aunt Lillian said. "And we are grateful for all you've done for us, honey. Let's give Mac a round of applause boys, come on," Lillian said. With a little more prodding from her, Bennett and Leshaun broke into a full round of applause.

"Uhm, thank you. I'm not sure if that's an appropriate time to clap. But thanks. Anyway, that's as bad as the bad news is going to get," I said. "Now here's some good news for you guys."

I set the checkbook on my lap and popped the pen cap off with my teeth. "All the money you guys have given me, all the cash that Bennett has busted his tail for, all that money? I put in a savings account for you guys. I didn't spend it. I'm not even going to keep it. It's for you guys."

"What?" Lillian said.

"For real?" Bennett said.

"Yep. I love you guys. Leshaun, you're like my little brother or somethin'. I aspire to have your type of swagger, dude. And, Bennett, I just wanted to show you that hard work pays off. You've been putting in the work. Now it's time for the payoff. Bennett, man. I had my doubts about you. I don't agree with everything you do in your life. But I couldn't be prouder to call you my cousin, dude. You're a top-notch guy and an inspiration. And, Lillian, you're just such a pure person. I've learned so much about life and being a person through you. I just . . . I'm proud of you for being the nucleus of this household."

"Oh, Pookie, you're just the sweetest thing!" Lillian yelled.

"You know, Lillian? It's not me being sweet. Your son worked his butt off and deserves this money. And you inspired us all. Why don't you take this money and go get started looking for a nice lil' apartment? There's tons in this area, renting right now. You guys could be moved in in a week, week and a half if you find one," I said.

I decided to donate a little money myself, throwing in some extra cash and wrote the check out for $5,000, handing it to Bennett.

"Man . . . hell yeah," Bennett said. He stood up and stuck his hand out. "You my nigga for life, Mac." I shook his hand and hugged him.

"Bennett. You're my friend and cousin for life," I said.

"Leshaun, honey, you just plan on movin' your ass in with us. Okay?" Lillian said. "We'll hide you from the cops for a while."

"On Crip, nigga," he said, throwing up a C sign to Aunt Lillian. She smiled and closed her eyes.

"It's Raining Men" began playing on my phone. I opened my texts, and while the rest of the family celebrated the news, I got a surprise of my own.

CHRISTINA: By chance are you hungry?

ME: Yes actually, why?

CHRISTINA: I had to return a sweater at this boutique I shop at, which is pretty close to your area. Wanna take me out to eat?

ME: You're by my house right now?

CHRISTINA: Yes. It's not a coincidence. I kinda decided you were going to take me out to eat tonight.

ME: Okay. Sure. Wanna meet me here in 15?

CHRISTINA: Sure, what's your address?

ME: 12345 Fake Address St.

CHRISTINA: Oh, you can't give me your real address because this is an internationally published book, right?

ME: Exactly. So for a deus ex machina, I'm going to just telepathically provide you with my address so you can meet me here in 15 minutes.

CHRISTINA: Perfect. See you soon!

"All right family, I'm gonna get ready to go on a date. The new girl is coming by!" I said.

"Ay, wait, Mac. I'mma go get somethin' real quick, aiight? Don't leave yet. Okay?" Bennett said.

"Uh, okay. I'm gonna change clothes, then go wait outside for Christina so she can find the house, okay?"

"Fa sho. I got somethin' for both you and the new girl. Leshaun come peep this shit too, Cuz."

I was guessing he was going to give us Molly powder, or Xanax, or a joint, or something we would throw away up the street. Either way, he was being very nice, and I had to get ready.

Black-Belt Ceremony

I stood outside on my driveway waiting for Christina. Across the street and one house to the right, Edgard was removing Jean Paul's training wheels from his bike while his son sat on the driveway, drawing a picture. Mariam sat in the crisp, evening sun.

A black Range Rover pulled up to my house and slowed to a stop in front of it. I had no idea Christina drove such a dope-ass car.

The window rolled down. "Hi," she said, smiling wide.

"Well, hello," I said. "Nice car."

"Thanks. It was my mom's."

The front door opened and out came Bennett and Leshaun.

"That must be Bennett. And what's the other kid's name again?" she said.

"Leshaun," I said.

"Thaaaat's right. Leshaun."

"What up? How you doin', girl? Welcome to Da Mafia house. I heard you a boss bitch. My nigga Mac kinda feelin' you, so you must be good shit!" Bennett yelled.

"I've heard good things about you too, Bennett!" she yelled.

"For real?" Bennett yelled.

"Yep! But I better stay away from you. I heard you're quite the expert at making chicks feel bad about your ex-girlfriend Leah," she yelled.

Bennett and Leshaun started laughing and walking down the driveway toward us.

"Don't give my secrets away, mothafucka!" Bennett said, sarcastically.

"I won't. Your secret is safe with me. Mac was telling me about all of it today over text. I gotta make someone bow to the KK at some point in my life," Christina said.

"Word up. Okay, so I wanted to kick a lil' sumthin' for y'all. Jus' to wish you luck on yo' date and shit. Dis is jus' some shit I was workin' on. Tryin' to expand niggas' minds and shit."

We stood silently as he flipped through some pages in his notebook.

"Aight, y'all. Dis one is called, 'Gregarious Gangsta,'" he said.

He proceeded to rap the lyrics for us:

Yo.
I'm a gregarious gangsta, lugubrious thirst.
I flummox meloncholy niggas with vociferous ominous words.
I refrain from utilizing curses or showing ephemeral insolence
    to bitches.
I'm nefarious, gratifying, and rapacious in cobalt stitches.
I'm a orthogonal symbiotic nigga with—

But suddenly a booming voice cut Bennett off: "Well, well, well. Looks like we got some racism going on up ova here!"

From the side of my house emerged Franklins, the Yorkshire terrier; Milton Cole, my backyard neighbor; and Carletta Cole, Milton's enormously big, black, beautiful (according to herself) and proud of it, wife.

"Man, fuck! Why I can't ever finish my raps! Fuck!" Bennett yelled.

"Now which one of y'all was just yellin' some old racist shit at my house? Huh? Bow to the KKK?" Carletta yelled.

Carletta Cole was no less than four hundred pounds of pure corn syrup and bleached flour–fed fat cells. She was wearing a nightgown that was the size of a parachute and sported very short, butch hair.

Christina appeared mortified. I stood in front of her to make sure Carletta didn't try to dogpile/smother her.

"Y'all wanna yell some ole KKK shit at my husband? Huh? Y'all wanna make fun of his stutter? Do ya? Well that shit don't fly with Big Mama. We don't do racism around here on the wireless internet. No, we sure do not." Up within about fifteen feet of us now, she was looking each of us in the eyes, one by one. You could hear her lungs laboring to suck in adequate oxygen, making it sound like she was choking, but it was just her breathing. Milton stood behind her quietly.

"Chill. Ain't nobody here racist. These are all my friends," Leshaun said, "It was a inside joke. Damn."

"A inside joke, was it?" Carletta said. "Whas' yo' name?"

"Leshaun, aka Loony. So fall back—ain't nobody racist over here."

"How do I know you ain't a slave bein' told to say that by these white devils?" she pressed him.

"Haha, what? A slave? Yo, go on with that shit."

"Hmmm. Nope. I don't believe you. You on the payroll, Dejuan."

"Leshaun. Not Dejuan. Not Tyquan. Not Tyshaun. *Le-shaun,*" Leshaun said.

"So who was it?" Carletta said. "Which one of you wants to get beat the fuck down, right now on this driveway?"

She poked her bottom lip out and eyeballed all of us back and forth. She was *furious,* like she was ready to eat someone maybe. Part of me started to seriously worry about this.

"Oh. My. God," Christina whispered.

A little too loudly. D'oh.

"It was *you!*" Carletta said, barreling toward Christina. "Bitch, don't you see Big Mama could eat you alive? Now you better go over and kiss my husband's feet before I tear yo' face off."

For her part, Christina said nothing.

"Leave her alone. She didn't do anything," I said, remaining tightly in front of Christina. "Like Leshaun, our *black* friend, told you. It was a joke. It has nothing to do with you guys. It was an accident."

"Four-hundred-thirty-nine years of oppression wasn't no accident, white boy. Yo' little girlfriend about to get body slammed like WWE wrestlin'. Get out of my way before I reverse suplex you too."

She clearly loved and studied professional wrestling because she was doing a great impression of the Rock, making the same face he did in the intros. Except she was five times bigger than him, and five million times uglier.

"Now I'mma count to three. And if by the time I get to three, this little skinny bitch ain't kissed my beautiful handsome prince Milton's feet and apologize for traumatizin' him, I'mma DDT her into this driveway."

Edgard picked Jean Paul up and gave him to Mariam, who carried him into the house. He stood quietly, staring at what was transpiring in our driveway, before pacing backward into the dark pit of his garage's shadows.

"One . . ." Carletta said, cracking her knuckles.

I felt Christina latch onto my back. As intense of a situation as this was, it felt good to be touched by her for the first time.

"Two . . ." Carletta said, crouching down into the same stance as an NFL linebacker. "Move out the way, honkey. This is woman-on-woman business."

I had no idea what was going to happen when she said "three." It felt so inevitable that I was going to be in a bonafide fistfight with this giant woman that I began quivering, waiting for it. I knew Brazilian jujitsu, but it's not exactly easy to perform the mounted triangle choke on a woman who is five times bigger than you.

Here it comes.

"Thr—"

My front door slammed open, nearly shattering. Every single person in the driveway was startled by the noise and twirled around to see where the noise came from.

Mercedes. And she was revved up. "Nah, fuck dat, nigga! This right here is gangsta-bitch-on-*fat*-bitch business!" she yelled.

Carletta stood back up and cocked her fists back, ready to throw a punch. Mercedes began to unhook her earrings and hand them to Bennett. Bennett looked at me. I looked at him.

"Sorry, homie, she slept in da basement last night. Dat sex just too good, mane. I'm weak for it," Bennett said.

I didn't care. A crisis was under way—Mercedes had burst out of my front door like an act of God, but she and Carletta were about to massacre each other in the driveway.

"What? You wanna get put in the sleeper hold, lil' white girl?" Carletta said.

Mercedes walked up to Carletta without a skip in her step and put her nose against Carletta's.

"I want yo' 958-pound ass to listen to me real fuckin' carefully. My name is Mercedes. No, that ain't a nickname, my mama named me Mercedes. She in prison for grand theft auto. She used to steal Mercedes cars. She gave birth to me in prison and named me that. Now. Every single mothafucka you see here in this driveway knows I'm about the craziest fuckin' bitch that ever lived. They see you and think about Twinkies, and HoHos and Snickers ice-cream bars and too much Dr Pepper and shit. They see me and think about blood, missing teeth, and crackin' a bitch's skull like I wanna hold her fuckin' brain or somethin'. Now I got some really mothafuckin' friendly advice for yo' water-buffalo-lookin' ass. If you lay a *finger* on that beautiful girl right there"—she turned to smile at Christina—"who I haven't met yet but I hope to soon"—she turned back to She-Rock and continued to point at the rest of us—"or you lay a *finger* on Mac right there, or you lay a *finger* on Leshaun right there, or you even *look* at my king right there, my royal beast of love, Bennett, fuck a *finger*, ho. You even *look* at Bennett like you wanna hurt him, or fuck him, or touch him, I'm gonna have ten different ambalaaances pullin' up in about ten minutes.

"I'm sure yo' brain is digestin' some cheesecake and egg rolls right now, so you didn't even take da time to do the math on what I just said right there, but yeah, *bitch*, I said ten ambalaaances. And nine of 'em gonna be just for *you*. One of 'em is gonna be for your funny-lookin'-ass husband and his skippin'-CD-talkin' ass. And after

I send your husband and all nine parts of you to the hospital, I'mma pick that ugly-ass dog up off the driveway and I'mma *eat* him."

Mercedes took two steps back. "*Now play with me, bitch!*" she yelled and cocked her head side to side like a fundamental, classic ghetto chicken head, snapped her fingers twice, crossed her arms, and stared Carletta dead in the eyes.

Carletta swallowed the lump in her throat as her confidence hesitated. There was dead silence on the driveway. Mercedes didn't even blink. Her heart was made of iron. She was rabid. Fearless. She looked through Carletta's soul.

Carletta shook her head and began walking back through the yard she emerged from. After a moment, Milton and Franklins followed, but before she cleared the house, Carletta turned around and stared at Mercedes.

"You got issues. You got issues, white girl," Carletta said. Then she vanished behind the house.

Mercedes approached Christina and stuck her hand out. "Ay, baby. I'm Mercedes."

"Thank you for . . . not letting that lady . . . eat me," Christina said as she shook and smiled.

Mercedes nodded, then swiveled her head my way. "Mac, honey, sorry I was sneakin' up in yo crib and shit."

"Save it; you're an angel. That was the greatest thing I've ever seen. They were about to piss themselves."

"Fuck that, y'all chill. Fuck them dumb-ass niggas. I wanna finish my rap! I ain't get to finish my fuckin' rap!" Bennett said.

Bennett began flipping through his notebook again.

"Okay. I'mma start this shit over. Dis one called 'Gregarious Gang—'"

"Bennett, baby, please don't rap that one. Please? I hate that shit," Mercedes interrupted.

"How come?" Bennett said.

"Because all you did was pick a bunch of fuckin' big words out of the tyrannosaurus book. I told you when you was writin' that shit last night, it wasn't gangsta enough. Do a different one, baby. Do the one you wrote for me on Valentine's Day, boo . . ." Mercedes said.

"Nah . . ." Bennett said shyly. "Harper hated when I rapped that type of shit. I wanna impress Christina so she likes our family and shit."

"Bennett, quit tryin' to impress people and be the fuck yourself, baby, c'mon. Do the one you wrote for me. It'll be a good way to send them on their first date, boo boo, c'mon."

"You really want me to do that one?" he asked.

"Yeah, what was it called again?"

"'Sex wit a Thug Bitch.'"

Christina stuck her head close to my face. "Harper's your ex, right? The terrible one?"

"Yep," I said.

"I wanna hear 'Sex wit a Thug Bitch,' Bennett. Seriously. Please?" Christina said, turning to Bennett.

"Really?" he said.

"Yes. Don't do 'Gregarious Gangsta,' my friend Mercedes does not like that one," she replied.

"Okay, den. Here go 'Sex wit a Thug Bitch.'" Bennett fastly flipped through his notebook to locate it. "This is more of a love song and shit. . . ."

"Oh, I like love songs," Christina said.

"*Okay, niggas!*" Bennett yelled, loud enough for the entire neighborhood to hear. Loud enough to echo into Edgard and Mariam's garage. "*Here go dat love shit.*"

You got dat thug bitch pussy, dat thug bitch kitty,
you da baddest mothafuckin bitch in Kansas City,
dat thug bitch pussy, dat thug bitch lovin',
I come and beat it up after a long day of thuggin'.
You my thug bitch, bitch, you hold my cock when I pee,
I don't gotta get violent, you bust yo glock for a G,
don't got just one gun, you got two nine-ahs,
one is named Brad, the other one is Angelina.
I love dat big booty, how it jiggle for a gangsta,
she a China doll bitch, her nipples will amaze ya.

We rob banks together, my bitch is hella paid,
She's da baddest thug bitch da Jesus eva made.

"Dat's how dat one go right dere," Bennett said.

"Yay!" Christina said, clapping.

Mercedes followed. "Boo, you so mothafuckin' good with them lyrics. Mmm!"

"I love the part about how Mercedes has two guns named Brad and Angelina, Bennett. Pretty genius if you ask me," Christina said.

"Well, thanks and shit." Bennett looked almost bashful as he said, "I hope y'all have a good date."

"It will be a wonderful date," she said.

And that's when I heard Mercedes correct Bennett with a soft, loving voice, "Baby, my two guns are named Jay-Z and Beyoncé. You're thinkin' of my old guns."

Let Us Prey

From the house across the street and one to the right, Edgard emerged shirtless from his garage holding a machete. His eyes were bright yellow and filled with ultraviolence. It looked like he wanted to send someone to meet his or her psychopomp, chopped into bits. He crossed the street to speak to us, with his machete on his shoulder.

"*Where big woman?*" he yelled. "*She scare boy.*"

"Holy shit, that guy has a sword! What the fuck is wrong with this neighborhood?" Christina whispered as he approached.

His skinny body was covered in scars and lashing marks. He had five very large exit-wound scars from what appeared to be from a splattering of buckshots.

"Uhhhh . . . hi, Edgard. You okay, man?" I asked, nervously.

"*Where big, fat woman? Jean Paul afraid to ride bike. He fear big, fat woman. I kill for nothing to protect boy. I lose arm. Where woman?*"

"Oh, I took care of that bitch, nigga," Mercedes said as she popped a stick of gum into her mouth.

"*Who is 'nigger' for?*" Edgard asked.

"Who is what?" Mercedes replied.

"*'Nigger'? Who is for? Who you say 'nigger' for?*"

"Uh, come on playa, it means lik—" Mercedes said before being cut off by Bennett:

"No one, man. We aren't sayin' it like that, doo," Bennett said.

"*No! I say 'nigger,'*" Edgard asked. "*You call Jean Paul 'nigger' when your skin milk?*"

"No, no, we didn't say anything like that. We love Jean Paul! No one was speaking about him," I said, not really sure what I was trying to accomplish.

He stood closer to Bennett and Mercedes, dangling his machete to kneecap height.

"*You scream every time,*" Edgard said to Mercedes. "*You scream loud. Make loud scream every time Jean Paul scared of you.*"

"Nah, mane, she ain't tryin' to be—" Bennett replied, but was cut off.

"*Shhhh! Why you say 'nigger' any time? Why you say? You see cool sun and clean water? You not say,*" he said.

Everyone was getting much more tense. Edgard could smell the fear on all of us. Most likely, if I had a hunch, because he was acting crazy and, well, carrying a machete.

"*I kill two beggars in Somalia for steal bread from wife. I kill all you for scare boy.*"

Edgard turned around and showed us his back. It had a giant suture scar, from the nape of his neck all the way down beyond his waistline. It looked like a giant alligator tail in scar-form, running down his back. To this day I have no idea what the scar was from, but I think all of our imaginations lit up imagining how his life had brought him that.

"Damn, mane. You're a thug for *real*. Look, doo, we don't wanna say that word like that about you. We are so sorry. Your son Jean Paul! Haha! He's great when he draws!" Bennett said, in a high-pitched, high-spirited voice.

"*Dross? Drawse? Draws?*" Edgard asked, sounding it out.

"Yeah! Draws! Jean Paul, draws great pictures. He's so cool!" Bennett said, opening his notebook, showing one of his own drawings. "Jean Paul is so good at drawing! Look at this, Jean

Paul is so much better!" He pointed to a picture he drew of a fat woman.

"Jean Paul drawing yes. Yeah!" Edgard said, cracking a smile. He began studying Bennett's drawing and giggling. After flipping through a few more pages of Bennett's drawings, Edgard was laughing hysterically.

"Hahaha! You drawing of shit. Hahaha!" Edgard said.

I turned and gave everyone a glance to indicate they really should join in and laugh.

"Yeah, Bennett. Jean Paul is *so* much better than you at drawing! Hahaha!" we all said, in some form or other, in unison.

"Okay, man. Hahaha. I give Jean Paul. He laugh and shit on. Hahaha!" Edgard said, ripping a picture out of Bennett's notebook.

Bennett began chuckling. He seemed very relieved, as we all did, that Egdard's mood was lightening up a bit. He didn't even acknowledge the fact that Edgard had ripped one of his drawings out and compared it to "shit."

Edgard studied us all head to toe and turned around, walking back to his house. Once he was inside, we all let off a deep sigh of relief and chattered about what had just happened.

Even afer the neighbors' garage door was long closed, Bennett kept staring across the street and one house to the right. I knew he was looking in that direction because he was still focused on Edgard. He'd been visibly moved by the scars and markings on Edgard's body; I was sure he'd never seen anything like it. As I watched him watch the house, I got the sense that something inside of him changed because of it. Perhaps not a full transformation, but a seed was planted.

"Are you ready to go, boo? My car is up at the park, we gotta go get it." Mercedes kissed Bennett on the cheek.

Bennett approached me with his hand out. I shook it and hugged him.

"I ain't no bitch or nothin'. So don't think dis mean I'mma stop bein' G as fuck. But I just want you to know dat I love you," he said.

I had to fight tears for a second.

A quick one.

C'mon. It was the most vulnerable thing he's ever said in his life.

"I love you too, little cousin. If you ever stop bein' G as fuck, I'm gonna be very upset with you," I said.

Mercedes nudged my cousin. "Come on, baby, let's go. A thug bitch is hungry."

Bennett gave his typical elongated five to Leshaun and began to walk off with Mercedes. He made it about a driveway-length away and turned around. He flashed a C sign. Then he dropped his hand, briefly hesitated, and lifted it back up, flashing a peace sign.

I flashed a peace sign back. Bennett and Mercedes turned around and walked off, toward the park. Leshaun vanished. No, seriously. I have no idea where he went. He was swallowed by the shadows and obscurity of the book's dramatic and fucking awesome ending.

I looked over at Christina, wondering what she thought of all that had happened. "So uh. Yeah. I know my family is crazy. And a crazy lady almost ate you. And the other just threatened to execute all of us with a machete. But . . . if you're still interested in going on a date with me, I know a great place in the neighborhood," I said to Christina.

She jingled her car keys and smiled.

"Come on, baby, let's go. A thug bitch is hungry."

ne no mo! u ...
the girliest text messa
a female language i ble
inja star a :) is my sord
it wrks luv me they bo
ersent fluant langauge
a i say kk and they bo
ushin spy wit. speak jus
z B gittin wit other bit
soft and sweet 2 eacJo
ennett. i know wat wa
I Dats fabulus And kk an
they think im sinstive
ar dat song dat g

Bennettz aPen-dix
of Gangsta azz Poettry

wait a minite..

what about all the otha
good stuf i write...

mercedes found a bitch number on my phone she mad as fucc aint given me no kitty.. i got crip balls

> Were you texting girls?

duh nigga.sum of us like 2 git pussy. not all us sit arund jaccing off 2 gay porn eating low fat yogert like u

> What are you gonna do about it?

get her a e pill or sing bruno mars to her all soft then hopfally fuk

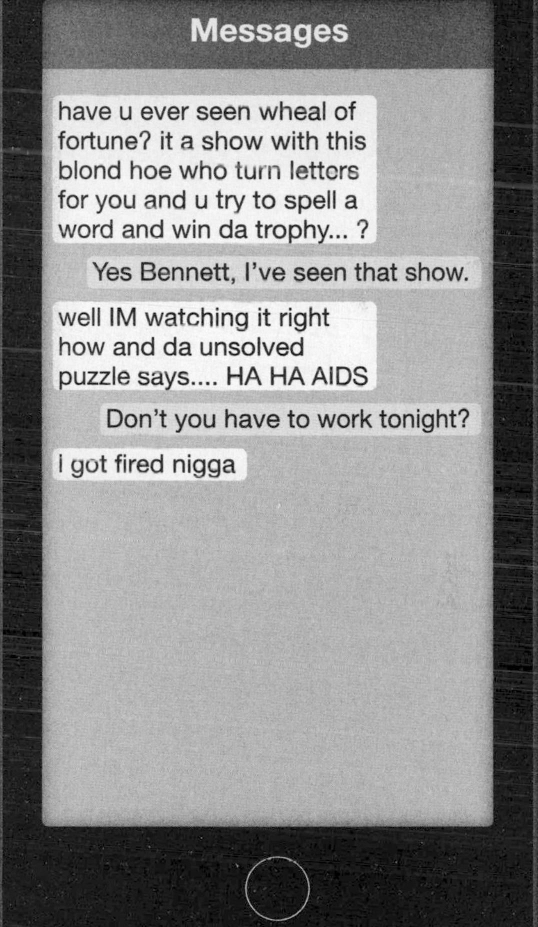
Messages
have u ever seen wheal of fortune? it a show with this blond hoe who turn letters for you and u try to spell a word and win da trophy... ?
Yes Bennett, I've seen that show.
well IM watching it right how and da unsolved puzzle says.... HA HA AIDS
Don't you have to work tonight?
i got fired nigga

im babysittin for my
girls sister right now

a wierd car keep driven by

What color? Whose is it?

half mexican but we dont
kno who tha daddy is..

my girls sistr is a hoe. she
got crabs that have aids

No man, I meant the car.

it mite belong to this dude Chris

The car or the baby?

Messages

Can you text me Lee's #?

ay.. yea when Im done haven sex ill find it

You text during sex?!?!!!

yep dis money dont stop jus cuz i wanna fuck a ho ! i hustle 24 hours a week

Your girl is a trooper.

i aint fucken My girl .

What if you get an STD?

Re-tard i showr rite after i cum b4 Stds can actavate

Mac Lethal

Messages

ay my nigga how du ur boys like da chronik ? fire HuH?

> I forgot to text you about that. Yeah, they like it.

> Everyone has asked me why you put chocolate mints on their bags of weed though.

cuzz i am a firm beleiver in exilint custommer service

> Haha. So you put chocolate mints in the bags of weed you sell?

ya an bassball cards for big orders

Messages

Why do I always end up in the friend zone with girls?

well first off nlgya you cant be compashionit !u such a Lame around bitchss.. u be talkin bout kowalla bears and bluebary muffins and shit

LoL,, hoes thnk ur a vary good lissener. U make dem hot choclat and talk abut Team edwrd

u cant be talkin bout snuggling on da beach durin a brisc sunset as seegalls fly in a hart shape

Messages

i stoll a porno from my freind CJ and it got all asian peopel in it.

Yeah? And? What's wrong with Asian chicks?

nothin.but even da dudes is chinesse n shit.like there diks r all yello n tiny

i forced myself 2 jack off anyway cuz i didnt wanna be racest. but i feel like i raped myself cuz i didnt enjoy it dat much :(

i wuz raped by a asian porno

Messages

man why da bitches dat wnat me most always gatta be crazie and ugly..

like i can pull a fly hoe no problemo but da bitches dat hit on me all aggresave faces look like a germen sheppard asshole

Excuse me??

i jus had some bitch sweat me for my numba. bitch look like golam in lord of da ring. bitch was all like BENNett my preshas lol

Messages

man i brang dis bitch over to succ my dik but she wuz like Can we watch a movie so i said sure baby

she puts in marley and me

a gangsta like Bennett wuz crying like a bitch !!

i cudnt stop blowen my nose from crying when she wuz given me head. i blew it 2 hard and farted

What! What did she do??

da bitch gagged and left :(

Messages

i hate u my girlfriend mercedes bump dis drake cd all day.... dis guy wear puppy dog print boxers man.

I'm in tears.

i bet ur in tears cuz u listen 2 drake.... it says alot about u. i thikn u prolly take bugs outside instead of kill them..

i bet u cry tearz of joy when u see ponies frolocking by da meddows

u smell like a gay kitten

Messages

Nigga I hate my new cell fone

Why?

Bcuz i has dis fuccin auto correction bull shit on it

Yeah? So?

Well how da fucc it kno wat i wanna say

I wuz textin my girl earlier about gittin a puppy and i try to say "You should get an adoption instead"

But my phone change it with out askin

So i ended up textin my girl "You should get an abortion shithead"

Messages

i took 3 big ass bong hits at my nigga Craig house den watch a show about black holez

a black hole is dis thing in space Dat can crush plannits and u can travel thru time in dem

do u think butt holes are da same.? if u travel thru a girls butt hole u can go to anotha dimenseion ?

Dats where they get da name Asstronat nigga.!

Sigh. Goodnight dude.

MAC'S ACKNOWLEDGMENTS

I'd like to thank my wife and baby's mama, Christina, for providing me an amazing marriage, the premise to base a love story on, and a joyous lump of a son, Rocky. Thank you for helping me navigate through this crazy book-writing experience, and for your honest but always tender criticism.

I'd like to thank Rockwell Carlin Sheldon, aka Rocky, my son. I love you more than you'll ever know in your entire life ever. Thank you for reinvigorating my life. You can't read as of now, but one day you'll be able to, and you'll be able to brag at school to all the kids that your dad wrote a book and theirs didn't.

I'd like to thank my dad and sisters, D. Warren, K. Rose, and H. Evelyn.

I'd like to thank my mother. We miss you.

I'd like to thank my stepmother, M2.

I'd like to thank my friends Joe, Seven, Paul, Alvie, Triebel, Patric, Jason, Ben W., Cody, Dutch, Approach, and Simon.

I'd like to thank my other family: Vaughn, Rick, Payden, Brenen, Christian, Morgan, Noah, Eli, and Aiden.

I'd like to let you know that James Lynch always wins.

I'd like to thank my HDMMA family: Jason, L.C., Travis, Bryan, Mike, Brandon, Brandon 2, Erika, Deron, London, R.J., Rachel, D.T., Macall, Poston, Henry, English Dave, HD on 3!

I'd like to thank Jason Bircher and KCBJJ, and Devin Pirata and Dragon Family.

I'd like to thank my William Morris Endeavor family: Bradley, Avi, Erin, Erin, Miles, Margaret, etc.

I'd like to thank Adam Wilson and Gallery Books. Thanks for believing in this.

I'd like to greatly thank Bennett, Mercedes Cruz, and Aunt Lillian for the strangest, most amazing summer of my life. I hope this book doesn't offend you. Know I love you.